Chasing Hairy

Chasing Hairy

A Novel of Sexual Terror

MICHAEL FLEISHER

Authors Choice Press
New York Lincoln Shanghai

Chasing Hairy

Authors Choice Press
an imprint of iUniverse, Inc.

iUniverse books may be ordered through booksellers or by contacting:

iUniverse
2021 Pine Lake Road, Suite 100
Lincoln, NE 68512
www.iuniverse.com
1-800-Authors (1-800-288-4677)

Originally published by St. Martin's Press

ISBN: 978-0-595-47557-5

Printed in the United States of America

To
Ray Kelly

Chasing Hairy

It's hard to know exactly where to begin all this, whether I should start with Ken Pedersen directly or whether I should lead off with the lie I told about how my father was dying of leukemia.

I grew up in New York City, my parents have been divorced since I was four, and in the summer of my senior year in high school, after I had already been accepted for admission to the University of Chicago, I fell in love with Lisa Holland, an incredibly sexy woman of twenty-two who had already been married and divorced twice, both times with the same guy. Because I was determined to stay in New York so I could be with her, and since the deadline for applying to colleges had long since passed, I wangled an appointment with the dean of admissions at Columbia University and talked him into letting me file a late application for admission by giving him this line of bullshit about how my poor father was dying of leukemia. My dad, I explained, had kept his illness a secret as long as he could, which was why I had just found out about it, and now that I knew the end was coming, I wanted desperately to attend a college close to home so that I could remain by his bedside during his last remaining months.

I don't really know whether my little scam would've worked or not, I don't really know whether they would've eventually approved my late application or turned me down, because two or three weeks later it all became irrelevant, Lisa found out I was only seventeen years old—and not the twenty-one I'd pretended to be—and dropped me like a lead balloon, and I went off to Chicago, heartbroken and desolate, determined to show Lisa what a fool she'd been for leaving me by studying hard and becoming a famous writer. And when I arrived on the U. of C. campus, my home became a hamster-sized cubicle in Hodgkin Tower, an eight-story men's dormitory that previous generations of students had nicknamed "the Zoo."

· 4 ·

All kinds of lunatics lived in the Zoo, including "the Mad Bomber," Jeremy Hirsch, who had blown off three of his fingers in high school playing with explosives and who used to get his rocks off by setting off miniature bombs in the showers and stairwells; Ernie Munger, a.k.a. "the Whip," who used to practice cracking his bullwhip outside on the front lawn and then demonstrate how tough he was by burning holes in his forearms with lit cigarettes; and six-foot-six Marty Bernstein, we called him "the Stork," who would get sloppy drunk every night and stagger through the hallways sobbing "I'm not stupid, somebody please believe me, I'm not stupid," and who eventually joined the Marines and got killed in Vietnam after he'd gotten kicked out of college for violently assaulting a clothes dryer in the dormitory laundry room and using a claw hammer to tear it apart.

But of all the crazed individuals I got to know during that first orientation week, when we'd spend our days listening to asshole speeches by members of the faculty and administration and our nights drinking beer and smoking reefers and shooting the shit mostly about pussy, the guy who piqued my interest the most, and the guy I eventually got to know best, was definitely this weird guy from New Mexico named Kenneth T. Pedersen.

Ken Pedersen wasn't my roommate—my roommate was Brian Davidson, an affable New York WASP with curly blond hair and wire-rimmed glasses who wrote saccharine love poems and nursed the ridiculous dream of one day becoming a great poet—but Pedersen did live on my floor, in a tiny room by himself at the far end of the hall.

Pedersen was an intense, chaotic, hyper little guy with enough excess energy stored up inside him to drive a ten-ton locomotive or light up the entire city of Los Angeles. He was fairly short, about five foot two, but he was also fairly stocky, with muscular arms and a powerful body. He had soft gray eyes that smouldered like white-hot charcoal whenever he got angry and sparkled like Roman candles when he got excited, and he had dark brown hair, long enough to tumble over his collar, and bushy eyebrows flecked with gray, and a full beard that made him look like a short version of Abraham Lincoln. And when he would talk, he would gesticulate wildly, waving his arms about, like a sexually aroused windmill or an octopus on LSD. But the thing that people remembered most about Pedersen, the thing you'd never be likely to forget about him once you'd heard it, was that laugh of his, a laugh you'll never hear duplicated except maybe in your nightmares, Pedersen could turn it on or off anytime he liked, it would start off more or less normally, like a normal laugh, and then it would get louder, its pitch would increase and it would get louder and louder, finally it would reach this incredible crescendo, so that unless you'd heard it lots of times before, you'd feel certain you were in the presence of a person whose mind had just snapped.

Ken Pedersen's mother, Marjory Pedersen, was a psychiatric social worker in Taos, New Mexico, and his father—that is, his real father—was a professional gigolo plying the lonely widow circuit somewhere out on the West Coast. When Ken was just a youngster, five years old or maybe six, his father had deserted the family and headed west, Ken hadn't seen hide nor hair of him since, and two years later his mother had married Arthur Pedersen, an accountant for a real-estate development firm, who had then legally adopted Ken and made him his own son.

I didn't become Ken Pedersen's friend right away by any means, it was several months before we really started to become close, but I guess what turned me on to him right from the beginning was that I was horny for pussy like every other guy on the floor and I was amazed by the wonders he could do with the pig book.

The pig book was our name for the Freshman Class Directory, a booklet distributed by the university giving the name, address, and a mug shot of every student in the incoming freshman class. The pictures weren't that good, all you could see was the head and sometimes part of the shoulders, but since all the chicks in the class were in it, and since the pictures were generally good enough to enable you to distinguish the pigs from the pretties, or, in Pedersen's terminology, the skags from the succulents, the book came to be used as a sort of Yellow Pages of pussy, which is why all the guys called it the pig book.

Every evening right after dinner Pedersen would emerge from his room, step to the pay phone mounted on the hallway wall, and riffle impatiently through the pages of the pig book. "God damn it," he'd mutter. "What kind of a god damned pig book is this? You can see their faces but you can't see their god damned tits. How in the name of Fucking H. Christ are you supposed to pick out a hairy if you can't see their tits?"

Once Pedersen had found a girl he wanted, he'd pull a

penny out of his pocket and activate the pay phone by spinning the penny down the quarter slot. Eventually, Ma Bell found out that all the pay phone had inside it was a shitload of pennies and pulled the phone out of the dorm, but by that time Pedersen had taught practically every guy in Hodgkin Tower how to make even foreign calls from pay phones for just a few cents apiece.

"Hello?" Pedersen would call out enthusiastically once he'd gotten that night's succulent on the phone. "You don't know me, but I'm Kenneth T. Pedersen of Taos, New Mexico, living over here on the fifth floor of Hodgkin Tower, and I was just leafing casually through the, uh, Freshman Class Directory, eager to acquaint myself, as much as possible, with my fellow students, when suddenly a stiff breeze blew through my window and blew open the pages of the directory to your name and picture, and, well, I just took one look at your picture and I knew that fate—that's right, fate—had intended for us to meet and get to know one another better.

"So I earnestly hope," he would continue, by now gesticulating wildly, the telephone receiver notched securely between his left shoulder and his ear, "I earnestly hope you won't make light of a modern man who's still enough of a romantic to believe in fate, and that you'll be good enough to join me this evening for a cup of—what's that? You say you will? Why that's just fantastic, my dear. Would eight o'clock suit you, or would nine o'clock be better?"

It was an uncanny technique, it never failed, and so you can understand why it wasn't long before practically every guy in the dormitory began crowding around the pay phone every night after supper to watch Ken Pedersen sift through the pig book and give the pig of the evening his line of bullshit.

Another incident that made Pedersen famous was the time he literally scaled Wharton Hall in order to fuck Margo Kendricks. Wharton Hall was this girls' dormitory building made of glass and concrete which was situated across the campus from Hodgkin Tower, and every night at ten o'clock, every night at ten exactly, there was this creamy blonde named Margo Kendricks who used to pose in front of her seventh-floor window in sexy black lingerie and do this mouth-watering striptease in front of her window. And after she'd unhooked her bra and slipped out of her panties and dropped them to the floor, she'd gyrate slowly in front of the window, squeezing her tits in both hands and licking the nipples with her tongue, and then she'd press her hairy pussy up against the window while holding up a huge sign that said FUCK ME in large red letters, knowing full well that there was no way on earth any man could get inside the girls' dorm.

Well every night at 9:30 the crowd would start to form, in the beginning just a few guys showed up, but after word got around there began to be hundreds, they'd gather on the lawn in front of the dorm and overflow the sidewalks into the street, when Margo Kendricks appeared at her window they'd start yelling and screaming at her to take her clothes off, every now and then you'd catch somebody off on the sidelines beating his meat.

And then one night, out of nowhere, there was Pedersen, somehow he had managed to anchor a rope to the flagpole up on the roof, and when Margo Kendricks appeared at the window and started doing her strip, he dashed to the base of the dormitory and started climbing the wall. Margo Kendricks couldn't see him coming, he was pressed too close to the dormitory wall, his body tightly hugging the concrete wall, and when a great roar went up from the crowd below, I'm sure she never suspected that the loudest cheers were for the miniature Abe Lincoln inching his way up the wall.

The fact is that by the time she saw Pedersen it was way too late. She had just pressed her cunt against the window glass and was reaching for the FUCK ME sign when suddenly Pedersen's smiling face appeared at her window. Clutching his climbing rope tightly in his left hand, he shattered the window with a blow of his right fist—the exultant crowd below scattered as shards of broken glass began hurtling toward the street—and then he climbed into Margo's room and grabbed her by the wrist and dragged her toward the bed.

Her bed was far back inside the room, so none of us actually saw Pedersen fuck her, and when I asked him later if he had actually done it, he just looked at me gravely and shook his head. "It's always preferable to stick it in their mouth, Sy," he replied sternly, his right index finger waggling out at me from a right hand that was now swathed in a gauze bandage where it had been cut by window glass. "Never forget that, because their pussy is filled with corrosive juices that have the chemical power to rot your dick off." And then he turned his back on me and ambled off down the hall.

It was also during orientation week that I started making it with Heather Thomas, a gorgeous spade chick from Pennsylvania with olive-brown skin and long black hair and soft, brown, almond-shaped eyes. She had large thighs and small breasts with thick black hairs growing in a ring around her nipples. The daughter of a steelworker and a part-time domestic, Heather had come to the U. of C. to study foreign languages, I never knew a black person who studied as much as Heather did, and in addition to all her homework and classes she worked part-time in a leukemia lab at the university hospital, taking blood samples from the fingers of small children dying of leukemia and mounting them on microscopical slides. Sometimes late at night, when no one else was there, we'd sneak into Heather's lab and make love on the white-tile floor, all the while trying, as best we could, to shut out the insistent babble of the scrubwomen out in the hall.

Pedersen landed a part-time job in the hospital, too, he worked alone at night in a huge cancer research lab taking care of these thousands and thousands of white mice, generations and generations of them, that were being bred in the lab under controlled conditions to help scientists find a cure for cancer. Pedersen's job was to feed all the mice and clean out their cages, and also to assign each new mouse a permanent inventory number by making notches in its ears with a special punch. The ear punch was similar to a train conductor's ticket punch, and by punching two holes in the mouse's left ear and two in its right, according to a special clocklike code, it was possible to assign each mouse a different four-digit number, up to a total of 9,999 different mice.

Some nights when Ken would arrive at work he would find one or two of the mouse cages set off to one side, along with a handwritten note saying that these mice were to be "sacrificed," and that meant that he was supposed to kill the mice in those cages because they had been used that afternoon in some sort of experiment. Now killing these poor mice was the one laboratory chore that Pedersen simply could not abide doing, so he used to just ignore his instructions and carry the mice outside and let them loose in the bushes. Eventually the scientists found out what Pedersen was doing and fired him, but the doomed mice he spared are still out there somewhere, so if you ever hear of some horrendous cancer epidemic sweeping Chicago, you'll know that Ken Pedersen was personally responsible.

When classes finally got under way in the first week of October, Pedersen and I were in only one class together, an afternoon English class where we spent the first few weeks discussing *Hamlet.* Pedersen adored *Hamlet,* you could even say he was obsessed with it, and whenever he could fabricate an excuse for reading a few passages aloud he liked nothing better than to snatch my copy off my desk, because he never bothered to bring a copy of his own, and leap to his feet, he would stalk and prance about the room, clutching the book in his left hand but hardly ever needing to glance down at the lines, as he recited all the parts in turn, endowing each character with its own special voice and mannerisms, and all the while he would be gesticulating wildly, like a drowning seaman treading water while frantically waving to an invisible ghost ship.

There were a lot of students in the class who resented Pedersen's histrionics, but I soon came to regard them as the only good reason for attending that class, if only because everyone else seemed to regard the play as some sort of sanctified religious tract, devoutly reciting from it aloud, when their turns came, in grave ministerial monotones appropriate to a wake. I remember there's this one scene in *Hamlet* in which Hamlet tells Ophelia that "I could interpret between you and your love, if I could see the puppets dallying," and the annotations in the back of our textbook version glibly explained away this line with some contrived bullshit explanation about Elizabethan puppet plays and the "dalliance" of puppets. On the day we discussed that scene in class, it was Pedersen who leaped to his feet, his arms waving and his eyes flashing, crying, "Can't you see he's talking about her tits, god damn it? The dallying puppets are Ophelia's tits." And even though Professor Henning, who taught the class, sometimes got a little exasperated at Pedersen's antics and probably wished that his most enthusiastic student were a little more subdued, I would sometimes glance at Henning while Pedersen was reading aloud, and I would get the distinct impression that Pedersen was the main reason Professor Henning liked to come to class, too.

Our English class met four afternoons a week, right after lunch, and Pedersen almost always arrived about fifteen minutes early, carrying some large, expensive book under his arm. The books were invariably weighty tomes on philosophy, religion, or ancient history—Pedersen never brought the same book twice—and every afternoon his preclass conversation would be peppered with aphorisms and nuggets of wisdom gleaned from the particular book he happened to be carrying that day.

Often, for example, we would talk about pussy. "If there is one quality that is indispensable to the successful pursuit of the elusive hairy," Pedersen noted one afternoon, in utter seriousness, after arriving in class toting a massive biography of Mahatma Gandhi, "that quality is perseverance. As Mahatma Gandhi once put it, 'Perseverance opens up treasures which bring perennial joy.' Now Gandhi obviously wasn't just talking about pussy, Sy, but you can easily see that the Mahatma's wisdom certainly applies to what we've just been talking about."

Now Pedersen never actually read these books of his, beyond perusing the dust jackets and maybe leafing randomly through the first few pages, but he did acquire sufficient knowledge of a superficial variety—a quotation here, a fact there—to make it appear to his less savvy observers that they were dealing with an eclectic, profoundly well-read person. And once Pedersen had absorbed one of Mahatma Gandhi's quotations, he could effortlessly conjure up dozens of impressive facsimile quotations entirely on his own, so that if one had never been exposed previously to Pedersen's technique, it would appear that his store of Gandhian wisdom was virtually inexhaustible.

I always knew that Pedersen never really read those books he brought to class, but what did puzzle me was how he managed to afford them, and eventually I worked up the courage to ask him.

"It's simple, Sy," he replied with an ingenuous grin. "I don't afford them. I steal them."

"From the campus bookstore?" I asked.

"Right," he nodded, "from the campus bookstore. Sometimes, of course, they don't have exactly what I want in stock, so I get them to special order the titles I want, and then I simply walk out without paying for them."

"Good grief," I exclaimed. "How many books have you managed to steal that way?"

"Oh, just a few, Sy," he winked. "Just a few. Just enough to quench my inexhaustible thirst for the world's treasure trove of knowledge." And then, having given me the only answer he was willing to give me, he punched me in the shoulder, hard but playfully, and threw back his head and began laughing uproariously.

The truth of it is that I didn't find out just how really inexhaustible Pedersen's so-called thirst for knowledge actually was until the middle of November, when my next-door neighbor knocked on my door and summoned me to the phone.

"Sy," whispered the urgent voice on the other end. "It's me—Ken. You've gotta do me a favor—fast."

"Look, Ken," I replied impatiently, "I'm studying. What—"

"Go to my room. Right now. It's open."

"Okay, but—"

"Inside the room you'll find some cartons filled with books. Just drag them the fuck out of there as fast as fuck you can and stack them up in your room. I'll—"

"My room?" I exclaimed. "For Christ's sake, Ken. What—"

"Please, Sy, just go and do it. I can't really talk to you now."

"Can I talk?" I asked.

"Yes," replied Pedersen, "you can. But I can't really answer."

"Is something wrong? Has something bad happened?"

"Yes."

"And it has something to do with these cartons of books you've got in your room?"

"Well, not necessarily. But it could have."

"It has something to do with books generally."

"Right."

"You got busted in the campus bookstore."

"Exactly." Pedersen paused. "The university's got private dicks staked out in the bookstore disguised as students," he whispered, almost inaudibly. "God damned sneaky sons of bitches. They've—"

"Was one of them a blond guy," I asked, "with short curly hair and a straw-colored crewneck sweater?"

"Yeah. He's the one who busted me. But—"

"I saw him in there this morning," I noted. "He was leaning against one of the bookshelves reading a newspaper. I didn't think he really looked like a student, at least not like a student on this campus. He looked more like—"

"Sy, look," hissed Pedersen, cutting me off, "they're gonna search my room, so you've gotta—"

"Don't worry," I said reassuringly. "I'll do it right now."

"Whew!" he sighed. "Thanks a lot. I swear, Sy, I don't know how the cocksucker ever managed to tag me. All I took was a goddam pencil, Sy. A goddam thirty-nine-cent Scripto mechanical—"

"Forget all that for now," I interrupted. "I'll move the books. Where are you now?"

"Campus security office. They're gonna take me over to the dean's office to set a date for me to go before the disciplinary committee. I'll be back at the Tower in time for dinner. But I heard the blond sonovabitch say that since all they got me on was the pencil, they was gonna search—"

"Don't worry," I repeated, "I'll move them. See you at dinner."

"Good," he whispered. "Thanks a lot, Sy." And then he hung up.

When I raced down the hall to Pedersen's room and flung open the door, I remember that I gasped a little. It was only a tiny room, smaller than most of the rooms, in fact, because his room only accommodated one person instead of the usual two, but stacked up in that room from floor to ceiling, packed so tightly together that you could barely negotiate your way around them to get to the bed or sit at the desk, were these cartons filled with hardbound books, I would say there were close to forty cartons containing, all in all, some two thousand books.

It took me about an hour and a half to move those cartons, to lug them one at a time down the hall to the room I shared with Brian Davidson, and I didn't finish doing it any too quickly, either, because within moments after I'd gotten through stacking the final box I saw two men exit from the stairwell—one was the blond guy with the crewneck sweater but the other one I'd never seen before—and stroll down the hallway toward Pedersen's door. Obviously, though, there was nothing left to find there and within two or three minutes both men left.

My roommate Brian could be pretty finicky about some things and I was afraid he'd blow his top when he found Pedersen's hoard of books piled up in our room, but in the end he accepted the temporary inconvenience like a pretty good sport, and three days later Pedersen and I borrowed a couple of hand trucks from the dormitory superintendent and wheeled them over to the post office for shipment to Pedersen's mother in Taos, New Mexico. God knows what he told his mother about how he acquired all those books, but knowing Pedersen, whatever story he told her was probably a good one. And since all the university had on Pedersen was the theft of a thirty-nine-cent pencil, they eventually let him off with just a slap on the wrist.

But I think Pedersen was really grateful to me for moving those books out of his room that day, because it was right after we shipped the books out to New Mexico that he invited me into his room to read me his journal. I remember it was after dinner, around ten o'clock at night, Pedersen's room was still as small as ever, of course, but without all those boxes it seemed empty and spacious. Pedersen pulled his desk chair out from under his desk and offered me a seat, and then seated himself in the green naugahide armchair close by his bed.

The armchair reminded me of one my father used to have before my mother divorced him, I was four and she was twenty-three, we went to Reno, Nevada, together on an overnight train, when night came we slept in a berth near the roof of the train, the berth had a picture window and switches for the lights, you could make our berth blue inside or all pink and white, I remember I played with the lights awhile and then I fell asleep, in the morning I woke up and I looked out the window, thick rings of fog clogged up the sky, it was as though a giant were puffing smoke rings high in the sky.

In Nevada we stayed at a motel across the road from a ranch, the horses at this ranch were kept in a big corral right across from where we lived, there was a cowboy named Tom there, I don't remember his last name, he used to catch wild horses and tame them for the ranch, he blew his nose without using a handkerchief and rolled his own cigarettes using only one hand, I liked him a lot but my mom didn't marry him, we went back to New York City and married a lawyer instead, Tom used to let us feed the horses, in the morning we'd cross the road from the motel and feed bread to the horses, slices of white bread and pieces of apple, those horses could eat a whole slice of white bread without even taking a bite, then I got pneumonia, I was sick in the motel with a case of pneumonia, Tom came to visit me and so did the doctor, penicillin was new then, if it hadn't been for penicillin I would have died there, there was a lawyer back in New York City who loved my mother and wanted to marry her, while I was sick in Nevada he sent me a phonograph, it was the old-fashioned kind that you wound up by hand, the phonograph was painted red and on each side of it there was a yellow decal duck, but one of those decal ducks had torn, so one of the ducks was missing a head, a record came with the phonograph, it was a record of a man singing Mother Goose rhymes, I played that record over and over, and over and over, at night the man would get sleepy, he would get tired from all that singing, and my mother would say let the man sleep, darling, let him rest till tomorrow, so I would let him rest while I rested, all through the night, but early the next morning I would put my record back on the phonograph and wake the man up again, he would always sound rested when I woke him up again, I played that record on that phonograph over and over, I never stopped playing it, my fever passed, the pneumonia went away, and finally I was well again.

On the floor in front of Pedersen's armchair lay a large white ceramic ashtray with a parade of blue horses prancing around the edge, and inside the ashtray lay a plastic tobacco pouch, a book of matches, and an old, yellowed meerschaum pipe. Pedersen reached down and picked up the empty pipe, sucked on it tentatively two or three times, and then leaned toward his bookshelf and pulled down a composition notebook with a marbled black-and-white cardboard cover. Then, moving the pipe to one corner of his mouth and clenching it carefully between his teeth, he opened the notebook reverently and began to read aloud from it.

"I, Kenneth Tobias Pedersen, a lifelong resident of Taos, New Mexico, the United States of America, being carnally knowledgeable of one Sandra Rosemary Share, known informally to me as Sandy, do hereby enter into the keeping of this journal, which is to be about my penis mostly, and about all the wondrous things that he and I have done together."

Throughout the previous spring, while he was still a senior at Taos High, Pedersen had had a torrid love affair with a sixteen-year-old girl named Sandy Share, the daughter of a man who drove a cement truck. The journal, in which Pedersen made entries for a period of fourteen weeks, was a day-by-day account of their romance.

> Saturday, March 25th. I left the house around 11:00 A.M. and drove the 20 miles or so out to our regular meeting place on Cortes Boulevard. I feel like a paranoid having to sneak around like this, picking her up so far from her house, but with old man Share on the warpath the way he

is, it just seems like the safest way to play it. Last week he called up the house and told Marjory he'd strangle me if he ever caught me hanging around his daughter again. I'd love to have it out with the sonovabitch, but probably the best thing for everybody is for me just to cool it.

I was supposed to meet Sandy at 11:30, but when I arrived she wasn't there. I was pretty sure I was on time, but I couldn't really be positive since for some stupid reason or other I'd forgotten to wear my watch. Anyway, a few minutes later she showed up and jumped in the car, and I gave her one of those soft kisses just behind the ear that turn her on so much, and she started stroking my cock through my jeans and I said she'd better cut that out unless she wanted me to crack up the car and couldn't she even restrain her horniness until we'd got out near the river.

I saw that she had thrown this big wicker picnic basket in the back seat, or at least in this place where the back seat used to be before we took it out, and I started to laugh, and when she asked me what I was laughing about I asked her what kind of lunch were we *not* going to eat today, cold chicken or ham sandwiches or what? She giggled, and I said I'd rather nibble on her pussy lips than on any damn ham sandwich, and she stopped giggling and said, "Oh, Ken," in that way of hers as if she was disappointed with me for being so vulgar, even though I know she really loves it. I remember that when I first met her she didn't understand that when I would talk about her hot wet pussy and her juicy cunt-lips, it was because I really loved her.

Then I pretended I was angry, really pissed off at her for being late, and she said how did I know she was late, I wasn't even wearing my watch, so I gave her some b.s. about how in Viking times the fearless Pedersen clan had been rewarded for its valor in battle by being given the power to tell the exact time by just looking at the sun, that this power has been passed through the generations from generation to generation, and that that's how I was able to tell she was exactly seven and a half minutes late. I had her going there for awhile, giving her my best intense, earnest voice and some of my best Stanislavski gestures, but when I told her my Viking magic extended to being able to tell the exact time even if there was no sun, like in the midst of a thunderstorm, she turned sideways in her seat and sank her teeth into my shoulder and I damn near totaled the car into this huge outcropping of rock.

We drove to our favorite shady spot, the overhang we discovered the first time we took a drive together. We always say we're going to try different places next time we come out, but for some reason we never seem to do it, we always just come back to the same old place. Then we spread the tablecloth under the overhang and put rocks on the corners of the tablecloth, and I got the picnic basket from the car and put it on the tablecloth. She said there were ham and cheese sandwiches in it, and I said she shouldn't have brought ham because coyotes are allergic to ham and since we're not going to eat the sandwiches anyway, we're just going to leave them out here for the coyotes like we always do, the coyotes would eat the sandwiches and probably get sick from them.

"Last time you told me the coyotes were Jewish and wouldn't even *touch* ham sandwiches," she said, and we both looked at each other and started laughing.

Then I put my arms around her and I kissed her, it was a good, long, wet kiss, and I reached down and felt her pussy through her cotton skirt and I told her I could feel the hairy palpitating. "Oh, Ken," she said scoldingly, "it doesn't palpitate, for god sakes," and we kissed again and this time she put her hand down between my legs and felt him. I could feel him growing and getting hungrier. He was really big by now, so I lay her gently down on the tablecloth and moved the picnic basket to one side so her head wouldn't hit it, and then I stood back up and stripped, and she sat up and unbuttoned her blouse, and unhooked her bra, and pulled her skirt over her head, and folded everything neatly near the basket.

"Why do women do that?" I snapped. "Why do women, in the midst of lovemaking, have to stop and fold everything?"

"You don't want my father to see me come home all rumpled and start putting two and two together, do you?" she asked.

> Then I lay down beside her. He was big and throbbing. Sandy has three long hairs growing out of each nipple. I named the ones in the left nipple Flopsy, Mopsy, and Cottontail, and the ones on the right I named Winken, Blinken, and Nod. Sometimes I would pull them out but they would always grow back. "Cottontail looks even bigger today," I said.
>
> "Oh, Ken, don't you ever know when to shut up?" she whispered.
>
> "You have the biggest, floppiest cunt-lips I ever saw," I said. "And look, it *is* palpitating."
>
> "Ken, please," she whispered.
>
> I put him into her. The way he gurgled and splashed in there, you wouldn't believe it's been less than a full day since he had a taste of the hairy. Sandy came five times, and when he finally came, it felt like the whole world was being flooded with jism.

The journal went on like that, page after page, day after day. There was an entry for almost every single day of that spring. On the evening of May 4th, however, Sandy's father, enraged at having learned that his underage daughter was still seeing Pedersen secretly, drove past the Pedersen yard in his pickup truck and fired a shotgun blast over Ken's head. Arthur Pedersen was terrified and advised Ken to stop seeing the girl—"For gosh sakes, Ken," he'd pleaded, "can't you just find yourself a less dangerous girl friend?"—but Marjory Pedersen had stood by her son and telephoned the police. Arrested briefly, then released on a few dollars' bail, Sandy's father retaliated by locking his daughter in her room and refusing to let her leave the house. For three weeks Pedersen was unable to see her. The last entry in the journal was dated Friday, May 26th:

> It's been 22 days since that cocksucker started locking her in. Twenty-two days equals 528 hours equals 31,680 minutes. I don't think I should sit here and take this shit. I think I should do something.

And there the journal ended. Pedersen gently closed the journal and returned it to its place on the bookshelf. It was almost 2:30 in the morning. He had been reading nonstop for over four hours. He reached down for his tobacco pouch and filled his pipe with tobacco and lit it, then leaned back in his armchair and began quietly exhaling puffs of smoke.

"What happened then?" I asked.

"What happened when, Sy?"

"What happened afterward? What happened after the last—"

"Well," he replied quietly, puffing on his pipe, "the night I wrote that last entry I went to her house. I waited till after midnight when I knew the cocksucker would be asleep, and I climbed this cottonwood tree outside her window and tapped on her window, and she let me in and we fucked.

"Then while we were fucking he must've heard us, because he busted in and grabbed me and started beating the piss out of me. I tried to fight back as best I could, but he had way too much size on me, so he got on top of me and his legs had my arms pinned and he was just beating the piss out of me. My face was all swoll' up and my eyes were all bloody and swoll' up so I couldn't really see him, but I was yelling and cursing and I remember for a minute I couldn't see any light coming through my eyes and I was afraid I was blind, that he'd blinded me, and I thought, 'Oh, god, I'll never be able to read again. Somebody will always have to read things to me.'

"And Sandy, she was just hysterical. Women don't undeistand violence, Sy, it's just not part of a woman's world, so she got hysterical and she was trying to pull him off of me but he just kept beating the piss out of me, so finally she ran to the phone and called the sheriff, and the sheriff came, before the sheriff came she broke this lamp over his head but it didn't do any good, except for a minute I remember I got an arm free and I tried to give him a sock, but anyway finally the sheriff came and they pulled him off of me.

"So they were holding him, you know, they were holding him and trying to help me up, because I was all puffed up, and all bloody, and I just went crazy, I grabbed this pair of scissors off Sandy's dresser and I went for him with the scissors, I screamed I was going to kill him and I just went crazy and went for him with the scissors.

"But the troopers grabbed me, two of them grabbed me, they grabbed the arm with the scissors and tried to wrestle me to the floor, but I kicked one in the balls and I punched the other one in the gut and laid him out, and two of them had to let go of Sandy's father and grab me because I was so crazy it took four of them to hold me down even though I was all bloodied up and pummeled up. I can't explain it any better than that, Sy. I just went completely crazy."

"What happened then?" I asked.

"The ambulance came and they tried to get this straitjacket on me, but I got my arm loose and decked this one doctor and just fought them. It took five or six of them to hold me, and finally they just held me down so I couldn't move and injected me with something until I passed out."

"And then?" I asked softly. "What happened then?"

"I'm not sure I know what happened then, Sy, because it was right after that that I had my breakdown. I was institutionalized for two months, and then I went home again. And to this day I don't know for sure why I had it, I can't really say why I had that breakdown. Except that I know somehow that my real father is the key to it. He's somewhere out in California and he could tell me. If I could find him, if I could sit down with him face-to-face and I could look him in the eye and he could look me in the eye, and I could ask him, he could tell me why I had that breakdown. And I've got to find him, Sy, I've got to ask him, because until I find out why I had that breakdown, I'll never find out who I really am."

Soon December came and the semester was over, the guys in Hodgkin Tower who were through with exams began trickling out to their Christmas vacations, the Mad Bomber said he was going to visit his mom in New Jersey and pick up some more of the stuff he needed for making more bombs, the motorcycle nuts were revving up their motorcycles and setting off down the frozen highways together. But a couple of us still had the physical science exam to get through, so we were sitting around the dorm, it was around 11:30 at night, we were sitting around with our phy sci books asking each other questions about black box radiation and formulas for mass and inertia and whatever else we thought they might ask us, my roommate Brian was helping us out with it, explaining a lot of the stuff to us, because he'd already taken the course the previous summer, and even though it seems pretty weird, because Brian wasn't really into science at all really, somehow he had a knack for the stuff and he was able to explain a lot of the stuff that just seemed crazy and inexplicable to all of the rest of us.

Anyway, we were sitting around about 11:30 P.M. drilling each other on this horrible stuff when Pedersen came bursting into the room, waving his arms like a maniac, yelling, "Drop everything! Put down those fucking books! Everybody get down to my fucking car this immediate fucking instant!"

"Come on, Ken," I remarked. "We can't possibly go anywhere now. Tomorrow's the phy sci."

"What the fuck's this all about, Pedersen?" somebody asked.

"Fuck the phy sci!" shrieked Pedersen, who had not stopped waving his arms for an instant. "Just fuck the phy sci, god damn it! I am going to show you assholes the biggest fucking pair of gazobs you ever saw in your whole fucking life!"

"Forget it, man," somebody said. "We've all got the phy sci to worry about."

"Whose gazobs, for chrissake?" asked somebody else. "Whose gazobs you talking about, Pedersen?"

" 'Jugs' Moran's gazobs," cried Pedersen animatedly.

" 'Jugs' Moran?" yelled somebody. "Who the fuck is 'Jugs' Moran?"

"She's this incredible stripper, you idiot," retorted Pedersen loudly. "She's this incredible stripper down at the Follies, and she has these two incredible succulent juggerinis that are about the size of the dino balloon in the Thanksgiving Day parade, and she's been performing five shows a day at the Follies, which is where I have been all day, watching her all fucking day, and tonight is her last night and rather than keep her all to myself I jumped into my car and drove all the fuck way back here so I could share her with you, which lord knows I didn't have to do, you ungrateful idiots, because can't you see that twelve o'clock's the last show and that we'll have to shag ass like crazy if we're going to make it?"

By now Pedersen was yelling at the top of his lungs, and getting hoarse from the yelling, and coughing as he tapped on his watch to underscore the imminent arrival of the twelve midnight show.

"Come on, Ken," scolded Brian, "these guys can't waste their time on big tits. They've all got the phy sci to—"

"And what's more," interrupted Pedersen, sensing that the moment had come to unveil the capper, "what's more," he cried, stabbing the air with his forefinger, "I have decided to pay the hairy one hundred balloons to do the trick with me."

"Ken," I exclaimed skeptically, "where on earth would you get your hands on—"

"A hundred dollars?" yelled somebody in sheer disbelief. "You're going to pay this bimbo a hundred bucks for a ball job just because of her big tits?"

"You haven't seen them now, have you?" asked Pedersen, sly as a fox, knowing he had made everybody forget all about the phy sci.

"How pathetic," mumbled Brian, awed and fascinated.

"Now come on, damn it," screamed Pedersen, turning his back on us and racing out the door. "I got room for six more in the car."

I looked at my watch. It was twenty minutes to twelve. "If we're going to go," I remarked, "we'd better hurry. It's twenty minutes to twelve and it'll take us at least twenty minutes to get there."

"Then let's get the hell outa here," cried the Mad Bomber, hurling his phy sci book savagely against the wall, and within seconds we were out of the room, bolting down the hall to the elevator, then becoming impatient with waiting for the elevator and racing pell-mell for the stairs.

"Hey!" called out somebody from the doorway of his room. "Where the hell you guys goin'?"

"To the Follies," yelled Brian. "Pedersen's going to shell out a hundred buckaroos to fuck some stripper with eighty-inch tits."

"Eighty-inch—!!" gasped the newcomer. "Great googa mooga! Can I come, too?"

"No way, man," I shouted back. "Ken's car is already full up."

"That's okay," came the reply. "I'll get Gary to take me in his car."

And before you knew it we were this four- or five-car caravan, roaring out of the dormitory parking lot, zooming down the lakefront drive toward the Follies Burlesque House on lower State Street—singing at the top of our lungs, "Heigh-ho! Heigh-ho! We're off to the burlesque show! We pay two bits to see two tits. Heigh-ho! Heigh-ho!"—parking the cars on side streets and racing, huffing and puffing, there must have been twenty-five of us, up to the ticket window to plunk down our four bucks apiece just in time for the start of the twelve o'clock show.

It was a weeknight and the theater was about half empty—there was this urine-and-semen smell to the place that made you think of popcorn covered with rancid butter—and when we got to our seats, altogether we took up practically two full goddam rows, the show hadn't really started yet and there was this pitchman type guy on the stage in a soiled brown suit waving some book with a brown paper cover and giving a pitch for people to buy it.

"Hey, Brian," I whispered. "You oughtta write about this place in one of your poems."

"It's all so sick," sniffed Brian.

". . . and how many of you men," the man with the book was proclaiming, "how many of you men out there, once you've found yourself a little gal who's willing, can say with assurance that you really, truly know exactly what you have to do to get her motor started? And once you've got her motor started," he continued, waving the book and shaking it over his head, "how many of you men out there can honestly say that you really know what you have to do to keep that motor running?

"Now this little book that I hold in my hand answers all these vital questions. It contains over one thousand mysteries and little-known facts about the female anatomy that will both amaze and astound you! For only twelve-fifty, that's twelve dollars and fifty cents, the world's most gifted and successful questers after the female mystique, the greatest lovers of all time, will tell you, in their own words and with numerous diagrams, pictures, and other illustrative materials, how you can achieve the incredible success with women you have always craved for."

"After he finishes pitching the books," whispered Pedersen, who was seated directly in front of me, "he sells some nudie pictures and then some French ticklers and then those pint-sized scum bags that just cover the head of your cock. Then the show starts. They've also got a clown. He's pretty funny. The jokes are all pretty old, but you know they have this timeless quality about them, this mythic, collective-unconscious quality that—"

"Pedersen, you're full of shit," I whispered.

"Ha," laughed Brian.

"And don't forget 'Jugs' Moran," continued Pedersen, ignoring my remark. "She's fourth. That's the star position."

The first stripper was plump, with pink skin and red hair and the kind of small pink nipples on large-sized tits that I have always thought were dull and uninteresting. Anyway, she was definitely not my kind of shit, but in front of me Pedersen was murmuring, "Oboy, oboy," and lasciviously rubbing his hands together.

"What a zaftig hairy she is, Sy," he whispered ecstatically, without bothering to turn around. "Isn't she a zaftig hairy, Sy?"

"You know those aren't my kind of nipples," I replied.

"Oh god damn, Sy," he spat disgustedly. "You and your goddam oreos. But don't worry. Wait'll you see 'Jugs.' That bitch has got a ton of oreos."

"Oreos are cookies," I noted, by way of correction.

"Just wait'll you see 'em."

The zaftig one with the pink nipples, I think her name was Honey Suckle, climaxed her act by turning her back on us and pulling her G-string down over her ass and shaking her buttocks at us in time to the music, which made me vaguely nauseous, and then she turned face front and gave us a quick flash of her clean-shaven pussy before skipping offstage to mild applause.

The next stripper was really sharp, nice tits, big hairy twat, the kind of chick you'd expect to see in the centerfold of one of the glossier stroke mags. She posed sexily on the stage in this slinky black negligee, and some bald guy in the front row yelled out, "Oh baby, you *know* I like that," and she cooed back, "I know you like me, but do you really *love* me?" And the guy yelled back, "I *really* love you." And she cooed again, "Would you like to get up on this stage with me and really love me?" But when the poor bald slob actually got up out of his seat and started to clamber up onto the stage, she knelt down and put a hand on his forehead and pushed him away, saying, "Better get back to your seat, lover. I was only kidding," and out of the corner of my eye I could see a huge guy with a crewcut in a black tie and tuxedo striding down the aisle toward the bald guy, but when he saw the bald guy going back to his seat he turned back up the aisle again and went back to his seat in the very last row.

After the second stripper, there was this comedy routine, with the guy who'd been selling the books dressed up as a broken-down drunk, staggering around under a street lamp with a bottle of whiskey. Then another drunk walks up to the first drunk and tricks him into letting him take a swig of his whiskey, and before long the second drunk has drunk up all of the first drunk's whiskey and the first drunk is all alone on the stage with an empty whiskey bottle.

Then a succulent chick walks out, and she's carrying a bottle, and the drunk figures he'll trick the succulent into letting him drink her whiskey just like the second drunk tricked him. So he tricks her into letting him take a swig out of her bottle, but as soon as he takes a big pull on the bottle he goes "Blagh!" and spits the stuff out all over the stage.

"Hey!" he yells. "What are you trying to do, kill me? That isn't whiskey!"

"Of course not," she replies sweetly. "I never said it was whiskey."

"Well, what the hell is it then?" demands the drunk.

"I'm on my way to the doctor," answers the chick. "You just drank my urine sample."

That punch line brought down the house, and after the laughter had subsided we saw the third stripper, who was flat-chested and sort of boyish but still kind of sexy in a boyish sort of way, and after she had finished her routine the emcee came out onto the stage and announced, "Ladies and gentlemen, fresh from triumphs throughout the United States and in command performances before the crowned heads of Europe, a young lady whose anatomical attainments will tantalize and astound you, the star of our show, the one and only 'JUGS' MORAN!"

To the semisweet blare of prerecorded trumpets and the staccato roll of prerecorded drums, "Jugs" Moran glided out onto the stage, clad in sheer black stockings and garter belt, transparent black bikini panties, and a transparent black baby-doll negligee open all the way down the front. A small black maid's cap perched atop a mane of peroxide-blond hair, and her feet had been crammed into a pair of narrow open-toed spike-heeled shoes whose steely chromium heels glinted garishly in the glow of a color-changing spotlight. At waist height she carried a large silver platter, and resting on the platter were her gigantic tits, these two incredible monster tits with gigantic aureoles that must've been at least half a foot across. A roar like an earthquake went up from the midnight crowd as she set down the tray on a small table at center stage and then whirled away from it with a sensual flourish, tossing her baby-doll top to the wings, unleashing those great, incredible tits in all their pink and purple splendor, letting them glide across the stage with her like a pair of lascivious, bald-headed dwarves. Her face had a dumb, tired look, like the kind dumb people have when they are bored and tired, and she swirled about the stage on a pair of legs that seemed almost too thin to support her torso while her eighty-inch tits soared obscenely after her.

"I think I have lovely legs, don't you agree?" she asked aloud, her hollow voice dripping with vacuousness, pausing in mid-glide a moment as though to give those amazing mammaries time to catch up with her. "Everywhere I go, men tell me how beautiful they are. What do you think?"

Another monster roar went up from the crowd, a sailor across the aisle was jerking off into a handkerchief, the glare of the color-changing spotlight glinted blindingly off the chromium high heels as "Jugs" deftly brushed her panties with her fingertips and sent them gliding to the floor, then gingerly knelt down and picked them up again, her right breast slouching on the stage like a half-deflated beach ball. She held the panties to her face and sniffed the crotch obscenely, then flung them into the third or fourth row, where they were ripped to shreds by the three or four salesmen, or whatever they were, who managed to lay hands on them.

"Oh, wow!" cried Pedersen ecstatically. "Oh, wow! I sure wish I'd been the one to catch those panties."

"What the hell for?" I yelled back. "What in god's name would you do with them?"

"Cut out the crotch," screamed Pedersen. "Cut out the crotch and smoke it in my pipe."

With other strippers, pulling off their G-string and flashing you their pussy is the climax of their act, but "Jugs" Moran kept right on going, tying those two incredible tits in knots, stuffing them in her mouth and sucking greedily on the aureoles, and then lying on her back and squeezing them, first one then the other, while licking her lips and moaning loudly with simulated ecstasy. And then she was gone, and the rafters rang with thunderous applause.

"Ken," I asked moments later, as the bouncer-ushers flung open the alley exit doors and we flowed out with the rest of the crowd into the garbage-strewn street, "how on earth are you going to fuck that bitch? If you tried to get anywheres near her, you'd be smothered by her tits!"

"That's just what'll be so exciting to find out," replied Pedersen. "Exactly how she manages to get them out of her way while she's fucking. Isn't it amazing the tricks she does with 'em? I read an interview with her where she said she never uses any silicone, because if you fill 'em up with silicone then they lose all their bounce and you can't do stunts with 'em."

"It's going to be incredible to see what she looks like in street clothes," I noted. "It must be a major fucking undertaking just to keep those babies strapped down so you can carry them around from place to place."

"Well you'll find that out soon enough," replied Pedersen, stuffing his meerschaum into his mouth and reaching into a side pocket for a book of matches, "because I'm going to stand right out here in the street till the hairy comes out of there and then take her to the nearest hotel for a fuck job."

"What makes you so sure she'll go for it?" I asked.

"All these hairies fuck and suck on the side, Sy," explained Pedersen patiently. "They can't make any real money stripping, so they supplement their income with fucking and sucking."

The street was cold and quiet now, the sailors had all scattered to hit the late-night bars, and the lights on the Follies marquee blinked into darkness. In the garish neon window of a topless bar across the street, a painted slut with purple lips and an expressionless face swung back and forth on a wooden swing trying to entice you into the bar to spend your money, back and forth, and back and forth, she wore a red sequined bra and panties and white cowboy boots and a matching white hat, and every time she swung forward you could see the soft flesh of her thighs not quite touching, and her big lumpy pussy straining to break the sequins on her panties, as though she had a big catcher's mitt stuffed in her panties.

Years later I made friends with a spade cop who lived in my neighborhood, his wife was a sexy Spanish bitch with silky black hair all the way down to her asshole, and I remember she told me she used to work as a bar girl in that place with the swing. "Most of them gurls you call B-gurls," she explained in her thick Spanish accent, "they is good gurls. They no fuck with anybody but their hoosbans. They talk to you, maybe if they really like you they give you some kinda hand job—you know what is a hand job, Sy?—but it's joost be a job joost like any other job. They ain't none of them gurls whores, baby. At night they finish up work an' they go home to their hoosbans just like any other workin' womens. You unnerstan' me what I'm tellin' you, right, Sy? You unnerstan' me, right?"

Anyway, so that night me and Brian and the other two or three guys who'd stayed behind to watch Pedersen proposition "Jugs" Moran, we went across the street to this doughnut shop so we could get in out of the cold and drink a cup of coffee and maybe eat some doughnuts while Ken waited outside the stage door for the platinum-blond stripper with the eighty-inch tits. Somebody ordered a jelly doughnut and started eating it out as though it were a jelly-filled pussy, and Brian said whoever it was was being disgusting, and everybody laughed, and meanwhile we all watched Pedersen through the plate-glass window, he was standing across the street, all alone in the alleyway outside the stage door, wearing his suede ranch jacket and smoking his meerschaum and for some reason looking even shorter than he actually was. Mounted behind a pane of glass at the front of the darkened theater was this five-foot-high picture of "Jugs" Moran carrying her tits on the silver platter, and way up high, way up high above the marquee, was a gigantic color-tinted black-and-white photograph of some anonymous stripper of long ago, that picture must have been five feet wide and twelve feet high, the stripper in it was a green-eyed blonde with red sequined pasties, and she had a thick snake of some kind, a python or maybe a boa constrictor, coiled around her waist and thighs, obscuring her pussy.

One by one, the strippers from the Follies came out of the stage door and disappeared down the street, their stiletto heels clack-clacking on the pavement as they clack-clacked down the refuse-littered, neon-puddled street into the early-morning winter night.

"Maybe we missed old 'Jugs,' " I mused half aloud. "Maybe she left already and none of us noticed her."

"How could anybody not notice all them tits?" somebody asked, munching a doughnut, and then, suddenly, through the doughnut shop window, we all could see her, carefully closing the stage door behind her and mincing down the alleyway in short, mincing steps, wearing a short, tight-fitting brown leather jacket with a brown fur pillbox hat atop her head. Somehow she looked smaller than she had onstage, and frailer, and you had to look really hard to see that underneath that leather jacket she still had both those gigantic tits.

Staring out through the doughnut shop window, we saw Pedersen step up to greet her, holding out his hundred dollars and saying something we couldn't hear because we were too far away to hear, and then we saw "Jugs" smile, a friendly and appreciative but at the same time condescending smile, and then, without once breaking stride, she stepped briskly past Pedersen, past him to the curb, where she was taken gallantly in tow by two tuxedo-clad gangsters, who escorted her to a waiting Mercedes limousine and roared away with her into the night.

And so it was already well past 3:00 A.M. when Pedersen and Brian and myself wandered into a dingy sailors' bar nestled between a tattoo parlor and a pornographic book store so that we could get ourselves drunk on three or four pitchers of beer. When Brian started to tease Pedersen about striking out with "Jugs" Moran, Pedersen deftly changed the subject by observing that there was some good-looking pussy in the bar but that you didn't stand a chance of scoring it because of the cunt-blockers.

"What the hell are cunt-blockers, Pedersen?" asked Brian, with that dodo's grin he sometimes got from drinking too much beer.

"Cunt-blockers," replied Pedersen, with all the saintly patience of a parent trying to teach his brain-damaged kid to eat an ice cream cone without smearing the ice cream all over his face, "are these lame guys who have got all kinds of sharp-looking pussy jammed up against the bar, and even though they don't stand a snowball's chance of actually getting any of it themselves, still"—now he jabbed a forefinger skyward for emphasis—"they will *block* you."

"You're out of your mind, Pedersen," sighed Brian, shaking his head. "One of these days, I'm going to write a poem about you."

"You're too late, motherfucker," retorted Pedersen. "Sy is going to write a *book* about me. Maybe *lots* of books about me. Isn't that right, Sy?"

"Yes," I affirmed. "That's right."

"No kidding," exclaimed Brian, drunkenly impressed. "No kidding," he repeated, mulling it over to himself. "How about you guys give me a lift to the airport, hey? I got a seven-thirty plane to catch and it'll be almost five o'clock by the time we get there. No point my going back to the dorm now anyhow."

"That depends on where you're going," replied Pedersen testily, deliberately slurring his words, pretending to be a lot more drunk than he really was. "Where you going, Brian?"

"You mean where's my plane going?" asked Brian uncomprehendingly.

"That's right, god damn it," yelled Pedersen at the top of his lungs, feigning sudden anger over nothing, one of his favorite devices for knocking people off-balance. "Whether I take you to the airport or not depends on where in god damn hell your plane's going. Now are you going to tell me where it's going, or—"

"I-I'm going to New York, Ken," stammered Brian, taken aback. "I'm going to spend Christmas with my folks in New York."

"I'll bet they're rich sons of bitches," snarled Pedersen.

"What's got into him?" whispered Brian to me.

"Nothing," I replied. "Come on, Ken. Are we going to give Brian a lift to his plane or not?"

"Of course we're giving him a lift," exclaimed Pedersen, draining his beer mug and then slamming it defiantly down on the tabletop. "Come on, Sy. Get the lead out. We're giving Brian a lift to the airport."

It was still pitch dark outside as we hurtled down the throughway en route to the airport, Pedersen driving with one hand while swilling beer from one of the numerous quart bottles he always kept stashed beneath the front seat, Brian on the passenger side drinking too, and me in the back seat staring dumbly at the onrushing highway, helpless to avert the horrendous crash I assumed was coming, but feeling, nonetheless, that as a matter of principle someone ought to be watching the road. Drunk or sober, Ken Pedersen was, without exception, the world's worst driver, even though he always thought of himself as one of the best. I remember about six of us took this trip to New York with him once, it was his car, he said, and by god he intended to drive the whole way nonstop, by himself, and if the rest of us didn't like it we could all go fuck ourselves, and I remember how we drove on and on, mile after terrifying mile, careening back and forth across the white line like a drunken meteor out of control, all attempts at persuading Pedersen to relinquish the wheel voluntarily ending in failure, until finally, at this Howard Johnson's somewhere in Pennsylvania, the passengers in the car just finally mutinied, we grabbed Pedersen, and confiscated his keys, and we threatened to lock him in the trunk for the rest of the trip unless he agreed to sit quietly and let the rest of us drive.

Now, as we approached the airport, the sun was starting to glint through the leaden sky like a twenty-five-watt bulb, and the lights atop the control tower were blinking signals in red like eyes made of blood. We left Brian sitting on a bench outside the United Airlines entrance, he was staring at the ground and shaking his head back and forth for no apparent reason, and then we waved goodbye to him and careened out of the airport parking lot and hurtled away again into the morning. It was the last time anyone ever saw him alive.

I overslept that morning and got to the psy sci exam twenty minutes late, not that it probably made any difference, I knew I'd be lucky just to pass the thing anyway, and afterwards I got together with Heather for a late breakfast, actually it was more like lunch, before going downtown with her to buy her some stuff she needed, clothes or something, I can't remember exactly what. We had this argument because Heather said we couldn't go downtown until she'd changed from her blue jeans into a dress, which pissed me off no end, because Heather would wear blue jeans to school seven days a week, but if she was going to go into a department store to spend her money, she didn't think it was ladylike to go unless she put on a dress. Anyway, it was while we were on the elevated subway headed downtown that I saw the headline for the very first time:

UNITED FLIGHT TO N.Y.
CRASHES ON TAKEOFF
DEATH TOLL HIGH

"Heather," I shouted, "come on. We've got to get off this train."

"Why?" she snapped. "This isn't—"

"Heather, please," I insisted. "We put Brian on a United flight—"

"There's millions of United flights," replied Heather.

The next stop was a local stop, where there wouldn't be any newsstands, so I waited till the next stop, it was an express stop but they didn't have any newsstand there either, so we rushed downstairs to the street and bought a *Sun-Times* from one of those boxes on the street where you put in your money and take out a paper.

Quick as I could, I scanned the article about the plane crash. "Heather," I exclaimed. "Flight 304. Everyone on the plane was killed. Flight 304 was Brian's plane. I know it was."

"A-Are you sure?" stammered Heather, her lip starting to tremble.

"Damn it," I cursed angrily, "why don't they give a passenger list?"

I threw down the newspaper and dragged Heather across the street toward a phone booth, almost getting us both killed by oncoming traffic.

"What are you going to do?" gasped Heather.

"Call United," I replied. "Got a dime?"

"Yes, here!" she said.

But the man at United said they wouldn't release the names of passengers until the bodies had been identified and next-of-kin notified. I slammed the phone in the motherfucker's face.

"What did they say?" asked Heather.

"They won't tell us," I replied. "Give me another dime."

"I don't have another dime," she said. "Here, use a quarter. But, hey! Who're you calling now?"

"The *Sun-Times,*" I replied.

"The *Sun-Times?*" she repeated. "But what will—"

"Sun-Times?" I yelled into the mouthpiece.

"Sun-Times," chimed a female voice. "Who are you calling?"

"City desk, please," I replied.

There was a pause on the other end of the line, followed by a series of clickety-clicks. Then, somewhere within the bowels of the *Sun-Times,* a telephone rang.

"City desk. Greeley speaking," said a voice.

"I-I'm calling about the plane crash," I shouted, trying to surmount the very loud office noise in the background. "The United crash over at O'Hare. I want to know if—"

"Just a minute," replied the voice. "I'll put you through to Hal Stark on that."

There was a long pause punctuated by clicks as the man at the city desk waited impatiently for someone to transfer my call.

"Damn," he muttered to himself. "When will those dumb—"

"Switchboard," cut in a female voice. "Are you flashing?"

"Yes. Put this call through to Mr. Stark, will you please?"

"Mr. Frank Stark?"

"No, Hal Stark. Harold Stark."

"Yes, sir. One moment please. I'll put you through."

Another pause. More clicks. And then the sound of another phone ringing.

"Whoops, I'm sorry," interjected the operator. "I gave you 2106 and you want 2107. Just a moment please."

"What's happening?" asked Heather. "Who are you speaking to?"

"The operator," I replied. "She—"

"Mr. Harold Stark's line is busy," trilled the operator.

"Damn it," I hissed. "All I want to do is find out about—"

"Your line is free now," cooed the operator. "Here you are, sir. Thank you for waiting."

"Hello," I said. "Is this Mr. Hal Stark?"

"That's me," answered the voice at the other end. "What can I do for you?" It was the voice of a young man, resonant, authoritative, like the kind you hear on the local news reporting to you from the scene of a tragic fire where four firemen died.

"I'm calling about the plane crash this morning," I explained. "I want to know if Brian Davidson was among the—"

"Everyone on the plane died," noted the reporter resonantly. "Incinerated. Was this fellow Davidson on the plane?"

"I'm not sure," I replied. "That's what I'm calling about. He was on his way to New York. He might've been on the plane, but—"

"You a relative?" asked the reporter.

"No," I answered. "A close friend. Just . . . can you tell me if—"

"Just a second. We just got hold of a passenger list. It's going into the evening edition. But just hold on a second. I'll check it to see if your friend's on it for you."

There was a clunk as he dropped the receiver on his desk, followed by a long silence broken only by the shuffling of papers. And then—

"Sorry I dropped you there, fella. Here we go. Jacobsen, Henry. Albano, John. Milgroom, Lawrence. O'Neil, Frederick. Sorry it's not in alphabetical order. Wait a minute. Here it is—Davidson, Brian. He was on there, all right."

"Does that list mean he was definitely on the plane?"

"It means he definitely signed up for the flight, all right. Unless he changed his mind at the last minute or didn't make it to the airport in time to—"

"Not much chance of that," I noted sadly. "A friend of mine and I drove him to the airport about two hours early. We—"

"Then I'm afraid he's gone," commented the reporter. "They were incinerated, every last one of them."

Heather heard him and started to cry. Tears welled up in her gigantic brown eyes and she covered her face with her hands and sobbed into her silly wool mittens. "Oh, Sy," she whispered. "Poor, poor Brian."

"You say you were a relative of this Davidson fella?" asked the reporter.

"No," I answered. "A friend."

"You mind if I ask you a few questions?"

"What kind of questions?"

"Was he *from* Chicago, or what?"

"No, he was from New York," I replied. "We were students at the university together. He was on his way home to New York to see his parents."

"On his way to New York to spend Christmas with his parents?"

"That's right."

"Do you know . . . do you know if he had any presents with him," asked the reporter, ". . . if he was carrying any presents home with him to give to his parents?"

"Not that I know of," I replied.

"Then if he was carrying presents, you don't know what the presents were, do you?"

"No," I answered, "I don't."

"Do you know what he wanted to be, what he was studying to be? If he had his eye on a career in—"

"A poet," I said. "He wanted to be a poet."

"A poet, eh?" mused the reporter. "That's—"

That's when I hung up.

Heather went back to Pennsylvania for Christmas to see her folks, and Pedersen went back to New Mexico to be with his, so I was really the only one who went to the funeral. I tried to get Pedersen to make the trip with me, but he just said, "Aw, Sy, I wasn't really ever close to Brian like you were, and besides, you know a really sad funeral wouldn't be my bag and I'd probably just wind up hitting on some pussy there and making everybody mad at me," so I ended up going to the funeral all by myself, hitchhiking, making it all the way from Chicago to New York in eighteen hours flat.

I wasn't really the only one who attended Brian's funeral, of course, but I was the only one I knew, the rest were all people he'd known from high school, plus his parents and relatives and maybe a smattering of family friends. We sat on folding chairs in the chapel of the Charles F. Brodhurst Funeral Home, across the street from a red brick public school, and we stared somberly at this vase they had which contained everything that was left of Brian after the crash. I'd been to one or two funerals before that, I guess, but I'd never been to one like that, where all you did was sit in complete silence and stare at a vase. I remember wondering to myself whether they'd actually gone to the trouble to find Brian's ashes, I mean the ones that actually belonged to Brian, or whether they'd just swept together one huge pile of ashes and then divided them up into separate little piles, one for each passenger who'd been on the plane. I remember wondering about all that and thinking that I'd really like to ask someone, but realizing that I'd better not, because if I did they'd think that I didn't really care about Brian.

My grandfather died when I was twelve years old, and I went to his funeral wearing charcoal-gray slacks and a bright red blazer with shiny brass buttons. My grandfather, meaning my father's father, had been a jeweler in Germany, and when the Nazis came to power he fled Germany with my grandmother, carrying with him his entire stock of gems, rubies and emeralds and other precious gems, wrapped in pieces of tissue paper inside delicate chamois bags. Sometimes, when I was little, he would take out one of those chamois bags and sit me on his knee and pour diamonds and rubies into his hand and show me how they gleamed and sparkled in the light, but his face was covered with bristly white stubble, it used to scratch me hard whenever he kissed me, and he had a phlegm-choked laugh that made me frightened, and so I didn't like to sit on his knee but my father used to make me. The bright red blazer I wore to his funeral was the most wonderful jacket I've ever owned, but my father told me, god knows how many times he told me, that all of our relatives thought I must have hated my grandfather because I wore a bright red jacket on the day of his funeral.

And so as we stared at that vase in the Charles F. Brodhurst chapel, all the other people in the chapel were probably thinking solemn thoughts, god knows about what, maybe thoughts about Brian's beautiful poetry or about Brian's soul floating to heaven, and I knew that if I told any of them what I was thinking, that I just wanted to know whether those were really Brian's ashes in the vase or whether that was just a fair share of the ashes from some horrible, gigantic pile of ashes, I knew that they'd all think I hated Brian just like they'd thought I'd hated my grandfather.

Then some kind of clergyman came into the chapel, we all stood up, Brian's mother wore a black veil and was sobbing, and Brian's father had to hold her up to keep her from falling, even though he was crying, too. All I wanted to do was get the fuck out of there and maybe go to a movie and afterward chase some hairy, but instead I stayed, of course I stayed, while the clergyman recited this sickening eulogy that would've made Brian barf if he'd been there to hear it.

Then everybody stood up, the folding chairs all squeaked in unison, and filed silently out of the chapel into the lobby. That's when I spotted this succulent hairy, a blond chick, I was sure she must've been Brian's girl friend in high school because she looked just like a girl he'd told me about, only now she was with this guy, this clean-cut football-player type in a three-piece brown suit with a brown overcoat folded over his arm, or at least she looked like she was with him, it was hard to tell, and I figured if I moved fast enough I ought to be able to catch up with her before she could get out of the lobby. "Excuse me," I would say, "my name's Sy Wiener. Were you a close friend of Brian's?" And then whatever she said back, as long as she wasn't with the football hero, I'd jump right on it, and maybe if I played my cards right I could get her to have dinner with me that night and we could console each other by—

"Excuse me," said this woman's voice behind me, "are you Sy Wiener?"

It was Brian's mother. She was a dark-haired woman in her early forties, attractive, maybe a little overweight, she wasn't crying anymore and she had pulled her veil away from her face and put it up on top of her head. She extended a puffy little right hand and I shook it, and when I glanced furtively over my shoulder to check where my blond hairy had gone to, my blond hairy was gone, gone with the wind.

"Yes, I'm Sy Wiener," I replied. "I want you to know you have my deepest sympathies, Mrs. Davidson. Brian and I were, at school we were—"

"Yes, I know," she said quietly. "Brian told me all about you in his letters. He admired you very much and respected your criticisms of his poetry."

"He would've been a great poet," I said, as convincingly as I could.

"He may not be dead, you know," remarked Mrs. Davidson. "You see, we think there's still a chance that Brian may not actually have been on that plane at all."

"B-But," I stammered, "we—"

"Yes, I know you took him to the airport, and I know he was booked on that flight. But no definite proof he was actually on the plane has been produced. The remains were too . . . too . . . they couldn't really be properly identified. There's always the possibility that while Brian was sitting on that bench waiting for the plane, some thief hit him over the head and left him lying in an alley somewhere. For all we really know, he may be wandering around Chicago somewhere, dazed, suffering from amnesia, not aware of who he really is. It's a possibility worth investigating, don't you agree?"

"Y-Yes, I guess so," I replied nervously, "but it seems very—"

"I know the chances seem remote," she agreed. "But we must not give up hope. That's why Brian's father and I have hired a pair of private detectives to comb Chicago in the event Brian may still be alive."

"I-I certainly wish you the best of luck," I stammered. "I—"

She reached out suddenly and grabbed my sleeve. "But if . . . if the worst happens," she went on, "and we lose all hope, Mr. Davidson and I would like to publish a commemorative volume of Brian's poetry. You're probably more familiar with his work than anyone. If we do publish the volume, would you be willing to edit the material for us, as a last favor to Brian?"

"Of course," I answered. "I'd be happy to."

The next semester came and went, and soon it was summer. The university wouldn't let you live in the dormitory during the summer, so Pedersen and I rented this apartment maybe a half mile away, five big rooms for eighty-five bucks a month on the second floor of this dilapidated two-story firetrap nestled at the center of a garbage-strewn slum. Downstairs was Mike's Grocery, where you could buy stale doughnuts every day and which got held up on the average maybe six times a month. There was a pool hall a block or so down the street, and when you walked up the flight of stairs to our apartment, the mongrel police dog owned by the Puerto Rican woman who lived across the landing from us would snarl behind her Fox-locked door like a werewolf gorging itself on human entrails by the light of the moon.

In a small foyer just inside our front door, there was a set of brass coat hooks fastened to the wall, and right after we moved in we agreed that if you came home and there was an article of clothing hanging on one of those brass hooks it meant that the other guy had some hot pussy jammed in his room and you should be careful not to barge into his room. The apartment had three bedrooms—mine faced the street—and at night the streetlight near my window lit up my room like daylight and a huge neon sign across the street changed colors constantly like an electronic chameleon, washing the wall above my bed in waves of many-colored light.

At night I'd go to work in the billing department of the University of Chicago Press, operating a computerized IBM billing machine that cranked out the invoices for the books that individuals and bookstores had ordered by mail. I worked up there alone at night with this spade cat named Walter who operated a second billing machine just like mine. He was a cool dude, this Walter, he had this thin moustache that made him look like a black Clark Gable, only Walter's principal occupation was being a pimp, at night he'd arrive at work late and spend an hour or two on the telephone getting in touch with the ho's in his stable—"Hey, baby, how much bread you gonna have for me tonight? Oh, no, baby, you know a hundred ain't where it's at. Whyn't you see if by midnight you can't maybe work it up to two-fifty"—and then he'd put in maybe an hour on the billing machine, he had this way of jamming up the machine with a torn IBM card to make it look like the machine was busted so he couldn't work anymore, then he'd leave the building and roar away into the night in his chrome-festooned pimpmobile, he had some incredible cunt working for him, too, I used to joke with him could he maybe let me have a free whiff, but he'd only laugh and say he couldn't even let his best friend touch his grade-A shit for less than forty dollars, or maybe, for a good friend, he'd settle for twenty. Anyway, long around mid-June or so Walter contracted spinal meningitis and they took him to the hospital, they put him in a room with three or four other guys who had the same thing and they rammed an elephant-sized hypodermic needle up into his spine and tried as best they could to suck all the meningitis out, the three or four other guys in Walter's room, they all died, Walter stayed alive awhile longer and then he died, too.

So I arranged for Pedersen to inherit Walter's job, at night we'd walk from our apartment to the U. of C. Press, sometimes Ken would wear white ducks and these spades would stop us in the street, asking us did we work at the hospital and was Ken a doctor and was there maybe any way we could steal them some drugs. From around ten o'clock at night till two in the morning we'd sit all alone in this tiny machine room, no one else in the goddam building but us, sitting back-to-back in front of these giant billing machines, watching the IBM punch cards rattle along their slots, cranking out invoices, passing the time by improvising obscene songs and singing them above the clatter of the billing machines at the top of our lungs:

Row, row your fucking boat
Gently down the fucking stream,
Merrily, merrily, merrily, merrily
Life is but a big fat wet dream!

The job didn't pay much, god knows, under two bucks an hour, but if you really busted your nuts you could get your night's work quota completed in four hours and then monkey with your time card to bill the company for eight, and then me and Pedersen would walk on home and pop up some popcorn and break out a few beers, and sometimes we'd fix ourselves one of those Kraft macaroni and cheese dinners that you can buy for maybe sixteen cents a box.

It was a good summer, that summer, Heather was home in Pennsylvania visiting her folks, writing me maybe a letter a week, and meanwhile I was fucking all these succulent hairies, like Donna Marie Jefferson, this divorced red-headed bitch from Chattanooga, Tennessee, she'd been married to this Hungarian guy three years till she got a divorce, she hated Negroes, "Sy, I just don't understand it," she whispered to me one night, "how you can possibly stand to live in a neighborhood with so many niggers."

"It's not something that bothers me," I replied.

"They're just like cockroaches, aren't they?" she purred, rubbing her thighs up against me and nibbling my ear. "They come crawling out of the woodwork as soon as it gets dark."

A few minutes later, up in my bedroom, after I'd turned out the light and started to unhook her bra, she whispered, "No, not that, I never even let my husband take off that," and then she lay down on the bed and hiked her skirt up over her thighs and wriggled out of her sopping wet panties and spread open her thighs to give me a whiff of the hairy. I grabbed her by the hair and ripped off her bra and then held her down while I pulled all her clothes off. "You sure do look good naked," I said admiringly.

"I hate you!" she hissed at me through tobacco-stained teeth. "I hate you!"

I climbed on top of her and rammed in my choad all the way to the root.

"Ohhh, I hate you," she moaned. "You're the only man who's ever had me naked. Even my husband never had me naked."

"I don't believe you," I said.

"Oh, it's true," she moaned. "It's true. I'll give you all you want tonight, but I'll hate you in the morning because you've shamed me."

And then there was Antoinette, this skinny light-skinned spade bitch who worked at Mike's Grocery Store, once when Pedersen and I were flat broke she slipped us some macaroni and a six-pack for free, and soon afterward I started popping her even though she had no tits to speak of and never would blow me. Instead she'd close her eyes when we'd fuck and pucker her lips like a gorilla, and hiss like a snake. "Oh Daddy," she'd hiss, "don't stop, Daddy. Whatever you gonna do, please don't stop. I'll do anything so you won't stop, Daddy. Anything you want me to."

"Will you suck it for me?" I'd ask.

"Oh yes, Daddy, anything. Anything, Daddy. I'll take it in my mouth and suck it for you, but don't stop, Daddy. Whatever you gonna do, please don't stop."

But when I'd pull my cock out of her pussy and try to stick it in her mouth, she'd only giggle and turn her face away and giggle some more, and I'd have to shove it back in her cunt and fuck her till I came.

Tony had this girl friend named Francetta who had dark brown skin and big brown eyes and a big pouty mouth that looked like it could handle maybe six or seven dicks at once. Sometimes Tony and I would go over to her place, Francetta would be straightening her hair with Dixie Peach or ironing a blouse, and she'd smile at me over her shoulder with that semen-swallowing mouth of hers and she'd say, "Antoinette, honey, if that cute white boy wasn't tied down to you, you just better *believe* I'd be jumping all over his face, honey."

She used to drive me wild, that Francetta, and so finally I decided to try to get the two of them up to my place and fuck them both at once. The idea was for me to invite them up to the apartment to spend an evening with Pedersen and myself, and then we'd get them wasted on gin and Pedersen would vacate the premises and let me ball them both myself. The night we did it, though, Pedersen got really swacked on beer before he ever got home, and when Francetta finally showed up about half an hour after Tony, Ken ignored our plan and went right after it. I don't think Fran really dug Pedersen especially, but he took her into his bedroom and after about fifteen minutes or so I could hear her through the walls saying, "Okay, honky child, if you really wants it *that* bad, this big black momma's sho' nuff gonna let you *have* some." It was the only time I ever tried to fuck Francetta, and pretty soon after that I stopped seeing Tony too.

Probably the high point of that summer, it was late July, or maybe it was early August, I forget, it was probably late July because it was the same month that Pedersen knocked up Elaine Willoughby and she had the kid on April 20th, I remember that for certain, anyway the high point was when my dad, my real dad, the one whom I said had leukemia when I tried to bullshit my way into Columbia University, well he had this management conference out in Chicago that month, so he figured as long as he was flying out there on the company's money he might as well stop by and pay me a visit. If IBM hadn't been paying the freight, you can believe me he wouldn't have come.

The weekend he was supposed to fly in, Pedersen was planning to spend the whole weekend with Elaine, she was this anemic-looking graduate student in the biology department, Pedersen said he had met her in the cafeteria or someplace, who looked like she'd just crawled out from under a rock, or like a vampire victim in a horror comic who's had all her blood sucked out. But Pedersen was planning on spending the whole weekend with her at her place, which meant our place would be empty except for me and my dad, and we figured I'd put my dad up in the spare bedroom we had, which we never used but which had a bed in it anyway, the spare bedroom adjoined my bedroom and overlooked the street, just like mine did, and even though it was kind of small, it had the advantage of not having a streetlight glaring right in through the window, or a neon sign splashing colored light on the walls, and Pedersen lent me a couple of sheets and a pillowcase and a quilt for my father to use during his visit. I took the sheets and stuff and put them aside to put on the bed when he came, I know it sounds trivial to even mention the sheets and pillowcase, but later on my dad made this incredible scene about the sheets which I think made me really see him clearly for the very first time.

Friday night Pedersen and I worked till two-thirty or three in the morning at the U. of C. Press, then we stopped at a bar for a couple of beers, and then Ken went straight to Elaine's while I went home alone and, after staying up so late and having had so much beer to drink I guess I overslept, because I ended up waking up too late to meet my dad's plane when it landed at the airport. I mean, I never actually told him I'd meet his airplane, all I really had was this note from him saying he had to attend this sales conference and he'd be arriving in Chicago on Saturday morning on such and such a plane, I thought if he expected me to meet the plane he should have said so but Pedersen thought I should take a bus out to the airport and meet the plane anyway, and so I guess I never really made up my mind about whether I was going to meet the plane or not, I just set the alarm clock and went to sleep, but when it went off the next morning I was so damn wasted that I just flicked the thing off and went right back to sleep.

The plane was due in about 11:45 and I didn't even get up till just after 12:30, so I was still eating my breakfast around two in the afternoon, which is something I still do, getting up real late and eating bacon and eggs and toast and coffee at around two in the afternoon, then staying up all day and through the night to right around dawn, so I was still in the middle of eating breakfast, and I remember I was reading this book of poetry Pedersen had,

The Gypsy Ballads of Garcia Lorca, and in the middle of breakfast the doorbell rang, and I jumped up and raced down the stairs, because there was no way to ring a buzzer and let anyone in, you had to just go all the way down to the ground floor and see who it was and let them in yourself, which was a real pain in the ass when kids, mostly smart-aleck spade kids, would ring the bell just to get you pissed off and then go run and hide before you could get downstairs. So there was my dad at the door holding these two canvas suitcases, and even though, as I said, it was the middle of the afternoon around two P.M., before I opened the street door and let him in I could see through the glass door panels that he was glancing anxiously up and down the street, like when it's late at night and you're afraid you've been followed and if the person you're visiting doesn't let you in right away you're terrified you'll get your throat slit by a spade with a razor.

"Hello, Simon," he said when I opened the door. "When you didn't meet the plane I thought I'd come right to your address."

My father's probably pretty average, I guess, he was in his forties then, full head of hair, middle-age paunch, pale blue eyes, and skin like the underbellies of catfish when you catch them at night and jerk them out of the water. And he's got this look of his, this one patented look, of someone who has been deeply wounded emotionally, and also offended, received a deep emotional wound and also been deeply offended, so he is both terribly hurt and at the same time filled with righteous anger, and out of tact, out of good taste and good breeding, he is trying to conceal the stinging hurt he feels and also restrain his righteous anger, but some crosses are too heavy for even the strongest man to bear, and if something soothing doesn't happen right away, he is going, in spite of himself, despite the good soldier that he is, to be forced to spew forth this cloud of stored-up hurt mixed with righteous anger.

"I-I'm sorry I missed the plane, Dad," I apologized, as contritely as I could. "You see—"

"No explanations necessary," he sighed, picking up both his suitcases and lumbering wearily past me into the vestibule and up the stairs. "How many flights is it to your apartment? It's hard for me to climb stairs with the problems I've been having. Especially carrying two heavy suitcases. Did I mention in any of my letters about the problems I've been having?"

"No," I replied. "You didn't. What kind of problems?"

"Later," he answered. "I'll tell you later. First I want to get up these stairs so I can put down these suitcases. How many flights did you say?"

"Just one," I replied. "The door's open on the right. Would you maybe like me to help you carry those suitcases?"

"No, no, that's all right," he insisted. "I might have used the help a minute ago, but now that I'm already a third of the way up the—no, forget it, I'll be fine, as long as my back doesn't—oh, damn, which door did you say it—"

"The one on the right when you reach the landing," I repeated. "It's open."

"Oh god," he blanched, climbing the stairs, nearing the top, suddenly blanching as the Puerto Rican woman's police dog started snarling and growling, growling and snarling, lusting for the chance to tear out the gizzards of whatever poor nigger might try to rip off the Puerto Rican woman's apartment. "Oh god," gasped my father. "That's not *your* dog, is it?"

"I'm thinking of buying it," I replied.

"You're thinking of—what are you smiling at?" he snapped. "What do you mean you're thinking of buying it?"

"I mean it's a handsome dog and I'm thinking I might like to buy it from my neighbor to keep as a pet."

My father staggered across my threshold with a martyred stagger and dropped the canvas suitcases on the hallway floor with a self-pitying thud. As I entered behind him and slammed the door, he turned and fixed me with an angry index finger.

"Don't try to be a smart-aleck with me," he warned, shaking the finger. "I didn't travel nine hundred miles to be—"

"I wasn't being a smart-aleck," I insisted. "I just said that—"

"I know what you said," he said.

He slouched in the foyer beneath the brass coat hooks and surveyed the apartment critically just as far as he could survey it without taking any steps, peering into my bedroom, which lay to his right, then peering down the long hallway toward the living room, straight ahead, unable to peer into the guest bedroom, which would be his room, because the door was closed. He didn't like what he saw, but pointedly refrained from making any comment, determined to make me feel that the apartment was beneath his standards, unacceptable, while at the same time making me believe, if he could manage it, that he was far too polite a guest to actually say openly that the accommodations were unacceptable.

"Do . . . do you have an Alka-Seltzer," he asked, "or something for the stomach? I have this—"

"No Alka-Seltzer," I replied. "How about aspirin or—"

"Aspirin upsets the stomach," he said. "Can you make me a cup of tea?"

"Yes," I answered, "we have tea. I'll make some. Come on in and sit down."

"Should we leave the luggage here?" he asked.

"Sure," I replied, "why not?"

"Well, someone, your friend, whoever lives here," he began nervously, "they might—"

"The only person who lives here is my friend Ken Pedersen," I noted, taking a pot out of the pantry to boil the tea water, "and he's spending the weekend with his chick, so he won't be back until you're gone. You're leaving Sunday, right?"

"What's the hurry?" asked my father.

"There's no hurry, Dad," I replied. "I only—"

"How do you live like this?" he asked with a wistful sigh.

"Like how, Dad?"

"Like this. In this apartment. This neighborhood. Aren't you—"

"No, Dad, I'm not," I replied impatiently. "The university's in this neighborhood. This is a good apartment because it's within easy walking distance of the university. My friends all think I'm lucky to have—"

"What's that pot for?" interrupted my father.

"I'm going to make the water for your tea," I replied. "Don't you—"

"Don't you have a teakettle?" he asked.

I didn't answer.

"I guess it doesn't really matter," he said finally. "But use two teabags. Make it really strong. And with two sugars. And squeeze in some lemon. Do you have any—"

"No," I replied. "I don't have any lemon. But I can go downstairs and—"

"No, no," he said. "I don't like being alone in strange places. Stay. Without the lemon's fine."

"Are you sure?" I asked. "It's just—"

"No," he insisted. "It's fine. Really."

■ ■ ■

That evening he took me to Sir Lancelot's Pub for dinner. It was this expensive steak place for businessmen that was listed in his little blue American Express book—he kept calling it Am-Ex, "Let's go here," he said, "they give it an asterisk in my Am-Ex"—and the waitresses there were all dressed like old English serving wenches, and my dad kept getting pissed off at me because I kept craning my neck to stare at their tits, there was this one waitress trolling past with a really heavy set of tits, instead of paying respectful attention to his fatherly bullshit.

"Well," he remarked, poring over his filet mignon, medium, with mushroom cap and parsley sprig and platter of cottage fries, "how are you getting on at the university?"

"I hate it," I replied.

He set his fork down at the edge of his plate and grasped his steak knife in the fingers of his right hand.

"Why do you hate it? Wasn't I right when I said it was nothing like high school, that you'd be able—"

"Well I don't know about that," I remarked, cutting him off. "Remember that time in high school when I wrote a composition for English class about a marijuana party I'd attended in Greenwich Village and Mr. Baker gave me an F on it just because it was about marijuana?"

"Yes, Simon, I recall that incident. You were very upset about that, and rightly so, and I assured you that a thing like that could never—"

"But that's exactly why I brought it up," I went on, "because something like that has happened again. Last semester I wrote a short story on my own, called 'The Dress,' about a teenage boy who has an affair with his mother. I showed it to my adviser, because I was very proud of the story and I hoped that maybe she'd use it to help me get admitted to an advanced creative writing course that freshmen usually aren't allowed to take. And you know what the bitch did? She xeroxed my story and dropped it in my file in the dean's office, along with a handwritten note to the effect that the content of my story was a clear indication of my urgent need for psychiatric care, as a result of which I found myself summoned to the dean's office a few days later so that she could ascertain whether—"

"Do you mean to tell me," interrupted my father incredulously, "that someone on the university faculty actually tried to use a short story you'd written as the basis for recommending that you submit to psychotherapy? I can't believe it."

"You can believe it or not. It happened."

"Well, all right," relented my father tentatively. "Let's say it happened. It's something to be concerned about, I'll grant you that, but not a basis on which to judge an entire university. That place will be good for you, Simon, believe me. It's the perfect place for a boy of your brilliance. It will help you—"

"I hate it," I repeated. "I think I'm probably going to quit."

He resumed eating, slicing V-shaped chunks out of his filet like a groom dissecting a wedding cake. "Oh," he remarked, feigning a tolerant curiosity, "what will you do instead?"

"I'm going to quit school and be a writer."

"That's admirable, Simon. Admirable. You know how proud I am of your writing. But while you're doing this writing, how will you live?"

"I have a job," I replied.

"Oh," he mused aloud, chewing, reaching into the corner of his mouth to retrieve a fugitive piece of gristle, "what kind of job?"

"I operate a billing machine at the University of Chicago Press."

"I see. A sort of clerical job. Do you enjoy it?"

"Not really," I admitted. "But it's close to home and I can work four hours and they pay me for eight, so it's—"

"Tell me," he interrupted, "how long do you think it will be before you'll be able to support yourself through your writing?"

"I don't know that," I replied.

"Do you think it might be ten years?" he asked, depositing the captured gristle triumphantly on the edge of his plate. "Do you think it might be ten years before you could earn enough money by writing to quit this job you have?"

"It's possible," I replied. "But—"

"It's more than possible," he went on, "it's virtually certain. William Faulkner wrote and published four or five novels and still couldn't support himself through his serious fiction. How do you think your writing stacks up against William Faulkner's?"

"It's not as good," I admitted.

"I know you think that I have some ulterior motive for all this," he remarked, "that I'm saying all this because I want to hold you back. But the truth is that I just don't want to see my favorite son . . . you are my favorite son," he smiled.

"I'm your only son," I noted dryly.

"That's right," he laughed. "That's why. I just don't want to see you wasting your life operating a billing machine just because you're a little impatient."

"I hate school," I insisted. "It's a goddam waste of my time. All I'm doing is—"

"You're absolutely right," he agreed. "Most of the people you meet in school or anyplace else in this world are morons. And most of the things you have to do in life are boring. But if you stick with school and hang in there and get yourself a law degree, then you can have some security, and an interesting, challenging life, and in your spare time you can write all the great fiction your heart desires. What do you say?"

"I say that school is boring and I think I'm going to quit."

"Do you think, as a favor to me, you could try to stick with it for one more semester, maybe get Professor Henning to get you into some special courses, and see how you feel about it then?"

"Okay," I replied. "I'll probably do that."

■ ■ ■

Later we left the restaurant and strolled down the street beneath the elevated subway tracks.

"Do you remember," he began, "how when you were in high school you got all involved in that theater group they had there and with that drama teacher you liked so much, Mr. Small, or whatever his name was?"

"Yes," I replied.

"And after you'd done such a professional job in that play about the convicts, you told your mother you were thinking about becoming an actor, and I told her you were far too intelligent to sacrifice the great career you had ahead of you in favor of a squalid life in the theater? She was so afraid you were going to do it. But I was right, wasn't I?"

"You were wrong," I commented.

"You just like being contrary," laughed my father.

■ ■ ■

It was almost 1:00 A.M. by the time we returned to the apartment, and the Puerto Rican police dog went insane as we climbed the stairs to the door.

"I could stay at a hotel," remarked my father.

"It's up to you," I replied, unwilling to twist his arm like I knew he wanted me to, "but there's plenty of room here. You're perfectly welcome to stay here if you want to."

"But where would I sleep?" he asked. "I can't sleep on the couch, and I don't want to sleep in your friend's room. What if he comes back?"

"He won't be coming back till after you're gone," I noted, "but you're not going to sleep in his room anyway. We have a spare bedroom. Here."

I flung open the door and flicked on the light. Outside a police car screamed through the night.

"The bed," he said nervously. "There . . . there are no linens on it."

"There are fresh linens in this drawer," I explained. "Come on, we'll put them on."

"Are you sure they're fresh?" he asked. "I don't want—"

"Straight from the laundromat," I replied. "I promise."

He reached out and accepted them with the look of a man who has been asked to spend the night in the bedclothes of a leper.

"Why didn't you put them on the bed before I came?" he whined.

He glanced anxiously out the window. "Hey!" he exclaimed suddenly. "What was that noise?"

"I don't know," I answered. "I didn't hear any noise. Now come on, let's put the sheets and stuff on the bed so you can get some sleep."

"Why didn't you do it before I came?" he asked again.

"Look," I replied irritably, "don't try to start anything with me. The sheets are clean. It will just take us two minutes to—"

"I'm not starting anything," he pouted. "You're a gifted boy, but you're selfish. Very selfish. When you're expecting a guest for the night, it doesn't even have to be your *father,* you—"

"Please stop it," I cut in, as I snatched away a sheet from the top of the bundle and started shaking it out. "I don't want to have to listen to it. Go ahead. Put down the rest of that stuff and help me get this sheet straight."

"Look," he remarked, pointing. "There's a hole in it."

"So there is," I agreed. "Does it matter?"

"Of course it matters," he insisted, his voice rising to a petulant whine. "I'm going to be sleeping on that."

"I'll get you another one," I replied, relenting. "I just hope we have another clean sheet in the house."

I went into Ken's room and searched through his chest of drawers. I found another sheet in the bottom drawer. It was green.

"Here," I snapped, holding it out for examination, "a brand new one. It doesn't matter that it's green, does it?"

"Of course not," sniffed my father.

We put the linens on the bed and the quilt on top. "I don't think it'll get cool enough for the quilt," I observed, "but in case it does—"

"Thank you," replied my father. He went to the closet and rummaged among the hangers.

"Do you have a wooden hanger for me to hang my suit on?" he asked.

"Yes," I nodded. "Go ahead. Get undressed. I'll get you one."

"And a chair," he added. "I'd like to have a chair to hang my shirt on."

"Coming right up," I said obligingly.

When I returned with the chair and the wooden hanger, he was standing at the windowsill in his undershorts, his palms pressed against the windowsill as he stared down into the street.

"It's a pretty lively street," I commented, "but don't worry. The noise won't keep you awake, even with the window open."

"We're not very high off the street, are we?" he observed anxiously.

"Second floor," I replied. "Right above the first floor. It's an old Chicago custom."

"You don't have to be sarcastic," he snapped, trying to sound angry but his voice trailing off involuntarily into an anxious whine. "I was just wondering . . . wondering . . ."

"Wondering what?" I asked.

". . . whether someone could . . . could climb up here while I'm sleeping," he whispered.

"I don't think so," I replied, as reassuringly as I could manage. "I'm quite sure you'll be safe."

He turned from the window. "Could . . . could you make me a cup of tea?" he asked, his eyes darting to and fro. "I think I'd like to have a cup of tea."

"Sure," I nodded, and went into the kitchen to make it. I was heating the water when he appeared in the kitchen doorway. He was fully dressed, his tie hanging loosely around his neck, and he was perspiring although it wasn't hot.

"Did you ever have any mice in this apartment?" he asked.

"We've caught two since we've been here," I replied. "How come you're dressed?"

"I don't think I'm well," he replied. "I think it would be better if I spent the night at a hotel. Will I have any trouble hailing a cab?"

"I'll have to call one for you," I observed. "Do you still want the tea?"

"No," he answered. "Maybe I'll have some later, at the hotel."

"The cab probably won't be here for fifteen or twenty minutes."

"That's all right," he said softly. "I'll have some later."

The cab company said they'd have a cab out front within thirty minutes.

"You sure you want to go to a hotel?" I asked.

"Yes," he replied quietly, "I think it would be better. If . . . if anything were to happen to me, it would be . . . safer. . . ."

"Oh, brother," I murmured.

"You don't care about me at all, do you?" he asked.

"No," I admitted, "I don't think so."

We sat in silence. An alarm clock in Pedersen's room started buzzing loudly, and I ran down the hall and shut it off. Then the cab came, and I carried my father's suitcases down the stairs and shoved them into the back seat.

"Goodbye," he said weakly.

"Goodbye," I replied.

The taxi roared away into the night.

I turned back toward my apartment and started up the stairs. Outside in the street, two winos were arguing over a bottle of Thunderbird.

"If you don't give me that bottle," whined one wino threateningly, "I'm gonna pull out my knife and cut off your ear and use it to wipe my asshole with."

"Oh yeah?" retorted his companion tauntingly. "Oh yeah? Well let's just see that knife. Let's just you show me what kinda knife you got."

■ ■ ■

When I was around twelve I went to this carnival set up in an armory near my house, I have always liked carnivals and circuses and magic, and the husband and wife who operated one booth there had a daughter, she was about my age or maybe two or three years older, she had thin lips and dingy blond hair, god I really wanted to fuck her, she was probably just some ignorant little cunt from the boonies, but it intoxicated me that she never had to go to school and could just ride around the country with the carnival fucking and sucking. There was a high wire strung maybe thirty feet above the ground where a trio of high-wire artists would perform two or three times a day, and a rope ladder descended from the high-wire rigging all the way to the armory floor.

Once every hour, this drunken sailor would stagger out onto the midway, actually he wasn't really a drunken sailor at all but a carnival performer dressed in a sailor suit, and he would stagger out onto the midway as if he were drunk and climb up the rope ladder high into the rigging, all the while weaving about drunkenly and pretending to lose his balance as though he had wandered up there by accident and might fall off any second and get himself killed.

To strike up a conversation with this carnival chick, I told her that my dad had once worked in a carnival doing that same drunken-sailor routine, and that one day an onlooker, believing my dad was actually a drunk in danger of falling, had climbed up the ladder after him in an effort to help him, he had grabbed hold of my father's legs in the midst of his acrobatic routine, my dad had lost his balance, and he and the other man had plummeted sixty feet to the ground, the other man wasn't too badly hurt, he just had a broken ankle or something like that, but my dad had busted his back in the fall and been paralyzed from the waist down and would remain confined to a wheelchair for the rest of his life.

■ ■ ■

I was fast asleep the next day and the phone was ringing. I had to get out of bed to answer it because it was on my desk on the other side of the room, and my eyes burned and the muscles in my back ached, like they always do when you've overslept and gotten way too much sleep.

"Hello," I answered weakly, still half asleep. "Who—"

"It's two o'clock in the afternoon," observed my father with barely restrained exasperation. "Where the devil have you been? I called you this morning but you were out."

"Sleeping," I replied.

"Sleeping?" he repeated incredulously. "For twelve hours?"

"Yes," I answered.

"You mean, when I called you earlier you were home and you didn't even hear the phone ring?"

"Yes," I admitted, "that's right."

"But I let it ring and ring."

"I didn't hear it," I said irritably, "because I was—"

"I was very sick last night," he whined. "Didn't you even care enough about me to call the hotel this morning to find out how I was feeling?"

"I was sleeping," I repeated. "You just woke—"

"Look," he said tersely. "I just called to say goodbye. I'm attending my conference this afternoon and then I'm taking the seven o'clock plane home. I'll eat dinner on the plane. I may not see you again for a long time."

I didn't reply. For a moment we were both silent.

"I'm very sorry the way this visit worked out," he said finally.

"I'm sorry you're sorry," I replied.

"No you're not," he snapped. "You're not sorry. You're too selfish to be sorry. You're too selfish to care about anything or anybody but yourself. Someday you'll learn how wrong it is not to care about other people. I only hope that by then it won't be too late for you."

"Anything else?" I asked wearily.

"Yes," he replied, "there is. Last night in my hotel room, I read that short story of yours."

" 'The Dress'?"

"Yes," he answered, " 'The Dress.' It's very, very good. I'm very proud of you. Maybe one day you'll be the writer I always hoped to be but wasn't."

"Maybe," I agreed.

"One more thing," he remarked. "It may be a long time before we get to talk again. While I'm here, is there anything . . . anything at all . . . that you'd like to know about your mother and me?"

"What do you mean?" I asked.

"I mean about your mother and me. Our relationship . . . the divorce. . . . Is there anything at all you'd like me to tell you?"

"No," I replied.

"I admire you, Simon," he observed casually, "but I don't respect you. Goodbye."

It was about a week later, maybe two, when I heard Pedersen bounding up the staircase and the Puerto Rican police dog snarling its head off and then Pedersen opening the front door, slamming it behind him, and then kind of hop-skipping in the general direction of my room, where I was busy typing a letter to Heather on this battered Underwood electric typewriter I had just bought for peanuts, it made a really loud humming noise whenever you turned the motor on, so if you wanted to be able to think straight you had to turn the power off whenever you stopped to think and then turn it on again when you were ready to type. It was a pain in the ass, that typewriter, and eventually it just broke down on me altogether and I've never used another electric typewriter since.

"Hey there, Sy," yelled Pedersen, poking his head in my door and yelling at me as though I were a half block away, "how'd you like to be best man at my weddin'?"

"Are you getting married?" I asked, turning off my Underwood and settling back in my rickety old swivel chair.

"I am if the frog dies," he replied. "Right now, it all depends on the frog."

Pedersen was wearing this brown wool cabbie's cap, a cap we'd purchased together in this junky army-navy store a block and a half down the street. The store had been owned by this ill-tempered Jewish cat, a survivor of Auschwitz, until one day about six months ago some spades broke in, tied him to a wooden chair, helped themselves to a few armloads of sneakers and sports coats, and then blew the poor guy's brains out before leaving the store. Pedersen had bought this wool cabbie's cap at that army-navy store, and now he jerked it off his head with a sudden jerk and began shifting it from hand to hand and then wringing it with both hands, like a sailor singing a song in *South Pacific.*

"Elaine thinks she's pregnant," sighed Pedersen, wringing the cap. "She went today to have a frog test. So if—"

"I thought they used rabbits," I remarked.

"You can still get a rabbit, Sy," he explained, his face breaking into a sunshine smile. "Don't worry, old buddy, they still have plenty of rabbits available. But frogs are a lot cheaper. Today the big move is to frogs."

"What happens if she's pregnant?" I asked.

"Why, I marry her, damn it. Didn't you hear me ask you if you wanted to be my best man? What are you, deaf or something? Unless, of course, *you* want to marry her."

"How about an abortion?" I asked.

"Illegal," he replied.

"So's stealing from the bookstore," I noted.

"You know I'm a totally honest citizen," he retorted. "I don't know any abortionist."

"There's this Dr. Stanley Barnwell up on Cottage Grove," I suggested. "He did one for a friend of Heather's. He said it would cost five hundred dollars, but as soon as he saw the chick was white, he upped the price to seven hundred and fifty."

"You mean this guy Barnwell is a coon abortionist?"

"Right."

"Where in hell would I get seven hundred and fifty dollars?"

"Maybe we could raise it somehow," I replied.

"How?" he asked.

"I don't know. We could sell some of those books you stole."

"I'm not selling my books for no goddam mother-fucking abortionist," snapped Pedersen, feigning indignation just for the fun of it. "Besides," he continued, now breaking into a grin,

"Elaine would never go for it. I been beating her over the head for two days to say she'd get an abortion and she won't go for it. It's against her religion."

"What religion?"

"The Catholic religion. Where're you from, Wiener, Africa? Catholics are—"

"So you're actually going to marry her?"

Pedersen scowled. "What's the matter? You against marriage?"

"No," I stammered, "but—"

"Well you ought to be," he snapped. "Marriage is terrible. A terrible institution. Especially for men. My father was married—and look at him. He's a god damned gigolo chasing after rich old ladies for whatever they've got in their pocketbooks. And my mother, she—"

"I thought you liked your father," I interjected. "You always—"

"I do," he replied. "I do. But marriage is still a terrible thing, Sy. Don't ever get married."

"I'm not getting married, Ken. You are."

"Ha ha! Very good, Sy. That's right. I am getting married. She's a lovely girl. I want to get married. It'll be good for me. Just what I need to—"

"Do you love her?" I asked.

"Love her?" he barked at me with a bogus frown while silently savoring the question. "Of course I love her. I love all the hairies, you know that, Sy. What kind of a question is that? I love them all—big ones, little ones, hairy ones. No, you're right, Sy. I abhor those little wispy hairless ones. They disgust me. I could never love a woman who didn't have a big bushy hairy."

"Does Elaine have a big bushy hairy?"

"Yes."

"Do you love her?"

"Who? Elaine or her hairy?"

"Elaine."

"Of course I don't love her. What're you crazy, Sy? I'm going to marry her. You're going to be my best man. I never said anything about loving her."

"Do you think you're going to want to live with her for the rest of your life?"

"Rest of my—! Ha ha! Very funny, Sy. Very funny. I'm not about to spend the rest of my life with that flabby little cunt just because she's pregnant. I may be a little insane, but I'm not crazy."

"But you're going to marry her, Ken. You said—"

"Marriage doesn't necessarily mean forever, Sy," replied Pedersen. "My father got married. It didn't mean forever with *him.* My mother got married—twice. It didn't mean forever when she married my father and I certainly hope it won't mean forever now that she's married to Arthur, because Arthur's a goddam moron."

"All right, Pedersen," I sighed, "you've worn me out. If you don't love Elaine, exactly why are you going to marry her?"

"Because, Sy," he replied, a bit patronizingly, "you do not knock up a hairy and then not marry her. It just isn't done. It's bad for the fucking kid. It gives the little bastards serious complexes. What the fuck's the matter with you, Sy? Don't you like children?"

"No," I admitted. "I don't."

Pedersen chuckled. "I don't like them either. But for a long time you don't have to worry about them. The mother takes care of them for a long time till they're ready to go off to college. All you do is just go off to work in the morning and when you come home at night you give them a little pet on the head. The women do all the hard part. Waking up in the middle of the night, vomiting—the women do all that. Stop looking at me like that, Sy. Jesus H. Christ, man, *you're* not getting married, for Christ's sake. *I'm* the one who's getting married."

■ ■ ■

The wedding took place three weeks later, August 14th I think, Pedersen's lukewarm psychologist mother and nincompoop adoptive father flew in from New Mexico the night before, they took Ken and Elaine and me out to dinner and we all had a pretty good time I suppose, except that the nincompoop, whose name was Arthur, insisted on telling these idiotic jokes after which he'd chuckle moronically to himself—he chuckled like a comic book, heh heh heh—as if the jokes were richly laden with all sorts of private significance.

Elaine was a good four years older than Ken, but she had this definitely infantile quality about her, you could easily imagine her seated in a high chair banging baby food jars together, like some important part of her had never grown up. On the whole, however, she seemed to be taking the whole scene pretty well, considering she was pregnant with a baby she didn't want and that she was also about to marry Ken, which as far as I could tell she didn't want either. Still, though, we all had a pretty good time the night of that dinner, and for all I know Elaine had even managed to convince herself, god knows how, that she really loved Ken Pedersen and was absolutely thrilled to be carrying his child.

The next morning, the day of the wedding, the Pedersens picked Ken and Elaine and me up in a rented car and drove us out to Elaine's mother's house in the Chicago suburb of Winnetka. Elaine's father had been a policeman on the Winnetka police force for twenty-three years and then had committed suicide by shooting himself in the mouth with less than a month to go until his retirement. Elaine once told Ken that the reason her old man killed himself was that he felt his life would have no meaning once they made him quit the force, but Ken always maintained that the real reason he did it was because the prospect of living at home with Mrs. Willoughby was too terrible to face, and once I'd met Mrs. Willoughby I was certain he was right.

Mrs. Willoughby weighed in at two hundred and twenty-five pounds and had views that made the John Birch Society seem like an organization of leftists. When she learned from Elaine, five months later, that Ken's best friend had married a Negro, she concluded that I must be part of the international Communist menace and actually sat down and wrote a letter about me to the FBI, which the silly sons of bitches probably still have in their files.

The wedding was an informal affair, held in a small chapel not far from Mrs. Willoughby's house, and after the ceremony was over and done with we all went back to the Willoughby homestead and drank champagne and gorged ourselves on wedding cake while Elaine's uncle Farley clicked away at us with his Kodak instamatic.

"All dressed up in that sports jacket," I whispered to Pedersen, "a guy could almost mistake you for the bridegroom."

"It's a great life," he exclaimed expansively, a stein of beer in one hand and a huge hunk of rose-topped wedding cake in the other. "You ought to try it. Soon as Heather comes back to school, you two are going to come up to our place for a good home-cooked dinner. I think she could use some friendly advice regarding the timely termination of your bachelor status. You know, the lord above never intended for us to—"

"When did you say the baby was due?" I whispered behind my hand.

"April, you cocksucker," he replied, and then he threw back his head and began laughing uproariously.

September came and the leaves began falling, covering the ground with a crazy quilt of breathtaking colors, who could possibly describe all those beautiful colors? Once my father had an idea for a novel about a pair of young lovers, she would be a waitress and he a student at Princeton, and so we drove out to Princeton in my father's Packard one hazy afternoon in September, we brought along a picnic lunch, hard-boiled eggs and chicken salad sandwiches, we brought a wire egg slicer to slice the hard-boiled eggs with, and we brought along a thermos bottle, no, two thermos bottles, one filled with coffee for my dad and the other filled with apple juice for me, we drove out to Princeton and parked the car and sat on the running board and ate our picnic lunch, I couldn't have been very old then, eight years old or maybe nine, it was late September and the leaves were falling, covering the ground with incredible colors, red and yellow and a score of other incredible colors, my dad had a pad with him, a long yellow pad, and he sat cross-legged on the running board and stared up at the trees and wrote down all the colors, every color he saw he wrote down on that pad, but the novel about the young lovers never got written, and so when the summer turns to fall and the leaves cloak the ground in their coat of infinite colors, I always recall that trip to Princeton, that haunting symbol of my father's failures.

Soon the school year began again, and even though I'd all but promised my dad I'd give it one more semester, when the time came to register I just didn't bother, I dropped out of school but held onto my job at the U. of C. Press. Then Heather came back to school from her summer in Pennsylvania, she moved back into her dorm while I stayed in my apartment, but on weekends she would sign out of the dormitory to visit some fictitious relative and we would spend the weekends together.

One night we went to Ken and Elaine's place for dinner, and while the salmon casserole baked in the oven Ken lighted his meerschaum pipe with a wooden match and entertained us all by snatching two copies of *Cyrano de Bergerac* off his bookshelf and then jumping around the living room playing the part of Cyrano while I slouched in his green naugahide armchair and read the part of Roxanne. "Come on, Sy," he would interrupt exuberantly, waving his arms about, "put more tits and ass into it, boy. More tits and ass."

Getting married had changed Ken Pedersen, now he was into being the head of the household, the lord of his castle, shouting out commands to his compliant Guinevere like an expansive King Arthur. "What's wrong with you, woman? Can't you see this man's glass is almost empty? Another beer this instant! We can't have my best friend sitting over there with an empty glass of beer!"

"We're out of beer," replied Elaine.

"What's that you say? Out of beer?" he cried incredulously. "The Pedersen family, out of beer? Surely you jest, I say! Surely—"

"It doesn't matter," I interjected. "One beer's enough for me before dinner anyway. Maybe you—"

"What? One beer's enough, you say?" cried Pedersen, stabbing the air with his forefinger like Cyrano wielding his foil. "One beer is never enough. You know that, Sy. One beer is never enough. Come on. We'll drive down to the store this instant and acquire some more brew."

He tossed me my pea coat and threw his suede ranch jacket across his shoulders like a cape. Elaine appeared in the doorway of the kitchen. "The casserole is almost ready," she said quietly.

"Then hold the god damned casserole," cried Pedersen, slamming his fist into his palm for emphasis. "Take whatever steps are necessary to prevent the sonovabitch from getting overdone before we get back. Add some new ingredients if you have to, by all means pour in some brand new ingredients."

"I-I'll try," promised Elaine.

I gave Heather a kiss on the cheek and then Pedersen and I walked out the door.

"Marriage is a wonderful thing," he bellowed, throwing his arm around my shoulder as we clambered down the two flights of stairs to the street. "It's a wonderful thing. Especially with a woman like Elaine. Why, she makes it—"

"I think we're out of earshot now," I whispered as we neared the first floor landing.

"Ha ha! Good," he laughed, punching me playfully in the shoulder. "That's good. I don't know how much longer I could have kept that up. It's terrible being married, Sy, just terrible. You have no idea how terrible it is."

"Oh, really?" I asked wryly. "When's the baby due?"

"You sonovabitch," he cursed. "You god damned sonovabitch. Why do you have to ask about the baby all the time? Isn't there anything else you can ask about? Don't you think about anything besides babies, for Christ's sake? Here I'm trying to talk to you about what it's like to be married, and all you can think about is a little bastard who hasn't even been born yet. Besides, who knows, he may not ever be born. And if he is born, I may decide to flush him down the toilet."

I laughed.

"You're right," he shrugged. "I couldn't do it. I could never flush my own flesh and blood down the toilet." He crammed his hands into his jacket pockets and stared solemnly down at the ground, as if the realization that he was emotionally incapable of flushing a baby down the toilet was fraught with significance and profoundly humbling.

"What's so terrible about your marriage?" I asked.

"I'm married to Elaine, Sy," he replied. "You know that."

"I see your point," I agreed, nodding my head.

"She's nothing but a vacuous, uninteresting, stupid little cunt," he exclaimed. "What in blazes did I ever marry her for?"

"You got her pregnant," I answered.

"Yes, yes, of course," he mumbled, thrusting his hands further into his pockets. "Of course."

We climbed into his Dodge and hurtled down Cottage Grove Avenue toward the liquor store. "A man should be king of his castle," proclaimed Pedersen, as his car barreled insanely down the nighttime street. "I don't have to ask you, Sy. I know you agree with that."

"I do," I replied.

"You agree and I agree," continued Pedersen soberly, "but Elaine does not seem to want to accept the fact that I am the king of the castle."

For a few minutes we drove on in silence. Only a passenger who had transcended his fear of death entirely could possibly converse with equanimity while Ken Pedersen was driving.

"It wouldn't really be so bad," he said finally, as he fishtailed wildly back across the white line to his own side of the street in order to avoid a head-on collision with an oncoming bus, "if it weren't for the 'Bee.' That cocksucking bitch is—"

"What's the 'Bee'?" I asked.

"Who," he corrected.

"Okay, Ken. Who's the 'Bee'?"

"Cocksucking sonovabitch," he muttered.

"Ken," I demanded impatiently, "are you going to—"

"Mrs. Willoughby," he replied. "Elaine's fucking mother. My fucking sonovabitch mother-in-law."

"The one time I met her I didn't like her either," I remarked.

"Do you know what she does?" exclaimed Pedersen, his voice rising. "Do you know what—"

Now our car hurtled across a busy intersection, through a red light, as Pedersen suddenly turned halfway round in his seat, ignoring the road completely, in order to be better positioned to gauge my reaction to what he was about to say. There was a horrendous shrieking of brakes to our immediate left as some more mundane, run-of-the-mill driver swerved sharply to his right to avoid a collision that probably would have meant instant death for us all.

"What the fuck was that?" snapped Pedersen annoyedly.

"That man back there just saved our life," I replied, as calmly as I could.

"Oh," he exclaimed indifferently. "Are you listening to me?"

"Watch the road," I said.

"But are you listening?"

"Yes."

"I was starting to tell you about Mrs. Willoughby. She hates me. She never wanted Elaine to marry me."

"Does she know about the kid?" I asked.

"She's not supposed to, but I bet Elaine told her. The hairy fink."

"What does she do?"

"What does who do? Elaine?"

"You were about to tell me what Mrs. Willoughby does," I replied.

"She calls up the house every day while I'm at school. The crafty bitch knows exactly when Elaine's at home and I'm away, and she calls, sometimes as much as two, three times a day."

"And?"

"And she tells Elaine that I'm a ne'er-do-well and a Communist and that she never should have married me."

"You?" I exclaimed incredulously. "A Communist?"

"It's just a word with her," explained Pedersen. "She doesn't mean anything political by it. She just says Communist the way we use cocksucking sonovabitch. Or mother-fucking cocksucking sonovabitch. Or—"

"How does Elaine feel about the calls?" I asked.

"She cries a lot. The 'Bee' plays Elaine the way Heifetz plays the goddam violin. She knows every chord, Sy, every goddam fucking chord. Every day she calls up maybe two, three times and tells Elaine how she ought to pack her bags and leave me and go back to Winnetka."

"Wait'll she sees the baby," I laughed. "She'll change her whole tune when she sees the baby."

"What baby?" asked Pedersen, staring intently out the windshield smiling from ear to ear.

"Your baby," I replied. "The one who's going to make you a proud daddy and Elaine a proud, happy mommy."

"One of these days," muttered Pedersen darkly, "me and the 'Bee' are going to have it out with knives."

Don't ask me why I finally proposed to Heather, because I honestly haven't the foggiest notion. A long time afterward, during an argument we had right around the time of the separation, Heather said that I never would have married her if she hadn't been black, and looking back on it now, it could be she was right.

It was a cold wintry night in November the night I proposed, Heather had been working late in the hospital leukemia lab, and I remember I finished my shift at the U. of C. Press and then dropped by the hospital to pick her up and walk her back to her dorm. We were sitting at a table in the hospital's all-night cafeteria, drinking hot coffee to help get us ready for going out in the cold, and Heather had lifted her coffee cup up to her lips, all I could see of her face were her soft brown eyes looking out at me over the rim of the coffee cup, and it was in that split second that I decided to marry her.

"How would you like to get married?" I asked her.

Her eyelashes fluttered gently and her pupils widened, the coffee cup still covered her mouth but I could see her eyes widen, and maybe that's why I asked her to marry me, so that I could see those eyes widen with a mixture of love and surprise in them.

"Do you mean it?" she asked quietly.

I stared at her sweet face and started to laugh.

"You do mean it, don't you, Sy?"

"Of course I mean it," I replied.

"When?" she asked.

"Well," I said, thinking it over, "women reach majority in this state at eighteen years of age, which means you're okay. But I won't legally be an adult here till I reach twenty-one, so either I've got to get my parents' consent, or—"

"They ain't exactly gonna be breakin' their necks to give you permission to marry one of us colored girls, sugar," cooed Heather in one of her infrequent Negro impersonations.

"It's either that," I continued, "or else we get married in some nearby state where men reach majority at eighteen or nineteen."

"Like?" she asked.

"Indiana, or maybe Michigan. I have a buddy in the law school. I'll ask him to check it out."

"But you won't change your mind?" she asked softly, raising her cup to her lips again to make the question seem casual.

"Why you askin' me that?" I joked. "You about to change into a pumpkin or somethin'?"

"Oh, Sy," she exclaimed, "I'm so happy!"

"Get that goofy-looking grin off your face," I chided jovially, draining my coffee cup. "You look positively ridiculous."

We left the cafeteria and skipped off down the street like a couple of nuts.

"No more living in the dormitory!" exulted Heather.

"Fucking and sucking every night of the week!" I cried.

"Hush yo' mouth, honky," scolded Heather playfully. "Race you back to the dormitory. And don't forget. Last one there has a Jewish bump on his nose."

"Guess what?" proclaimed Heather two weeks later.

We were in the bathroom of my apartment, I was sitting on the edge of the bathtub, keeping her company while she did her hair, and she was standing in front of the mirror in a terry cloth robe, her electric comb plugged into a wall socket, daubing her long, thick black hair with Dixie Peach, straightening it with the metal comb, and then wrapping it, a curl at a time, around huge wire rollers that looked about two inches in diameter and maybe four inches wide. Watching her do it, it was as though I'd been watching women do that all my life, even though before I'd met Heather I'd never seen a woman do it before.

"Go on," prodded Heather. "Guess what?"

"Columbus was really a Negro," I replied.

"I thought you told me he was Jewish, Sy."

"He was," I replied, "and someday they're going to prove it."

"I got a letter from my parents this morning. They want us to spend Christmas with them."

"How'd they find out we were seeing each other? I thought you'd decided not to tell them because you were afraid your father would have a fit."

"I changed my mind."

"You told them we're getting married, didn't you?"

"No."

"What did you tell them?"

"Not that."

"Tell them I'm busy Christmas. I don't feature traveling seven hundred miles just to get killed by some girl's blood-crazed father."

"I told them I've been dating you for awhile and . . . and that we've discussed the possibility of getting married. That's all."

"So now they want me to come to Pennsylvania so they can kill me."

"They just want to meet you, that's all. Come on, Sy. They're my parents. You're going to have to meet them sometime."

So we went. Pedersen drove us as far as the Chicago Skyway entrance ramp, and from there we thumbed it, hitching past Gary, Indiana, whose steel mills befoul the highway in a cloud of sulfurous brimstone mist, then across Ohio into Pennsylvania, arriving at the Muskrat Valley turnoff at ten o'clock the next morning, hyper from lack of sleep, our appetites dulled by a turnpike diet of Twinkies and vending machine coffee.

The Thomases lived in a dilapidated farmhouse not too far from the turnpike, with a chicken coop out back housing maybe fifty, sixty chickens and the closest neighbor out of sight behind a hill two hundred yards or so away down a winding, rut-filled road. Heather's father was a great, dark-skinned man clad in faded denim overalls and an old plaid woolen shirt worn thin at the elbows. Muscles rippled in his forearms like strands of steel cable, and a thick black vein bulged in his forehead like a snake coiling and uncoiling over his eyes. Even though his close-cropped black hair was liberally speckled with white, you'd never have guessed he was sixty years old.

Both Heather's father and mother were standing in the front yard as we opened the gate and stepped into the yard, our feet cold and muddy up to the ankles from walking down the road, which was all half-frozen mud. Heather's mother, a light-skinned, wiry black woman who looked fifteen years older than her husband even though she was actually a few years younger, had skin the color of light-brown caramels and silver-gray hair tied in a single whiplike braid that hung down her back. She had a pair of old-fashioned wire-rimmed eyeglasses perched on her nose, the lens over the left eye as clear as a window, the one over the right eye thick and almost translucent, so that the eye peering through it seemed somehow huge and distorted.

When we entered the yard, Heather's mom rushed up to her and gave her a hug and then put out her hand to me and, when I appeared hesitant, leaned over and gave me an affectionate peck on the cheek.

"Good to see you both," she exclaimed warmly. "How'd you all get here, anyway? Swim through the mud?"

"We walked from the highway," I replied. "It was pretty muddy all the way, all right. Must've been a good two miles."

"Three," she corrected, turning toward her husband. "Three's right, isn't it, Daddy?"

"That's right," nodded Mr. Thomas. "It be three miles from the highway, almos' on the nose."

"Come on inside, you two," chimed in Mrs. Thomas. "I'll make you both some lunch."

We stepped across the front yard and entered the kitchen. "Marcia and Charlene went up to Auntie Jeanne's for Christmas," continued Heather's mother brightly, as we took off our coats and hung them on pegs. "They said to say hello to you all and they're sorry they won't get to see you while you're here." Striding to the kitchen sink and taking up a paring knife in one hand, Mrs. Thomas suddenly turned and peered at me scrutinizingly over her eyeglasses. "Marcia and Charlene," she explained, "is Heather's sisters."

"I know that," I replied.

"If you're gonna marry into this crazy family," she went on, now turning her back to me and deftly peeling a cucumber with the paring knife and cutting it into slices, "I guess it only makes sense you learn who all the people are."

"Mother," scolded Heather, "you—"

"Well, it's true, ain't it?" chirped Mrs. Thomas, eyeing me over her shoulder with a not entirely benevolent twinkle in her eye.

"Yes," I admitted. "It's true."

"I don't know what in blazes you want her for," she went on, as she withdrew a giant loaf of white bread from the refrigerator and dropped four slices into an oversized toaster. "You two want your BLT's on toast, don't you?"

"Fine with me," I replied.

"Me too," said Heather.

"She can't cook," continued Mrs. Thomas merrily. "And she can't keep house, that's for sure, less'n college has taught her somethin' that I never—"

"No," I agreed, "you're right. Her dormitory room at college looks like a cyclone hit it."

"Sy," exclaimed Heather with amused indignation.

Mrs. Thomas laughed heartily. "Well at least he has some idea of what he's getting hisself into," she said cheerfully, pulling the slices of white bread out of the toaster and tossing them onto a pair of cream-colored plates with all the aplomb of a short-order cook. "But has she told you yet," she added darkly, skillfully smearing the toast with mayonnaise and then laying on slices of cucumber, lettuce, tomato, and freshly cooked bacon, "that she absolutely hates children?"

"It's just as well," I cut in, having decided it was time to thwart her. "I don't really like them either."

"Then what's the point of gettin' married then?" asked Mr. Thomas, clearly bewildered but not wanting to offend.

"Well," I began slowly, carefully choosing my words, "I think—"

"Andrew," snapped Mrs. Thomas to her husband with what she hoped would pass for good-natured annoyance, "let the kids eat. Can't you see they're dying to have something to eat?"

■ ■ ■

After lunch Heather started helping her mother clean up the kitchen, and Heather's dad invited me to go for a walk with him around his place.

"This be my chicken coop, Sy," he proclaimed proudly, as he slipped the latch on the chicken-wire gate and we entered the tiny fenced-in yard. "Be careful now. They'll peck you if'n they don't know you." He held up a swollen index finger. "Sometimes peck you even if they do know you," he laughed.

"You raise the chickens for money?" I asked. I have a loud voice, but it was all but drowned out by the chickens, which, indignant at our intrusion, now squawked and screeched and flapped around us.

"Excuse me?" inquired Mr. Thomas, cupping a hand to his ear.

"Do you sell these chickens to people?" I repeated, as loudly as I could.

"You want one?" he shouted, indicating the flock of flapping chickens with a wave of his hand. "Go ahead. Which one you want?"

"I only mean why do you raise them?" I asked.

"Pets," he replied simply, pursing his lips and nodding his head as he contemplated the simple wisdom of his answer. "Chickens is smart birds. People think they's dumb, but they ain't dumb. They smart." He paused. "Smarter'n most people, you know what I mean?" he added, chuckling softly to himself.

"And I guess every morning you get fresh eggs from them, too," I remarked.

"Oh, yeah. Momma comes 'roun' and takes the eggs from 'em every day. Some she keeps, some she gives away. But I don't keep these chickens for layin' eggs. I keeps 'em 'cause I likes to watch 'em and hear 'em cluckin' and scratchin'. You can hear 'em cluckin' and scratchin', can'tcha?"

"Sure," I laughed. "I'd have to be deaf not to hear 'em."

"They's pretty loud, ain't they?" he agreed, and we both smiled.

We left the chicken coop and circled behind the house, where a steep, rock-strewn embankment descended to a shallow, swift-running stream. He sat on a rock close by the stream and reached into a pocket of his woolen shirt and pulled out a pair of gumdrops, retaining a green one in the palm of his hand while he extended me an orange one between a massive thumb and forefinger.

"Gumdrop?" he offered.

"Sure," I replied, and took it.

He popped the green one into his mouth and chewed on it thoughtfully. "You smoke?" he asked.

"No," I answered. "I don't like the taste."

"Me neither," he nodded. "I told my daughters not to smoke, but they're grown or close to grown and they won't listen. Ruins your health."

"I've gotten Heather to cut down a little," I remarked, "but she gets mad when I keep after her to quit."

"Womens is stubborn," he observed. "Ain't no man alive gonna make 'em do what they don't want to do."

"Amen," I muttered.

"What's that?" he asked.

"I said 'amen.' "

He smiled broadly and then broke into a laugh. "If I had it to do over again," he went on, absentmindedly tossing a pebble into the brook, "I think I'd be a farmer. I think bein' a farmer was what I'd liked to be. But when I was comin' up I was wild, always jivin' around. I joined the Army. I never gave any thought about the future. Didn't seem like the colored man hardly had him a future. I got out of the Army, I got married, I had my children. I had to take care of 'em, had to put bread on the table. No time to think about farmin' and savin' to buy land and bein' a farmer. So I went to work in the steel mill. Been in the steel mill now better'n thirty-five years. You can bet that's a long time, thirty-five years."

He twisted his body slightly and gestured southward, toward a sulfurous yellow cloud on the far horizon. At this distance it was hard to see, but there it hung, hovering like a pus-filled jellyfish over the valley.

"There it is," he noted gravely. "Day and night. Seven days a week. Fifty-two weeks a year. Day and night. It never stops."

He paused a moment and dug his thumb and forefinger deep into the innards of his right shirt pocket. When the search proved fruitless, he surveyed his left pocket, this time with more success. "Another gumdrop?" he asked.

"No thanks," I replied.

"It's a red one," he remarked amiably, thrusting it toward me for closer examination. "Red ones always be good."

"No thanks," I repeated.

"Up to you," he shrugged, and popped it in his mouth.

"Have you worked at the same mill all those years?" I asked.

"Nope," he replied. "Worked for Jones and Laughlin for six years, maybe seven. Then came the steel wars. We fought for the union. We fought for our right to have a union. I got fired. Lost all my seniority. Lost everything I had. Had to start all over again. Then I went to work for Armco. Been there ever since. That's where I am now. But if I'd held onto that seniority, I'd probably be a foreman today."

"What do you do there?" I asked.

He gripped his right thigh with both hands and stiffly held out his leg. "Well before my leg up and went bad on me—"

"What happened to your leg?"

"Blood clot in it."

"A thrombosis?" I asked.

"Yes," he replied. "'Bout the size of a half-dollar."

"You mean it's still there?"

"No," he answered, shaking his head. "It's better now. Clot's all gone now. But that don't mean the leg is good like it used to be. They can't give it back to you like it used to be."

"I'm sorry," I said. "I interrupted. You were telling me—"

"I used to be a laborer," he went on. "But long as we got the union, the steel mill pays pretty good. That's why I stayed in. Had a wife and three childrens to support. But even then, it's no place to spend your life in."

"Why not?"

"Once," he continued, staring into the stream and tossing another pebble into the stream as though he were going to ignore my question, "me and a buddy, he was a white fella, we was crossin' this catwalk over the vat, and the railing give way and we fell, and I grabbed the ledge of the catwalk with my fingers, but he didn't, but he managed to grab hold my leg."

"Jesus Christ," I exclaimed softly. "What happened?"

"I started to hollerin' 'Pull us up! Pull us up!' and they ran and pulled me up, but he couldn't hold on that long and he fell down into the vat."

He paused a moment and stared up at me.

"I don't know what you all want to be," he said quietly, "but do you think somethin' like that could happen to you on a job you'd likely get after goin' to college?"

"No," I admitted. "I guess not."

"That's why I want Heather to finish college," he continued. "I don't want my children workin' in no place like a steel mill or scrubbin' floors on their hands and knees like their mother done."

"I don't want Heather to leave college," I replied, a little defensively.

"I know that," he said.

"What did they do about the man who fell in the vat?"

"What do you mean?"

"Did they pull him out and bury him, or what?"

"Oh," he shrugged, "they ain't nothin' left of a man like that—that steel be's so hot. He's just gone soon's he hits the steel. So they just cool down the steel what's in the vat and then they take it outside somewhere and they bury it."

"Is there some reason they can't use the steel because the man was killed in it?" I asked.

"No," he replied thoughtfully, "ain't no reason. But they just buries it all the same. Ever since I hurt my leg, I can't do that kind of work no more."

"What do you do now?"

"I'm a scarfing inspector. You know what that is?"

"No."

"It's not important what it is. It just lets me sit down so I'm not on this leg so much, that's all. Mostly I sit down on this one chair and prop my leg up on this other chair and I keep an eye on the ingots as they come down the slide. That's all."

He stood up, leaning on the rock with one hand to help take the weight off the leg that had suffered the blood clot. I hadn't noticed it before, but now I could see that he limped a little. We didn't climb up the embankment toward the house, instead circling around back toward the chicken coop along a mostly flat meadow littered with the wintry skeletal remains of scraggly underbrush.

"You ever hunt?" asked Heather's father finally, breaking the silence.

"No," I replied. "I don't like hunting."

"I don't hunt anymore either," he nodded. "When I was your age, lord, I used to hunt all the time. These woods around here was full of deer. Prob'ly they still is, even now. I used to take my dog and go out and hunt 'em."

"Heather said you had a dog," I remarked. "A German shepherd. Where is he? I don't see him around."

The reply came slowly. "He be dead."

"I'm sorry," I said. "What—"

"Don't tell Heather," he went on. "She liked that old dog. I used to let him run loose, you know, big dog like that. You can't keep a big old dog like that in the house."

"He got hit by a car?" I asked quietly.

"My neighbor, he was always complainin' about the dog runnin' on his property. Never did no damage, just chased rabbits over there sometime. You know how dogs chase rabbits."

"Yes," I replied.

"Well, he just left some food out for him last week and killed him. Left some food out for him with ground glass in it and killed him."

"Good god," I murmured under my breath.

"Can't understand how someone could be so mean as to go and do that to a dog," he muttered introspectively, shaking his head, "but you know what?"

"What?"

"There's plenty'a people out there what'd be happy to go out and do that to people. They'd like to do to people what that man done to my dog."

Now we passed by the chicken coop and a weatherbeaten old red doghouse and made our way slowly toward the ramshackle front porch of the house. A few steps short of the porch, he stopped.

"I don't want you to think that I care you're white," he remarked. "Mrs. Thomas, I think she cares, but I don't care. You know when I was comin' up, Mrs. Thomas's people didn't want her to marry me neither, on accounta they said I was too dark for her and not good enough to marry her. I ain't forgotten. Just because the years passed, I ain't forgotten. And I ain't gonna do to my daughters what was done to me."

"I don't know what to say," I replied.

"Don't say nothin'," he answered. "Just take good care of my daughter. Just look out for her and see that she finish college and get a good education. Today a man can't hardly pick up a pick and shovel without he's got hisself a good education."

"It's damn near true," I agreed.

"You bet it's true," he insisted. "But remember this—I ain't prejudiced. You and me, we both have the same blood. If you was to cut my arm and put the blood over here, and cut your arm and put the blood over there, ain't no man on earth could tell them two bloods apart. I know that, even if half the rest of the world don't want to believe it.

"And one more thing," he added gravely, "and then prob'ly we's talked enough. I've prob'ly 'bout talked your ear off already."

"I enjoyed it," I remarked.

"Make yourself some good friends. Heather's a good girl. All my daughters is good girls, but Heather is a good girl. If you got Heather, you got yourself a good girl. Now go out and make yourself some good friends to go along with her."

"I don't think I know what you mean, Mr. Thomas."

"You wouldn't believe how many friends I had," he went on, "when the larder was full and all of my friends was invited to come eat at my table. But when I got poor, and the time come I couldn't feed 'em no more, that's when most of those friends was gone."

▪ ▪ ▪

That evening Mrs. Thomas served up a fried chicken dinner with sweet potatoes and collard greens, and then Heather and I cleared away the dishes and let her mom and dad demolish us in a few hands of whist. After the card game, we all started off to bed, Heather and her parents to upstairs bedrooms while I was tucked away in this tiny guest room just off the kitchen.

"Heather," I whispered, "you think you can come down to my room later?"

"I'll try," she replied softly, then kissed me gently on the cheek and started up the stairs.

For almost an hour, I lay on my back on the cot in the guest room, absentmindedly counting the holes in the acoustical-tile ceiling, until finally I heard muffled footsteps on the staircase and then looked up to see Heather standing in the doorway in her bathrobe and nightgown.

Even though I was really wasted from the trip and the dinner, I was still ripe for some succulent pussy, but Heather pointed toward the ceiling and whispered that her parents' bedroom was directly overhead and that, even with the acoustical tile, if we tried to fuck they would probably hear us. I was about to settle for a blowjob, Heather had kneeled down by the cot and taken my cock in her mouth, when suddenly I heard footsteps and a rustling sound coming from the kitchen.

"Heather? Heather, dear? Are you there?" chimed a syrupy, singsong voice.

"Yes," answered Heather, scrambling hastily to her feet. "I'm in here with Sy."

"Oh," stammered Mrs. Thomas, poking her bespectacled face into the guest-room door. "I just felt like some sort of midnight snack, that's all, and when I looked in your room to see if you might like to join me, I—"

"There was just something we wanted to talk about," I snapped annoyedly, cutting her off, letting her know I was onto her game.

"I didn't mean to interrupt anything," she apologized nervously. "If this is—"

"Don't worry, you didn't," I replied tersely.

"Are you sure?" she asked.

"Is there something you want, Mom?" inquired Heather, trying not to sound impatient.

"Well, yes, Heather, there is," answered her mother. "If Simon will excuse us for a moment, perhaps we could talk for a moment out on the porch. You won't mind excusing us for a moment, will you, Simon? Just for a little woman talk?"

"Of course not," I replied.

They walked through the kitchen together and opened the screen door and walked out onto the porch. "Quiet, dear," I heard Mrs. Thomas whisper, "we don't want to wake your father." Then the porch door clicked shut and everything they said dissolved into mumbles.

I didn't trust the bitch. I didn't trust that bitch for a minute. So I pulled on my blue jeans and tiptoed into the kitchen and stood just inside the porch door and listened.

". . . patient with you," Mrs. Thomas was saying.

"I-I know that," replied Heather, sounding a little bewildered. "But what's—"

"And with your sisters," continued her mother. "We've always been careful to be patient with them too."

"Mother," interrupted Heather impatiently, "I still don't understand what you're—"

"You was the first we had," her mother went on, the urgency rising in her voice. "For a time, you was all we wanted. And then we had Marcia. That was enough for us. Two was all we wanted.

It wasn't till a long time after that we had Charlene. A long time after. She was an accident. Don't you ever tell Charlene she was an accident, you hear? That's a dark secret and you've got to keep it secret."

"Yes, Momma."

"When I came pregnant with Charlene, we didn't expect it. We had two fine children already and all we could do to feed 'em. We hadn't thought about no more children. I talked about it with your daddy. 'Maybe we should get rid of it,' I said, 'get rid of it before it's born.' Your daddy said no, that would be wrong. 'We'll have it,' he said, 'we'll have three fine children. We'll love it like we love the other two.'

"Your daddy was already near forty-five or forty-six. He was out of work on accounta they was havin' a big steel strike. Men forty-five or forty-six, they don't want no more children. They want to lean back and enjoy the ones they got. But not your daddy. 'If the good lord sends us another one,' he said, 'then we'll have another one.' So Charlene was born. Now we got three lovely daughters. You and Marcia and Charlene. We love 'em all the same 'cause they all came outa my body the same. Except the oldest. You're the oldest. You always feel somethin' special in your heart about the oldest."

"What are you trying to tell me, Momma?" asked Heather.

"Hush up," snapped her mother, "an' let your momma speak. Is that what they teached you in college, to interrupt your own momma before she's had her chance to speak? Is it? Is that what they teach you?"

"No, Momma."

"I worked as a maid. Every day I could get work, I worked as a maid. I worked on my hands and knees for Mr. Charlie and Mr. Charlie's women. They say 'Fetch this,' I fetch this. They say 'Fetch that,' I fetch that. They say 'Be a good nigger, Ruby Thomas,' I be the best nigger I know how. I work on my knees like a good nigger till my hands be raw. Five days, six days, seven days a week. Sometimes I pray there be eight days a week so I could work a eighth day on my knees for that two, three dollars a day. Some weeks your father couldn't get no work. Only I could get work. So he take care of the kids, of you three kids, while I go work. 'Yes, ma'm. No, ma'm. Thank you, ma'm. Anything I could do to please you, ma'm.' It made me fit to vomit, but I said it, rubbin' my hands raw and my knees raw I said it so we could put milk on the table for our babies, so we wouldn't have to watch our babies die for havin' nothin' on the table to eat.

"Once we had nothin' to eat. They was hard times and we had nothin' to eat. No work at the mill, no domestic work neither. I say, 'Andrew, what we gonna do? We have no milk for the children.' Your father he say, 'I'll get some milk somehow. I'll get some milk even if I haves to steal it.' So he goes out, he goes down the road and he steals a quart of milk from off a white man's porch, and he brings it on home, brings it on home so you and your sisters will have milk to help you grow strong. And that big man, your father, that big man who is so strong and you've seen him do it, you know he can take a bar of iron, like a tire iron from the car trunk and bend it in half if he wants to, he goes into the back there, out there where we built the chicken coop, and he starts to cry, a strong man like him crying because he had to make himself a thief to feed his own children."

There was a long silence. "Why are you telling me all this, Momma?" asked Heather softly.

"You know Mrs. Eason who lives up on Crabtree Road? That Mrs. Eason I wrote you I do work for maybe two, three days a week?"

"Yes, Momma, I remember."

"She's an old white woman, seventy years old, maybe even seventy-five, she's all crippled up, can't get around no more, lays up in her bed upstairs watchin' teevee. Can't hardly even get up outa bed by herself. All crippled up. Can't look after herself. Needs someone else to come and look after her. You know who looks after her? You know who?"

"Yes."

"*I* look after her, that's who. Two days a week, three if I'm lucky, I go up to that pussy old white woman's house and I look after her. White people can't even get by in this life without they got their nigger to help look after 'em. I clean her house, I change her bed, I wash the linens and the dirty clothes and I cook her up some meals so she'll have somethin' to eat during the days I ain't there. She's an old woman. She sits up there in bed in her nightdress and sometimes she shits in her nightdress and I take the nightdress off of her and clean up the shit with my own two hands. And you know what she does? Answer me. Do you know?"

"No."

" 'Listen here, Ruby,' she says. 'When you're downstairs,

you're not sitting down on any of my furniture, are you?' 'No, ma'm,' I say. 'Because I won't have no colored sitting down on any of my chairs or any of my couches. You come here to work, Ruby. I pay you good money. I don't want to find you sitting down.'

"And when I make her her lunch, when I make her some tuna fish or soup or some kinda sandwich, you think I'm allowed to take some and have a sandwich for myself? No, I ain't. I bring my own lunch. I bring my own sandwich by myself in a little paper bag. 'You're not eating any of my food, are you, Ruby?' she asks me. 'Because I can't be havin' any colored eating up my good food.'

"And when I want a glass of water, I'm doin' all this heavy housework so I get thirsty and I want to go get myself a glass of water, you think I can just take a glass out of the cabinet and pour myself a glass of water? Is that what you think? Well, I'll tell you what I do. There's a special glass she has, a special jelly-jar plastic glass, and it's just for me, that pussy old white woman went out and got this old plastic jelly jar somewhere just for me, just so when I want a drink of water I won't be drinkin' it from any of her fine five-and-ten-cent-store glasses. 'Now Ruby,' she says, 'when you're drinking water down there, don't you be drinking it from out of any of my glasses, you hear? You take care to drink it out of that special glass I bought you. I won't be having no colored eating off of my dishes or drinking out of my glasses.' "

For a moment the voices on the porch fell silent.

"Why'd you bring that white boy here?" asked Heather's mother sharply.

"You invited him," replied Heather.

"I'm tellin' you this, Heather," continued Mrs. Thomas, her voice as biting as an acid bath, "and you better listen to me, 'cause I mean what I'm tellin' you. You try to marry that white boy, and I'll have it annulled. I'll get down on my hands and knees and I'll work on my hands and knees till my hands are bloody and there's not a breath of life left in my body. But so help me god, I'll have it annulled. You understand what I'm tellin' you, girl? You understand what I'm tryin' to tell you?"

"Yes, I do," answered Heather quietly. "Now goodnight, Momma. I'm going to bed."

I scurried back through the kitchen and paused just inside the guest-room door. The porch door creaked open and I could hear Heather step into the kitchen and then begin to ascend the stairs.

"You understand what I'm tellin' you, don't you, Heather?" called out her mother's voice from the porch.

If there was an answer from the staircase, I did not hear it.

Three weeks later Heather and I drove up to Michigan to get married, at least we tried to get married, in the end it turned out we had to drive up there twice. The first time, Ken and Elaine drove us up there, we set out early on a Friday morning, and since none of us had taken the time to eat any breakfast, we pulled in at a drive-in doughnut stand just outside Chicago and loaded up on a sickening array of different-type doughnuts plus coffee to wash them down with in plastic cups. Then we tore off down the open highway toward Michigan, with Pedersen gripping the steering wheel with his right hand and waving a caramel-custard doughnut out the window with his left and periodically prevailing upon Elaine, who was sitting next to him on the front seat, to steady the wheel and steer the car so that he could free his own right hand for drinking coffee out of his plastic cup.

"Come on, Ken," complained Elaine. "Put down the coffee and take the wheel back. This isn't safe."

"I can see you don't know much about Pedersen's driving," I called out from the back seat, where Heather and I were holding hands. "We're probably a lot better off with Pedersen's hands *off* the wheel than we'd ever be with them *on* it."

Pedersen whooped with joy and launched into his genuine simulated lunatic's laughter, sloshing his coffee all over Elaine and drenching his beard with caramel custard. "You should of got yourself a doughnut like this one, Sy," he shouted, setting his coffee cup down on the dashboard and resuming his terrifyingly erratic control of the wheel. "It's just like eating out a hot, wet pussy."

"Ken!" chided Elaine indignantly.

"Women are incredible, aren't they, Sy?" yelled Pedersen, wiping his beard with the sleeve of his khaki windbreaker. "Take Elaine here. When you get in bed with her, she flops all over the place throwing her cunt in your face, moaning and flopping around to get you to eat out her pussy. But then if you openly compare cunt-slop to caramel custard, which is after all delicious, she gets pissed off at you. What the fuck, man, how you gonna figure?"

"Beats me," I admitted.

"Both of you cut it out," scolded Heather.

"Cut what out?" yelled Pedersen.

Heather was digging her thumbnail hard into my wrist. "Better change the subject, Pedersen," I remarked with a slight wince.

"I'm really glad you two are getting married," noted Pedersen brightly. "There's nothing like being married. Pretty soon you and Heather'll be wanting to have a kid. Can't get married without having a kid."

"I don't know if we want a kid," replied Heather.

"Our little bastard's due in about three months," continued Pedersen. "I'm going to teach the—"

"Stop calling him a bastard," snapped Elaine.

"Ha ha!" laughed Pedersen. "Why not? It seems to me that—"

"Ken," I interrupted tactfully, seeing that Elaine was becoming really annoyed, "are you sure you know where our turnoff is?"

"Turnoff?" exclaimed Pedersen. "Of course I don't know where the turnoff is. I just *aim* this thing. You want me to navigate, I charge extra."

"Better hand me the map then," I remarked. "It's up there on the dash."

■ ■ ■

When we finally arrived at St. Joseph, a tiny Michigan town near the Illinois border, we stopped at the courthouse and said that we wanted to buy a marriage license. The clerk there asked to see our blood test, and when I told him we hadn't had any, he directed us to a hospital about two miles away.

"We have to go to the hospital," I told Pedersen when Heather and I returned to the car.

"Why," frowned Pedersen, "you sick?"

"Blood test," I explained.

"You'll fail," said Pedersen solemnly. "They'll probably find out about your old syphilis."

"Syphilis?" exclaimed Heather.

"He's just being funny," I explained. "Come on, Ken. It's not far. They gave me directions."

At the hospital they took blood samples and gave us some receipts, and said we'd have to come back in three days to get the results.

"You mean we won't be able to get married today?" I asked.

"That's right," replied the man in the lab coat. "You can't get the license without the results, and we won't have the results till the middle of next week."

"What!?" exclaimed Pedersen incredulously when I told him the news. "You're not getting married? It's not fair. It's a gyp. We've been ripped off."

"I'm sorry," I replied. "I should've checked about the blood test. We'll have to come up here again sometime next week. If you can't make it, Heather and I can probably take the bus."

"I feel cheated," pouted Pedersen.

"Why?" asked Elaine.

"I want them to be as happy as we are," cackled Pedersen maniacally, slapping her thigh, and then he floored the accelerator and we hurtled homeward.

The following week, Pedersen's car was in the shop for repairs, so Heather and I went down to the Trailways terminal and drove up to St. Joseph by bus. The bus left us off in front of the courthouse, so we had to walk the two miles to the hospital to get our blood test results and then walk two miles back to the courthouse to pick up the marriage license. There was fresh snow on the ground, so the walking was hard and pretty slow, every now and then a car would come by and we'd try to shag a lift, but we ended up walking the whole four miles without anyone giving us one.

Back at the courthouse, on the second floor, the clerk gave us our marriage license and told us that if we went to the judge's chambers one flight down, the judge could probably marry us right away. I remember we were midway down the long flight of stairs when suddenly a state trooper wearing mirror-lensed sunglasses and wielding a nightstick called out to us to step to one side of the stairway, and then a column of manacled men, six or eight of them, all linked together by a long heavy chain connecting their manacles, clanked up the steps with the state trooper following grim-faced a few paces behind them. The prisoners were all in their twenties—some white, some black—and as they brushed by us on their way up the staircase, the last man in line, a Negro as handsome as the handsomest movie star, smiled at us wryly and then quietly clanked his manacles with a slight upward motion of his wrists and then shrugged his shoulders and shook his head from side to side ever so slightly.

"Oh, Sy," whispered Heather. "He's so beautiful."

"He probably killed four people in their sleep," I replied.

"No," she said quietly, "he didn't. He just couldn't have."

When we got to the judge's chambers on the ground floor of the courthouse, his secretary told us that we were ten minutes late, the judge was about to start court proceedings for the day, and she suggested that rather than wait till late afternoon when the judge would be finished, we have the ceremony performed by a justice of the peace who owned a hardware store in Mason Harbor, about ten miles away.

We took a cab to Mason Harbor and asked the driver to please wait for us outside the J.P.'s hardware store so that after the ceremony he could drive us back to the bus station to catch our bus back to Chicago.

Inside, the hardware store was empty except for the proprietor standing behind the counter and a farmer in white overalls picking out a new rake.

"Can I help you folks?" inquired the proprietor, a gaunt, wiry man in his early fifties with a light brown crewcut flecked with gray. He was dressed in faded blue jeans and a flannel shirt with the sleeves rolled up, and he wore a blue apron that tied in the back. He wasn't wearing eyeglasses behind the counter, but he took a pair out of his shirt pocket soon afterward so he could read from the Bible.

"Are you the justice of the peace?" I asked.

"Sure am," he replied brightly. "You two folks figurin' to get married?"

"That's right," I answered. "The judge in—"

"Hey, Peter," he called out to the farmer, while simultaneously lifting up the hinged slat in the counter so that he could step out from behind the counter, "think you can take care of yourself for a few minutes while I marry these folks?"

"You bet," replied the farmer.

The proprietor led us across the length of the store, past great piles of tar paper and ax handles and huge kegs of nails, to a door made of unsanded wooden planks. Behind the door, inside a medium-sized room, was a polished mahogany rolltop desk that looked as though it might have adorned the office of an oldtime railroad baron a hundred years ago, and piled all around the room, so many of them that it was hard to negotiate a path around them, were gigantic burlap sacks brimful with chicken feed. At one corner of the room stood an old wooden coatrack, and on it hung an old tweed jacket with leather patches sewn onto the elbows. The hardware proprietor removed his apron and hung it on the coatrack, then took down the jacket to wear in its stead.

"Wait a minute," he exclaimed suddenly. "Law says we got to have two witnesses. You folks bring any witnesses?"

"We've got a cabdriver waiting outside," I suggested. "He could be a witness."

"Good idea," nodded the proprietor. "I'll go get Pete. Old Pete just loves weddings. I just hope he doesn't go all to pieces on us, sentimental as he is." He winked at Heather and scurried out the plank door back into the store.

Along one wall of the room was a large sheet of plywood set on sawhorses, and piled high on the plywood were leaflets published by the John Birch Society. On the wall above the makeshift table were certificates identifying the proprietor as a justice of the peace, a sponsor of the local Little League, and a bowling league champ. An old patriotic poster in an antique gilt frame showed a blue-eyed blonde draped in a gossamer floor-length version of the American flag and bore the legend, "Our Country / Right or Wrong / Our Country" in large red block letters.

Within moments the store owner returned with the farmer and the cabdriver. Reaching into the pocket of his flannel shirt, he pulled out a pair of horn-rimmed reading glasses, then put them on and playfully peered over the lenses at Heather. "You can still back out of this if you want to," he smiled. The farmer and the cabdriver both laughed.

From the top drawer of the rolltop desk, the proprietor withdrew a softbound edition of the King James Bible and opened it to the place marked by the book's own red ribbon bookmark. Tucked between the pages of the Bible was a typewritten sheet of paper containing the words of the civil marriage ceremony.

"We're not religious," I remarked. "There's no need to—"

"It's your wedding," he replied, smiling indulgently. "But take it from me, if your marriage turns out to be anything like mine, and lord only knows most marriages do, you're gonna need all the help from the man upstairs you can get."

The farmer and the cabdriver looked at each other and laughed again, and the farmer pulled off his cap respectfully and held it in his hands behind his back, spacing his feet about three feet apart. The whole ceremony couldn't have taken more than about two minutes, with the hardware proprietor reading slowly and deliberately from the typewritten sheet tucked into his Bible and then concluding with a reading of one of the Psalms. Then he looked up.

"Have you got a ring?" he asked.

"N-No," I stammered. "I guess we forgot."

"That's okay," replied the proprietor. "My wife never wears hers anyway."

"Mine neither," said the farmer over my shoulder, "and we've been married goin' on thirty-two years."

"I now pronounce you man and wife," announced the proprietor. For a moment, no one spoke. "Well, what's the matter with you?" scolded the proprietor gently, slapping his Bible shut. "Ain't you going to kiss her?"

Heather and I kissed, handed the proprietor a ten-dollar bill, thanked the cabdriver and the farmer for being our witnesses, and then took the cab back to the bus station for the journey home.

That same afternoon Heather moved out of her dormitory and into my apartment, and that night she telephoned her folks and told them what we'd done. Old vulture-eye refused to believe it, she kept insisting we were lying to her so we could live together in sin, and eventually she even went so far as to call up this nephew she had in Chicago and ask him to come over to our house and take a look at our marriage license. After awhile, though, she started writing letters to Heather about how much she liked me and how thrilled she was that I was her son-in-law, it's amazing how the in-laws will suck ass once they see they can't stop the marriage, but I didn't much give a shit whether Heather's mother liked me or not, and during the two years we were married I don't think I even saw the Thomases again, though I do seem to remember Heather's going back to Pennsylvania for a visit once on somebody's birthday.

I was sound asleep around 7:30 in the morning about three months later when the phone started jangling, and when I answered it there was Pedersen. He was talking a mile a minute, even faster than usual, and even though I couldn't see him I was certain that, wherever he was, he was waving his arms like a psychotic windmill.

"Sy, wake up. It's me, Ken. How the fuck are ya?"

"Same way I always am at seven-thirty in the morning," I yawned. "Exhausted. In case you've forgotten, I—"

"Forget all that, Sy," he shrieked into the receiver. "Elaine just dropped the kid. I'm a father."

"Congratulations," I replied, now beginning to awaken. "A boy or a girl?"

"Damn it, Sy, I don't know if it's a boy or a girl. How the fuck am I supposed to know that? It's a kid, that's all. I'm the father of a goddam kid."

"Come on, Ken," I repeated wearily, "is it a boy or a girl?"

"I-I'm not sure," he stammered, feigning bewilderment. "It's got this disgusting little shriveled-up dork. Does that—"

"It's a boy," I observed dryly. "Tell me, how's Elaine?"

"Fuck Elaine, Sy," exclaimed Pedersen. "You've gotta pull on your clothes and come down here to the hospital and see my kid."

"Ken," I groaned, "I've gotta get some sleep. How about after I wake up? How late are they—"

"What in the fuck is the matter with you, Sy? Didn't you hear me? I am a goddam parent. By the time you finish sleeping, the kid'll be graduating from college. You've—"

"I'll be right down there," I capitulated, and hung up.

■ ■ ■

Through the glass partition of the nursery we watched a black-skinned nurse in a starched white uniform and face-mask hold up Pedersen's newborn son for us to see. The nurse was about forty, with an ass about a yard wide, but she also had these fat, sloppy, monster tits that you could tell would flop down to her knees like medicine balls if she ever unhooked her gigantic bra. I was awestruck.

"Shit, Pedersen," I exclaimed in a whisper, "when have you seen such horrendous tits?"

"Tits!?" reprimanded Pedersen, striving unsuccessfully to keep his voice low. "What's the matter with you, Wiener? This is a fucking hospital. You're not supposed to think about tits in a hospital. You're supposed to be looking at my fucking kid."

Now some people think that newborn babies are ugly, but I have always liked them better at that stage than when they reach the age when you are supposed to think of them as human beings.

"He looks just like Mrs. Willoughby," I remarked, with as serious a face as I could manage.

"Better not say bad things about him," warned Pedersen. "You're his godfather."

"What's a godfather?" I asked.

"What do you mean, 'What's a godfather?' Where you come from, Wiener, Africa?"

"Jews don't have godfathers," I explained. "They—"

"Godfather," he interrupted, frowning, "means that anytime we get sick of the kid, we can give him to you, and you have to take him into your own home and raise him as though he were your own son."

I laughed.

The nurse bent over and set the baby down again, oh how I longed to wallow among those tits, and then Pedersen smiled moronically and waved to the nurse with a childlike wave and we turned away from the glass partition and strolled away down the hospital corridor.

I once met a guy named Mac who'd been in a veterans' hospital during the war. His arms had been in bandages and his legs in casts, and he swore there'd been this sexy black nurse there with huge heavy tits and thick purple lipstick who came on duty every night and used to give blowjobs to every guy in the ward. How could anything be more agonizingly exquisite than getting your cock sucked under circumstances like those?

"Have a cigar," offered Pedersen.

"I don't smoke," I replied.

"You're supposed to take one," he insisted. "It doesn't matter whether you smoke it or not."

I took the cigar and stuck it in my pocket. "What's his name?" I asked.

"I want his first name to be Jordan," replied Pedersen, "but Elaine wants his middle name to be Alexander, after her father, so there'll have to be some kind of change."

"Why?" I asked. "Why can't you have—"

"You can't have a kid called Jordan Alexander Pedersen, Sy."

"Why not?"

"The initials, Sy. The initials. The other kids'll call him Jap. You can't have the kids going around calling your kid a Jap."

"I never thought of that," I admitted.

"Maybe I'll change his first name to Marlon," continued Pedersen thoughtfully, "after Marlon Brando."

"Then they'll call him Map," I noted.

"Beats the hell out of Jap," observed Pedersen.

We reached the lobby and exited from the hospital through the big revolving doors. An April breeze was sweeping up candy wrappers and whisking them down the street.

"Come on," exclaimed Pedersen suddenly, yanking my arm. "Let's go!"

"Let's go where?"

"The strip show," answered Pedersen. "They've got a new stripper down at the Majestic named Lada Bazooms. Sings a song on a ukulele and stuffs a banana in her cunt. They say she's got a voice like a frying pan, but—"

"I can't, man," I said apologetically. "I've just gotta go get some sleep."

"You can sleep later, man," cajoled Pedersen. "This is—"

"No, really, Ken. I can't. I'm really bushed."

Pedersen stuffed his hands in his pockets and sadly shook his head. "There's something dead wrong with your priorities, Wiener," he announced solemnly. "Something about your priorities is sadly fucked up."

"Take care, man," I apologized, "and have a good time."

"Don't worry, I will," he waved, and whistled off down the street.

It was three or four weeks later when it happened, on a weekend morning around 3:00 A.M. Heather was under the covers, sound asleep, but I lay on the edge of the bed, wide awake, eyes burning, unable to fall asleep.

That night, Heather and I had gotten into bed and done some fucking, Heather was not especially good at fucking, and after pulling and puffing and heaving and coaxing in order to eke out Heather's one lone orgasm, I told her that I wanted her to give me a blowjob.

Now Heather may not have been much at fucking, but she was downright pathetic at giving a blowjob, even though, lord knows, I tried everything I knew to teach her. You see, a real blowjob must be done with love, by a woman who loves the feel of cock and the taste of come. Heather would blow me if I asked her to, but she never really learned how to caress the tip or lick the head, and she did not learn to relish the swallow as a woman should, so that instead of closing her eyes gently and moaning softly and drinking the come with the grateful ecstasy of a woman who loves come, she would always start to jerk away at the initial spurt and I would have to hold her fast by the hair to keep her from pulling away, and then, when I shot my wad and filled her mouth with it, she would start coughing and gagging and choking. If, as Ken Pedersen once told me, there are only two kinds of women in this world, swallowers and spitters, you'd have to say Heather was definitely a spitter.

And so on this night, don't ask me why I got the urge on this particular night, I decided that I wanted to stand upright while Heather knelt at my feet and blew me, because until that night I never had had a woman actually kneel down at my feet and blow me.

"I want you to kneel down and eat me," I whispered, as I climbed to my feet and stood upright on the bed.

"Why do you want me to do that?" she asked.

"I just do," I replied.

"You've never wanted me to do that before."

"I know that, Heather," I snapped, "but now I—"

"I think the reason you want me to do it," she continued softly, "is because you need to feel you have power over me."

Suddenly my eyes began to burn, the way they do when I become incredibly angry, and Heather must have seen a flicker of that rage reddening my eyes, because her soft brown eyes suddenly widened, a look of fear flitted hurriedly across her face, and lifting my now-flaccid penis toward her mouth, she whispered, "But that's all right. I don't mind. It's a—"

"Get away from me, Heather," I hissed angrily.

"I didn't mean anything, Sy. Here, let me—"

"Leave me alone," I said threateningly, climbing down beneath the covers, my eyes burning. "Leave me alone. I'm going to sleep."

She shrugged slightly and kissed me on the back of the neck and slid down between the sheets and nodded off to sleep, but I could not sleep, I lay on my side on the edge of the bed, staring across the room toward the half-open window, my eyes burning. And then the doorbell rang.

"M-My god," cried Heather, awakening with a start. "Wh-What was that?"

"The doorbell," I spat contemptuously, as though I were talking to the village idiot. "I'll get it."

"But Sy, who on earth could it be?"

I started to answer her. I was about to say, "How the hell should I know who it could be?" And then the doorbell rang again.

It was Pedersen. He was slouched in the doorway, leaning against the doorjamb, scowling up at me like a sleepy, malevolent dwarf.

"Ken," I exclaimed. "What in—"

He straightened up stiffly and took a half step backward, trying to point at me with an unsteady index finger but unable to succeed in holding it steady, so that instead he seemed to be using his finger to inscribe an invisible circle around my head. "Ken," he chirped, his eyes glowering, drunkenly mimicking my own surprise. "What in—?" And then he collapsed on the floor and began laughing hysterically.

"I have decided to pay you a visit," he announced when the laughter had finally subsided, "because you are my friend."

"You're drunk," I muttered aloud to no one in particular.

He cocked his head thoughtfully to one side and frowned, as if giving what I had just said the utmost consideration. "You might say I've had a whiff of the berry," he admitted finally, "yes."

Now Pedersen staggered into the foyer, weaving unsteadily. Heather had put on a bathrobe and slippers and come to the door.

"Is the coon home?" chirped Pedersen cheerfully.

"He's drunk," I told Heather apologetically.

"As a skunk," she added contemptuously. "I'll go to the kitchen and make us all some coffee."

"What did she mean, 'skunk'?" inquired Pedersen with a sly, paranoidal look.

"Ken," I whispered. "Are you really drunk, or are you just pretending?"

He cocked his head to one side again, and thought again, and then he cupped his hand over his mouth and leaned toward me conspiratorially. "I'm drunk as a skunk," he confided furtively. "But don't tell Heather. She doesn't like drunks."

"I don't think she likes you at all," I replied quietly. "And you're not going to help matters by calling her names."

"I didn't call her names," pouted Pedersen, pointing an index finger abstractedly at the ceiling. And then he paused for an instant, cupped his hands megaphone-style around his mouth, and bellowed loudly toward the kitchen: "I CALLED HER A COON!"

"Ken," I hissed. "Shut up."

"You don't like drunks either," he muttered irritably.

"Don't be ridiculous, Ken. After all, I drink, too."

"Oh, you drink, all right," snarled Pedersen contemptuously as he lurched down the hallway toward the living room, all the while staring back at me over his shoulder to appraise me with a falcon's eye, "but you don't *really* drink."

"What does that mean," I inquired indignantly, "I don't really—"

"You drink like a Jew drinks," he snapped.

Pedersen spread himself face down on the living room couch as though he were intending to fall asleep, then suddenly sat bolt upright and began staring intently at the blank gray wall on the far side of the room.

"How long would you say it is, Sy," he began, with a wistful sadness in his voice and a tender, faraway look in his eye, "since you really had a good, strong-scented whiff of the hairy?"

"I don't know, Ken," I laughed, gesturing pointedly toward the kitchen. "That's a very difficult question for me to discuss at this time."

"Remember 'Jugs' Moran's tits?" recalled Pedersen reverently.

"Whose tits we talkin' about?" inquired Heather cheerily, suddenly gliding into the living room with a tray containing a pot of coffee and related accouterments.

" 'Jugs' Moran's," I replied. "A stripper at the Follies. Ken was especially fond of her."

"She had eighty-inch tits," proclaimed Pedersen in awestruck tones. "Sy was pretty fond of her, too."

"How does he take his coffee?" asked Heather, changing the subject.

"I take three—" began Pedersen, gesturing vaguely at the

coffee tray and then breaking off what he was saying in mid-sentence. "I take three—"

"Three sugars and lots of milk," I interjected.

"My god," mumbled Heather, spooning in the sugar. "Is he gonna drink it or make candy bars out of it?"

Pedersen drew his cup to his lips and sipped his coffee in silence.

"Are us little colored girls allowed to stay in the parlor and listen to the white folks' discussion?" asked Heather defiantly, glaring at Pedersen, her hands on her hips.

"Don't let what he said before bother you," I said soothingly. "He doesn't like Jews either."

"Hah!" exclaimed Heather, plopping herself down into a canvas butterfly chair. "Nobody likes *them.*"

For about a minute nobody spoke.

"This scene we got here is just like one of them old race jokes," announced Heather wryly. "Here we are, all in a room—a white person, a colored person, and a Jew."

"Where's a Jew?" shouted Pedersen, suddenly snapping to attention and springing to life. "Where? Where?"

"You're not really drunk, are you, Pedersen?" I asked.

"Yes," he answered solemnly. "I really am."

"Did you and Elaine have a fight?" I asked.

He didn't answer.

"Did you and Elaine have a fight?" I asked again.

Pedersen set down his coffee cup and leaped to his feet. "God damn it, Sy!" he yelled. "God damn it! Would I be sitting here at three-thirty o'clock in the fucking morning if I hadn't had a god damn fight with Elaine?"

"What was it about?" I asked.

"His mother-in-law," interjected Heather smugly.

"My mother-in-law," mumbled Pedersen glumly.

"And the baby," added Heather.

"Let me tell you both something about babies," screamed Pedersen, whirling suddenly in a half-circle to point an accusing index finger first at me, then at Heather. "Just let me tell you something."

"Tell us what?" I asked.

"They stink up the house," cried Pedersen. "They shit up the house and the whole fucking house stinks from all their fucking goddam shit."

Heather giggled.

"It's not funny," muttered Pedersen resentfully. "How would you like to live in an apartment that stank like a pile of shit?"

"I wouldn't," I admitted.

"They're not civilized," continued Pedersen. "They're just not civilized. They're not even human, for Christ's sake. They're monsters. They're little fucking monsters."

Heather giggled again.

"What do you mean?" I asked.

Pedersen paused dramatically. Drunk as a skunk or sober as a judge, Ken Pedersen was a past master of the dramatic pause. "They make hideous noises," he whispered darkly. "They gurgle and shit and vomit and make unearthly, hideous noises."

Now Pedersen paused again, suspiciously surveying the room around him with the eyes of an eagle. And then suddenly, without warning, something deep inside him shifted gears and his arms began waving like a pinwheel in a tornado. "Do you comprehend what I'm trying to tell you, Sy? Can you possibly comprehend what I'm trying to tell you? How would you like to live in the same fucking house with an absolutely disgusting little fucking gargoyle that makes hideous unearthly noises and gurgles and shits and vomits? That can't even pronounce a single fucking English sentence? That all it knows how to do is shit and vomit? In the middle of the night, it vomits. In the morning me and Elaine have a fight about how the kid kept me up all night with its wailing and vomiting, and so then Elaine gets upset and *she* vomits. She and her kid, Sy, all they do is take turns vomiting. Everything that goes on in my house is a goddam fucking symphony of vomiting."

By now Pedersen was shrieking at the top of his lungs.

"Calm down, Ken," I urged quietly. "Just tell me, what did you fight about tonight?"

"God damn, Sy," he whined hoarsely, a melancholy exasperation coloring his voice. "Haven't you been listening to anything I've been telling you? Didn't you hear me explain about the shit and the vomit?"

"Yes," I replied apologetically. "I did. I'm sorry."

"And my mother-in-law," continued Pedersen with a whine, "haven't you been listening to everything I've been telling you about my mother-in-law?"

"You haven't told us anything about your mother-in-law," observed Heather.

"She calls Elaine up on the telephone two or three times a day to try to browbeat her into leaving Ken," I explained.

"That's right," affirmed Pedersen. "Come on, Sy, you tell me. Don't you think I have the right to throw Mrs. Willoughby out the window?"

"Yes," I answered. "If anybody ever had the right to throw his mother-in-law out the window, you do."

"And don't forget, Sy," exclaimed Pedersen, "the kid is Elaine's fucking kid. I never wanted any kid. I hate kids. I never asked her to go into the hospital and shit out that fucking little kid. It was never my idea. You do understand that."

"I do, Ken," I replied soothingly, putting my arm around his shoulder. "Come on. We'll put you in the spare bedroom and let you get some rest."

Pedersen cocked his head to one side and looked up at me smiling, his eyes twinkling up at me with a mischievous twinkle. "Can I stay here forever?" he asked poignantly.

"No, Ken," I laughed, "I don't think so. Come on. Let's get you to bed."

As we started out of the living room, Ken looked back over his shoulder at Heather, she was still seated in the butterfly chair drinking her coffee, and flashed her his warmest, most disarming smile, for Pedersen had a smile that could make you forgive him almost anything. "You're a wonderful woman," he said softly, zapping her with megavolts of tenderness and sincerity. "I'm ashamed that I called you a coon."

"Thank you, Ken," replied Heather warmly, and she smiled.

With one arm hanging limp and the other slung across my shoulder, Pedersen negotiated the narrow hallway leading to our small spare bedroom. Once or twice he swerved drunkenly, bumping me up against the hallway wall, and once when I looked down at him I could have sworn I saw the shadow of a mischievous smile flit instantaneously across his face.

"Were you really drunk in there?" I asked skeptically.

"Yes," he answered frankly, as he paused to steady himself momentarily against the bedroom door. "I was drunk as a skunk."

"But you weren't the least bit drunk while we were walking down the hall just now, were you?" I asked.

"That, Simon me lad," he whispered hoarsely, in his best

imitation Irish brogue, "you'll never know, even up to the day they bury you," and then he flung open the bedroom door and threw himself like a sack of stones onto the bed.

There were more nights like that over the next couple of weeks, nights when Ken and Elaine would have these incredible fights and Ken would storm angrily out of the house and turn up on our doorstep in the middle of the night, usually carrying this zippered blue-and-gold canvas athletic bag emblazoned with the Taos High School insignia, sometimes stone sober and, at other times, either totally swacked or pretending to be so.

I remember one night he showed up, it was pouring down rain, and there he was standing on our doorstep, like a half-drowned little boy who had run away from home. "Shit," I exclaimed in mock disgust as I helped him inside, "pretty soon we're gonna have to start charging you rent for the room," and I remember he looked up at me with this pathetic forlorn look, I know that look intimately because my father was born with it stamped on his face, and I started to apologize, I was about to say I was sorry for having said what I'd said, when suddenly I saw one of those patented Pedersen smiles just starting to ooch out of hiding from the corners of his mouth, and then the next thing I knew he was breaking into this enormous grin, an enormous, gigantic, toothpaste-selling grin, and then he punched me in the shoulder, playfully but hard, he was standing in the hallway, sopping wet and drenched to the skin, and then he held up his high school gym bag, which he used to carry his overnight stuff in, and he said, "See that sonovabitch, Sy? Do you see that sonovabitch? I'm going to put a revolving door on my apartment and buy me a set of wheels for this sonovabitch, so that next time I have a falling out with that dumb cunt of mine, I can wheel this little sonovabitch over here instead of going to all the trouble of carrying it."

"Is that you, Pedersen?" called out Heather, who had just put down her knitting and started down the hall.

"I was just explaining to Sy," announced Pedersen, holding his gym bag aloft, "about how I'm—hey, wait a minute! What the fuck am I standing here all sopping wet for? Come on there, woman! Let's see you hustle into the kitchen and make me some hot coffee. Your old pal Ken Pedersen is here to see you people safely through the lonely night ahead." And then he put down his gym bag and started telling stories a mile a minute, pretty soon he was waving his arms around like an oversexed windmill, and I knew that whatever the fight had been about, somehow Ken Pedersen had managed to come out of it all right.

So Pedersen slept at our house several nights during that period, but it wasn't until midsummer, July or August, that the really serious fight occurred, the one that made poor Pedersen's life so crazy and more than anything else probably led to the slashing. It was a sticky, humid, unpleasant night, Pedersen and I knocked off work early at the U. of C. Press, and then we stopped by a tavern on the way home for a couple of beers. I hadn't been home two hours when the telephone rang. It was Elaine, wailing and sobbing and sounding hysterical.

"Oh, please!" she shrieked frantically. "Please! Oh my god, I'm so afraid. Hurry, Sy! Please! I'm terrified he'll kill the baby!"

"You're afraid Ken will?" I shouted into the mouthpiece. In the background I could hear bellowing and the thud of heavy objects hitting the floor. "Elaine! Tell me, for Christ's sake, what's—"

"Oh, please!" she sobbed. "Please! H-He's gone crazy!"

"I'll be right over," I yelled. "Here, Heather," I shouted, thrusting the receiver into her hands, "talk to her. Try to get her to calm down. I'm going over there."

"She's hung up," shrugged Heather.

I ran out the door and raced down the street. Ken and Elaine's place was only a few blocks away, on the third floor of a five-story walk-up. The lobby door was locked when I arrived, so I pressed all the house-phone buttons at once, tore through the door as soon as someone buzzed me in, and then bounded up the three flights of stairs to the Pedersens' apartment and started banging on the door like a maniac. The door opened slightly, barely a crack, and Elaine squinted out at me fearfully over the door chain. "Oh, thank god!" she exclaimed gratefully. "Thank god!"

Inside, the living room looked like a cyclone had hit it. Overturned furniture littered the floor, sheets of white typing paper were strewn everywhere, and a cheap chrome-plated pole lamp had been knocked over against a low bookcase, so that half the room had been plunged into eerie near-darkness while the other half was bathed in garish, blinding light. Pedersen stood in a weird half-crouch near his portable metal typing table, wearing cutoff blue jeans without any shirt, his belt buckle was undone, and he was cursing at the top of his lungs at old Mrs. Willoughby, who stood about twelve feet away from him, quaking with fear, struggling against panic to hold her ground, Pedersen was kind of scrunched down real low, he was kind of craning his neck and also bending his wrist in this weird way and pointing an index finger in her direction, his face was blotched with purple and contorted with anger, his hands were shaking and his whole body was trembling, and in the next room you could hear his kid screaming his fucking head off.

You should have seen Mrs. Willoughby. I don't think I ever saw anybody scared like she was scared, but she was standing her ground, her eyes fixed on Pedersen, uncertain whether to stand her ground or take flight, and when she heard me enter the room she kind of glanced to her right to look at me for an instant, she took her eyes off Pedersen just for an instant, and then her eyes darted back to him again, her eyes were wide with fear, there was this involuntary twitching around the corners of her mouth, and there was this relief in her face, this everlasting relief that at last someone had arrived on the scene, altering the human equation slightly, perhaps reducing the chances that she would be murdered by Pedersen.

"Do you see this?" she shrieked like a madwoman, shrieking at me while her eyes remained frozen on Pedersen. "Do you see this? You disgusting degenerates? You filthy degenerate hippies? I knew you were no good. I knew both of you were no good the moment I laid eyes on you. Both of you. Do you hear me? Scum! Do you see what this rotten scum degenerate has done to my daughter? If only Elaine's father were alive, he'd take care of you both. He'd take care of you, all right. He'd—"

"Now look, both of you," I said softly, trying to calm them down. "Try—"

"BITCH!" screamed Pedersen hysterically, suddenly uncoiling to his full height and arching his fingers as though he were about to lunge for Mrs. Willoughby's throat. "GOD DAMNED STINKING FUCKING BITCH!!"

Mrs. Willoughby paled and backed away, it was only a step, but that was enough for Pedersen. He seized his Smith-Corona typewriter off the typing table, hoisted it in both hands high over his head, and hurled it at Mrs. Willoughby with all his might. It missed her head by a foot and thudded to the floor, but by now Mrs. Willoughby was in mortal fear.

"GOD DAMNED BITCH!" shrieked Pedersen, the words catching mucus in his throat and turning all gravelly as he advanced on her with his arms extended, flexing and unflexing his fingers like claws. "DIRTY MOTHER-FUCKING GOD DAMNED BITCH!"

Mrs. Willoughby spun on her heels and ran for her life. She made it to the door and tried to get out the door, but Elaine had double-locked the door from the inside after I entered, and in her mortal terror Mrs. Willoughby could not get it open.

"GOD DAMNED MOTHER-FUCKING BITCH!" bellowed Pedersen.

"Stay back!" shrieked Mrs. Willoughby, huddling terrified against the door. "S-Stay back!"

Elaine was half-crouched in a far corner, clinging desperately to the wall, her hands trembling uncontrollably and her face white as a sheet. All at once Mrs. Willoughby sprang for the telephone on a nearby end table—"Y-You're a madman," she shrieked. "I-I'm going to call the police!"—but Pedersen got there before she could reach it, and, slamming his hand down onto the receiver with a look of maniacal glee, tore the telephone cable out of the wall and hurled both telephone and cable through the living room window to crash in the courtyard three stories below.

Mrs. Willoughby aged ten years in an instant. It was the funniest thing I ever saw in my life. "C-Come, Elaine," she whispered hoarsely, fearful of what Pedersen might do to her if she used her full voice. "G-Get the baby and—and come on. W-We've got to get out of here."

Elaine cringed in the corner and did not answer. Mrs. Willoughby tore into the adjoining room and emerged moments later with the baby wrapped in a blanket. She reached out to

Elaine and tugged her by the hand. "Come on, girl," she urged, the terror thickly clotted in the back of her throat. "Come on. W-We've got to get out of here."

Elaine abandoned her corner dumbly, like a cow being pulled out of mud. "A-All right, Mom," she murmured dazedly. "A-All right."

I raced to the door and unlatched the door for them, and in less than a second they were gone.

"How about a beer, Sy?" offered Pedersen brightly.

"How are you feeling, Ken?" I asked, a little uncertainly.

But he was already in the kitchen, burrowing for a beer inside the refrigerator. "I threw just about everything else at that fucking bitch," he chuckled, "but you'll notice I was careful not to throw any of the beer."

"You really outdid yourself this time, Ken. This apartment is a holy wreck."

Pedersen took a leisurely pull on his beer and wiped his mouth on the back of his arm. There was a tranquil, self-satisfied smile on his face, like that of a man who has finally gotten around to performing some long-overdue backyard chore. "The Smith-Corona set her up pretty good," he observed matter-of-factly, "but it was really the telephone that put the whole scene over"—now he took another long, slow pull on his beer before gazing straight at me with a twinkle in his eye—"don't you agree, Sy?"

I had to laugh. "I sure do," I replied. "Five'll get you eight she peed in her pants."

Pedersen punched me lightly in the shoulder. "I bet she did, too," he said softly. "I bet she did, too."

"Elaine was terrified," I observed. "She was afraid you were going to hurt the baby."

"That's just Elaine projecting, Sy," explained Pedersen casually.

"What do you mean?"

"She's just projecting, Sy. Projecting her fantasies onto me. She hates the baby and wishes he were dead, but she can't bring herself to admit her hatred, even to herself, so she accuses *me* of hating the baby and fantasizes that I'm going to kill it. It's very elementary stuff. I'm surprised you didn't see through it yourself."

"Where on earth did you learn all that stuff?" I asked.

"Well, you can't very well recuperate from a nervous breakdown without picking up a little of that stuff," he replied, tossing his empty beer bottle in a trash can and rummaging through the refrigerator for another. "But also, I've had lots of long conversations with Marjory, that's my mom, about psychology and related subjects, especially concerning my own inner feelings and motivations. You'd really like my mother if you ever got to know her, Sy. She's a sensitive, highly intelligent woman."

"But you do hate the kid," I persisted. "You do wish the kid had never been born. If Elaine thinks you hate the kid, you can't just dismiss it as a fantasy."

"Oh, sure," agreed Pedersen, finally locating his new beer and wrenching off the bottle cap by hooking it onto a counter ledge and slamming it with his fist, "but just because I have the fantasy doesn't mean I have any intention of actually acting it out. Elaine would just *like* me to act it out, because—"

"There's the maniac, officer," yelled Mrs. Willoughby's voice from the doorway. "He forced my poor daughter to marry him and now he's threatening to strangle her baby."

Two uniformed policemen preceded Mrs. Willoughby into the living room, the older of the two with his revolver drawn, the younger one, a rookie in his twenties, nervously fingering his in its holster.

"And that's his crazy friend," shrieked Mrs. Willoughby, pointing a bony index finger at me. "He's the hippie who goaded my daughter's husband on while he was trying to kill me."

Both cops were white, which made me nervous. Spade cops are almost always more sympathetic. The older cop, a white-haired veteran in his early fifties, took an unbelieving look around the demolished room and silently slipped his revolver back in its holster.

"What exactly happened here?" he asked.

"Would you guys like a beer?" offered Pedersen.

"Can't," replied the veteran politely. "We're on duty."

"I might have some apple juice," suggested Pedersen.

"What's the matter with you?" screamed Mrs. Willoughby at the two policemen. "Aren't you going to put the handcuffs on them before they kill us all?"

The older cop turned to his partner and gestured toward Mrs. Willoughby. "Harris," he began, "why—"

"Didn't you hear what I was just telling you?" cried Mrs.

Willoughby, "about how my own husband was a police officer for—"

"Harris," repeated the older cop, "take Mrs. Willoughby down to the car with the young lady and the baby. I'm sure they'll all be more comfortable down there."

"Right," replied Harris, and with that he began shepherding Mrs. Willoughby toward the front door. On the way out, she shot Ken a hateful fuck-you glance over her shoulder and then Harris slammed the door behind them and they both were gone.

"I'll take that beer now," said the policeman.

Ken handed him a fresh bottle and the cop lifted it to his lips and took a long, slow pull on it. Then he turned slowly in a tight circle, taking in the entire room, before tipping his hat back on his head and scratching his head thoughtfully with the fingers of his right hand. "What the holy fuck did you guys do in here?" he exclaimed finally in clearly appreciative amazement. "It looks like a fucking—"

And then suddenly Pedersen caught his eye and they started to laugh. They laughed so long and so hard that pretty soon I couldn't help but laugh along with them. We were all standing in the middle of an apartment that looked like it had been hit by a hurricane, one window was completely smashed and there was junk and debris all over the place, and here we were laughing so hard that pretty soon our sides were sore and all we wanted to do was stop.

The cop picked up a fallen end table and set his beer down on it and then pulled a pad and ballpoint pen out of his back pocket. Laughing aloud one last time, he wiped his mouth on his forearm and poised his pen above his pad.

"What happened?" he asked.

"Well," began Pedersen earnestly, "that fucking Mrs. Willoughby never—"

"Willoughby's the battle-axe down in the car," interrupted the cop.

"Right," replied Pedersen. "She's my mother-in-law."

"I'm so sorry," consoled the cop sarcastically, and then he laughed again.

Ken laughed, too. "She never wanted me and Elaine to get married," he explained. "Ever since the wedding day, even *including* the wedding day, she's been calling Elaine on the telephone eight times a day and bullying her and badgering her about how I'm no good for her and how she should pack up the baby and leave me and come back home and live with her. I work at night and go to school days, so mostly she calls when I'm away at school or away working. If I'm home when she calls, she just hangs up, because she knows if she ever pulls any of that shit with me I'll sew up her god damn cunt for her."

"So what happened tonight?" asked the cop.

"Well, tonight I went to work as usual, but me and Sy here got off early on account of a card sorter was busted, and so we stopped off someplace for a beer and then I got home a few hours early. You see, Elaine wasn't expecting me that early because—"

"I understand," nodded the cop. "So what happened then?"

"So I got home and when I'm about to put my key in the lock I hear that fucking—I hear Elaine crying her eyes out and old Mrs. Willoughby browbeating her about what a worthless bum I am. So I figured I'd had enough of that shit and it was about time I—"

"You rip the phone out of the wall?" interrupted the cop.

"Yeah," replied Pedersen. "What makes you ask about that?"

"That really threw her for a loop," answered the cop. "You wanta know somethin'? I've always wanted to do that."

"Why don't you do it sometime?" suggested Pedersen.

"When would I?" asked the cop.

"Next time you have a fight with the old lady," shrugged Pedersen.

The cop shoved his ballpoint pen and pad back inside his pocket and took a last admiring look around the room. "Aw, no," he replied thoughtfully, shaking his head. "Me and the wife, we been married twenty years. We been happily married twenty years. We never have fights like this."

"You sound like a lucky man," I remarked.

"I am," agreed the cop. "But you know somethin', you fellas? I'm a Protestant. You fellas Protestants?"

"Uh-huh," nodded Pedersen.

"Well my wife's a Catholic," continued the cop. "And her old lady, you wouldn't believe it. When me and my wife wanted to get married, that fucking old garbage bag pulled every trick in the fucking book to get us to break up. You know what I mean?

She pulled every fucking trick in the book. Now we been married twenty fucking years. Can you beat that?"

We shook our heads. No, we couldn't beat that.

"Listen," said the cop, "there's no need for me to report this. Just a family quarrel. I ain't got enough paper on my work sheet to report every goddam family quarrel."

"Thanks, officer," I said gratefully.

"But the old lady down in the car is pretty worked up," the cop went on. "You better let us take her and your wife and kid back to her place—she said she lives in Winnetka or someplace—for the night and then tomorrow you go out there and smooch it up with her and fix it all up and bring her back here."

"Okay," replied Pedersen.

"But for tonight," repeated the cop, "better to just let your wife spend the night with her old lady. It'll help calm everybody down. Better for everybody."

The cop turned to go. He walked to the door and put his hand on the knob and then turned back toward us again. "You know how to handle it, don'tcha?" he remarked, gesturing toward Pedersen. "You just go out there tomorrow and kiss her up a little and maybe give her a little hot dick. No matter how sore they are, they can't resist a little of that hot dick."

"Thanks," laughed Ken. "I hope you enjoyed the beer."

"I didn't drink no beer," replied the cop with a wink. "Remember, I'm on duty."

The policeman's footsteps receded down the hallway and clumped down the stairs.

"I guess I ought to be getting home, too, Ken," I remarked, "unless you want me to stay here with you for awhile."

"I know Heather doesn't like me very much," said Pedersen plaintively, "but could I maybe come stay at your place tonight? Because—"

"Sure, Ken," I replied reassuringly. "Heather doesn't—"

"—because god damn it, Sy, I'm feeling awful lonely."

The next day was warm and sunny, but with a warm wind sweeping in off the lake. I remember the wind that day because in the afternoon I bought a bagful of fried shrimp and took a walk through the park, eating my shrimp and watching all the hairies twitching along, holding down their cotton dresses to prevent the wind from blowing them up over their face. There is only one thing more sexy in this world than a succulent hairy with her dress billowing up over her thighs in the summer wind, and that is the spangled goddesses you see at the circus.

When I was a kid my dad would take me to the circus, they had a freak tent at the circus when I was a kid, plus there'd always be horrible little men with warts on their faces and change aprons around their waists, these men always wore change aprons like the men who sell newspapers, they sold little cardboard boxes with plastic windows in them, through the plastic windows you could see painted turtles and dying chameleons twisting, squirming, dying inside the windows. I remember I wanted to buy one of the chameleons, but my dad always said no, the chameleon was sick, he said, it was sick and would die soon after we got home, I promised I would take good care of the chameleon, but my dad said the turtles and chameleons were all very sick, they would die soon no matter how well I took care of them, it made me feel yellow inside and sick to my stomach to think of all those poor little creatures, trapped in those boxes, clawing, scratching, dying to get out, dying by the thousands as soon as they got home, dying by the tens of thousands as soon as they got home, thrown down toilet bowls by little boys like me, little boys who thought it was all their fault, whirling away down toilet bowls into oblivion, whirling away forever, clawing, scratching.

The most wonderful women on earth live in the circus, their

costumes are so wonderful they make your eyes burn, they fly through the air, they never grow old, I still recall one of them, a long-haired blonde clothed in diamonds and emeralds, she lowered herself gracefully from the high wire and took a smooth rubber bracket gently between her lips and spun round and round up there, high above the tanbark, holding on by her ruby lips and whirling in starlight, till my eyes burned and my head throbbed with excitement and my little boy's knuckles turned white as I clutched the sides of my chair. I have never longed for anything as much in this world as I longed for that emerald goddess atwirl in the starlight.

■ ■ ■

The following evening I got home from some shopping to find Pedersen in the kitchen, slaving over a hot stove, and Heather in the living room listening to madrigals playing on the hi-fi.

"I see you put him to work," I remarked, kissing her lightly on the cheek. "What's he making?"

"Chili," called out Pedersen from the kitchen, where he was now stirring his steaming concoction with a big wooden spoon. "Down-home, red-hot, red-devil, sonovabitch chili."

"I thought Red Devil was the name of a paint remover," I quipped, whereupon Pedersen hooted with glee, spooning himself up a huge wooden spoonful of chili, helping himself to a modest taste of it, and then playfully clutching his throat and miming the grotesque gestures of a man howling with pain.

"You seem chipper tonight," I remarked.

"Chili's almost ready," replied Pedersen, scooping some up and downing another mouthful. "Just needs a little more turpentine."

"What happened that you're so cheerful?" I asked. "Mrs. Willoughby get eaten alive by a horde of white ants?"

Pedersen set down his spoon and hooted again.

"Did you speak to Elaine today?" I asked.

Pedersen was spooning the chili into these small wooden bowls we had that Heather always used for salad. If I had done that, she would've started screaming her fucking head off, but when Pedersen did it she said nothing. "Better than that," answered Pedersen. "I drove up there this morning, while the 'Bee' was away at work."

"Oh yeah? What happened?"

"The front door was locked," he continued, "and nobody answered the bell. So I went around to the back and climbed in a window, and when I got upstairs I found Elaine taking a bath in the bathtub."

"What did you say to her?" I asked.

"Not a fuckin' thing, Sy. I didn't say a fuckin' thing. I just walked over to the bathtub and pulled up the plunger thing to let out all the water, and then I took off my clothes and I fucked her right in the bathtub. Right there in the bathtub, Sy. She was sopping wet and everything. Her tits were sopping wet, her pussy was sopping wet, everything was sopping wet. And Sy, it was terrific, absolutely terrific. Best hunk of twat I ever had in my life. You and Heather oughtta try it. It was terrific."

"I just knew there hadda be *some* technique that might get Sy inside a bathtub," joked Heather.

"Anything else happen while you were there?" I asked.

"Anything else!?" exclaimed Pedersen. "What else had to happen, for chrissakes? I just finished telling you, Sy. I fucked Elaine right in the god damned bathtub."

The chili had been brought to the dining room table by now, along with a box of Saltine crackers and a couple of beers. Heather and I dug in, but Pedersen held back to savor my reaction. Everyone else I knew always loved Pedersen's chili, but for me it was always like eating red-hot sand laced with strychnine. I uttered an agonized gasp and groped blindly for a beer bottle while Pedersen put his sleeve to his mouth to stifle a bogus guffaw. Then Heather started slapping me on the back and the two of them started laughing uproariously.

"It's awful hard being Jewish, ain't it?" chortled Heather.

"Ken," I interjected, determined to bring an end to this particular aspect of the evening's entertainment, "I understand that you fucked her in the bathtub, but are you and Elaine going to get back together again or what?"

"Of course," he replied matter-of-factly. "She and the baby'll be home in a day or so."

"Did she actually say that?" I asked.

"She didn't actually have to say that in so many words, Sy," replied Pedersen condescendingly. "When a man and a woman love each other, they communicate in numerous ways other than words."

I guffawed. Even Pedersen was smirking. "This hypothetical man and woman we're talking about," I began, "just how exactly did you say they communicated with one another?"

"With their bodies, Sy," replied Pedersen. "With their eyes. God damn it, Sy, what's wrong with you? I already told you how I went up there and climbed in the goddam window and fucked her in the goddam—"

The phone rang, cutting Pedersen short. "Answer it, will you, Heather?" I asked.

"Why me?" complained Heather, rising from her chair. "Why do I have to answer it? Why don't you answer it?"

"Because you're the only woman," I answered casually.

"And the only coon," chimed in Pedersen.

"Hello?" called out Heather into the mouthpiece. "Yes, he's here. He's having dinner. Should I—"

I rose from my seat and reached for the receiver. "Who is it?" I asked.

"It's not for you," whispered Heather, cupping her hand over the mouthpiece. "It's Mrs. Willoughby. She wants to speak to Ken."

Ken rose from the table and made his way to the easy chair next to the telephone. Cradling the receiver in the hollow of his left shoulder, between his left shoulder and his ear, he slouched down in the easy chair while Mrs. Willoughby began talking and picked up the pad and pencil which lay on the end table next to the telephone and began intently sketching small doodles of clowns.

Somewhere among my files I still have the doodles Ken Pedersen made on that day, along with other doodles that he'd made on other days. Almost always they were of clowns, sad clowns and happy ones, clowns smiling and frowning, with big bulbous noses and gaps between their teeth and those cone-shaped dunce caps with three or four pompons lined up vertically down the front. Mostly Pedersen drew clowns when he doodled, but there was also a gnarled old witch riding a broomstick and a pipe-smoking sea captain with a misshapen nose. The clowns nearly always had bold block letters printed across them spelling out words like PEDERASTY and FELLATIO and BESTIALITY, and Pedersen would rework the letters so many times that he always ended up making holes in the paper.

Ken Pedersen had bushy eyebrows, and his forehead moved

around a lot more than most people's. Heather and I couldn't hear what Mrs. Willoughby was saying on the phone, from the dinner table it all sounded like so much Minnie Mouse chatter, but I do remember Pedersen didn't even get a word in edgewise, he just sat there with the phone notched in his shoulder, doodling clowns on the phone pad, his eyes fixed on the pad and his brow furrowed, as though he were concentrating more on those clowns than on whatever it was Mrs. Willoughby was telling him. At the very beginning after he'd gone to the phone, Pedersen sort of opened his mouth every now and then as though he were trying to say something, but after a few minutes he didn't even do that, he just sat there furrowing his brow, with this blue vein starting to stand out on his brow, leaning hard on the pencil and drawing and redrawing those lines on the paper. Finally, it was bound to happen the way he was leaning on it, the pencil point broke, and Pedersen lifted the broken pencil up close to his face for a second and stared at the broken point for a second and then he carefully placed both the pencil and pad back on the end table and carefully lined up the pad with the pencil vertical alongside it. Perhaps he might never have spoken at all if it hadn't been for that pencil breaking.

"Now look here," he began angrily, "you god damned—"

Suddenly the Minnie Mouse chatter on the other end stopped. There was a loud click on the far end of the line. Pedersen stared quizzically at the mouthpiece for a moment and hung up the phone, then extracted a worn little brown address book from his trousers pocket, consulted it briefly, and dialed a number from it. "This is a toll call to Winnetka, Sy," he said softly. "I'll pay you back as soon as the bill comes."

"Forget it," I replied.

Cradling the receiver between his shoulder and ear again, Pedersen reached for the pad again and tore off the page containing his doodles. Then, reaching up from his easy chair, he snatched an aluminum pushpin out of the small corkboard mounted on the wall over the telephone and tacked his doodles up on the cork. I'll bet he let that number he'd dialed ring thirty times before he finally hung up.

Then Pedersen dialed the number again. This time someone answered on the very first ring, but Pedersen listened for just a moment or two and then hung up the phone again. Then he dialed the operator.

"Operator," he said quietly, "I just called 566-0972 in Winnetka and got a tape-recorded message saying the number is no longer in service. The phone number belongs to my mother-in-law and I'm sure there must be some mistake. Do you think you could check it out for me? The name is Willoughby, Frances Willoughby. The address is—"

Through the receiver, I could hear the soft buzz of the operator's voice.

"But you see, this is my mother-in-law," repeated Pedersen. "My wife is up there visiting her, and I've got to—"

The operator's voice buzzed again, this time more briefly. Pedersen hung up the receiver, shaking his head in mild bewilderment. He rose from the chair and walked into the kitchen. "Got any more beers in here?" he called out.

"In the refrigerator," answered Heather.

"What happened?" I asked.

Sounds of rummaging emerged from the kitchen.

"Don't you know where the opener is by now?" cried Heather. "It's in the—"

"Got it," replied Pedersen loudly. "Here it is."

Now Pedersen appeared in the kitchen doorway and took a long pull on his freshly opened bottle of beer.

"What'd she say?" I asked.

Pedersen dropped the arm grasping the bottle limply to his side. "She said I'm nothing but a piece of filth and Elaine wants nothing whatsoever more to do with me and I should never try to see Elaine again as long as I live."

"That's nice," cooed Heather sarcastically.

"Anything else?" I asked.

"Jesus Christ, Wiener," exclaimed Heather. "Isn't that enough?"

Pedersen took a deep breath and exhaled nervously. "She said she'd have me arrested for trespassing if I tried to go out there again. Can you beat the shit out of that?"

"And what happened when you tried to call her back?"

"The operator said she'd had the phone disconnected and got a new, unlisted number instead."

Pedersen crossed the room and started down the hallway toward the front door.

"Hey, Pedersen, where're you going?" I called out.

"I can't reach 'em on the phone, Sy."

"You mean you're going out there?"

"I'm going to have a heart-to-heart with Mrs. Willoughby and bring Elaine back home with me," Pedersen explained, pausing at the front door with his hand on the knob.

"Wait a minute," I cautioned, following him to the door. "Maybe you should wait till tomorrow. See if—"

"What's going to happen tomorrow, Sy?" he asked with a shrug.

He was right. I couldn't think of anything. "Want me to come along?" I offered.

"What do you want to come along for, Sy?" asked Pedersen, opening the door wide. "You know how you hate the shitty way I drive."

"You sure?" I called out.

But by then he was already gone, skipping down the stairs and out the downstairs door, whistling a song into the summer night.

We didn't notice the knife was missing till later that night, when we started washing the dinner dishes before going to bed.

"Sy, did you put the butcher knife somewhere?" asked Heather.

"Not me," I replied. "What makes you—"

"It's just not in the drawer," she exclaimed. "I always put it in the middle compartment of the middle drawer."

"Check the other drawers," I suggested. "Maybe I put it in a wrong drawer by mistake."

She checked, but it wasn't there either. I was about to say that maybe Pedersen had put it someplace while he was cooking his chili dinner, but I never got to say it because that was when the phone rang.

"Is this Chicago, 362-0909?" inquired a male voice at the

other end. There was a lot of background noise coming through the receiver, typewriters clacking and phones ringing, and the guy on the phone sounded sort of distracted, as though he were talking to me but busy doing something else with his hands.

"That's right," I replied. "Who—"

"This Simon R. Wiener?" asked the voice.

"Yes, that's me," I affirmed. "Can—"

"Simon R. Wiener? 362-0909?" repeated the caller, as if all this time he had not been listening.

"That's right," I answered impatiently. "Who the hell is this?"

"Hendricks, Mr. Wiener," replied the man at the other end. "Sergeant Hendricks, Winnetka police. You know a fellow named Pedersen? Kenneth T. Pedersen?"

"Yes, I do," I replied. "He's a friend of mine. He—"

"Congratulations," intoned the sergeant dryly. "Wait a minute, Mr. Wiener. I've got something I've got to attend to here."

"Who is it?" asked Heather.

"You say you know this Kenneth Pedersen?" repeated the man on the telephone.

"Yes," I reiterated. "He's a friend of mine. Now what the hell's the matter? Is anything wrong?"

"You could say there's something wrong, Mr. Wiener, yes."

"Well suppose you tell me what it is," I said annoyedly.

"Okay, Mr. Wiener. Your friend just slashed up his mother-in-law with a butcher knife. Slashed her up pretty good."

"H-He did?" I stammered incredulously. "He—"

"I just told you he did, Mr. Wiener. You got some reason I should say it again?"

"D-Did he kill her?" I gasped. "Is she—"

"Not for want of tryin' he didn't," said the voice on the phone. "He stabbed her maybe twenty-eight times."

"But she's alive?" I asked again. "She's all right?"

"If you call bein' in shock and covered with blood and maybe she'll never use her right arm again bein' all right, I guess you could say she's all right, sir, yes."

"But she's alive," I persisted. "She's not—"

"That's right, Mr. Wiener, yessir."

"And what about Ken? Have you got him there?"

"Not here, Mr. Wiener, no sir."

"Well have you got him in jail, or—"

"We got him over at the hospital, Mr. Wiener. St. Francis' Hospital. Same hospital where he put Mrs. Willoughby."

"Hospital? Good god! What's the—"

"Fell down a flight of stairs resisting arrest, Mr. Wiener. Busted up his arm and needs some stitches in his face. He's over at the hospital now gettin' those stitches sewed in his face."

"C-Can I see him?" I stammered.

"Not tonight you can't, Mr. Wiener, no sir."

"Tomorrow?"

On the other end of the line, there was a pause. "I suppose tomorrow you can, yes. Just come around to St. Francis of Assisi Hospital in Winnetka anytime after ten A.M. tomorrow morning and ask at the desk for Sergeant Hendricks, that's me, or Officer Claremont. One of us'll be there. Also if you want you could bring him along some extra underwear and maybe a toothbrush."

"Okay," I replied. "I'll be there before noon anyway. Thanks for—"

"Oh yeah," interrupted Sergeant Hendricks, "one more thing. This Pedersen character was bloodied up pretty good from that fall down the stairs. You know, his mouth was pretty bloodied up and he couldn't talk too good, but he asked us would you call his mother in New Mexico and maybe fill her in."

"Sure," I answered. "And I'll be—"

"Fine," interjected the sergeant tersely, and then he hung up.

"Anyone want to fill the colored-girl contingent in on what's going on?" inquired Heather.

"Sure," I replied casually. "You know that meat knife you were just looking for?"

Heather nodded.

"Well Ken just finished using it to hack up Mrs. Willoughby."

Heather's eyes narrowed. "What the hell are you talking about?" she asked peevishly, suspicious that I was pulling her leg.

"I'll explain in a minute," I promised, reaching for the little file box where I kept my phone numbers. "Right now I've got to call Mrs. Pedersen."

The woman's voice on the other end of the line sounded disoriented and sleepy.

"H-Hello? Who—"

"Mrs. Pedersen?" I asked. "Is this Mrs. Pedersen?"

"Yes," replied the drowsy voice. "Who is this?"

"It's me, Mrs. Pedersen. Sy Wiener. Ken's friend in Chicago. I have to speak to you."

"Oh? A-Are you in Chicago?" she stammered uncomprehendingly, still not yet fully awake.

"Yes," I replied. "I'm sorry to wake you up, but I have to speak to you."

"I'm afraid we're sleeping, Sy. Do you think you can call back tomorrow?"

"I know it's late, Mrs. Pedersen, but there's been a serious accident and Ken's in trouble."

"Ken? In trouble?" she exclaimed, suddenly alert. "Just a moment, Sy. Let me slip on a robe and pick up the phone downstairs so I won't wake anyone up. Don't hang up. I'll be just a minute."

There was a pause of at least a minute, maybe even two or three. Pedersen's page of clown doodles smiled and glowered on the corkboard. The voice that finally came on the phone again was wide awake, calm and collected, rich with the synthetic reasonableness of professional understanding.

"I'm sorry to have kept you waiting," intoned the new voice. "Now tell me, what exactly seems to have happened?"

"I don't know all the details myself," I explained, "but I just got a call from the Winnetka police. They say Ken tried to kill Mrs. Willoughby with a butcher knife. She's alive, but injured— I don't know exactly how badly. Ken is in custody."

"You say Ken's in jail?"

"No. Ken's in the hospital. The policeman who called me said that he suffered a broken arm and some facial cuts and bruises while trying to resist arrest. They have him in the same hospital as Mrs. Willoughby. I'm going to visit him there tomorrow."

"Did they say how this happened, Simon?"

"They really didn't," I replied. "The cop who called me was pretty antagonistic. Mrs. Willoughby's late husband was a Winnetka policeman, remember? But from what I could gather, Ken got into some kind of confrontation with Mrs. Willoughby during which he slashed her up repeatedly with a butcher knife."

There was a long pause at the other end. "A psychotic episode," she mumbled introspectively.

"Excuse me?" I asked.

"A psychotic episode," she repeated. "Mrs. Willoughby obviously did something that drastically provoked him. Ken experienced a similar psychotic episode once before in his life, the spring before he—"

"Was that the thing involving Sandy and her father?" I asked.

"Yes," replied Mrs. Pedersen. "It was."

"There's not much else I know," I admitted. "I'm going up to see him tomorrow. Is there anything you want me to do, about lawyers or—"

"I guess I'm going to have to come up there myself," she mused aloud. "I have consultations tomorrow that can't be cancelled, but I'll fly up there Friday and take a cab to Winnetka straight from the airport. Where did you say they have Ken?"

"St. Francis of Assisi Hospital, in Winnetka."

"Fine, Simon. Thank you. And thank you very much for calling me. Now I think we might as well hang up. I don't think there's any more we can accomplish on the telephone until—"

"Mrs. Pedersen," I exclaimed suddenly. "There's something I'm worried about that I think you ought to know."

"Yes?"

"Ken and Elaine had a fight yesterday, and he's been staying with Heather and me until he and Elaine could patch it up."

"This background information will undoubtedly be valuable, Simon," observed Mrs. Pedersen with reasoned detachment, "but we'll have plenty of time to—"

"You don't understand," I went on. "Ken had an argument with Mrs. Willoughby on the telephone earlier this evening and then he rushed out of the house and drove up there to Winnetka to have it out with her. Well, what I'm worried about is that now one of our butcher knives is missing."

"Oh?"

"I don't know if our knife is the one he used or not, but if it *was* the one he used, that may indicate premeditation of some kind and make Ken vulnerable to—"

"Do the police know about your missing butcher knife?" asked Mrs. Pedersen.

"I don't think so," I replied. "At least if they do, they didn't—"

"Then we won't worry about it now," she said. "Thank you, Simon. You've been a good friend to Ken. He thinks very highly of you. But now I think we've done all we can for tonight. I'll be speaking with you again soon. Goodnight."

The hospital was pretty much like any other hospital, you figure a hospital's a hospital, they're places you go when you're sick, except that this one had huge colored murals of Batman, Superman, and other comics heroes splashed across the lobby walls.

I once made friends with a spastic named Carl who worked as a therapist with retarded children and lived in an apartment hotel about two or three blocks from the University of Chicago campus. Inside his room, he had this gigantic collection of comic books, thousands and thousands of them, he kept them all in plastic bags so the dust wouldn't get on them, he had all kinds of comics, every kind you could think of, super-heroes and Donald Duck and even the old scary horror comics. And hung up all around his room, hung up in aluminum picture frames all around the room, were obscene paintings of comic-book heroines, Wonder Woman and Sheena, Queen of the Jungle, he would write letters to his favorite cartoonists commissioning paintings of Batgirl and the Catwoman and dozens more I never heard of, he had one painting of Sheena being fucked by a black panther, and another of the Catwoman giving Batman a blowjob.

Right before you reached the hospital admissions desk you passed by the gift shop, seated in the front window was a colossal toy dog with roly-poly eyes, a huge red tongue, and a body covered with soft pink fur, and all at once I thought how funny it would be to buy that pink dog and show up in Pedersen's room with it as a get-well gift. But the price tag on the sonovabitch turned out to be $120, so I decided Pedersen would just have to get along without it.

When I got to the front desk, I just stood there a minute waiting for someone to notice me.

"Excuse me?" I said finally.

This one nurse turned around. There wasn't much to her, mid-to-late thirties with corn-fed, wholesome-looking, fair-to-medium-sized tits, but she had this incredible mouth, this fantastic pouty mouth that looked like it could suck off a nine-pound penis, it reminded me of old Mac's story about the nurse who used to come into his room at night and suck him off while his legs were broken during the war.

"Can I help you?" she inquired pleasantly.

"I hope so, ma'm," I replied. "Is Sergeant Hendricks here? Or Officer Claremont? I'm—"

"I'm Claremont," intoned a husky voice off to my right, whereupon a heavy-set uniformed policeman of about fifty, with a grayish-brown crewcut, eased himself out of a wooden folding chair near the wall and began ambling toward me. "I'm Officer Claremont," he repeated. "Sergeant Hendricks isn't here. Won't be here until—"

"I'm Simon Wiener," I explained. "Sergeant Hendricks telephoned me last night. I said I'd be up here this morning to—"

"Oh yeah," interrupted Claremont, nodding his head. "You're the friend of the wisenheimer up in 313, right?"

"Ken Pedersen," I said.

He nodded again, his expression indicating his profound irritation at having to carry on a conversation with someone who was obviously so dense. "What you got in the overnight bag?" he asked.

"Just a few things I threw together," I replied. "Some socks, a toothbrush, a few—"

"Throw it up there on the counter," said the cop.

"Will you need me, Dave?" asked the corn-fed nurse.

"No, Irene, thanks," replied Claremont. "I'll take this kid up there myself soon's I have a look at this stuff."

The nurse eyed me warily for a second, then turned back to her clipboards.

"She's got a nice mouth," I remarked in a low voice.

"Who, Irene?" asked the cop indifferently.

"Right," I replied. "The nurse. She's got a—"

"She's old enough to be your mother," snapped the cop. He gestured casually toward the overnight bag. "Go ahead," he demanded. "Open it up."

I unzipped the canvas overnight bag and watched Officer

Claremont sift lackadaisically through the contents. I could probably have hidden a sawed-off shotgun under the socks and gotten away with it. "Okay," he said finally, "close it up and c'mon."

He turned and led me down another cartoon-festooned corridor to the elevator, then turned away from it and headed for a stairwell. "It's not worth waitin' for it," he said tersely. "We'll take the stairs."

We climbed two flights to the third floor and made our way along a maze of corridors, these devoid of cartoons and painted a flat white.

"Isn't this is a pretty big hospital for a community of this size?" I asked.

"What's that?" he answered, his mind, if he had one, apparently on something else.

"Isn't this a pretty big hospital," I repeated, "for a—"

"Oh yeah," he nodded. "It's the only hospital for thirty miles. We get a lot of business in here." He paused a moment. "Still," he added, "your friend's the only psycho I can remember us having in here. You actually a friend of this psycho?"

"His best friend," I admitted. "He's not really a bad guy. A little crazy maybe, but not really crazy. I wish he hadn't done what you people say he did."

Officer Claremont shook his head in bemused dismay. "The woman your friend slashed, Mrs. Willoughby, her husband was an officer with us for maybe twenty years."

"Twenty-three," I corrected amiably.

Claremont shook his head again. "You boys both at the university down there?" he asked.

"Ken is," I replied. "I'm not. I work."

We arrived at the door to room 313 and Officer Claremont reached out to grab the knob. "You college boys need to let off steam," he began, "I wish you'd swallow some goldfish or steal some panties like we used to do. I guess it was pretty silly, that stuff we used to do, but at least we didn't hurt anybody."

Claremont opened the door and we entered the room. Pedersen was lying on his back in the bed, his right arm encased in a plaster cast and his left wrist handcuffed to the head of the bed. His bruise-blackened eyes peered out from a mummification of bandages, and his lips were swollen and clotted with blood.

Officer Claremont unlocked the handcuffs and hooked them around a loop in his belt. "Go ahead," he remarked, gesturing toward my overnight case. "Give him the stuff. Fifteen minutes, then you gotta go."

"Thanks," I replied. "I—"

"Don't thank me, fella," he snapped, striding out of the room and slamming the door behind him. "We're gonna send this clown away for just as long as we can."

Ken swung himself up into a sitting position and began shaking his recently handcuffed left wrist to bring back the circulation. I set down the overnight bag and walked over to the window. A wire screen had been nailed over the window from the outside, and I remember peering absentmindedly through the screen, trying to calculate how many knotted-together sheets it would take to reach the ground.

"How many sheets you figure I'd have to tie together to get out of this place, Sy?" joked Pedersen.

"That's just what I was wondering," I laughed. "Probably three or four would do it. What do you think?"

"I don't even have three or four sheets," replied Pedersen. "I only have one. No, two. I only have two sheets. What kind of fucking sinkhole hospital is this, they don't even give you enough goddam sheets to escape from your own room?"

"Maybe you could requisition some extras," I suggested.

Pedersen extended his broken arm in the direction of my overnight case. "What you got in there, Sy?"

"Oh, some socks, underwear, a pair of blue jeans, one or two other things."

"What other things?"

"A machine gun."

Pedersen laughed, or at least he tried to laugh. His lips were all swollen and puffy, and his laughter came out muffled and all distorted, like a man trying to gargle underwater. "Wouldn't that be funny?" he chuckled. "MACHINE-GUN PEDERSEN FLEES HOSPITAL. ESCAPING MANIAC ELUDES—"

He paused for a moment in mid-sentence, shaking his head in silent amusement at the absurdity of trying to flee the hospital.

"Did you call Marjory?" he asked finally.

"Yes," I replied, "I did. I called her as soon as I learned what happened. I'm afraid I woke her up."

"That's okay," smiled Pedersen. "Marjory sleeps too much anyway. What'd she have to say?"

"She said she'd be up here tomorrow. She said she had some

important appointments today. Tomorrow was the earliest she could make it."

"That's Marjory for you," sighed Pedersen tolerantly. "She's got all these clients who count on her. She never lets them down. Once she makes an appointment with one of them, she won't let hell or high water stop her from keeping it."

"I don't like her," I admitted.

"You should, Sy," scolded Pedersen. "She's a brilliant, alive, sensitive person."

"Okay," I said.

Pedersen laughed. "What else did she say?"

"Not much. She thanked me for calling her, said she'd fly up here tomorrow, that's about it."

"I hope I'm still here tomorrow," remarked Pedersen thoughtfully. "They may have moved me to the jail by tomorrow."

"Between you and me, Pedersen, your mother exudes all the warmth of a battery-operated dildo."

"What do you mean, Sy?"

"Well, if she was upset at the news of your being in the hospital," I replied, "she sure kept it pretty well hidden."

"My mother's getting hysterical isn't going to help me out of this jam I'm in, Sy. Besides, a psychiatric social worker has a duty to maintain her objectivity. Becoming overly involved can be fatal."

"They won't let me stay long," I remarked, glancing at the door over my shoulder. "While I'm here, tell me what the hell happened."

Pedersen briefly lifted up his cast-encrusted arm, paused a moment, then set it back down again. "Well," he began, "I was sitting in a chair in the living room when the cops came. Two of 'em grabbed me out of the chair and beat the piss out of me. And then, you know that staircase in Mrs. Willoughby's house leading down to the basement?"

"No," I replied, shaking my head, "I never—"

"Well," he went on, "it leads from the kitchen down to the basement. After they beat the piss out of me, they dragged me into the kitchen and threw me down the stairs. That's how I broke my arm. I also got an incredible bump on my head."

"What about Elaine?" I asked. "Couldn't she—"

Pedersen cocked his head quizzically to one side and examined me incredulously through one blackened eye. "It was Elaine's mother I hacked up with the butcher knife, Sy."

"Ken," I whispered hoarsely, "what the fuck happened at Mrs. Willoughby's house?"

"I don't really know," replied Pedersen thoughtfully. "There are these forces buried deep within my psyche, Sy, that I've never been able to fully understand. That's why I've always relied on people like you and Marjory to—"

"Come on, Ken," I prodded. "Tell me about what happened with Mrs. Willoughby."

"Okay," he said with an uneasy laugh. "Don't get mad."

"I'm not mad."

"There's not much to tell, actually," he began. "You remember when the 'Bee' called me up at your place."

"You mean last night, during dinner."

"Sure, that's right. She called me names and said she was going to see to it that I'd never be able to see Elaine again, and then she hung up on me. And when I tried to call her back, it turned out she'd changed her phone number to an unlisted number. And you remember, Sy, how I'd already told you how I'd gone up to Winnetka and fixed it all up with Elaine on my own. You remember how I'd fucked her in the bathtub. If you're going to get a handle on this whole bizarre set of events, Sy, it's very important that you—"

"Go on, Ken," I said.

"Well," he continued, "when I found I couldn't get the 'Bee' back on the telephone, I became incredibly angry, because suddenly I realized the true extent to which that disgusting hairy was trying to manipulate and control me. So when I went into your kitchen to find myself another beer, I took your and Heather's butcher knife and stuck it inside my shirt, figuring I'd drive up to Winnetka and do whatever was necessary to—"

"Then it was our butcher knife you used?" I asked.

"No," replied Pedersen. "It wasn't. Because on the way up there I cooled off a little, so I pulled over to the curb somewhere and threw your butcher knife in a refuse basket. I'm sorry."

"About what?"

"About your butcher knife. I'll buy you another one."

"Forget it."

"No, really," he insisted. "I'll buy you another one." Suddenly the shadow of an impish smile stole across his battered face and his gray eyes began twinkling mischievously.

"So you threw the butcher knife in the ashcan," I noted. "Then what?"

"Then I drove up to Mrs. Willoughby's house and pounded on the front door."

"Didn't she answer the doorbell?" I asked.

"I was seething with anger, Sy. When you're seething with anger you pound on the door."

"Okay," I nodded. "Go on."

"How are you going to be a writer," he complained, "if you don't have any sense of the dramatic?"

"Come on, Ken," I urged impatiently. "The guy outside said fifteen minutes. So you pounded on the door. Then what?"

"Mrs. Willoughby came to the door in her nightgown. Nine o'clock at night and she's already wearing her nightgown. Be thankful you didn't have to see it, Sy. It was positively revolting. That elephantine belly, those flabby, withered tits, that—"

"Did she let you in?"

Pedersen chuckled. "You asked me what happened, Sy. I'm not going to be able to communicate what happened in any meaningful way unless you give me a chance to re-create it for you in all its—"

"What did she say when she saw you at the door, Ken?"

Pedersen put his hands on his hips and craned his neck like a turkey. "She said, 'What do you *mean* by coming out here uninvited at this time of night without even having the *decency* to call first?' "

I chuckled. "What did you say?"

"I said, 'Look here, you decrepit old bitch, I couldn't possibly have called you to tell you I was coming out here because you changed your god damned phone to a god damned unlisted number.' "

"What did she say to that?"

"She didn't say anything. The old disgusting hairy tried to slam the door in my face. Here I am, the perfect gentleman, visiting the home of my own mother-in-law, where my loving wife and my darling infant son—"

Pedersen was really excited now, waving his arms wildly as his voice grew louder and louder.

"Shhh," I cautioned, gesturing over my shoulder in the direction of the door. "Okay, she tried to slam the door in your face. What did you do then?"

Pedersen dropped his hands to his sides and lowered his voice. "I gave the door a good solid kick before she could close it, and forced myself in."

"Okay," I nodded. "Then what?"

"She told me to get out of her house, and I told her I wasn't going anywhere until I got what I came for. Somehow we'd gotten all the way to the dining room, so all this I'm telling you took place in the dining room. Then she asked me what exactly had I come for, and I told her Elaine was my wife and the kid was my kid and I was god damned pissed off at her for attempting to sabotage our marriage and that I'd come up there to get Elaine and the baby and take them home with me. So we started arguing. And you know what, Sy? She was doing all the screaming and yelling and losing her temper, and I was just being cool and in perfect control and giving her a piece of my mind, which, as you know, I'd wanted to do for a long, long time."

"Then what happened?"

"Elaine wandered into the room. That is, she didn't wander into the room exactly, but my back was to the dining room door and Mrs. Willoughby was facing me across the room, she was facing the dining room door, and Elaine came and stood in the dining room doorway so that I couldn't really see her, in fact I didn't even hear her, but I could see in Mrs. Willoughby's eyes that someone was standing there, so I whirled around and saw Elaine standing there."

"What did you say?"

"Nothing. I didn't have a chance to say anything. Mrs. Willoughby said, 'Elaine, I want you to go back upstairs like a good girl. I'll take care of Ken myself.' And you know what Elaine did, Sy? Elaine said, 'Yes, Momma,' and turned right around and walked out of the room and went back upstairs without saying another word." Pedersen paused a moment to catch his breath. "But that wasn't really so bad, Sy. Not really. It was what she said. That's what got to me."

"What who said?"

"What Mrs. Willoughby said about taking care of me. Can you imagine that? The gall of that bitch? She was going to take care of me. Like the fact that I was seething with anger didn't worry her at all. The fact that I had driven all the way up there to have it out with her didn't bother her at all. None of it bothered her, because all she had to do was take care of me."

"What did you say to her?"

"I didn't say anything. I remember my hands were at my sides. My fists were clenched. There are these Hindus in India who clench their fists all their life, so that eventually their fingernails grow all the way through the palms of their hands and out the other side. They do it for self-discipline, to show their self-discipline and inner spiritual strength. That's how hard my fists were clenched, Sy. I felt they were clenched so hard that I could practically feel the fingernails growing through to the other side. And I didn't feel angry. I didn't feel angry at all. I just felt my fingernails growing through the palms of my hands and this wave of inner peace washing over me, quenching my anger with inner spiritual peace. I was going to leave. In my mind I decided to leave, but when I tried to move I was rooted to the spot. I tried to move but I couldn't. Something irresistible was rooting me to the spot. And that's when I started to tremble. The wave was washing over me and the fingernails were growing and I was standing on this spot and trembling. I think I was cold. I think I was trembling because I was so damn cold."

"And what about Mrs. Willoughby?"

"She was frightened. Her eyes were wide and she was frightened. I think she was frightened because she thought I was trembling with anger, but the real reason I was trembling was because I was cold. 'Why are you trembling like that?' she asked me."

"What did you say to her?"

"I didn't say anything. I wanted to tell her how cold I was, but for some reason I couldn't. There was a sideboard in the dining room against the dining room wall, and on top of the sideboard there was one of those silver things with a carving set and also a butcher knife resting alongside it. I was rooted to the spot and my fingernails were growing, they were growing so loudly I could hear them growing, crunching and growing through to the other side. The crunching was growing louder and louder. I knew I had to unclench my fists and somehow get away from that spot. The knife was on the sideboard and I grabbed it. Then I went into the living room and flopped down in a chair.

I thought about reading a magazine, but I was too tired for reading. Soon afterward, the police came."

"What about Mrs. Willoughby?"

"She was in the dining room, Sy, covered with blood."

I glanced at my watch. I had been in the room about thirty-five minutes. I wanted to do something to show Ken I loved him, but for the life of me I didn't know what to do. So I put my hand on his shoulder, because it seemed like all I could do. "I'm going to have to go now, man," I said. "They've already let me stay here longer than they said they would."

Pedersen stared down at the floor and sadly nodded his head. Then suddenly he came alive again, flipping his legs up on the bed and propping himself up against the headboard with his one good arm bent behind his head.

"Now before you leave, Sy," he announced, "I want you to take a good long look around this room and memorize every last detail of this entire room."

"What for?" I asked.

Pedersen's eyes sparkled like starlight. "How are you going to be able to write that book about me," he asked, shaking his head slowly from side to side as though irked at having to explain the obvious to a moron, "without giving a complete description of this ridiculous room?"

■ ■ ■

Outside the hospital it was a warm, dry morning. In the park across the street, a Revolutionary War cannon basked in the sun and a little girl in pigtails, ten or eleven, skipped along a pathway, dutifully followed by a shaggy Newfoundland dog. In the meadow beyond, a sandy-haired boy—clad in blue jeans and a T-shirt emblazoned with the slogan "Be kind to kids"—ran to and fro in the grass, skillfully playing out his twine, as he struggled to launch a shimmering aluminum-foil kite far into the azure sky.

Pontiac, Illinois, is a wr[illegible] community in the midwestern heartland that nestl[illegible]ying toadstool in the darkening shadow of the Illinois [illegible]ntiary, a forbidding maximum-security fortress of st[illegible]oncrete that casts its oppressive gray eminence over [illegible]vn like a suffocating Btfsplkian cloud. A high stone wall surrounds the prison, and in one of its recesses is a gray metal door identified with a small sign bearing a single sterile word: RECEPTION.

I parked my new second-hand Datsun on the tree-lined street bordering the wall, stretched in the noonday sun, and strode toward the door.

"It's too bad they won't let us little colored girls inside the prison," Heather had pouted earlier that morning.

"It's got nothing to do with your being a colored girl," I assured her. "Besides his parents, he's only allowed to have one friend on the visitors' list. You know that. We tried to have you put on, and they—"

"Don't worry about it, Sy," she said gently, touching my arm. "It's all right. I'll do some studying and clean up the house while you're gone."

"Be back for dinner," I waved, as I headed for the door.

"Don't forget, Sy," she called out after me. "Say hello to the slasher for me."

The reception office was small and cheerless, with a government-issue couch upholstered in beige vinyl marred by cigarette burns, a half-dozen wooden folding chairs, and heavy ashtrays on bronze pedestals scattered about the room. Behind a small wooden counter equipped with a pair of telephones, a mammoth Rolodex, and some long metal file drawers filled with battered 5 X 8 index cards, sat a khaki-uniformed guard, and on the far side of the room, opposite the entrance, sat a second guard atop a high wooden stool, presiding over a second metal door fitted with a massive lock. Finally, on the walls of the room, forming a neat, continuous stripe extending almost three-quarters of the way around the room, was a series of 8 X 10 black-and-white photographs in black wooden frames, they were like the pictures they take of kids in summer camp, showing uniformed convicts playing softball, milking dairy cows, tending a garden, watching a movie, playing pool in the rec hall, and sitting in the dining hall contemplating dessert trays piled high with huge hunks of watermelon. A third guard lay sprawled on the couch, idly smoking a cigarette.

"Yes?" asked the smoker disinterestedly, glancing up as I walked in.

"I'm here to visit an inmate," I replied.

The guard took a last, heavy drag on his cigarette and smothered it out in one of the ashtrays. "Over there," he said finally, pointing toward the counter.

"Who are you here to see?" inquired the guard behind the counter.

I glanced briefly at the official letter I'd been carrying in my pocket. "Kenneth T. Pedersen," I replied, "inmate number 33190."

"Are you on his visitors' list?" asked the guard. "You can't visit the inmate unless—"

"Yes," I answered nervously, "I am. I'm on the list. My—"

"Say, Larry," interrupted the guard behind the counter, leaning over to his right so that he could look past me, "do you have an extra cigarette over there?"

The guard on the couch shook a cigarette partway out of his pack, ambled slowly across the room, and proffered it to his friend behind the counter. "Thanks," remarked the guard behind the counter. He inserted the cigarette between his lips and lit it with a paper match.

"What did you say his number was?" he asked finally.

"33190," I replied.

"And your name is?"

"Wiener. Simon Wiener."

"You a relative?" asked the guard.

"No," I answered, "a friend."

He took a long pull on his cigarette and leaned back comfortably in his naugahide swivel chair, bracing his knee against the counter and pushing back hard against the chair so that it now leaned precariously against the wall supported by only one of its three legs.

"You're sure you're on the list," he repeated. "Because we get a lot—"

"Yes," I said. "I'm sure."

"Inmate's name and number?"

"Kenneth T. Pedersen. Inmate number 33190."

The guard leaned forward in his chair now, settling it back with a metallic clunk onto all three legs. He gently rested his cigarette on the rim of a glass ashtray and began riffling through one of his dog-eared card files.

"What is your name?" he asked.

"Wiener. Simon R. Wiener."

"Got any I.D.?"

"Driver's license okay?" I asked.

"Sure," he replied.

I reached into my wallet and took out my driver's license and laid it on the counter. The guard didn't even bother to look at it.

"Over there," he mumbled, gesturing toward the guard seated on the stool near the door with the massive lock.

"I could use a lock like that on the door of my Chicago apartment," I remarked pleasantly.

"What do you have in your pockets?" asked the guard on the stool.

"Money," I replied. "Keys, handkerchief, wallet, comb."

"You can keep the money and the handkerchief," noted the guard, "but the rest you'll have to leave here. And that watch, you'll have to leave that here, too."

From a narrow wooden ledge beneath his stool he produced a small brown paper bag and wrote my name on it with a Pentel pen. "Put it all in here," he instructed. "You'll get it all back as soon as you come out."

"Okay," I replied.

He reached toward the massive lock, then paused a moment. "You'll have to leave those sunglasses you're wearing, too," he remarked.

"They're prescription glasses," I explained. "I need them to—"

"No sunglasses allowed inside the prison," he announced impassively. "You'll have to leave them here."

"Even though they're prescription?"

"They're sunglasses, aren't they?" he asked patiently.

"Yes," I admitted.

"No sunglasses allowed inside the prison," he repeated. "You'll have to leave them."

I took off my sunglasses and folded them and dropped them in the paper bag. "How come they have that rule?" I asked.

"What rule?" he replied.

"About the sunglasses. After all, it's not as if—"

"You want to see your friend, don't you?" asked the guard paternally, his voice completely devoid of any malice.

"Yes," I said. "I do."

Now the guard climbed down from his stool. Clutching the paper bag containing my belongings in his left hand, he spun the wheel of the massive lock and swung open the heavy metal door. I am nearsighted, but not severely so. Through the open doorway I could see a neatly groomed lawn, at the center of it was a small garden with tiger lilies and other flowers, and across the lawn, maybe forty yards away, rose a sprawling dungeon of gray stone, enterable by means of a pair of massive iron gates and dotted with windows set with iron bars all along its height and width.

"You just cross that yard," instructed the guard, "and give this pass to the guard at the gate. He'll tell you where to go from there."

"Thanks," I said.

"Don't mention it," he replied amiably. "And don't you worry about those sunglasses. They'll be right here when you get back."

I stepped through the doorway and began crossing the reddish flagstone path that bisected the lawn and connected the reception office with the prison gate. I wondered why the hell they wouldn't let me keep my sunglasses. I tried to imagine how they might be used as a tool of some kind or as a weapon in making an escape, but try as I might I kept coming up empty. The day had suddenly become overcast and chilly. I figured I might have rain on the way back home. I looked to my right and left, trying to see as much as I could of the prison and the grounds, but without my glasses everything started to get blurry at about forty or fifty feet, and so all I could see to my right and left was a wide expanse of blurry grass.

Behind the prison gate was another uniformed guard

mounted on another stool. I handed him my pass and he gestured to his right, toward a room marked: VISITORS. Convicts in gray linen shirts, slacks, and caps like baseball caps walked to and fro. Nearby, nestled in an alcove, was a small commissary, manned by an inmate, stocked with things like ice cream, candy, and cigarettes. Just about every painted surface had been painted gray, as though it was the only color they had in the whole goddam world.

Even the visitors' room was gray, and huge, with long rectangular wooden tables placed at right angles to one another throughout the room, so that the place reminded you of those mazes you see in puzzle books. On either side of the wooden tables was a row of wooden chairs without arms, bolted together, and running lengthwise down the center of each table was a thin wooden partition about six inches high. Just inside the room, on a wooden stool fronted by a table that looked sort of like a scrivener's desk in a nineteenth-century law firm, a uniformed guard in his fifties sat reading a newspaper. Except for the two of us, the room was empty.

"We got us a slow day today," he remarked good-naturedly, rattling his newspaper. "Sit anywhere you want. He'll be right on down."

I selected a table at the far end of the room, as far away from the guard as possible. I remember thinking that Ken would probably want to sit as far away from the guard as possible. There was a sign on the wall enumerating a list of visitors' regulations, but it was hard for me to read it without my glasses. One of the rules said it was forbidden to pass notes or other objects over or under the table.

And then I saw Pedersen enter the room. He was wearing gray slacks and a matching work shirt open at the collar, and a gray cap dangled from the fingers of his left hand. His hair had been cut in a convict's crewcut, and his Abe Lincoln beard had been completely shaved off.

"What made you pick this table?" he asked idly, as he seated himself in the chair across from me.

"I'm not exactly sure," I replied. "I—"

He glanced over his shoulder at the guard seated near the door. "You picked the table farthest from the door," he observed casually.

"How are you, man?" I asked.

Pedersen smiled wanly and tossed his cap onto the table. "This is a prison, Sy," he replied. "Remember? I pled guilty. They've got me doing one to ten for felonious assault."

"Judging by the pictures I saw," I joked, somewhat lamely, "you guys have it pretty cushy in here."

"What pictures?"

"In the reception office at the front of the prison, they have these photographs on the wall of prisoners playing softball and milking cows and eating watermelon. Reminded me of—"

"Cows?" he exclaimed. His eyes were sparkling now with the old Pedersen sparkle, and his voice rose, but just a little, like that of a man who has learned the hard way to keep his emotions under control. And I noticed right away that he did not gesticulate as he spoke, but that he kept the fingertips of both hands pressed against the tabletop, the muscles of his hands and his fingers twitching slightly as he spoke, like the legs and tail of a sleeping cat, involuntary, fearful movements that tell you that in its dreams, behind its eyelids, the furry creature is running for its life.

"Maybe they weren't cows," I quipped. "Maybe they were really elephants."

Pedersen smiled and his eyes sparkled. "I didn't know we had cows," he mused aloud. "I'll have to check on that." He paused a moment. "Whenever *Newsweek* comes out here, though," he added, "we do get watermelon."

"I'm not surprised," I noted. "The guys in the picture all seemed to be staring at their watermelons in disbelief."

"They were probably under orders not to touch the goddam melons till after the pictures had been taken."

"How are you doing, man?" I asked gently.

He smiled wanly again and stifled a nervous laugh by exhaling sharply through his nose while his fingertips drummed out a St. Vitus tattoo on the tabletop.

The guard at the door looked curiously over at us, licked his right thumb, and nonchalantly turned the page of his newspaper.

"How's Heather?" asked Pedersen.

"Just great," I replied. "She asked me to say hello for her. She wanted to come visit you, but they wouldn't let her get on the list."

Pedersen paused. "Even if she were on the list," he said finally, "they wouldn't have let her in here anyway."

"That's ridiculous. Why not?"

"They don't let in interracial visitors."

I frowned. "You're kidding."

"No," he said seriously, "I'm not kidding. If you're white, and ou have a spade wife or girl friend on the outside, they won't et her come visit you. And if you're black, with a white girl riend, same story."

"But how can they—"

"They just do," he replied. "They hassle you, ask for all kinds of weird I.D., whatever. I've made friends with this pimp named Rodney who's on my tier. He's married to a white woman on the outside. Whenever she tries to come, they just give her this bullshit and won't let her in. They just won't. They won't even let him have a picture of her. Whenever she sends a picture of herself, they steal it out of his mail."

"Jesus Christ," I exclaimed. "Can't he *do* anything?"

Pedersen shrugged. "A couple of his holes signed on as his sisters. They're black, so they visit him all the time. No problem."

"Holes?"

"Yeah, holes," replied Pedersen casually. "Rodney's a pimp. He calls them his holes."

"You mean 'ho's,' " I corrected. "It's a contraction of—"

"No," interrupted Pedersen, shaking his head, "Rodney calls them 'holes.' I'm certain. 'Ken boy,' he says, 'soon's you'n me's got outa this joint, ah'm gonna take you on down to Moline wi'f me an' set you up fo' a solid week wi'f two, mebbe three'a mah bestest, beautifulest *holes.*' "

His face had come alive with the enthusiasm of the imitation, but his normally expressive hands remained glued to the tabletop.

"They cut your hair off," I noted regretfully, "and your beard. I never saw you before without a beard."

"Individuality," chuckled Pedersen ironically, "is not exactly a value they cultivate here."

For several moments neither of us spoke.

"I'm trying to get transferred to a different tier," said Pedersen finally. "I want them to put me on a lower tier."

"What do you mean?" I asked, clearing my throat, because I was not used to conversing with my voice this low.

"The cells are in tiers," he replied. "I'm on the fifth tier. That's a high tier."

"So?"

"I want to get moved to a lower tier."

"I don't understand."

"Well, you see, after my orientation, they put me on the fifth tier and I kind of made friends with this guy up there. The joint is really run by the inmates, Sy. You've got to make friends with—"

"Come on, Ken," I interrupted. "You're losing me."

"I made friends with this guy. He used to play cards a lot. And I think he must've cheated some dudes, or at least some dudes thought he had cheated them, and so two weeks ago they just threw him off the tier."

"Then what happened?"

Pedersen blinked and slouched back in his chair. Then he leaned forward again and, placing his right hand flat on the table, began elevating it higher and higher off the tabletop in a series of jerky steps to illustrate the relative positioning of the first to fifth tiers. "The cells are in tiers, Sy," he explained, with the slightly worn-out patience of an overworked paraprofessional tutoring a retarded child. "The first tier is here. The second tier is here. The third—"

"I understood that," I remarked.

"I am on the fifth tier," he went on. "This dude I became friendly with was thrown off the fifth tier."

"You mean he died."

"Yes."

"And you're afraid—"

"I'm afraid," he continued, relieved that he was not dealing with an absolute moron, "that the guys who did it may decide they don't like me because I'm relatively new here and because I was a friend of his, not really that close a friend, but a friend nonetheless, and—"

"And do the same to you."

Pedersen smiled broadly. "Exactly," he nodded. "A lower tier is safer."

I smiled back at him. "Because it's closer to the ground."

"Precisely," he replied.

"Less far to fall."

"You've got it, Sy. By god, you've got it."

We looked into each other's eyes and laughed. Damn it if it didn't seem just like the old days.

"You know what?" I asked brightly.

"No. What?"

"They wouldn't let me wear my sunglasses in here."

"Your what?" exclaimed Pedersen.

"My sunglasses. I wore my sunglasses down here but they said I couldn't wear them inside here. They're holding them for me at the reception office."

"How come?"

"I haven't the foggiest. I thought maybe you'd know."

"I don't know either," he admitted.

"I was thinking maybe they were afraid you might use them in some sort of dramatic escape. Focus the sunlight through the bars of your cell window and use the lenses to set your mattress on fire. Then, in the confusion—"

"Yeah," replied Pedersen distractedly, "maybe that was what they thought."

He leaned back in his chair again and closed his eyes and cupped his left hand over his eyes like a man suffering from a migraine headache.

"Are you all right?" I asked.

"I have a job in the laundry," he said quietly, his eyes still closed, his thumb and middle finger now wrapped around the bridge of his nose, holding his eyes closed as though to keep out the light, "but I don't like it. I'm trying to get them to let me teach instead."

"Teach?"

He opened his eyes, his fingers still cupped around the bridge of his nose, and blinked at me uncertainly, as though for the last few seconds he'd forgotten I was there.

"They've got something like twenty-two hundred guys in here, Sy, and you know how many of them have high school diplomas?" He paused, but for only a second. "Six. Six in the whole goddam prison."

"Is that really true?" I asked.

"Six. And you know how many have had any college whatsoever?"

I shook my head. No, I didn't know how many had ever been to college.

"Me," he answered with a smile, dropping his left hand away from his face. "The average reading level is like around the fourth grade. You've got to send me in some books."

"What kind of books?"

"Any kind, so long as they're not like pornographic or radical. If you send those, they'll just confiscate them. They have a library here. I went up there one afternoon to see if I could find something to read, to keep me occupied, you have so much time on your hands in here, and I swear all they had was the Hardy Boys and *Tom Swift and his Electric Grandmother.* Stuff like that. Nothing—"

He paused in mid-sentence. "That's what you could send me. You could send me a Shakespeare. I've been devoting some time to thinking about my theories of *Hamlet,* but every time I want to look something up—could you do that? Could you send me in a Shakespeare?"

"Soon's I get home," I promised. "Anything else?"

"Just send anything. Anything. As long as it's—"

"As long as it's not *Tom Swift and his Electric Grandmother.*"

"Right," he nodded.

"So what's this about the teaching?"

"They have these high school equivalency courses. I've made friends with—"

"What are they? What are—"

"High school equivalency courses. The state offers this high school equivalency test for people who never finished high school. You pass it and you get a high school equivalency certificate which is supposed to be the equivalent of a high school diploma, except that if you go out looking for a job it really isn't.

"Anyway, a lot of the guys in the joint are working for their high school equivalency certificates, and they have some dip-shit courses like in math and English, taught by the inmates, to help these guys pass the test. I'd rather teach a few of those than work in the laundry, but first I—"

"You were saying you made friends with somebody?"

"Oh, yeah. Right. You see there's this psychologist who's in charge of—"

"The psychologist isn't an inmate."

"No, he's not. He's a guy with a psychology degree from the outside who runs the educational program, and he interviewed me and I've kind of struck up an acquaintance with the guy and he said he'd do what he could to get me out of the laundry and into maybe teaching a few new courses, like some more interesting courses for some of the smarter guys."

"Like the six guys who have high school diplomas."

Pedersen smiled, but his eyes darted nervously to and fro, alert to some impalpable danger existing solely in his imagination. "The psychologist guy is an asshole," he said disdainfully. "I know ten times more psychology than he does."

"Better not let him find that out," I suggested.

"Don't worry," replied Pedersen. "It's our secret."

"Anything else you want besides the books?" I asked. "Magazine subscriptions or—"

"No," he chuckled. "I've got those. You know what I've got?"

"What?"

"I've got a two-year subscription to the Winnetka *Herald.*"

"How come?"

"Because Winnetka's the place where my crime occurred. I figure if anything new comes up about my case, they'll probably print it in the Winnetka *Herald.*"

"What do you mean, 'anything new'?"

"My appeal," he replied. "I've got a new lawyer and I'm appealing."

"On what grounds?"

"On the grounds that the presiding judge erred in accepting my guilty plea without ordering me to undergo a sanity hearing."

"I don't understand."

"Well you see, I have a mental history, meaning my breakdown and everything. Well my old lawyer was an asshole and he persuaded me to plead guilty. But my new lawyer says that, given my history of mental instability, the court was legally obligated to give me a sanity hearing to establish whether I was competent to enter a plea, before accepting my guilty plea and sending me to prison."

"Do you think it'll work?" I asked skeptically.

Pedersen shrugged, extending his palms upward in a caricature of a derelict panhandling for a dime. "It's all I've got, Sy. Sounds pretty good, though, doesn't it?"

"Pretty good," I replied unenthusiastically.

Pedersen laughed. The guard at the door glanced briefly over at us. "You're too much of a pessimist, Sy," scolded Pedersen. "It's not good to be such a goddam pessimist."

"When will you find out about it?" I asked.

Pedersen smiled softly and his eyes twinkled. "Don't be so

fucking impatient, Sy," he chuckled. "These things take time."

It was time to go. As we got up from the table, the scraping of our chairs echoed loudly in the near-empty room.

"How come there are no other visitors?" I inquired curiously, as we ambled slowly toward the door.

Pedersen shrugged. "Weekday, I guess," he suggested tentatively. The guard on the stool stared down at us with the benign disinterest of a maître d'. I almost expected him to ask us if we'd remembered to pay our check.

"Anything else I can get for you, besides the books?" I asked, as we paused in the doorway.

"Well," he mused thoughtfully, trying to suppress a growing smirk, "if you could just sneak me in a big, wet, sloshy, mouth-watering—"

"Besides that," I said.

"Yeah," he replied, suddenly serious. "Stop by the commissary on your way out and buy me two dollars and fifty cents' worth of stuff. That's the limit you're allowed to spend. They'll send me the stuff after dinner. That's when they come around with it."

"What do you want me to buy you?" I asked.

"Just a chocolate malt and spend the rest on packs of cigarettes," he replied. "It doesn't matter what kind."

"But you don't smoke cigarettes, do you?"

"No. But around here they use 'em like money. If I have cigarettes, I can trade them for any other kind of stuff I want."

"Want some tobacco for your meerschaum pipe?"

"No use," he replied, shaking his head. "Some sonovabitch swiped it. But you could send me up some Rum-Soaked Crooks."

"What are Rum—"

"Cheap cigars, soaked in rum. And they're not half bad. Sort of like tossing down a shot of cheap rum while sucking on the exhaust pipe of a moving automobile."

I laughed. Pedersen laughed, too, and stuck out his hand.

"Come back soon, man," he said jauntily, struggling to hold down the emotion rising huskily in his voice. "I love ya, and I miss ya, and remember I ain't got no one else."

"You're doin' all right, man," I said encouragingly, shaking his hand and not letting go of it. "You'll make it."

"Sure I will," he said smartly, with a touch of sad bravado. "You know why I'll make it?"

"Why?"

"'Cause I'm tough," he replied. "I am one tough-ass sonovabitch."

Outside the visitors' room Pedersen flipped his gray cap back onto his head and walked briskly away down a long gray corridor. At the far end of the corridor he turned and waved at me, but he was pretty far away by then and without my glasses I couldn't see the expression on his face.

It was around the time that Ken Pedersen went to prison that I really started chasing hairy again, all at once it just seemed like I was into one strange pussy after another, Heather started bitching that I never wanted to fuck her anymore, maybe an occasional halfhearted pop on a Sunday morning, climb on climb off, that seemed to be about the extent of it.

By this time I'd quit my night job at the U. of C. Press and started working full-time as an editor on a crumb-bum encyclopedia that was operated as a tax shelter by a Chicago gangster and sold by door-to-door salesmen out in the sticks. This encyclopedia place was a fucking zoo, let me tell you, there was this emaciated spade cat who worked there, a guy about forty—he smoked Gaulois cigarettes and wore a different tweed jacket every goddam day of the week—who spoke fluent Parisian French and claimed he was the illegitimate offspring of some English earl, and then there was Allan, a sweet homosexual masochist who was the office librarian, every night he'd prowl the gay bars in his motorcycle jacket and skintight black leather pants, he'd pick a fight with some sadist who would beat the holy piss out of him, the next morning he'd be back at work again, kindly and soft-spoken, his eyes all blackened and his face covered with painful bruises.

But the redeeming feature of that fucking place had to be

the pussy, the entire office building was crawling with pussy, in fact it was in the lobby of that building that I hit on Mary Ellen, she had legs like a goddam soccer player with two watermelon-sized tits and long light-brown hair that fluttered like a spring breeze around her big, soft ass. I don't think it took me twenty minutes to get her to come upstairs with me and spread her thighs for me behind the Bibles.

Right behind the office cubicle where I worked was a kind of open warehouse area that was stacked to the ceiling with gigantic illustrated Bibles. I could never figure out what they were doing there, unless sometime before they started publishing encyclopedias, the company had been in the business of manufacturing Bibles.

Anyway, the day after I fucked Mary Ellen behind the Bibles somebody at the office told her I was married and after that she wouldn't even say hello to me anymore, but the real reason I'm even mentioning the thing with Mary Ellen is so that I can convey some idea of what was happening between me and Heather. I was pulling down pretty good money, but we were spending it like water, mostly on bullshit, and we were getting into debt at incredible speed. It had been months since I'd sat down to try to write any fiction. And when Heather started getting wise to the fact that I was out copping strange pussy, I started hinting that it would be okay with me if she found herself another lover, figuring that would take some of the heat off me.

Things got very weird between me and Heather after that, and in fact it wasn't very long after I fucked Mary Ellen that Heather showed up at the house one night with an archaeology student named Julian.

"Julian," she said, "this is my husband Simon. Simon, I want you to meet Julian. I met him in—"

"Nice to meet you, Julian," I said cheerfully, shaking his hand.

Julian was completely freaked by it all. Looking back on it now, he must've thought we were crazy, I guess we *were* crazy, but at the time it seemed like a good idea, a way of keeping Heather occupied so I could be free to chase the hairy. The three of us sat around the living room for awhile, drinking coffee and shooting the breeze, Julian acting all fidgety and glancing nervously around the room, and then finally I excused myself and ambled off to bed, I heard rustling in the living room followed by the clinking of coffee cups being washed and put away, I could hear Julian whispering frantically, wanting to know what the fuck was going on here, and Heather like a patient mother calming him down, and then they tiptoed into our spare bedroom and spent most of the night there, but I think the whole scene must've frightened Julian to death, because when I awoke the next morning Heather was in bed with me and Julian was gone.

We never talked about divorce, Heather and I, but after the time with Julian we began casually bringing other partners home with us, having them to dinner, sometimes teaming up afterward for games of whist or Scrabble—with Heather and me clucking to one another and exchanging anecdotes like an old married couple—before retiring to adjoining bedrooms for the remainder of the night.

Even when the separation came, just after Christmas, we didn't really think of it as the end of our marriage, but more like a continuation of it in a different form. On Christmas eve, Heather and I stayed up late, I was reading a book, some Russian novel or something, and Heather was knitting me a bulky-knit sweater that was going to be my Christmas present. She was sitting across from me, on the other side of the room, and all of a sudden she let out this little gasp and put down the sweater and started to cry.

"What's the matter, Heather?" I asked.

"I made a mistake," she sobbed, the tears welling up in her eyes and streaming down her face. "I'm going to have to unravel the right sleeve and do the whole thing over again. The sweater was almost finished. Now I'll never be able to have it ready for you for Christmas."

"How long will it take to reknit the sleeve?" I asked.

"Eight or ten hours," she replied, dabbing her moist brown eyes with a kleenex.

"No problem," I shrugged. "All we have to do is stay up all night and it'll be done by morning."

"Y-You mean, you'd stay up with me?"

"Sure I will. I'll sit here and finish my book and cook us up some hot coffee to keep us awake."

"I love you, Sy," she whispered.

"I love you, too, Heather," I replied.

The sweater was finished around eleven o'clock Christmas morning, and after we ate breakfast and opened our presents we went into the bedroom and had some of the best sex we'd ever had in all the time I'd known her. I still have that damn sweater, it's a bulky-knit white crewneck with wisps of black wool running through it like streaks of black peppermint in white saltwater taffy, but less than ten days later we split up all our possessions, the hi-fi and the books and the dishes and the furniture, and I threw my share into one of those U-Haul-It trailers and moved into my own place about twelve blocks away.

Every two weeks, almost like clockwork, I'd been driving down to Pontiac to see Ken Pedersen,but this was the first time I'd gone down there since I'd moved out on Heather. The prison was swarming with visitors that weekend in January, friends and relatives, I figured, who hadn't been able to make it up there during the holidays, and one of them, I remember, was this succulent Spanish chick with a long black ponytail and bright red nail polish and tight white pants and mile-high fuck-me platform shoes. She strutted into the visitors' room just ahead of me, and I thought to myself if she left the same time I did I'd follow her outside and maybe try to hit on her.

"Your old man on the inside?" I'd ask.

"Yes," she'd reply, her ponytail flouncing. "He rob a filling station. He got three to five for armed robbery. How about you? You got a friend in this joint?"

"I got a buddy inside for slashing up his mother-in-law," I'd tell her. "How about having a drink with me?"

"I no drink alcoholic beverages," she'd say.

"I'd really like to ball you," I'd say.

"What?" she'd say.

"Ball," I'd say. "I'd really like to fuck you."

"That's no way to speak to a lady," she'd say. "You always speak to a lady that way?"

"Sorry," I'd say.

"That's okay," she'd say. "I suck you off a little if you like be sucked off. My name is Mimi. You got a big car? Come on, I gonna suck you off while we go sit in your car."

"Hey, man," hissed Pedersen sharply, reaching across the table and grabbing my arm. "Stop gaping at the fucking hairy, you sonovabitch. You're here to visit *me,* remember? You can always gape at the goddam hairy."

"I'm sorry," I replied. "I—"

"Hot damn, Sy," whispered Pedersen lasciviously. "Look at those goddam pants she's wearing. You look close at her ass, you can see the goddam blood circulating."

We were sitting in our usual place at the back of the room, only today there were lots of people in the room, there were these little buzzing clusters of conversation all over the room, so you had to keep your voice low to avoid bothering other people a few feet away.

"You don't look so good, Sy," confided Pedersen. "What's been going on?"

"Nothing much," I replied. "But I'm not living with Heather anymore. I'm living alone, in my own place."

"Oh, wow," exclaimed Pedersen softly. "How's that working out?"

"Not too bad. I'm kind of glad to be away from Heather. But it's dreary. Most of the rooms don't have any light fixtures in the ceiling, and I haven't got any lamps yet. So when I get home at night I have to either eat my dinner in the bedroom or sit around alone in the dark."

"Got any pussy?"

"No money, no pussy."

"What've you been doing?" he asked.

"Working."

"Besides working."

"Writing. Well, anyway, sort of. I've been trying to start doing some writing again. Heather—"

"Sy, they turned down my appeal," said Pedersen.

"Oh Jesus, Ken. I'm sorry. I forgot to ask about it."

"That's okay," he replied quietly, shrugging his shoulders. "They just turned me down flat. But that's okay. My lawyer always said they'd turn me down. On the first appellate level, they turn everything down. Now we're taking it to the state supreme court. That's where we're going to win."

"This is the sanity-hearing thing, right?" I asked. "You're saying they were supposed to—"

"Right," he nodded.

"I hope you make it, man. I really—"

"I will," he replied confidently. "I can't lose. It's a brilliant argument."

"When will you know?"

Pedersen smiled nervously. "Who knows?" he shrugged. "Maybe in a thousand years."

I looked up. "The Spanish chick is leaving," I noted.

"You gonna go after her?" asked Pedersen curiously.

"No," I laughed. "I just wanted to watch those cheeks of ass twitch out the door."

"Lower-class women are lame fucks, Sy," cautioned Pedersen.

"I know that," I replied.

"They won't give you any head," he continued. "They go through their entire life without giving a single blowjob."

"I know," I repeated.

"Their whole life," he murmured, shaking his head slowly from side to side as he contemplated the awesome injustice of it. "When you think about it, it's positively amazing, isn't it?"

For a few seconds we just sat and stared at each other. In a corner of the room, a little black girl visiting her father started to cry. Somebody handed her a Tootsie Pop and she stuck it in her mouth and her eyes dried.

"I come up for parole in eight weeks," remarked Pedersen.

"That's not the same as the appeal."

"No," he replied. "This is parole. I go up before the parole board in eight weeks. My sentence was one to ten, so that means after a year I come up for parole."

"It hasn't seemed like a year."

"Yeah, Sy, it has."

"Oh, I'm sorry," I apologized. "I didn't—"

"That's okay," replied Pedersen.

"You think you'll get it?"

"I don't know. I hope so."

"I hope so, too," I said softly. "How does it work? What's—"

"We made a deal with Mrs. Willoughby."

"What do you mean?"

"Well, Mrs. Willoughby filed a suit against me in civil court for two hundred and fifty thousand dollars' damages."

"I don't think I understand."

"After I attacked her," explained Pedersen, "she filed this civil suit asking for two hundred and fifty thousand dollars in damages as compensation for the injuries and trauma she—"

"Even though you were sent to jail for the crime?"

"Sure. That's criminal. The suit is civil."

"She can do that?"

"Yeah."

"You mean, anyone who's the victim of a crime can go out and sue the perpetrator of the crime once he's caught?"

"Exactly."

"I didn't know that. Besides, the way it turned out, if I recall correctly, is that Mrs. Willoughby didn't suffer any serious injuries, just a whole bunch of superficial cuts. So what's the two hundred and fifty thousand dollars for?"

"C'mon, Sy," replied Pedersen impatiently. "This is legal schmeagel, you know that. She didn't have any permanent injuries, but she's got doctor bills, she's got trauma, she had a very traumatic experience."

"So what kind of deal did you make?"

"Elaine's met this guy and she wants to marry him."

"Ain't love grand!" I exclaimed sarcastically.

"And he wants to adopt our kid."

"He wants your kid to be *his* kid?"

"Jordan A. Pedersen is an incredible little kid, Sy."

"And Elaine's a wonderful girl," I added. "So what's the deal?"

"Well, in order to marry the guy," began Pedersen, "she's got to get a divorce from me first, and since you can't divorce someone who's in prison or a mental institution without their permission—"

"You can't?"

"It's very hard. Maybe even impossible. You can't just go out and divorce somebody while they're in prison. And also, they can't just go out and adopt my kid. After all, it is my kid."

"Go on."

"So we told them we wouldn't oppose the divorce and they could adopt the kid as long as Mrs. Willoughby agreed to drop her lawsuit against me."

"And they went for it."

"Yeah, they did. It's a good deal for them. Where would I get two hundred and fifty thousand dollars even if they won the lawsuit? All around, it's a—"

"But what exactly has this got to do with the parole thing?"

"Well, they're not exactly related," admitted Pedersen, "but we're hoping that by me being cooperative on the divorce and on the thing with the kid, maybe Mrs. Willoughby won't show up to oppose the parole."

"Run that by me once again?" I asked, blinking incredulously. "What has Mrs. Willoughby got to do with—"

"In Illinois," explained Pedersen, "the victim gets invited to testify before the parole board on the question of whether or not the convict should get a parole."

"You're putting me on."

"No, really," nodded Pedersen. "That's the way it—"

"You mean to tell me that when they want to decide whether a convict has served enough time and should be set free, they call in the *victim* of the crime and ask his *opinion*?"

Pedersen threw back his head and started to laugh.

"What's so goddam funny?" I exclaimed, but I was starting to laugh, too.

"The look on your face," replied Pedersen.

"I just can't believe it, Ken. I just can't believe that—"

"That's the way they do it," he said calmly.

"Democracy in action."

"Right on."

For a moment, Pedersen fell silent. "You would've liked Xavier Templeton," he said finally.

"Who?" I asked.

"Xavier Templeton," he repeated. "A friend of Marjory's. Xavier Templeton is probably the only anarchical pacifist in the entire state of New Mexico."

"Maybe the whole world," I agreed solemnly.

"No, really," exclaimed Pedersen earnestly. "You really would've liked him. He was a lot like you. A real nonconformist. When I was growing up he—"

"What did you say he was again?" I asked.

"An anarchical pacifist," repeated Pedersen. "He doesn't believe in war and he doesn't believe in government. He believes in total noninvolvement with all forms of government."

"Then he doesn't pay his taxes."

"Right," nodded Pedersen. "He doesn't pay his taxes. He says taxes only pay for wars and prisons, never for freedom."

"Does he put stamps on letters and drop them in the mailbox?"

"Yes," admitted Pedersen, "I think he does. I think he does make use of the postal service."

"Sounds hypocritical to me," I remarked. "Sounds to me like your friend Xavier wants to use the government whenever it's convenient for him without paying his share of the freight."

"You'd still like him," insisted Pedersen. "You'd like his ideas. When I was growing up he had a lot of influence on me. Taos isn't like New York. It's very conformist. Everyone's afraid to be individualistic. They're afraid of being called Communist. Xavier Templeton really lives out his ideas. And he's right about prisons, Sy. I never knew that before I came here, but now I can see he was really right. Prisons don't help anybody, Sy. They don't do any good at all when you get down to it. The whole world is a prison, Sy. We're all in a prison. In a way, you're in more of a prison than I am because at least I can see my walls."

He paused for a moment. He was leaning forward in his chair, staring down at his hands and rubbing the fingers of one hand with the fingers of his other hand, the way he sometimes did when he got really excited.

"A lot of my ideas about *Hamlet,*" he went on, "a large part of my whole theory about *Hamlet,* really consists of ideas that I took from Xavier and applied to Shakespeare. That's—"

"Couldn't we talk about something else, Ken?"

"Each one of us is a victim, Sy," whispered Pedersen softly.

"I know, Ken," I apologized. "I'm sorry. But whenever you get into your philosophy groove, it just drives me bananas."

Pedersen looked into my eyes and laughed. It was a soft, quiet laugh and his eyes were sparkling. There was this one laugh Pedersen had that I could never really be sure about, I could never tell whether it meant that I'd hurt his feelings or whether it meant he'd been bullshitting me all along and was laughing because I'd finally seen through his bullshit.

Then all at once the laughter faded. "You learn a lot about time in prison," he remarked with utter seriousness. "You learn a lot about time and space."

"What do you mean?" I asked.

"I'm allowed to write one letter a week," he went on, staring down at his fingers. "Just one letter a week. Usually I write to Marjory. Every now and then I write to you. They give you this special paper to write it with. You have to use their paper. You write your letter and then you put it in the envelope, unsealed, so that if they want to they can read it before it goes out."

"I think you've lost me," I admitted. "I—"

"They give you this paper," he continued quietly, an eerie intensity building in his voice. "You have to use this special letter paper that they give you, and the paper is ruled, it has lines on it like the kind they taught you to write on when you were a little kid in school."

"Time and space, Ken," I interrupted. "You were—"

"There are sixty-eight lines on each sheet of paper, Sy, thirty-four lines on one side and thirty-four on the other. And you have so much to say, you have so goddam much that you want to say, to get out of your system, when you're sitting in your bunk and the time comes to write that one goddam letter, you have so much to say you could just fill up those sixty-eight lines like that, as if those sixty-eight lines amounted to nothing."

He paused for a moment without looking up, greatly agitated, nervously rubbing the fingers of his right hand with the fingers of his left.

"So you stop yourself," he went on. "You've got those thirty-four lines on each side, that's all you've got, so you want to use them right, you want to say exactly what you're thinking, to really communicate for maybe the first time in your life, to tell anyone, even if it's just yourself, exactly what you're thinking, to really communicate, so you pick your words, you pick one word that seems right, and then, before you even put it down on the paper, you just discard that word and pick another word that seems like it's better, that seems to say it better, just so you can make that space you've got really count for something, make those thirty-four lines on each side really count, as if your whole goddam world had to be somehow crammed into that."

He paused again and looked imploringly up at me. "Do you understand what I'm saying?" he asked.

"Yes," I replied softly. "I do."

"That's what I meant about the time and space."

For a moment we were both silent. It was as though we were inside a glass case, like they have at the museum, and the buzz of all the other visitors in the room was on the outside of this case, where it was low, and subdued, and we could hardly hear it.

"I hope you get out of here soon, man," I said, glancing about. "I hope the 'Bee' lays off you and lets you get that parole."

"Are you going to go now?" asked Pedersen.

"Not if you don't want me to," I replied.

"No, it's okay," he said, holding his breath a moment, then exhaling. "If I were you, I wouldn't want to stay around here either. Just let me tell you about the movie."

"What movie?"

"Oh, we saw this shitty movie. I don't even remember the name of it. Every week we see some movie, and last week's was this ridiculous shitty movie about how one day the insects are going to take over the world."

"A science fiction movie?"

"No," he replied. "That's what we all thought it was going to be, but it turned out to be more like a documentary with this off-the-wall narration about how man would eventually wipe himself out and the insects would survive to take over the world."

"I thought it was the bats who were going to take over the world," I laughed.

"Hey, I remember that," exclaimed Pedersen. "That physicist we met at the U. of C. told us that, that someday the bats were going to take over the world. What was his name again?"

"I don't remember," I replied.

"Yeah, but I remember he told us that," continued Pedersen. "But no, according to this movie it's going to be the insects. But that's not really what I wanted to tell you about. What I really wanted to tell you about was the spiders."

"The spiders?"

"Yeah, they had this long thing on the mating ritual of the black widow spider. You haven't seen this movie, have you?"

"Word of honor, I haven't."

"Well, they had this incredible footage of the mating ritual of the black widow spider. You see, the female black widow is really huge, and the male is really tiny. So when it comes time for mating, the little male spider crawls up to the female and he does this sort of dance, this ritualized kind of mating dance, where he crawls all around her and touches her in this special way like to turn her on, and he has to do it just right, because if she doesn't like the way he does it, she'll just squash him right there and that'll be the end of it."

"Sounds familiar already," I noted wryly.

"Just listen," exclaimed Pedersen eagerly. "There's more."

He was excited now, in his element, his eyes sparkling, as his fingers pranced gingerly across the tabletop in a skillful rendition of the cautious yet enraptured mating dance of the male black widow spider.

"So first," continued Pedersen with a sly twinkle in his eye, "the male spider moves all around her. And then, when he figures he's got her juices all hot and flowing—bang!—he jumps on top of her and he fucks her."

"Then what happens?" I asked expectantly.

"Ah," exclaimed Pedersen, pointing a forefinger high in the air and leaning far forward in his chair to stare directly into my face, "now comes the incredible part. After he fucks her, the male has to escape. He has just a few seconds to make his escape."

Now Pedersen leaned back in his chair and paused dramatically. He stretched out his arms and placed his hands on the table. On the left was the satiated female spider, on the right would be the male, running for its life.

"For the male," continued Pedersen, licking his lips, "the most exciting part is the attempt to escape. Because if the male doesn't escape in time—you see, he's little, and the female's gigantic, so one big step of hers carries her as far as a lot of little steps of his. And if he doesn't escape in time: WHUMPF!"—Pedersen's left hand pounced sadistically on the fleeing fingers of his right, pinning them helplessly to the top of the table—"the female is on him like a shot."

Pedersen paused. "And do you know what she does then?" he inquired slyly.

"No, what?"

"She mashes in his head," snarled Pedersen, "and sucks out his brains."

"Yecch," I muttered nauseously. "Those are the kind of movies they show around here once a week?"

"You should have heard the crowd rooting for the male to get away," joked Pedersen.

"I can just imagine," I replied.

"It's like a contemporary love story, isn't it, Sy?"

It wasn't too long after that that Heather came over to visit me, and that's when the thing with the steak knife happened. I was living alone in this four-room apartment, it was a lot less depressing now that I'd bought a few table lamps, and so pretty much every day after work, unless maybe that night I had some hairy going, I used to come home from work and make myself something like a Kraft's macaroni and cheese dinner and wash it down with beer or Pepsi Cola. Sometimes, if I felt up to it, I'd peck away at this story I was trying to write about that summer when Heather was away and Pedersen and I balled Tony and Francetta.

I hadn't even seen or talked to Heather in almost two months, except for once in awhile she'd called me on the telephone about some bullshit, and once I'd caught a glimpse of her driving down Fifty-third Street in a green Triumph with some bearded spade cat at the wheel.

And then one night the phone rang, and when I picked it up the voice said, "This is Heather. Am I bothering you?"

"No, Heather, of course not. It's nice to hear your—"

"Because I wouldn't bother you, Sy, if it weren't—are you writing?"

"Yes," I replied, "but don't worry about it. It's—"

"What about, Sy? What are you writing about?"

"Oh, just a short story, about that summer you were away seeing your folks and Pedersen and I were running around together."

"The summer you were fucking that girl Tony?" She paused a moment, hoping I would answer. "You didn't think I knew about that, did you, Sy?"

"Look, Heather," I began, "I—"

"Don't worry, Sy. I didn't call about that. I just called because I need some typing paper. I'm working on this thing and it's late at night and I have no paper."

"You need the paper tonight?"

"Yes," she replied, "tonight. I want to come over, if I can, and borrow a few sheets of paper. I know you always have reams of it lying around, and I don't have any."

"Okay, Heather," I said. "Sure. Come on."

"That is, if I won't be interrupting anything."

My mind flashed on the spade I'd seen her with in the Triumph. "You won't be interrupting anything," I replied quietly. "There's nothing to interrupt. Come on over."

So she came over. I didn't want her to come over, because the way I felt about it now our marriage was over, and our relationship was over, and in addition I had this feeling, I know it is a crazy feeling but I had it nonetheless, this feeling that once Heather entered my new apartment, since we had been separated she had never been inside it, once she came inside it and took a long look at the furniture and the bookcases and the rooms and the walls, she would begin to possess some sort of awful power over my new life without her.

So at first I thought maybe I would just wait until she rang the downstairs doorbell and then I would come out into the hallway and hand her the paper, just hand her the paper in an envelope right there in the hallway, and then I realized that she would see the cowardice in that, she would sense I was too frightened to invite her inside, and that would give her even more power over me and over my life. So I decided to invite her into my apartment despite her power, although I did take the precaution of putting the paper, about thirty or forty sheets of it, inside a brown manila envelope, one of those manila envelopes with the two red circles that you tie the string around in a figure eight, because I reasoned that handing her the paper in an envelope would have a formal quality about it, a formal giving of paper by a man to a woman from whom he is now estranged, whereas just giving her the paper plain, without the envelope, would have a personal quality about it that might imply things I did not want to imply, that might suggest a closeness I did not want to suggest. And I gave her more paper than she wanted, a lot more than she'd asked for, because that would be my way of telling her that I did not want her to come back soon.

"Hello," she called out from the entranceway. "Mind if I

come in? The door downstairs was open, and so was your door, so I just—"

Already she had begun strolling around the apartment, surveying it from every angle, examining the hallway, the bedroom, the typewriter on the bed. I rushed forward and thrust the manila envelope full of typing paper into her hands.

"H-Here's your paper," I stammered. "I thought it would be easier to carry if I put it in this envelope. And I gave you a lot more than you asked for, in case—"

"I didn't really come about the paper," she replied softly. "I came because I want to talk to you."

My heart was pounding. "Okay," I said. "What about?"

"What about?" exclaimed Heather incredulously. "Sy, how can you ask me that? I'm your wife. You're my husband. I agreed to live apart for awhile because you said it would make our marriage better, because you complained that your identity was slipping away from you and that you needed to have a corner of your life to keep just for yourself."

"That's right."

"All right then. But now it's been almost two full months. We haven't even seen each other once in that time. This . . . this is the first time I've even been inside your apartment." She lowered her eyes and stared at the floor. "I-I think up excuses to call you sometimes," she whispered, "but you've never called me, not even once."

"I've been working on that story I told you about," I replied nervously. "It takes—"

"I don't want to live alone anymore, Sy. I'm lonely without you."

"Even with the bearded nigger with the green Triumph?" I asked, with the untroubled cruelty of an Auschwitz physician.

Her eyes narrowed slightly but her voice held calm. For a moment she contemplated a flat denial, like a chess player mulling over the consequences of castling.

"How do you know about that?" she asked finally.

"I've got my mojo working," I replied mischievously.

Heather laughed. "I believe you," she smiled. "Lord knows you certainly have some sort of mojo power over me. When we split up, I decided I needed a man around the house, so I went out and got one. But it wasn't just a man I needed, Sy. It was you."

She paused. There was a soft whistle of air as she took a deep breath, and then a whispered sigh as she slowly exhaled it. "I want to live with you again, Sy. Whatever I did wrong last time, I—"

"Oh, Heather," I blurted suddenly, without thinking, "can't you see it's all over between us?"

For the length of a heartbeat there was absolute silence. In the street outside, an old woman cursed at a cabdriver. Heather's lips trembled. Her eyes seemed to flash like lightning. When she moved, it was with the awkward desperation of oxen drowning in wet cement.

The dishes from my dinner were still on the table. I had made myself a steak that evening, charred on the outside and almost raw on the inside, with a plate of mushrooms and fried potatoes, and nestled on the edge of my dinner plate was a razor-sharp steak knife, it had a wooden handle with brass rivets and a wide steel blade and was modeled after the knives used by the butchers in the abattoirs of France, it was one of a set of six knives given to Heather and me as a wedding present and when we had separated we had divided them up, so now Heather had three of them and I had the other three, and when I said that it was all over between us, Heather fell silent for the length of a heartbeat, I saw her lips tremble, and then she lunged for that knife on the edge of my plate, almost as a man having a heart attack might lunge for the pills on the top of his nightstand, in his desperation not really remembering which pills to take, the red or the yellow, just lunging for something, anything that might hold off the seizure, anything that might keep the gnarled fingers of death from closing round his throat, and cutting off his air, and putting him to sleep, forever.

"If it's all over, Sy," replied Heather with chilling matter-of-factness, "then there's only one thing left for me to do. I'm going to kill you." And then she lunged at me, raising the knife high over her shoulder, gripping the handle till her knuckles turned white.

My mother was not an emotional woman, she was coolly rational and almost never spontaneous, as a boy I would have done anything to crack through that coolness to the embers of passion glowing beneath. Though I tried interminably, however, almost always I failed, I would say that nine hundred and ninety-nine times out of a thousand I failed, but sometimes I did not fail, sometimes I would say something, or do something, god knows what it was I would say or do, but whatever it was, I would say it, or do it, and all at once my mother would dissolve into anger, it was the only real emotion she ever showed me, and she would dissolve into it, like a mannequin dissolving to wax in the heat of a kiln, its synthetic hair burning, the plastic flesh dissolving, the eyes pouring out of their sockets and melting, everything melting, she would turn on me in an anger that I cannot describe, in an anger that remains utterly beyond description, and I would see what I had done, I would see what I had done and I would run from her, I would run for my life, I was very nimble, I was ten or eleven, I would leap across a bed, or a couch, and I would run from her, and she would come after me, if she caught me she would slap my face again and again, they were stinging slaps, and she would scratch at my eyes, trying as hard as she could to scratch my eyes out, she had long red fingernails, they were in fashion then, all beautiful women had them and my mother was beautiful, the fingernails would leave long red furrows down the sides of my face, furrows that began beneath my eyes and ran down my face, and so whenever she got angry I would run, we had a large apartment, you could run round and round it, it had seven rooms and a long hallway, you could run down the hallway and through the living room and back down the same hallway all the way to the kitchen, you could never be cornered, there was always a place to run, my mother could never trap me.

Sometimes I would chase my brother, he is not really my brother, he is my half-brother, a year after my mother divorced my father she married another man, my stepfather, and a year after that she gave birth to my half-brother, we grew up in that house together, pretending we were brothers, not half-brothers, now he is a homosexual who lives in Canada, and works at odd jobs, and plays the kazoo, he has duped my mother into believing he is attending college and making a documentary film about Canadian wildlife, but in the old days we were brothers, I was the big brother and he was the little brother, sometimes we would play together and I would chase him down the hallway, the very same hallway down which my mother chased me, but after chasing him around the house several times and getting him up to his topmost speed, I would chase him into the hallway and then, while he was racing pell-mell down the hall, I would circle round through the living room to the far end of the hallway and surprise him when he came racing out, he would let out a scream, a shriek, of excitement, and of fear, I would catch him in my arms and drag him to the ground, we would roll over and over on the living-room carpet, laughing and grunting until our strength was exhausted, and then we would lie apart on the carpet, staring up at the ceiling, exhausted, like a pair of spent lovers gazing up at the stars.

My mother never learned this trick, the trick of getting me up to top speed and chasing me into the hallway and then racing around through the living room and heading me off, perhaps this trick simply never occurred to her, or perhaps it occurred to her but she felt she was too grown up to use it, too grown up to use strategy as she chased me around the house, or perhaps she was too angry, too angry for strategy, and so she just chased me, older than I was, and slower, unable to keep up the frantic pace, until finally she grew too exhausted to chase me and just collapsed on her bed, or on the carpet in the living room, or on a couch in the living room, and sobbed and sobbed until her anger subsided.

Sometimes I would let her catch me, I would let her trap me in a corner or I would pretend to slip and fall, she would flail away at my face with her hands, she would dig her long red fingernails into my face and leave long bloody furrows running down my face, but at least then I would not have to see my mother cry, to bear the unbearable sight of my mother sobbing.

Raising the steak knife high over her shoulder and gripping the wood handle till her knuckles blanched white, Heather lunged at me. A swinging door separated the dining area from the kitchen, and there was this small brass knob on the inside of the door, inside the kitchen, so you could close the swinging door and lock yourself inside the kitchen. I ran into the kitchen and locked myself inside, and then I stood there, leaning against the door, breathing hard, listening in vain for some sound from Heather on the other side of the door.

On the wall of the kitchen was a telephone, a yellow telephone mounted on the wall, and I remember thinking I should call someone, but who should I call, what should I say to them, should I say that my wife was in the dining room, lurking there with a steak knife, waiting to stab me to death the moment I unlocked the kitchen door? I was hysterical I suppose, but at the time I did not feel hysterical, I felt sane, and safe, there was enough food in the refrigerator and the cabinets to last me almost two weeks, perhaps more than two weeks, there were pots and pans to cook the food in and utensils and plates, there was a telephone for communicating with the outside world, and, if I had to, if it was absolutely necessary, I could even curl up and go to sleep on the cool linoleum floor.

"Heather?" I called out tentatively.

But there was no answer.

"A-Are you there?" I asked.

Nothing.

Silently I unlocked the kitchen door and then retreated backward, against the refrigerator, staring in trepidation at the unlocked door.

Finally I summoned up my courage and opened the door. It made a long, loud squeak as it opened. The lamps in the dining room and living room had been turned out, so the apartment was almost completely dark, the only light being a thin stream of light seeping through the crack at the bottom of the kitchen door. Heather was sitting in a brown cloth-upholstered armchair, alone in the dark, staring vacantly down at her hands, which lay nervously clasped in the dark.

"You scared the hell out of me, Heather," I said, breaking the silence.

"Maybe I should kill myself," she whispered.

"Don't do that," I replied softly.

For the first time, she looked up. In her lap, her hands fluttered like butterflies in a jar of carbon tetrachloride. When I was a little boy, that is how I used to kill them, the monarchs and the mourning cloaks and the tiger swallowtails, I would put them in jars, empty glass jars, at the bottom would be a piece of cotton soaked in carbon tetrachloride, I would put the butterflies inside and screw on the lid, the butterflies would flap their wings, wildly at first, you hoped they would not spoil their wings by leaving too much powder on the sides of the jar, their legs would tremble and collapse beneath them and their antennae would curl grotesquely, the flapping of the wings would become slower, more graceful somehow, as peace descended into the jar, the wings would flutter, and stiffen, the butterflies would die.

"Why shouldn't I?" she asked quietly. "Would you miss me?"

"Yes," I replied. "I would."

She cocked her head to one side and put a forefinger absentmindedly to her lips, a little girl of seven toying with the tantalizing notion of being desperately missed. Then she rose from the chair and extended me her hand. "I'm grateful for all those moments of happiness we had together," she said.

I took her hand and held it. "So am I," I replied.

"I'm sorry I was such a pest."

"You weren't a pest."

"And I'm sorry I frightened you."

"You did frighten me," I admitted.

"Goodbye, Sy."

"Goodbye," I replied.

Heather walked calmly across the room and closed the front door behind her and disappeared into the shadows at the bottom of the stairs.

It was late the next day when the firemen finally broke into her apartment. The place was full of gas and Heather lay dead on the floor. This note, written in soft pencil, was found alongside her:

> My beloved Simon:
>
> I forgive everything and everyone. I am grateful for those wonderful moments of happiness. Sincerely I thank you. I regret that this is the only solution I have; I regret that I must hurt and inconvenience you but it is the only way I see. I love you with all my being. If there is a God I pray that he will show mercy and that this will be final. Please let there be nothing else.

The call from Marjory Pedersen came less than two weeks later:

"Simon, is that you? This is Marjory Pedersen. I'm calling from Taos. God, we have an awful connection. Can you hear me?"

"It's the decline of Western civilization," I replied loudly.

"The decline of what?" she shouted bewilderedly over the static.

"The decline of Western civilization. Western civilization is collapsing and this is one of the symptoms of the collapse."

"Oh, yes," she agreed, "that's right. I completely agree with you. Have you spoken with Ken? Have you heard about his parole hearing?"

"No. I missed a visit. I couldn't go last week. It's coming up pretty soon, isn't it?"

For a moment the static eased, but Mrs. Pedersen was still shouting. "It came up," she yelled into the mouthpiece. "They denied it. They wouldn't give Ken a parole."

There was a pause. "I'm sorry to hear that," I said.

"What's that?" she asked.

"I said I'm sorry."

"We all are," she replied softly. "It's just awful. It's—"

"When will they consider him again?" I interrupted. "When will he come up for review again?"

"Not for another eighteen months."

"That stinks," I commented. "He's already been in for such a—"

"We would've had a good chance if it hadn't been for that dreadful Mrs. Willoughby," blurted Mrs. Pedersen angrily. "She's been out to get Ken ever since the beginning."

"What do you mean?"

"The hearing. She came to the hearing. Didn't Ken tell you how we cooperated with Elaine in getting the divorce and the adoption with the tacit understanding that Mrs. Willoughby would reciprocate at least to the extent of not opposing Ken's parole?"

"Yes," I replied. "He did tell me something about that. He said that Mrs. Willoughby had sued him for two hundred and fifty thousand dollars, and that—"

"That lawsuit was ridiculous," exclaimed Mrs. Pedersen flatly. "She never would've had a prayer with it in court and she knew it. It was just harassment, plain and simple. The main thing we wanted was that she'd stand on the sidelines, at least be neutral, and not gum up Ken's chances for a parole."

"What did she do?" I asked. "Did she say something really damning at the hearing?"

The voice at the other end of the line rose an octave. "Did she say something damning at the hearing! Simon, do you know what that . . . that shrike did? First she had her doctor telephone the parole board and ask to have the hearing *postponed* for two weeks on the ground that the mere *thought* of appearing had caused her to suffer a nervous collapse."

"Did they postpone it?"

"No, they didn't. At least they didn't let her get away with that one. But when she did appear, she brought her doctor with her. All the time she was testifying, that bald-headed so-and-so sat next to her, comforting her and handing her pills to take and paper-cupfuls of water. Can you imagine the effect of that disgusting little charade on the parole board, Simon, sitting there and watching the victim of a knife attack being supported by her physician, twitching every which way and popping an assortment of multicolored pills?"

"You'd think that after a year," I began, "she—"

"That disgusting little Sarah Bernhardt," continued Mrs. Pedersen contemptuously. "Believe me, she belongs in a mental institution. I treat patients down here every day who—"

"Is her appearance really what fouled up Ken's parole?" I asked.

"Wait a minute," exclaimed Mrs. Pedersen. "I still haven't told you about the injuries."

"What injuries? I thought Mrs. Willoughby didn't suffer any permanent—"

"Exactly!" proclaimed Mrs. Pedersen triumphantly. "Exactly, Simon. You're exactly right. Immediately following the incident, she was treated for cuts at the hospital and almost immediately released. She hadn't sustained a single serious injury."

"That's what I thought," I replied. "I seem to—"

"You can't believe how disgusting that woman is, Simon. How vindictive. I'm not condoning what Ken did, but at least he—"

"So what did you mean," I interrupted, "when you said you wanted to tell me about the injuries?"

"That's what I'm telling you, Simon. Mrs. Willoughby showed up at the parole hearing with her doctor, and she had her arm in this huge sling and, Simon, she had this incredible bandage on her face like Boris Karloff in *The Return of the Mummy.*"

"You mean it was all completely phony?" I asked incredulously.

"Phony? Of course it was phony. Ken's lawyer objected, of course. He said that it was a matter of record that there had been no injuries of this magnitude. He offered to obtain affidavits from the hospital staff, from the police, records of her—"

"And did he do that?"

"No, no, there was no time for that. By that time the damage had already been done. They just said that they'd take note of our lawyer's objection in reaching—it's just that we were completely unprepared for an underhanded ploy like that. We knew she might decide to show up, yes, but we never—still, if you ask me, Mansfield, that's Ken's attorney, should have anticipated that something like that *might* happen and been prepared to counter it with—"

"But he wasn't."

"No, he wasn't. None of us were. The damage was done by then. I swear, Simon, sometimes I find myself wishing that Ken had finished the job."

She paused, and exhaled a deep breath. "I guess I don't sound very objective, do I?" she asked defensively. "I don't sound very much like a person with psychiatric training. But it's so offensive to me for that hideous woman to—"

"That's okay," I replied. "You're his mother. You're not supposed to be objective about something like this. And between you and me, I think she got what was coming to her, too."

At the other end of the line, Mrs. Pedersen allowed herself a short, nervous laugh. "I guess we really shouldn't be going that far, should we?"

"How is Ken holding up?" I asked.

"Ken?"

"Yes. How is Ken taking the business about the parole?"

Mrs. Pedersen paused, then cleared her throat. "Well," she began finally, "he's depressed, of course, but under the circumstances I'd say he was doing quite well. I'd say he was holding up admirably. And in spite of this setback he still has hope. We have high hopes that the state supreme court will grant his appeal."

"Ken told me about that," I remarked. "I hope—"

"Of course," continued Mrs. Pedersen introspectively, "when the parole decision first came down, Ken was quite upset. He would have liked to have had the opportunity to share his feelings with a sympathetic peer. But then, of course, you missed your regular visit."

"I'm sorry," I replied. "I wanted to visit him ten days ago. I just couldn't."

"I understand," observed Mrs. Pedersen coolly. "I know you would never have disappointed Ken unless there were some—"

"Heather committed suicide," I remarked icily.

At the other end of the line there was an incredulous pause. "Are you being serious, Simon, or—"

"No," I retorted coolly. "Actually this is all my idea of a tremendous joke."

"It's terrible news, Sy," replied Mrs. Pedersen gravely. "How are you feeling?"

I wanted to tell Mrs. Pedersen that I hated her, but instead I bit my lip and said nothing.

"You know," she went on glibly, never missing a stroke, "the pain and suffering which the act of suicide causes its victim are probably less destructive in the long run than the deep psychological scars that the act inflicts on those still living. I hope—"

She paused in mid-sentence, waiting for me to say something. But I said nothing.

"You needn't talk about it if you don't want to," she said finally.

"Good," I shot back irritably. "Then I won't."

For an uncomfortable moment, neither one of us spoke.

"I think I should get off the line now," said Mrs. Pedersen in a low voice. "I hope you begin feeling better soon, and I hope you'll be able to find your way clear before long to paying Ken a—"

"Don't worry, Mrs. Pedersen," I mumbled hoarsely. "I'll be going down to see him at the end of the week."

"All right, you meatballs," the voice of the sergeant boomed out, "before we start to fill out this medical history questionnaire, I want everybody to look down the sheet to question nineteen."

I was in a classroom-type room at the U.S. Army induction

center in downtown Chicago, taking the written part of my preinduction physical exam. Dropping out of college had made me ripe for the Vietnam draft, and Uncle Sam had finally dropped me a letter.

"Question number nineteen, for those of you meatballs who are too dumb to read," bellowed the sergeant from his lectern in front of the blackboard at the head of the room, "reads as follows: 'Do you now have, or have you ever had, *homosexual tendencies?*' "

A murmur of amused denial went up from the thirty or so draftees seated at their writing desks and wafted gently across the room.

"There it is," I thought to myself as I gazed down at the questionnaire. "That's the one. The question that's going to keep me out of the Army."

"Now," thundered the sergeant, as he leaned intimidatingly across his lectern, carefully scrutinizing the face of every draftee in the room. "Now," he repeated like a crack of thunder, "we don't have any *queers* in here, do we?"

The draftees in the room fell deathly silent. A few turned round and craned their necks to survey the deathly silent room.

"I didn't think we had any queers in here," boomed the sergeant belligerently, "but yesterday we had this meatball come down here in goddam *panties* and a goddam *dress.*"

The sergeant paused as though awaiting a response, but none of the draftees uttered a sound.

"You heard me," he bellowed again. "This goddam meatball actually came down here in goddam *panties* and a goddam meatball fucking *dress.*"

Now the draftees responded with a roar of laughter.

"Me," thundered the sergeant, raising himself to his full height and surveying the room with suspicious eyes, "I thought the guy would make a *fine* rice-paddy daddy." He paused, grasping the lectern with both hands, his eyes riding roughshod over every face in the room. "But the *shrinks,* they sent that meatball *home.*"

A few of the draftees turned in their seats and smirked at their neighbor, but a titter of laughter from the back of the room was stomped on by the sergeant's angry, sarcastic voice.

"If we keep sendin' meatballs home just 'cause they wanta run around in a goddam dress, how we ever gonna raise a goddam army to teach what-for to them motherfucking gooks in the Nam?"

The sergeant paused, glowering, long enough to allow the simple wisdom of his message to be absorbed throughout the room.

"So before we start to fill out this questionnaire," he roared, "I want everybody to pick up his pencil, like this, and put a big 'X' in the 'No' box on question number nineteen. Because," he continued, as he abruptly shoved aside the lectern and began lumbering toward the aisle of writing desks on the far side of the room, "before we go any further, I'm going to go around this room and see to it that every one of you meatballs has answered no to that degenerate god damned question."

The sergeant was stalking the aisles like a puma now, scanning the questionnaires, as the draftees grabbed up their pencils and scurried to check the "No" box on question nineteen.

"You can just bet your goddam ass we don't have any queers in this room," bellowed the sergeant. "Because if we did have, if we did have any queers in here, the cocksucker would sure be in some big trouble, wouldn't he? Because the rest of us would probably take that little queer outside and beat the holy shit out of him, wouldn't we?"

There was no answer. The thirty draftees were all much too busy answering no to question nineteen. Indeed, the other questions on the medical history form hardly mattered. The Army didn't give a shit if you now had, or had ever had, scarlet fever or pneumonia or tuberculosis. They could easily put you in the hospital and cure you of those things and then ship you off to kill gooks in the rice paddies of Vietnam. All the Army cared about in the whole wide world was whether you were going to go around sucking cocks once you got in the Army.

Except for the sergeant. He couldn't care less how many cocks you sucked once you got in the Army. He was a man with a mission, the sergeant, a man who had his priorities in order, he knew damn well that it was more important to raise an army of fighting men to crush the gook menace than it was to keep faggots out of the Army, and if after you'd killed a few gooks you wanted to lay back in your base camp and suck a few dicks, well by god that was okay with him.

The sergeant strode threateningly up and down the aisles, glaring down at the writing desks to satisfy himself that everyone had filled in the "No" box on question nineteen. It seemed as though I had no choice: just as the sergeant reached my place, I snatched up my pencil—they had given us only short pencils, without erasers—and crisscrossed the "No" box with a large black "X." He walked right by me without even looking at it, then returned to his lectern and said, "All right now. Begin."

I zipped through the remainder of the questionnaire and then sat there staring at it, wondering how in hell I was going to manage to keep out of the Army. And then suddenly I was seized by an inspiration: setting my questionnaire back down on the writing desk, I returned to question nineteen and drew an "X" in the "Yes" box—so that I had now answered the question both ways, yes and no—and then hastily scrawled out the yes "X" with my pencil, leaving the no "X" stand as is, thereby creating the false impression that I had initially answered yes to the question and then crossed out that response and changed my answer to no.

Later, when the time came for a final evaluation of all my test results, the physician in charge glanced uneasily down at my medical history form and then squinted up at me from behind the low wooden table that served as his desk.

"This question nineteen," he asked. "What's the answer supposed to be here on this question nineteen?"

"Question nineteen?" I stammered. "What question is that?"

The doctor blinked and cleared his throat. "This question here," he replied in a low voice, turning the questionnaire toward me and pointing at the number. "This question here about homosexual tendencies. Is the answer supposed to be yes or no?"

"It's supposed to be yes," I whispered timorously.

"You had yes," said the doctor, obviously discomfited, "but then you wrote no. Why did you write yes and then change your answer to no?"

I paused for a moment and glanced furtively about. "Because—" I began, and paused again.

"Because why?" snapped the doctor.

"Because the Army man who gave out the tests said we'd be in big trouble if we answered yes. He said—"

A second doctor, evaluating folders of test results at a table close by, overheard what I'd said and looked up from his work. "The sergeant said you'd be in big trouble if you answered yes to question nineteen?" he inquired softly.

"Yes," I replied.

For a brief moment the two doctors looked at one another. The doctor at the other table slowly shook his head. He reached into a drawer and pulled out a green slip of paper. "Give him this," he said tersely, reaching over to hand the green slip to my doctor.

My doctor accepted the slip and then handed it to me along with my examination folder. "Take all this down the hall to 213," he said matter-of-factly. "You're going to have to see the psychiatrist."

■ ■ ■

The psychiatrist, he was actually only a psychologist, was in his late twenties, handsome, with brown eyes and wavy light-brown hair. He was wearing a white lab coat, through the V of the lab coat you could see a navy blue necktie decorated with tiny red seahorses, and pinned to the upper left-hand pocket of the lab coat was a black identification pin with the name Dr. Rogers printed across it in white letters.

He opened my folder to the medical history form and glanced at it briefly, then rose from his desk and, placing one foot on his swivel chair, began gazing absentmindedly past me across the room. The room was more like a cubicle than a real room—small and gray, devoid of decorations or personal effects, furnished only with a gray metal desk and matching swivel chair, side chair, and wastebasket. White acoustical tile covered the ceiling, but several tiles had already buckled and one tile in particular seemed like it might fall any second.

"You know why you're here, don't you?" asked Dr. Rogers casually.

"No sir," I stammered nervously. "I don't."

"You don't have any idea?" he persisted.

"I suppose it has something to do with my answers to some of the test questions," I replied. "Am I in some sort of trouble?"

"No," he answered quietly, "you're not in any trouble. You're here because of what you answered on question nineteen." He paused and folded his arms across his chest, waiting for me to become defensive about question nineteen.

"Question nineteen?" I asked.

"Yes," he replied, nodding his head knowingly. "Question nineteen."

I stared nervously at my lap and shook my head in silent bewilderment.

"You don't remember question nineteen?" asked Dr. Rogers.

"No sir," I replied apologetically, "I don't."

"Question nineteen asked, 'Do you now have, or have you ever had, homosexual tendencies?' You answered yes to that question."

"Yes sir. I remember."

"What was your reason for giving that answer?" he asked.

"That was the true answer," I replied.

"Are you sure?" he asked.

"Yes sir," I answered.

Now Dr. Rogers picked up my folder and opened it again, cradling it in the crook of his left arm.

"You were married," he noted.

"Yes sir."

"For how long?"

"Two years, sir."

"And then you separated."

"Yes sir."

He closed the folder and set it back down on the desk. "Why?" he asked.

"Because my wife found out," I replied.

"About your homosexuality?"

"Yes sir."

"She must have been very upset."

"Yes sir, she was."

He clasped his hands behind his back and began pacing the floor slowly behind his desk. "You were having homosexual relations, then, during the period you were married to your wife?"

"Yes sir," I replied.

"With one person primarily, or with several?"

"One primarily."

"Who was he?"

"Excuse me?"

"What was his name?"

"Ken Pedersen. We were friends in college. We shared an apartment together during the period prior to my marriage."

"I see. And do you live with him now?"

"No sir. I live alone now."

"Your relationship with Mr. Pedersen has terminated?"

"No sir. He's serving a prison term. In the Illinois State Penitentiary at Pontiac."

Dr. Rogers paused. His facial expression did not change, but he paused a moment and reflected.

"What did he do?" he asked finally.

"He slashed a woman with a butcher knife."

"You say you live alone now?"

"Yes sir."

"And do you have other lovers?"

"Other lovers?"

"Other male lovers, besides Mr. Pedersen."

"Yes sir."

"And you have sexual relations with these male lovers?"

"Yes sir."

He stopped his pacing and turned slowly toward me, eyeing me closely, deliberately. "When you have these sexual relations," he asked, "what role do you play?"

"I don't understand the question, sir."

"Do you play the role of the man or the role of the woman?"

"It doesn't work that way. Nobody does that."

"Nobody does what?"

"Nobody's the man and nobody's the woman. It doesn't work that way. We're both the man and we're both the woman, I guess. It just doesn't happen in those terms."

"But what specifically do you do?"

I stared down at my hands and did not answer.

"What acts do you perform?"

"I-I don't mean to be uncooperative, sir," I stammered. "I don't want to get into any trouble. But I'm just not accustomed to discussing my personal life this way."

"I understand," replied Dr. Rogers sympathetically. "I don't think I'd like being pushed and picked at either. I just have to ask you a few more questions. Then we'll be through."

"All right," I nodded.

"I need to know what you do," he went on. "When you have relations with your male lovers, do you fellate them?"

"Sir?"

"Do you take their penis in your mouth?"

"Yes sir."

"And do they take your penis in their mouth?"

"Do I have to answer more questions like this?"

"No, this is the last one. Do they take your penis in their mouth?"

"Yes sir."

He picked up my folder and opened it and glanced at it again. "I notice that you answered yes to this question and then changed your answer to no. Why did you do that?"

I paused a moment. I cracked the knuckle on the middle finger of my right hand, and then the one on the middle finger of my left. "I was afraid I'd get in trouble if I answered yes. I was afraid I'd be kept out of the Army."

"You want to be in the Army?" asked Dr. Rogers, unable to prevent his voice from becoming tinged with surprise.

"Yes," I replied.

"Why, may I ask?"

"I love my country," I answered. "If my country is in a fight against communism, I want to do my part."

Dr. Rogers propped his left foot back up on his swivel chair and ran his right forefinger thoughtfully across his lower lip. "But given your . . . your proclivity," he began deliberately, "your emotional situation, do you really think you could serve effectively?"

"Why not?" I replied. "I'm strong. I'm smart. I'm willing to work. I'll fight as hard as the next man."

"But given your emotional situation," he repeated, "given the emotional situation we've just discussed, don't you think it would be impossible for you to serve effectively, living day in and day out with—"

"Look," I interrupted vehemently, "let's get something straight. Maybe you think anyone who goes to bed with a man has got to be some kind of a sissy. But that's not true. You've no business excluding me because of my personal life. My personal life is my personal business. Not the Army's. Not anyone's. I love my country as much as any man. I can work as hard and fight as hard as—"

Dr. Rogers was on the run. All he wanted to do now was to end that interview as fast as he could end it. He extended a limp hand to me across his desk.

"I admire your courage," he said quietly, "and your forthrightness. The decision isn't up to me. All I do is hand in my report. But in all honesty I have to tell you that when they get my report, they'll probably decide that you couldn't serve effectively, even though I know you feel strongly that you could."

I reached out and shook his hand. His hand had sweat on it, but mine didn't.

"Goodbye," I said. "And thank you."

"Don't mention it," he replied.

I walked slowly, solemnly out of the induction center and didn't start laughing until I was safely home. Ten days later the notice arrived in my mailbox: "Draft status 4F," it proclaimed. "Applicant medically unfit for service."

Coffee breaks were at 10:00 A.M. and 3:00 P.M. at the Mafioso crumb-bum encyclopedia where I worked, and every afternoon, rain or shine, I used to take my coffee break in the cafeteria downstairs in the lobby, because every day at that hour, every day without fail, there was this sexy older chick, I mean really older, like fifty-five or even sixty, who used to drink a cup of coffee at the lunch counter there from three o'clock until exactly twenty minutes after.

It's not that she was especially good-looking, but she had this incredible whorish ambience about her that used to drive me crazy. She had gigantic spready tits stuffed into this skintight bra, not your pointy headlight tits, but the kind that would have to cascade down to her waist whenever she unlimbered them, like beach balls suspended from a pair of elastic bands, and she used to wear these tight white cashmere sweaters with a little polka-dot scarf tied around her neck, so that I always used to imagine myself tearing off her sweater and unleashing those mammoth tits and then grabbing the tail end of that scarf in one hand and dragging her down onto her knees and making her blow me.

She had this long, matted, shoulder-length blond hair, the shit looked like it came straight from Woolworth's, and she had this huge mouth, covered with red or orange lipstick, that had no firm shape, her mouth was all spready, just like her tits, so that whenever she talked, like when she asked the waitress for a cup of coffee, her lips would kind of palpitate and tremble in this obscene, epileptic kind of way, as though they were quivering to excite your cock after you'd stuffed it in her mouth.

So it was a warm summer day just after three o'clock, instead of getting some fresh air like a normal person I was sitting at my usual table in the lobby cafeteria ogling those huge spready tits and that come-licking mouth, when all of a sudden a hand gripped my shoulder from behind, accompanied by the sound of a familiar voice.

"Wouldn't you know it," reprimanded the voice with amused disapproval. "I come all the way down here to see you, and I find you slobbering into your coffee cup over some obscene fossilized hairy."

"Ken!" I cried, whirling around in my chair. "Ken. God damn. What in—"

"I won't say she's the ugliest woman I've ever seen," he went on, peering in the direction of the lunch counter with an exaggerated squint, "but hot damn, Sy, she sure is the oldest. She's fucking old enough to—and what in god's name is that shit she's got on her head?"

"That's her hair," I replied. "You hold onto that with both hands while she takes it in her mouth. Otherwise you grab the scarf. And don't overlook those tits. They're—"

"She's fucking old enough to be your fucking grandmother," exclaimed Pedersen, shaking his head with amiable revulsion. "I mean, god damn it, Sy. God damn it." He pulled the chair directly opposite me out from the table and pushed the seat between his legs so that he was now sitting on it backwards, his arms folded across the back. "It's good to see you, man," he said with a smile. "It's real good to be on the outside and to have us both be on the outside together."

Ken Pedersen had soft gray eyes and bushy brown eyebrows with flecks of gray in them. He was wearing a worn blue gabardine suit with a wine-colored red tie, the suit was shiny in places where it was badly worn, like on the knees and elbows and on the underside of the forearms. And somehow, there was something that seemed weird about Ken Pedersen that day, some subtle combination of things that made it hard to pin down exactly what it was that made him seem so weird. For one thing, he looked incredibly pale. Inside the prison, somehow, he hadn't seemed so pale, maybe because the whole place was pale, or at least conducive to paleness, but here in the cafeteria, sitting backwards in the chair across from me, leaning on the back of the chair and smiling, he seemed very pale, and his lips didn't seem to move as much as they should when he talked, and he would blink at peculiar times while we talked, it seemed to me he was blinking a lot more than he should've been blinking, every now and then he would blink a few times in rapid succession, as if his eyes were tired, or as if the lights in the cafeteria were very bright, even though they really weren't.

And there was something else about Pedersen that seemed different, different from the Ken Pedersen I remembered: his gestures seemed different, sometimes more exaggerated than I remembered them, sometimes more understated, but always somehow different, as though he were an actor hired to impersonate Ken Pedersen and had not yet gotten the gestures down exactly right. Also, you have to know that Ken Pedersen was like a chameleon, somehow he looked different every time you looked at him. At the university, with his full beard and longish hair, he had looked like an impish leprechaun or a short Abe Lincoln, and inside the prison, wearing those gray prison clothes and with his hair cut short and his beard shaved off, he had looked like an auto mechanic or a dishwasher repairman. But now, with his thick eyebrows and gray eyes, dressed in his blue gabardine suit and looking so pale, he somehow looked older than he really was, middle-aged, like your father's brother who never quite made it, who was always trying to hide from everybody how really destitute he was, how the bills were piling up and the phone company was threatening to cut off his phone, so that he could act good-humored and put up a convincing front when he came to your house to ask your dad to lend him some more money.

I pushed my chair back onto its back legs and jammed my hands into my pants pockets and stared at Pedersen across the table. "You look good, man," I said brightly. "It's good to see you."

He smiled wanly, and there was a nervous quiver at the corners of his mouth. "I feel terrific," he replied softly.

"Well, tell me, god damn it," I exclaimed. "Tell me what the hell are you doing here. Did you go over the fucking wall, or what?"

He seemed about to launch into one of his famous hearty maniacal laughs, but then he thought better of it, and fell silent, and cracked his knuckles instead. "My appeal came through," he said quietly. "Remember I told you about my appeal?"

"Sure I remember," I replied enthusiastically. "Now come on. Tell me what happened."

"Well," he began, "it came through. They ruled—"

"Hey, wait a minute," I cut in. "Before you get started, can I buy you a cup of coffee or something? Do you—"

"No," he replied. "Thanks, but there's no time. I'm meeting Arthur at the airport in an hour and a half. We're flying back to New Mexico this afternoon. I just wanted to see you for a few minutes before I left."

"Well, I'm goddam glad you did," I exclaimed. "Okay, I'm sorry I interrupted. Get back to the appeal."

Pedersen paused and cleared his throat. "There's really not that much to tell," he began, "nothing that I didn't already tell you in prison. The state supreme court ruled that the judge in my case erred by not requiring me to undergo a sanity hearing before allowing me to plead. Because of my previous psychiatric history, including the fact that I was once institutionalized, they ruled that accepting my guilty plea in the absence of a sanity hearing constituted a violation of my legal rights."

"That's fabulous," I said enthusiastically. "Does that mean it's all over?"

"Don't know yet," he replied. "The supreme court reversed my conviction and remanded me to the custody of the Winnetka authorities. They're releasing me in my parents' custody pending—"

"Jesus Christ! Pending what?"

"Well, the way it works, Sy," he explained, "is that the reversal puts my case right back to where it was right after I attacked Mrs. Willoughby. My conviction is reversed, my guilty plea is nullified, I'm back to being legally innocent until I'm proven guilty. But obviously I did it, everyone knows I did it, if they want to they can start at the beginning and charge me all over again."

"Will they do that?"

"That's what we don't know. The way it works, the law gives them ninety days in which to bring the charges against me again.

If they don't do it within that time, I'm a free man. If they do do it, then I'll have to go through a sanity hearing, maybe a—"

"What would be their reason for deciding *not* to recharge you?"

"Well for one thing," he replied, "the sentence I got the last time was one to ten. I've already given them almost a year and a half of it. So there's a pretty good chance that even if I were found sane and convicted again, the judge would order me released for time served. That means Winnetka would have to foot the bill for a trial and it would all be for nothing."

"What about the possibility of Mrs. Willoughby bringing pressure on—"

"Well, that's a possibility. But another thing we've got going for us is that we're threatening to sue the state for damages for depriving me of my civil rights. And we're offering to refrain from suing if they'll just leave my case where it is and refrain from pressing charges."

"Sounds like you've got a good chance," I observed.

"A good chance," he nodded.

For a moment, we both fell silent. On the white-tiled ceiling above our heads, a fluorescent light tube was buzzing in its socket.

"Hey!" exclaimed Pedersen suddenly, reaching across the tabletop to jab me playfully with his fist. "I almost forgot. I almost forgot to tell you how I found out about my appeal."

"What do you mean, how you found out about—"

"I mean, god damn it, that I almost forgot to tell you about how I, Kenneth T. Pedersen, found out that I was on the very verge of becoming a free man again."

His gray eyes had brightened now, and his bushy eyebrows bounded up and down on his forehead like a pair of startled brown rabbits. And his face had started to come alive again from somewhere deep beneath the skin, there was something of the old Ken Pedersen in it, Ken Pedersen the rainmaker, the con man, the snake-oil peddler, I could see him thumbing slyly through the pig book, or giving an electrifying discourse on Shakespeare, or reading aloud from *Cyrano de Bergerac,* except that without his long hair and beard, and with the wan pallor of imprisonment still haunting his face, giving his features the pathetic quality of an elderly employee pleading for a meager raise, somehow he reminded me uncomfortably of a middle-aged former athlete wistfully recalling his bygone glory while watching the films of some long-ago game.

"Remember how I was subscribing to the Winnetka *Herald,*" he went on, "how I said they would be sure to carry any news about my case?"

"I remember," I replied.

"Well I was thumbing through that sonovabitch about ten days ago, right after your last visit, reading about some bake sale at the firehouse and the schedule for the Little League, and then all of a sudden there it was, Sy, this goddam headline, this god damned unbelievable fucking headline."

He paused and stared at me. His gray eyes were ashen embers with white-hot coals glowing just beneath.

"Come on, man," I urged, a little impatiently. "What did the goddam headline say?"

He snickered nervously for a second and then fell silent. Placing his hands side by side in front of his face, curled outward, like claws, he then spread them apart sideways to the right and left in a single, sweeping gesture, as if he were brushing his fingertips against the top and bottom of an invisible headline suspended before him in midair. "SLASHER," he intoned with solemn grandeur, "GETS SANITY HEARING."

I roared with laughter.

"I swear to god, Sy," vowed Pedersen with a broad smile, "that's what it said. 'Slasher Gets Sanity Hearing.' And then there was this article about the decision the state supreme court had just made in my case. That's how I found out about it. Two days before anyone notified me officially—my lawyer, or the prison authorities, or—"

"You mean, you learned you were about to be released from a goddam newspaper, even before your lawyer told you?"

"What can I tell you?" shrugged Pedersen. "He's an asshole. They're all assholes."

"Okay," I persisted, "but you knew over a week ago. How come you didn't get someone to call me and tell me—Mansfield, or Marjory?"

"I just wanted to surprise you, man. I just wanted to drop in on you and see the look on your face when I just dropped in on you." He smiled broadly. "And here I drop in on you and I find you with your cock all hanging down to your ankles over some calcified hairy that—"

I turned in my chair and glanced over toward the lunch counter. "She's probably gone by now," I noted.

"Fifteen or twenty minutes ago," replied Pedersen.

"Damn it, Pedersen," I exclaimed, "we ought to go out and celebrate this thing. Can't you and Arthur stay over in Chicago tonight and we'll—"

"No," answered Pedersen, shaking his head. "I'd like to, but no. We've got airline reservations, Marjory's waiting. Besides, it's best for me to get out of this jurisdiction as fast as hell I can. Out of sight, out of—"

"What the hell are you going to do in Taos, for Christ's sake?"

"Come on, man," pleaded Pedersen, forcing a wan smile, "I just got out of the joint. I just got out of the joint after better than fifteen months in the joint. Boy, have I got stories to tell you about the joint, Sy. Enough stories for a million books. But this is my first day out. Look at me, man. I'm wearing a suit. A god damned blue suit. God knows where Marjory dug up this ridiculous god damned suit. I'm just going back to New Mexico, man. I just want to go home to New Mexico and lie around in the sun and eat some good food for a change, and after two or three weeks of that maybe start to chase a little hairy."

"They have that in New Mexico?" I asked incredulously.

Pedersen stood up. His chair screeched like chalk on a blackboard as he pushed his chair back under the table. I got up, too. We shook hands and he took his free hand and slapped my shoulder.

"Oh, they have it," he replied with an easy laugh, "but after fifteen months I may've forgot how to chase it."

"Not you," I said reassuringly, and we both smiled.

Out of the corner of my eye I could see a trio of businessmen heading toward our table, seeing that Pedersen and I were about to vacate it.

"You'll keep in touch, won't you, fella?" I asked.

He squeezed my hand tighter and then released his grip and jammed his hands in his trousers pockets. "Don't be ridiculous," he snapped, his eyes laughing, "of course I will. And I'll send you a full account of exactly how Illinois decides to dispose of my case."

"You've got my address?" I asked uncertainly.

"Of course I've got it," he replied.

Spontaneously we reached out and shook hands again. The

businessmen had arrived at our table and were milling about acting impatient.

"And thanks," remarked Pedersen. "Thanks for all the visits. Thanks for everything. I couldn't have got through my time without you."

"Don't be ridiculous," I laughed.

"Are you men through?" inquired one of the businessmen.

"Yes," I answered irritably, "yes we are."

"We'll sit down then," remarked one of his companions.

Pedersen made his way down the aisle past the lunch counter and stepped into the revolving door leading out into the street. Just as he entered the doorway, he turned and waved to me. "So long," he called out. "Don't forget me."

And then he whirled through the revolving door like a slice of pie on a lazy Susan, and within less than an instant Ken Pedersen was gone.

That was 1964. It was the summer of 1964 when Ken Pedersen got out of prison and visited me in the cafeteria and then whirled away through the revolving door to fly home to New Mexico and become Marjory Pedersen's son again. And they never did prosecute him a second time for slashing Mrs. Willoughby. They just figured fifteen months behind bars was enough, I guess, and made up their minds to leave him alone.

I don't even think I heard from Pedersen after that until after I'd gotten back from Mexico. Maybe we exchanged a letter or two, but as far as I can remember we didn't even do that. Because it wasn't long after Pedersen went back to Taos that I met Laurie Meyers, and it wasn't more than two or three months after that that she and I decided, on the spur of the moment, to hitchhike to Mexico and stay there an entire year.

I met Laurie Meyers at the home of the saxophone player

who lived downstairs from me, his name was Willard, and sometimes, usually late at night, I'd bop down to his place and we'd fix ourselves some popcorn and Pepsi Colas and listen to Eric Dolphy and John Coltrane. One night, Laurie Meyers was there.

Laurie Meyers was a nineteen-year-old anthropology student at the University of Chicago who used to drive to and from school in a Lancia touring car that had been given to her as a high school graduation gift by her father, a multimillionaire textile manufacturer in North Carolina. During the Depression, Laurie's dad had been as poor as a churchmouse. He'd bummed all around the country in freight cars, working as a dishwasher and at other odd jobs—once he'd seen two hoboes stab a third man to death for a one-dollar bill—and yet somehow he'd saved up enough money to start his own textile mill, which he'd built into one of the largest textile companies in the entire state of North Carolina.

Laurie Meyers had clear blue eyes and soft brown hair and a voice as soft and warm as spring, but she also had a mind like a wolf trap and a willingness to try just about anything. We started living together within a week after we met, and a few months later, no more than four or five months after Ken Pedersen got out of prison, I decided I was sick and tired of working, so just like that I quit my job, Laurie took a temporary leave of absence from school, and we loaded up some knapsacks and packed ourselves off to Mexico for almost a year.

We spent seven or eight months in Oaxaca, where the climate is always like spring, and the rest of our time we stayed in the Yucatan, where we lived in an old wooden house near the ocean owned by a tugboat captain whom we'd met in Vera Cruz. By day we dozed in hammocks and swam in the warm tropical surf, and at night we gorged ourselves on shrimp and *tortuga* in a thatched-roof café, waited on by a sloe-eyed Mayan girl about twelve years old who wore thin cotton dresses and had lustrous black hair down to her shoulders.

To get from place to place we hitchhiked, often on massive tractor-trailer trucks, split-shifting through the mountain passes on cold, dark nights, once with a skinny, rodentlike trucker who pulled out his cock and waved it in Laurie's face because he assumed any woman traveling with a man must be a whore if she wasn't his wife.

I had thought about writing a novel that year we were away,

but somehow the time passed and I just never got to it. Mostly we just ate and slept, and wiled away the time, and argued about why we weren't having any sex. Because that was really the thing that loused it up between Laurie Meyers and me, the fact that even though she was really warm and nice, maybe *because* she was really warm and nice, she just never had that sexy something that some bitches have that makes you feel like a railroad spike has been hammered in your brain. So by the time we got back from Mexico our relationship was pretty much over, at least it was over for her, and within a month, maybe even less than that, she had moved out of my place and started making it with some other guy, an asshole graphic designer who had a runaway receding hairline and a face that looked like it belonged to some repulsive species of long-extinct reptile.

And it was right about then, right after we got back from Mexico and Laurie left me and moved in with the reptile, that the phone rang and sure enough it was Pedersen.

"Where you been, you horny fuck?" he cried, with the telephone probably already securely notched between his ear and his shoulder so he could be free to wave his arms about like a giant squid in a coital frenzy. "Where the goddam fuck you been?"

"Mexico, man," I replied. "Me and this chick I've been living with just got back from Mexico a few weeks ago and now she's gone and moved out on me and moved in with the Reptile."

"The who?"

"The Reptile."

"Hey," exclaimed Pedersen, "can you hear that static? Have you got that static on your end, too?"

"Yeah, I've got it."

"You want me to call you back?"

"No, it's okay," I replied. "I don't think it matters. Does it matter to you?"

"God damned phone company," he muttered. "God damn monopolistic—hey, remember all those practically free calls we used to make when I—"

"Sure, I remember. How could—"

"Remember that call we made to Kenya? The time we called all the way to Kenya and we said we wanted to speak to Jomo Kenyatta and we made them run all—"

"Uh-huh. I remember."

"Hey," remarked Pedersen abruptly, "you sound depressed. You depressed?"

"A little," I admitted.

"About that chick you went to Mexico with?"

"Uh-huh."

"What's this thing about a reptile? What kind of goddam reptile?"

"It's just a joke, man. She's living with some guy who looks like a reptile, that's all. So I—"

"What kind of reptile does he look like?" asked Pedersen curiously.

"God damn, Pedersen," I replied irritably. "I don't know what god damn—"

"You mean like a . . . a snake? Or an alligator? That kind of reptile?"

"More like an alligator."

"How the fuck can they do that?" he exclaimed in tortured bewilderment. "How the fuck can a woman leave a friend of mine and move in with some goddam alligator?"

"I don't know," I confessed, shaking my head. "I've been trying to work that one out myself."

"You've gotta go out and score yourself another hairy, Sy, that's all there is to it."

For a moment there was silence. There's never any static when you're silent, just when you're trying to talk.

"What have you been doing?" I asked finally.

"Oh, not a fuck of a lot. Living at home, going to school, trying—"

"Going to school where?"

"Oh, man, at the local college down here. New Mexico State College. It sure isn't like the U. of C., man. The students are so fucking stupid. Even the professors are stupid. And everybody's so fucking reactionary they make Ivan the Terrible look like fucking Lenin. Their idea of a philosopher would be A. A. Milne.

"So naturally I'm the smartest person around here and everybody is dying to know my opinion about everything. Being the campus intellectual is a very heavy responsibility, Sy. I'm trying very hard not to let—"

"What are you studying?"

"Oh, the usual bullshit. Some required math. English. I'm really into Shakespeare. My Shakespeare professor is really interested in me, especially in my theory of *Hamlet,* at least I thought he was until last week. Now I'm not so sure."

"What happened?"

"Well, they have this little theater here, so I've been doing some acting, some directing. It's very cathartic, Sy. Acting is very cathartic. Directing is very cathartic. It's all an entirely—"

"About the Shakespeare professor."

"I was getting to that. We have this theater. It's run by the college but it's become more of a community theater, and when we do a play there are usually people from the community who go out for parts in it, too. So I've been directing *Cat on a Hot Tin Roof* there, you know, Tennessee Williams'—"

"Go on—"

"—and Melinda Jenkins has been playing the part of Maggie."

"Who's Melinda Jenkins?"

"Don't you remember Melinda Jenkins? The chick who took thalidomide and then she announced she was going to Sweden to get an abortion in Sweden because she had taken the drug and it might result in her giving birth to a deformed baby?"

"Oh, sure, I remember. You mean, she—"

"Right. She's playing Maggie in my *Cat* production. Well, she is definitely not my shit, Sy, she is not my shit but she is definitely some people's shit, and if I look at her objectively, from an objective point of view, I would have to admit that—"

"The English professor. Let's get back to him."

"Okay, so this Jenkins bitch is in my production. And Samuel, that's the professor's name, Samuel, comes down to a run-through, and the next day, after class, he asks me would I come by his office.

"Well, I've been doing a lot of talking to Marjory lately. Those conversations have done a lot for me, Sy. Because getting to understand the complexities of my interaction with *my* mother, Sy, has been helping me get to the root of Hamlet's relationship with *his* mother. This is what I've been involved with while you've been away in fucking Mexico, Sy, this incredible business of Hamlet and Hamlet's mother.

"So when I went to see Samuel after class, as a matter of fact we're in the middle of reading *Hamlet* in class, I'm all bubbling over with my *Hamlet* theory, especially this new part I've just constructed about the triangle, the triangle between Hamlet, his mother, and his uncle. You know how I get, Sy, how excited and carried away I get, when I feel I'm on the track of some important new philosophical insight, so naturally when I get to Samuel's office, I start, with words, and with gestures, with both words and gestures, to lay out for him these valuable new concepts that I've been working with, that I've glommed onto thanks to my conversations with—"

"And he wasn't interested."

"How did you know that?"

"I guessed. Go on."

"Well, you're right. He wasn't interested. I'm in the middle of my first sentence, or maybe it was my second or third sentence, and he interrupts me, right out of the blue, and you know what that sonovabitch says?"

"No, what?"

"He says, 'Ken, I want to ask you something.' So I say, 'Go ahead, ask.' And he says, 'Do you suppose Melinda Jenkins fucks, Ken?'

"Do you understand the gall of that man, Sy? I'm in the middle of these new, these brand-new revelations about Hamlet and Hamlet's mother, and all this cocksucker wants to know, this character who's supposed to be interested in Shakespeare and intellectual pursuits, in the love of knowledge for its own sake, all he wants to know is if I think some twitchy second-rate actress screws!"

"What did you tell him?"

"I said, 'Of course she screws, Fred.' We're on a first-name basis, so I don't call him Dr. Samuel, I call him Fred. So I say, 'Of course she screws, Fred. They *all* screw.' "

"And what did he say?"

"What the fuck do I care what he said? I started to get back into my *Hamlet* thing, getting back into these very specific and original *Hamlet* revelations of mine, and all of a sudden the cocksucker interrupts me again."

"What did he say?"

"He said, 'Melinda Jenkins is married, isn't she, Ken?' So I said, 'Yes, Fred, she's married, and now I'd like to get back into this *Hamlet* thing of mine which I'm very into right now.' And he says, 'So when you said she screws, did you mean she screws for her husband, or do you suppose she screws for other men as well?' "

I laughed. "What did you say to that?"

"I was really exasperated, Sy. Really exasperated. I said, 'Look, Fred, do you want me to get you a date with the bitch?' "

"What did he say to that?"

"He said, 'Yes, Ken, as a matter of fact I would. And I'm glad you offered, because I wouldn't have wanted to impose on our friendship.' "

I laughed again. "Did you get him a date with her?"

"Of course not. I think he's a creep. I avoid him completely now. Melinda Jenkins fucks for anybody. She fucks for anybody who asks. If goddam creepy Fred Samuel wants to fuck her, all he has to do is ask. I'm not going to ask her for him."

"Why not?"

"Because if I ask her, then I'm going to fuck her myself, that's why. She's not my shit, Sy, I already told you she's not my shit. Still, if I ask her, I fuck her, it's only fair."

"Are you still in Samuel's class?"

"No, I dropped the class. The class is ridiculous. The class is so boring and stupid it makes me sick. But it's a small campus, it's a small community, Sy, with a small campus, so I still run into the guy every now and then walking across the campus. And every time he sees me, you know what that sonovabitch says?"

"No, what?"

"He gives me this hearty asshole wave, like we're still pals, and he says, 'Hey, Ken, are you working on that special project for me?' "

"What special project?"

"What are you dense, Sy? Fucking Melinda Jenkins is his special project. That's his asshole idea of a fucking code or something, calling it his special project. So I wave back at him and I say, 'Sure am, Fred,' and that's that. Just looking at the cocksucker makes me sick."

Pedersen paused. So did the phone static. It seemed like for an instant the whole goddam world paused in its orbit to contemplate what an asshole Pedersen's Shakespeare professor was for not having enough balls to approach Melinda Jenkins and fuck her on his own.

"Anyway," Pedersen continued finally, "the student body is so fucking stupid down here, Sy, all the girls even have blond hair, that down here I'm just this incredibly worldly, philosophical—I'm the only one with any real—Jesus Christ, Sy, I mean I'm pulling straight A's down here and I'm not hardly doing shit."

He paused again, this time to savor the wonderment of his straight-A average.

"And do you know what, Sy? Do you know what? I'm even in the *Who's Who of American College and University Students*! Can you beat the shit out of that? I, Kenneth Tobias Pedersen, have a complete biography in the *Who's Who of—*"

"Are you the only ex-con in the book?" I asked mischievously.

"Uh, I didn't exactly tell them that, Sy. I wasn't so sure it would be a good idea to tell them about that."

"Why not?" I persisted. "I would have thought that would be just your—"

"I'm conflicted about it, Sy. You've got me there. I'm definitely conflicted about it. On the one hand, I feel that the prison experience can be viewed positively, as a broadening experience, as a sort of Taoist window through which—"

"And on the other?"

"Well, on the other hand, and I would definitely say that Marjory has exerted a strong influence on me in this, I am trying to start a new life, to avoid these sort of existential pitfalls that—"

"Is that what Marjory calls them? Existential pitfalls?"

"No, that's my term. Hey, man, are you upset about something?"

"Yes, I guess I am. I'm upset about Laurie Meyers. I'm sorry. Go on."

"Well, it's a conservative community out here, Sy, and while I think that the prison experience was broadening in many ways, and even feel strongly in some ways that I ought to be sharing it with other people, if only to communicate somehow some of the meaning that it had for me, on the other hand this is a conservative community, you have to make your peace with reality, Sy, and there's just a lot of negative reinforcement out here in terms of—"

"So you left the prison part out of your biography."

"Right."

"What did you put in its place?"

"What do you mean?"

"What did you say you were doing during that year and a half?"

"I just extended my U. of C. thing. I said I was attending the U. of C. I do feel conflicted about it, Sy. I do. But I'm trying to listen to Marjory on things like this, trying to stop being the incurable romantic I've always been and start listening more to her point of view on things. She's an incredible woman, Sy."

"I don't like her, Ken. I think she's—"

"I know how you feel, Sy, but I think you're wrong in this case. She's an incredible woman. And she thinks highly of you."

"I don't believe it."

"She does. Really. I think she may have one or two psychological reservations, but basically—"

"She thinks highly of me but she thinks I'm crazy."

Pedersen laughed. "Maybe you have a point there," he admitted, "but I think on some levels she really likes you. And maybe, on some other levels, she feels a little competitive with you or threatened by you. But she still likes you and, in any case, she's been an incredible help to me during this period I've been living at home."

"How?"

"Well, for one thing, we've had a chance to talk. A real chance to sit down with each other and sort things out. We've been talking about my dad, my—"

"Arthur?"

"No, my real dad. The one who's a gigolo somewhere out in California. Marjory has an incredible number of incredible insights about him that have been really helpful to me in helping me shape my new perspective."

"Name four."

"You mean four insights?"

"Right. What insights has she had about your father that have been helpful to you in shaping your perspective?"

"Well," replied Pedersen slowly, "for example, she's helped me understand my attack on Mrs. Willoughby in terms of the unconscious meaning it has for me as an expression of unconscious hatred for my father."

"Hatred for your father? You worship your father!"

"Not unconsciously, Sy. Unconsciously I hate him for abandoning my mother and running off to California. And while in many ways I tend to idealize him, and the life he leads, Marjory points out, quite reasonably I think, that—"

"How about your attack on Mrs. Willoughby as an expression

of hostility toward your mother?" I asked.

"Marjory disagrees with that," replied Pedersen. "I did ask her about that, but she's explained to me that this rage and violence that I directed toward a woman was actually directed toward a woman as my psyche's way of denying the hatred I feel toward my father. It's a denial, Sy. I attack a woman, making it seem, on the surface, as if I hate my mother. Actually, I love my mother but, on some level, I hate my father. I conceal this patricidal hatred from myself by directing my rage against a woman who, superficially, appears to represent my mother."

"Very devious, your psyche."

"It's true," laughed Pedersen. "That's why I'm lucky I have Marjory to help me. You'd learn to like her if you knew her better, Sy. You'd certainly learn to respect her. I know you would.

"Anyway, that's one of the reasons Tracy and I are planning on moving to California. One, so that I can really try to get into some serious acting, and the other so that I can find my father, try to unravel the reason behind my breakdown, try to confront some of these—"

"Tracy? Who's Tracy?"

"Oh, man, she's my new woman. She's a really amazing woman, Sy. I don't think I've ever had such complete rapport with a woman before this. I—"

"More rapport than with Elaine?" I chuckled.

Pedersen laughed nervously. "Oh, definitely more rapport than with Elaine, Sy. I don't think I ever had any real rapport with Elaine. Underneath it all, she was a pretty superficial person, Sy. I don't think she ever really appreciated my complexities and my, let's call them existential contradictions."

"But Tracy does."

"Oh, yeah, she really does, Sy. She's really terrific. I told her all about my prison past and she accepts everything, she's just completely accepting of me. And she's been through a lot for me, Sy. A helluva lot. When she told her parents about me, and they learned I was an ex-con, they just freaked out, they just freaked out and threw her out of the house and told her to never come back. So she didn't. She moved in with us about three months ago and she's been living with us ever since. We're going to get married and move out of here as soon as she gets her divorce."

"Divorce?"

"She's married to this creep, Sy. This incredible creep. Army ,rgeant or something. Collects snakes. Can you believe that? Snakes? Anyway, she's been separated from him for about a year now and living with her folks, her divorce is due any week now, and as soon as she gets her divorce we're going to move out of here and move to L.A."

"What will she do in L.A.?"

"Well we're both actors, Sy. We're both deeply committed to acting, and of course Tracy is deeply committed to my philosophy as well. She's just terrific, Sy. Wait till you meet her. I've already told her all about you and about the book you're going to write about me. I've even started saving up my papers and pictures and stuff so it'll be all put away for you and organized for when you're ready to get started. Anyway, I've told her all about you and about how you used to visit me in prison, I really owe you for that, Sy, and about how you've designated yourself as my biographer. That's what she calls you, my biographer. She can't wait to meet you.

"Anyway, we're both of us deeply committed to acting, and by acting I mean acting, Sy, real mimesis, not any of your stoned-out, freaked-out psychodrama bullshit where you rip and tear at each other and then tell yourself that's got something to do with making yourself into an actor. We're—"

"What is she doing out there now?"

"Out where?"

"Out in New Mexico. With—"

"She's with me, Sy. I just told you that. She's out here with me, living with Arthur and Marjory and me, waiting for her divorce to come through so we—"

"Yes, I understand that. I mean, does she have a job, or—"

"Yeah. She's working as a sort of bookkeeper in this greeting card store part-time to earn some money, but mostly we're both up at the theater doing scenes and stuff. That's how we met, working at the theater."

"And in Los Angeles?"

"Well, I suppose in Los Angeles we'll both try to get jobs, and then we'll both be looking for acting work and I'll be trying to find my father."

"When do you figure you'll make the move?"

"Soon as the divorce happens, Sy. As soon as the papers come through we'll get married, and then as soon as that happens we'll move to California. Couple of months. Shouldn't be more than a couple of months. How about you, Sy? Now that you're back, what kind of plans have you got?"

"I don't know, man," I replied. "I think I'm going to pack my shit and go to New York and try to be a writer."

"You gonna get a job?"

"No, I'm going to try to avoid that, try to get myself some freelance bullshit. I've got a friend named Earl at the *Village Voice* who may be able to get me into rock and roll journalism."

"Rock and roll journalism? What the fuck kind of bullshit is that?"

"That's just what it is," I agreed, "bullshit. But maybe I can tear down some bread at it while I—"

"While you write the great American novel, right?"

"Right."

"I wish you luck, old man," he sighed. "You know I wish you luck. But New York's crazy, man. They're all crazy in New York. They're just like rats there, man, ripping and tearing, tearing and ripping. It's—"

"It's okay," I remarked. "I grew up there."

"I know. But it's different when you're growing up there, man. It's a lot different. You go back now, you're not a kid anymore, you're going to find yourself right in the midst of the ripping and tearing."

"Maybe," I replied, "but I've got to try it. It's the only game in—"

"You'd be a lot better off coming to California with Tracy and me," he continued. "Maybe we could even stay together. All three of us. What the hell? And that would give you a chance to observe me close up, firsthand, see how I—"

"New York, Ken," I replied. "I'm going to try New York."

"But you'll come out to see us once we're settled in L.A., won't you, Sy?" asked Pedersen hopefully. "Shit, you'll pay us a good long visit, won't you? Man, Tracy really wants to meet you, man. I've told her all—"

"I want to meet her, too," I remarked. "Don't worry. We'll stay in touch."

"We will, too, won't we, man?" he asked, the words suddenly catching in the back of his throat. "We'll always have something together, won't we, Sy?"

"Yes, Ken," I replied. "I think we always will."

"Goodbye, man," he said. "This fucking phone call has cost Marjory a fucking fortune."

"Goodbye, man," I answered. "And Ken—Ken, you take care."

New York is a hard-ass town, it will grind you up like lemon peel and toss you out like garbage, and probably the only thing easy about it is that unless you are lame and blind you can have your fill of bitches, you can see more succulent bitches trolling down Fifth Avenue on one spring afternoon than you will see in Chicago your whole goddam life, and they are all easy, except for your barbed-wire women's-lib bitches in their mechanics' overalls and round wire-rimmed glasses and T-shirts em blazoned with the Equal Rights Amendment, they are all on the prowl for easy dick. On Wednesday and Friday nights they dress to the nines and overflow the singles bars to overflowing, they mill about in the streets outside them, braying to one another like frightened sheep.

Fuck only knows how I got through that first goddam year. I sold a tiny article on Chicago blues to a cruddy magazine sold at discothèques, and I helped a professor at N.Y.U. rewrite a book he had written on Italian fascism. But the real way I survived was by working in an office three days a week writing entries for a shitty encyclopedia of the Bible, my job was writing all the geographical entries, from Abel-beth-maacah to Zuph.

And that was how I met Carol, because Carol worked for a pair of architects who had an office on the same floor, the two architects were never there, they were always away somewhere, so the first time I fucked her it was right in their office, I just took her into her bosses' private office and fucked her on this sexy red leather couch. Carol had hazel eyes and long blond hair, and even though she wasn't fat she used to wear one of those girdles, or panty girdles, or whatever the fuck you call them, you had to pull on that sonovabitch to get it off of her like you were fighting for your life against a gigantic rubber band.

She didn't really like to fuck that much, though, mostly she just liked to eat it, so after awhile we stopped making it in her bosses' office and she just started coming over to the Bible encyclopedia office once or twice a day—I had this tiny cubicle there where I worked at my typewriter—and sucking me off while I sat in my cubicle.

The whole year I knew her I was up at her apartment only once, and I remember that tacked up on the inside of her bedroom door was this gigantic photograph of her being fucked from behind by a German shepherd dog.

It was Carol who turned me on to Dane Christopher, Dane Christopher wasn't his real name but that's what he called himself, Carol gave me his name and phone number one day and told me I could probably work for him writing pornography.

"Can I help you?" answered a man's voice mellowly at the far end of the line.

"I hope so," I replied. "My name's Simon Wiener. I'm—"

"Oh, yeah," said the voice with a lilt of recognition. "You're a writer, a friend of Carol's, right?"

"Right."

"Yeah, right. She told me all about you. She's some chick that Carol, right?"

"Yeah. Right."

"Oh, yeah. I wish I had a million like her, all right. She'll do anything, that Carol. Don't have to pay her nothin' to do it. She just loves to do it, right?"

"Right."

"You ever seen that picture in her place of her screwin' the shepherd? She ever show you that one?"

"Yes, I was up at her place once. I—"

"That picture's really somethin', right? You know who took that picture?"

"No. Who?"

"I don't know. I thought maybe you knew. But that's some picture, right?"

"Yes, it—"

"Well, uh, listen, Mr., uh, what'd you say your name was again?"

"Wiener. Simon—"

"Oh yeah, that's right. Wiener. Well listen, Mr. Wiener. Bein' as how you're a friend of Carol's, there's no reason you should call me Dane Christopher, 'cause that's just bullshit, right? It's just some bullshit I use for the public, right? I mean, you never know who the fuck's gonna call you on the phone these days, right?"

"That's right," I laughed.

"Yeah," he chuckled, "that's right. Anyway, my name is Simonson, Peter Simonson. Dane Christopher's just somethin' I use for the public, the I.R.S., like that."

"I understand."

"You should call me Pete."

"Okay, Pete."

"Pleased to meetcha, Sy. You don't mind me callin' you Sy, do you, Sy?"

"No, of course not."

"Well, look here, Sy, because I don't want to waste your time and you don't want to waste my time. Carol says you're a dynamite writer, is that right?"

"Yes," I laughed, "that's right."

"Good, because what this business needs is some dynamite writers, you know what I mean? Now look, this is porno, right? These are your low-budget, what we used to call skin flicks, right?"

"How long are they?"

"About seventy-five minutes. They should be about seventy-five minutes and they should take place mostly in one room, or two rooms at the most, we don't want more than two interiors, and just exteriors that can, you know, be shot around the streets of New York."

"Can you shoot in the subways and places like that?"

"Yeah, we can shoot in the subways, but, uh, Sy, you know we can't have no fuckin' and suckin' on the subways, right?"

"Oh, sure," I stammered. "I just—"

"Don't worry, Sy. I know what you meant. You were just checkin' it out, right? Well, yeah, we can have some exteriors, like on the subways, like you said, but only around New York, and by New York I really mean Manhattan, right? We don't want to have to carry all our crap on the Staten Island ferry and crap like that, right?"

"Right."

"And we want about six fuck scenes. You understand me, right? Two interior locations tops, one room is really your best bet, and five, six fuck scenes. You don't need too much dialogue, but you've gotta make sure and leave lots of space for the fuck scenes, you know, the camera's grindin' and the people are just on top of each other fucking and sucking."

"But you do want some dialogue?" I asked. "You do want some semblance of a story?"

"Yeah, Sy. That's about what we want. Some sort of semblance. To make it in this business today, even in our end of the business, you can't make it without that semblance. So you go to it. But one thing."

"What?"

"When you do the dialogue, Sy, don't put too much dialogue on the pussies, you understand? Try to give the guys all the dialogue."

"Okay, but how come?"

"The cunts we get, Sy, they're too goofy to even get their names straight, you understand me? If you've got dialogue, try to give the guys the dialogue."

"Okay," I replied, "I will. Now tell me, how much do you—"

"We pay two hundred for a script, Sy. One hundred when you hand in the script, I mean after the script is approved, and the other hundred after we've finished making the movie."

"How long does that take?"

"What? Making the movie?"

"Yes."

"Oh, making the movie doesn't take long, but it may be a long time before I get to it. I mean, I'm working on one movie now, I got about fifteen, sixteen scripts in the drawer, it could take me a while before I get to it."

"And if I write scripts for you," I asked, "how many will you let me write?"

"Oh, I guess one a month if you're good. Carol says you're real good, so—"

"That means I'd be making two hundred a month. I can't live on two hundred dollars a month."

"You're right about that," he admitted. "The prices in this town will eat you up alive, not to mention the goddam inflation."

"But—"

"But that's how we do business, Sy. We pay two hundred if you're good. You want some time to think it over?"

"Yes," I replied glumly, "I would."

"Okay," he said amiably, "you think it over. You decide you want to give it a whirl, you've got my number, right?"

"Right," I agreed, and hung up.

So it was really the Bible encyclopedia that got me through that awful year, the Bible encyclopedia more than anything else, and it seemed like I was so worried about money all the time, so worried about money and preoccupied with earning it, that I could just never clear away any free time to do any serious writing, I don't think I wrote even a page of fiction that entire goddam year. And I was so goddam poor all the time that when a note came from Pedersen in April saying that he and Tracy were going to be married in May in a simple ceremony in his mother's home in New Mexico, and Christ he hoped I'd attend the wedding and maybe even stay on for a few days afterward, there was just no way I could afford the plane fare, so I had to write them a letter wishing them the best but saying I was sorry, I wouldn't be able to attend. I wrote them this cute note about how I'd been the best man at Ken's first wedding and so maybe, all things considered, it was just as well I was staying away from this one, but the real reason I didn't go was that I just couldn't afford it.

And the fact that I wasn't getting any writing done was wearing away at me, I would go through the day with a feeling of constant fear, fear that I'd never have any money and always be poor, fear that I'd never be a real writer at all, my father had wanted to be a writer and had never made it, now I was following in my father's footsteps, and I think it must've been that feeling of fear that was responsible in the end for my inspiration, the inspiration I had five or six months later, sometime in the fall.

I got the inspiration the same day I got blown by the chick with the stringy brown hair and rotted teeth, I've forgotten her name if I ever knew it, actually I'm not sure she ever actually told me her name, anyway if she did tell me, by now I've forgotten it, to me she'll always just be the chick with the stringy brown hair and rotted teeth.

I was living in a ground-floor apartment on East Twenty-eighth Street, the neighborhood had once been predominantly Italian, it was crammed full of Italian pastry shops and Italian fish stores where you could buy fresh fish, but now the neighborhood was changing, becoming more expensive, the Italians were moving out, to Staten Island and the Bronx, the fish stores and pastry shops were closing down one after another and the stewardesses and models were moving in.

I remember it was fall, my neighbor down the hall had flown home to Cleveland for her mother's funeral and I was taking care of her dog as a favor, it was a black-and-brown one, it looked kind of like a dachshund, and I was walking it home from an empty lot across the street from the Bellevue Psychiatric Hospital when suddenly I spotted this chick jaywalking toward me across First Avenue, and before I knew it there she was, standing beside me, hooking her arm in my arm, pressing her head warmly against my shoulder, saying, "Hi there. Okay if I walk with you?"

"No, of course not," I replied, my cock starting to harden. "Come on."

She was wearing a thin cotton dress, a cotton print dress that was worn and faded, and a maroon satin jacket that looked like it had once been emblazoned with some sort of high school emblem, it was a boy's jacket, the kind of jacket you'd buy when you were in high school, and she had stringy brown hair, matted is more like it, it was stringy and matted, like she never washed it, but what I remember most, the thing you would never forget if you ever saw her, was that she had a mouthful of rotted, decayed, revolting-looking teeth.

"What do you do?" she asked, pressing her head snugly against my shoulder.

"I'm a writer," I replied. "Or at least I—"

"Do you do your writing at home?"

"Yes," I nodded. "I do."

"Do you live around here?" she asked.

"Sure," I replied, "just a few blocks away."

"I'd love to see where you live," she sighed, and then she opened her mouth and gently sank her teeth into my shoulder.

"Do you live around here?" I asked, as we began to walk the few blocks to my apartment.

"No," she replied, "I don't live anyplace right now. I'm between things, because everything is sort of bewildered right now."

"Bewildered?"

"Yes," she answered matter-of-factly, cocking her head to one side and smiling up at me. "You know, bewildered."

"Oh," I nodded quietly.

"You have a nice dog," she remarked.

"It's not mine," I explained. "It belongs to a neighbor of mine. She had to go to a funeral in—"

"Is this where you live?" asked the girl.

"No," I replied, pointing to another entrance further down the street, "I live in that green building, three or four doors down."

"I'm glad you live there," she said cheerfully.

"Me too," I laughed. "What were you doing over on First Avenue?"

"Over where?" she asked.

"First Avenue," I repeated. "What were you—"

"Oh, just visiting a friend. I have a friend in Bellevue and I went to visit her, but now that I'm through visiting her I don't have anyplace to go right now because things are so . . . so bewildered right now."

"I remember," I nodded. "You told me that."

"You know what I mean, don't you, when everything gets all crazed and bewildered?" For a brief moment she fell silent. "You're a Scorpio, aren't you?" she said finally.

"Yeah, that's right," I exclaimed. "I am. How—"

"Because I'm an Aries," she replied quietly. "Scorpios are a big part of what's happening to me right now."

I turned my key in the lock and opened my apartment door. I leaned down and unhooked the dachshund's leash and it bounded into my bedroom and scrambled under the bed. I threw my sweater across the back of a nearby chair, hung the girl's jacket in the hallway closet, and put my arm around her shoulder. She quivered with excitement.

"You're really turning me on," she whispered. "Would you like to ball me?"

"I'd rather you just gave me a blowjob," I replied softly. "You'd like to blow me, wouldn't you?"

"I would if you're well hung," she purred. "If you're well hung, I'd—"

"I am well hung."

"Then I'd really like to," she whispered. "That way I wouldn't have to bother taking off my dress."

I took her into the bedroom and sat her down on the edge of the bed, then unbuckled my belt and let my blue jeans drop to the floor. Then I pulled out my cock. She moaned softly and looked adoringly up at me, her wan smile revealing a wide swath of hideously rotted teeth. "You really are well hung," she whispered.

"Go ahead," I said hoarsely. "Eat it."

She took the whole thing deep in her mouth, sucking it in right down to the root—I reached down and gently pulled her stringy brown hair back behind her head so that I could get an unobstructed view of my cock bulging in her cheeks—and then she drew my cock partway out of her mouth again and gently caressed the head with her lips and gratefully drank down the great wads of semen that spurted onto her tongue through her open lips.

"That was good," she said quietly, softly blotting her mouth with the back of her wrist.

"Yes it was," I agreed. I leaned down and kissed her on the cheek.

"I guess you want me to go now, right?" she asked.

"Well," I began, "I do have—"

"Don't worry," she said, "I understand. Do you still have my jacket?"

I zipped up my jeans and walked to the closet door. "Of course I still have it," I smiled. "It's in here."

"I'm so glad," she replied confidentially, as though she were divulging some intimate secret. "I hang onto that jacket, as if . . . as if it meant something. Do you know what I mean?"

"Of course," I answered. "We've all got things like that. I've—"

She threw back her head and laughed a hearty, wholesome laugh. "That's because you're a Scorpio," she exclaimed happily. "Leave it to a Scorpio to have all the bases covered. You know what I mean?"

"Of course," I nodded reassuringly.

Moments later she was out the door, skipping briskly down the street. I never saw her again, but it was that same day that I got the inspiration to haul myself out of the rut I was in, the rut of never doing any writing and of not being a writer, by selling all my jazz records and other junk and flying out to New Mexico for a couple of weeks to start writing that book I had always said I was going to write about Ken Pedersen. It wouldn't really be like writing a novel, I figured, but at least it would be something

I could sink my teeth into, something I really knew something about, it would be a biography of Ken Pedersen with pictures and documents and a complete narrative account of Pedersen's life. As soon as I got my inspiration, I ran to the phone and dialed Marjory Pedersen's number.

"Hello?" replied Marjory Pedersen's voice at the other end of the line.

"Hello, Mrs. Pedersen? It's me, Simon Wiener. I'm trying to get in touch with Ken. Can you—"

"He's not living here anymore, Sy," replied Mrs. Pedersen. "He and Tracy were married last May. They continued living here for awhile, but then they moved out to California about five or six weeks ago."

"Do you have a phone number for them?" I asked. "Could you give me their phone number?"

"I don't see why not, Sy. Is something wrong? What is it you want to call Ken about?"

"I want to fly out and visit him," I replied enthusiastically. "I've decided to write a book about Ken's life."

There was a chilly pause on the far end of the line. "A book about Ken's life?" repeated Mrs. Pedersen warily. "You mean, a fictionalized—"

"No," I blurted, "not a fictionalized account. I mean a biography of Ken's life, the real story of his life, with—"

"You mean," she interrupted, her voice now practically clogged with suspicion, "you mean this will be a book about Ken, with his real name and—"

"Yes," I said eagerly, "that's right. Ken and I—"

"Have you informed Ken about this project?" she asked.

"Yes, of course," I stammered defensively. "As a matter of fact, it may even originally have been his idea. We've been talking about it for years, even when—"

"Ken is very fond of you, Simon," interjected Mrs. Pedersen coolly. "He respects you a great deal. It's quite possible he was swayed by—"

"He wasn't swayed by anything," I snapped. "It's something he's practically begged me to do. He brings it up every time I see him. And it's a good idea. It—"

"It's possible that Ken hasn't yet fully considered the ramifications that might flow from such a book," she continued, "the impact it might have on his efforts to build a new life for himself and Tracy, for example, to say nothing of its implications for Arthur and myself. Tell me, Simon, if you don't mind my asking, what exactly would Ken stand to gain from this project?"

"I don't know," I admitted. "A percentage of the proceeds, possibly, but as of now I'm not sure there'd be any proceeds. Right now I haven't even got a—"

"I see," she interrupted. "Well I think this is a matter that merits further consideration by all of us, don't you agree?"

"Yes," I replied irritably, "I suppose it does. But for the time being, do you think I could just have his phone number?"

"Certainly, Simon. I'll look it up for you. Here it is. Area code 213. Phone number 876-9807."

"Thank you, Mrs. Pedersen."

"You're welcome, Simon," she replied. "It's always a pleasure to talk to you. Thank you for calling."

■ ■ ■

It was late the following day by the time I finally reached Ken Pedersen.

"Hey, you lucky sonovabitch," I exclaimed into the mouthpiece. "Guess what noted author-to-be is going to be sleeping in your house and otherwise mooching off you for the next couple of weeks while he starts writing the definitive story of your colorful life."

"Sy," inquired Pedersen uncertainly, "is that you?"

"Of course it's me, Pedersen. Didn't you hear what I said? After all these years, I'm finally going to sit down and write that book about your life."

"Gee, Sy," began Pedersen haltingly, apologetically, "it would be really great to see you. Tracy and I would both love it. She's dying to—"

"What the fuck's wrong with you, Pedersen?" I shouted. "Act enthusiastic, damn it. Ever since we were in college together you've been after me to write down every word you said so I could write a book about you. Well okay, now I'm—"

"Hey, man," he said reassuringly, "don't sweat it, man. I still want to do it. It's just that things have been a little rough out here, you know. A little rougher than I expected, that's all."

"What the hell is it, Ken? Is something wrong?"

"No, man, it's not that anything's wrong. It's just that we're both trying to land some acting work, which is really rough, and we haven't got a fuck of a lot of money, and so we're both out there looking for some kind of jobs to tide us over, and every time I go somewhere to apply for a goddam job they hand me this goddam form to fill out, they hand me one of those goddam application forms, and right there staring me in the fucking face they're asking me have I ever been arrested, have I ever been this or that, you know how it is, man, you know how it is with these goddam applications, I just never seem to know how to deal with them, that's all, I never know what to do, so mostly I just get up and walk out, you know, and after a while it gets . . . it just gets depressing."

"Can't you just lie on the forms?" I asked. "Can't you just say that—I mean, are they really going to check to find out if—"

"So it's not as if I don't want to *do* the book, man," he went on, as though I hadn't spoken, "it's not as if I don't want to do it. It's just that the prison experience is kind of hemming in on me, man, kind of getting to me in this new depressing way. And right in the middle of me being involved with this goddam depression, Marjory calls me on the phone and—"

"I spoke to her yesterday. She doesn't want me to do the book."

"I don't think that's exactly her position, Sy," whined Pedersen. "She's just trying to appraise it all rationally, that's all, trying to appraise it from a realistic perspective so she can—"

"Do you want me to call it off?" I asked irritably. "Do you want me to forget about it?"

"No, man," replied Pedersen pathetically. "No, I don't want you to forget it. I just want you to try and get into what I'm feeling, man. This whole job thing. The goddam applications. I feel hemmed in, man, that's all."

"So you'd still like me to come."

"Of course, man. Of course I want you to come. Tracy's dying to meet you, man. I've told her all about you and she's dying to meet you. Shit. Come on out. Stay out here a year. Stay as long as you goddam like. It'll be like old—"

"And the book. You want me to come out there ready to work on the book."

He paused. "Yeah," he said finally, "sure I do. I'll get all my shit together, my papers, my letters, maybe you'll even want to take a look at what I've written down so far on my *Hamlet* thing.

I just want us to talk about it a little, that's all, try to come to some consensus on the thing so there won't be any bad repercussions, that's all. You don't mind that, do you?"

"Of course not, Ken," I replied, trying my best to conceal my annoyance and sound sympathetic. "Of course not. But, some way or other, we'll do it, right? You still want to do it?"

"Sure I do, man. Come on out here. Come on the fuck out here just as soon as you can."

The first thing you notice after landing at the Los Angeles International Airport, after you've gotten off the plane and smiled goodbye at the stewardess and gotten your suitcase off that metal carousel thing, the first thing you notice when you step outside are the palm trees, because the airport is ringed with palm trees, there are palm trees lining the roads leading out of the airport, and there are even a few palm trees, perhaps half a dozen of them, growing inside the airport grounds as well. There is something about palm trees inside an airport that is very, very weird, and I remember I was standing there with my luggage, staring up at this palm tree, or maybe it was even a bunch of palm trees growing together in some fucking group, I was imagining Heather, bare-breasted, in a grass skirt, shinnying up a palm tree to pick me a coconut, she had a white gardenia pinned in her jet-black hair, which had been straightened with an electric comb and Dixie Peach, she was shinnying up the palm tree, her brown thighs, rubbed with coconut oil, gleaming like sexually aroused mahogany beneath her grass skirt, when all of a sudden there was Pedersen, in blue Bermuda shorts and a short-sleeved yellow shirt, a suntanned ex-convict who still blinked like a convict whenever he was out in the sun.

"How the fuck are you, man?" he exclaimed, punching me

playfully in the shoulder and reaching out to relieve me of my bag. "Shit, it's good to see you."

"I was thinking about those palm trees, man," I remarked. "I was thinking about Heather climbing up one of those palm trees to get me a coconut."

Pedersen emitted a short, nervous, patronizing laugh of the kind you customarily reserve for loved ones in the insane asylum. "Any hairies on the flight out?" he asked.

"Just one," I replied. "She was coming home to California after visiting her boy friend in Connecticut or someplace. I kissed her a few times, tried to get her to go back to the bathroom with me and fuck me in the bathroom, but no matter how much I worked at it I couldn't—"

"There's gobs of stray pussy in California, Sy," interrupted Pedersen reassuringly, as he opened his car door and gestured me into the back seat. "Wherever you go in California, there's an incredible quantity of hot pussy. I'm sure Tracy can set you up with all the pussy you can handle, probably even more than you can handle. So don't get uptight about the hairy on the plane, Sy, because chances are she wasn't even from California, she was probably from Peoria or some other weird place where nobody knows how to fuck, so just let me throw your suitcase in the goddam trunk and let's get the hell out of here, because I'm supposed to pick Tracy up at her job at ten after five, and her job is a good twenty minutes from here, unless we get all jammed up in the traffic."

The road out of the airport was lined with palm trees, one palm tree after another, an equal distance apart. "The smog is killing the palm trees," observed Pedersen casually, waving his arm out the window toward the equidistant palm trees. "Pretty soon, there won't be any palm trees left."

"I was just thinking about that," I commented. "I was thinking that they don't really belong in a big American city anyway, that living in a city with palm trees could have the potential to get you really weirded out."

Pedersen chuckled softly and shook his head. There was a bag of gumdrops in the glove compartment, and he reached in and took out the gumdrops and offered me one. "They're good," he remarked. "Try one. They're from a—"

"Heather's father used to eat gumdrops," I recalled. "He had this old plaid hunting shirt, you know those heavy woolen shirts like you sometimes wear when you go hunting, and he used to fill up the pockets with—"

"Did he eat the black ones?" asked Pedersen, his eyes sparkling like rhinestones in the rearview mirror.

"The what?" I replied.

"The black ones. Did he eat the black ones?"

"Pedersen, what the fuck are you talking about?"

"The gumdrops, damn it. I'm asking about the gumdrops. I'm asking did Heather's father eat all the gumdrops, or only some of the gumdrops, or did he have a favorite flavor, or did he always leave one flavor for last, but mostly I'm asking did he eat the black ones?"

"I don't know," I answered, a little bewildered. "What a goddam weird question. Why on earth would you ask a—"

"I always leave the black ones," noted Pedersen with the matter-of-fact nonchalance of the connoisseur. "I always leave the black ones, and when there's nothing left in the bottom of the bag but the black ones, that's when I throw the fucker away."

"I think Heather's father ate all of them," I mused aloud. "And I think he may have especially liked the red ones, because he—"

"So I would always ask myself," continued Pedersen, ignoring me, "I would always ask myself, if so many people are like me, and they throw the black gumdrops away, if all they do is sort of save them up at the bottom of the bag and then throw them all away, who, I would ask myself, who do the gumdrop people make the black ones for anyway, why do they even make the little sons of bitches if everyone is just going to throw them all away?"

He paused a moment, in order to allow the gravity of it all to sink in.

"What did you finally decide?" I asked.

"I decided that spades must eat the black ones," he announced with quiet conviction. "I decided that spades must eat the black ones, and maybe they throw some other color away. Maybe they throw the white ones away. But this is all theoretical and highly—"

"The white ones taste just like the black ones," I retorted. "It wouldn't make—"

"Not always," corrected Pedersen patiently. "That's not always true, Sy. You know that. Or at least you ought to. You ought to know that as well as I do. Sometimes the white ones taste exactly like the black ones, I'll admit that's true, but just as often they taste like cinnamon—"

"Like the purple ones."

"Yes, that's right, like the purple ones, and sometimes—"

"Why are you so fucking interested in all this?" I asked.

"I'm not interested in it," he replied calmly.

"But you must be," I insisted. "You've been—"

"It's a minor-league existential thing with me, Sy," he observed quietly. "Just a simple matter of a passing fascination with the ephemeral existentials."

"Oh," I replied, and the car fell silent. Even at relatively low speeds, Ken Pedersen drove an automobile with all the cautious deliberation of a Kamikaze pilot. At every curve, it seemed as though his mind's eye would construct an imaginary dotted line straight through the curve, and then Pedersen would send the car hurtling down that line as though he could transform the landscape by the mere force of his will. I always regarded it as a testament to my sanity that throughout the time I knew him I hated to drive with him.

"Are you working at some job, man," I asked him finally, "or just taking it easy, or what?"

"I've been looking, man," he replied. "I've been looking but I haven't been able to find anything. It's like I've been telling you, man, it's the prison experience. It's—"

"I know," I remarked. "We talked about it a little. I was just wondering—"

"Tracy's working," he went on. "Tracy's got this little secretarial job. It's keeping us going while we look for work as actors, which is a full-time job in itself, let me tell you. We're going to pick her up now. That's where we're going right now, to pick her up. She gets off work at five o'clock. I told her we'd pick her up at about ten after, but now I'm not sure we're going to make it."

"You think we'll be very late?" I asked.

"No," he replied, "not too late."

Tracy was standing on the sidewalk out in front of this low-level, three-story office building when we finally pulled up at the curb around twenty after five. She scrutinized me for a fleeting moment through the back-seat window, then opened the front door and climbed in the front.

"You know, Ken, I've been standing on that—"

"I'm sorry, honey," apologized Pedersen. "Sy's plane was

maybe five or six minutes late, and then the goddam traffic was—"

"Don't be too hard on Ken," I pleaded whimsically. "If you've ever driven with him before, you know he got us here as fast as the laws of thermodynamics would permit."

Pedersen laughed a hearty laugh, a hearty thank-you-for-getting-me-off-the-hook type laugh.

"You're Sy," noted Tracy, shifting around in the front seat to get a better look at me. "I've been looking forward to meeting you. Ken's told me so—"

"Pedersen only tolerates me," I joked, "because he knows I'm his biggest fan. I'm going to write a book about—"

"I know," she remarked. "I think it's a great idea. But Marjory doesn't think it's a great idea, does she, Ken?"

"Now come on, Tracy," pleaded Pedersen. "You know that—"

"You don't like her either, eh?" I laughed.

"No," replied Tracy, "I don't."

Her comment was followed by this acidic pause that probably could have eaten its way through the floorboards of the car

"What kind of a job do you have?" I asked.

"Asshole secretarial job," she shrugged disdainfully. "Asshole—hey, Ken," she squirmed around in her seat again so that now she had one foot on the floor, the other curled up beneath her on the front seat, "you know what that cunt-faced Harrison bitch pulled on me today? Can you imagine what she did?"

"More of the same?" inquired Pedersen.

"Exactly," Tracy exclaimed. "Exactly. The same damn shit as last week. Only today she did it with the SO-4s, while last week she—"

"What's going on?" I asked.

"Just office bullshit, Sy," explained Pedersen. "We'll be home any minute. Just your pure office-politics bullshit."

"It's not worth hearing about," added Tracy, "believe me. It's just not worth it. But it's so, so *exasperating*. It makes me—"

"So if you work all day nine to five," I asked, "does that make it hard for you to go out looking for acting work? Or do—"

"Well the reason I took this goddam job," she began, still irritated over the behavior of this "Harrison bitch" and the SO-4s, "the reason I took this job, as opposed to some other job, the reason I took it is that they said if there was an audition I had to go to, or if I had to go to a call-back or something like that, they would let me go and I could make up the time on Saturdays or after five o'clock. And for a while it was okay. It seemed like it was—"

"If you're an actor, Sy," interrupted Pedersen, "if you're an actor, you have to be free days. You can't just tell some producer that you can only try out for a part after five o'clock at night. Because—"

"I understand that," I replied. "Tracy, go—"

"Well, that's really all there is to it," she sighed resignedly. "That's really just about all there is to it. For a while it seemed that everything was really working out okay, and then this incredible cunt-lapping Harrison bitch started in with her SO-4s, which is just starting to make life impossible for me. Ken knows what I'm talking about, don't you, Ken?"

"Believe me, Sy," observed Pedersen solemnly, "believe me, this is one woman you wouldn't want to have curling up beside you on a cold winter's night."

"Ha!" exclaimed Tracy derisively. "That is the fucking understatement of the—"

"I promised Sy we'd hunt him up some pussy, Tracy," interrupted Pedersen. "I told—"

"Well you don't want Joni Harrison, Sy," remarked Tracy sardonically. "Believe me. I doubt if Joni Harrison has ever even seen a cock, but even if she—"

"You have my word," I vowed. "I will not go to bed with Joni Harrison." And we all laughed.

"You have gumdrops in the glove compartment?" asked Tracy, springing open the glove compartment.

"Yes," replied Pedersen, "they're—"

"I'm not going to find just a bag of black ones like I did last time, am I? It's not going to be like—"

"I got a new bag. It's in there, isn't it?"

"Yes," exclaimed Tracy, "here it is. I never used to eat this junk, Sy. Then I met Ken, and now I'm addicted to junk. You want some?"

"No thanks," I replied. "I had some a little while ago. Tell me, when you go out looking for jobs, for acting jobs, do you use the name Pedersen, or your maiden name, or what?"

Tracy held the gumdrop bag up to her face and peered at me suspiciously through the cellophane. "I don't use Pedersen," she replied. "I use the name Tracy Jerreau."

"Wow! What a wild name. Is that your maiden name?"

"No, it isn't."

"Listen, Sy," interrupted Pedersen nervously, "we—"

"My maiden name was Fogelson," noted Tracy.

"Fogelson?" I exclaimed incredulously. "You're Jewish? I didn't know you were Jewish."

"I'm not Jewish," she replied coldly. "I—"

"Of course you're Jewish," I went on. "With a name like—"

"I used to be Jewish," she amended coolly. "I used to be Jewish, but now I'm not."

"That's absurd," I replied. "You—"

"It's a religion," she continued. "I'm an atheist. I don't—"

"Me neither," I retorted. "But being Jewish isn't only a religion. It's—"

"If I'm Jewish," she snapped, glowering at me over the front seat, "if I'm Jewish, Sy, then so are you."

"But of course," I shrugged. "I never—"

"We're here, people," exclaimed Pedersen cheerfully. "We're here, and right here is my own private parking space which no one else may park in upon pain of death."

Now as I have said, Ken Pedersen was the world's worst driver, it was one of the dozen-odd ways in which he habitually attempted to race death to the crossing, but he was, in spite of this, an excellent parker, and he pulled into the parking space with all the aplomb of a brain surgeon.

"Only one turn," observed Tracy dryly. "You were lucky."

"That's not true," complained Pedersen. "Tell her, Sy. Tell her it's not true."

"No," I agreed, "it isn't. Ken Pedersen is the world's most determinedly reckless driver, but he is also one of the world's best parkers."

"Hey," exclaimed Pedersen, laughing uneasily. "You weren't supposed to say that. The part about me being one of the world's best parkers is true, of course, but—"

"I didn't mean to hurt your feelings, I mean about the Jewish business," I said to Tracy. "Honestly, I'm—"

"Forget it," she replied, trying to sound chipper but coming off as curt instead. "Let's get inside and pull together some dinner. I don't know about you guys, but I am famished."

■ ■ ■

The apartment was small and fairly compact, with white ceilings and pale yellow walls. A short hallway connected the miniature living room with the two bedrooms, one small the other tiny, that faced one another on either side of the hall. The walls of the hallway were papered with white 3 X 5 index cards containing pithy epigrammatical quotations from George Santayana and Themistocles and Alexis de Tocqueville, in fact from all those revered dead guys whose writings you always see plastered all over the place on those placards mounted inside glass cases at the entrance to churches. The living room, which was connected to a walk-in kitchen, had a pink princess telephone and a cream-colored portable Motorola TV, which was left on, virtually all the time, for the purpose of enhancing what Pedersen referred to as the "existential ambience" of the apartment.

"This," announced Pedersen, standing at the head of the hallway and gesturing expansively toward the scores of typewritten index cards papering the walls, "is my hall of philosophical speculation, containing the timeless wisdom of the great historical sages who have influenced me greatly in the formulation of my own philosophical formulations, not to—"

"Why did you get a place with two bedrooms?" I asked. "Don't the two of you sleep in the same bedroom?"

"Of course we do, Sy," clucked Pedersen, shaking his head. "Of course we sleep in the same bedroom. What kind of question is that, do we sleep in the same bedroom? Of course we sleep in the same bedroom. We sleep in the large bedroom over there. The small bedroom is for the kid."

"What kid?" I asked. "Are you and—"

Pedersen cupped one hand to his mouth. "As soon as Tracy and I have a little money saved," he shouted, loudly enough to ensure that Tracy would hear him in the kitchen, "we are going to have a kid. The tiny bedroom is for our kid."

"Who's going to have a kid?" yelled Tracy from the kitchen, over the noise of an electric mixer. "I'm sure as—"

"*You* are," shouted Pedersen. "Deep in her heart of hearts, every woman longs to—"

Tracy appeared in the living room, cradling a large green mixing bowl in the crook of her left arm while she assiduously stirred its contents with a fork held in her right. "I'm not having any kid, Pedersen," she chided seriously. "If you—"

"You know as well as I do that no woman is truly fulfilled unless she has given birth to a child, my dear," insisted Pedersen, now launching into the mellifluent array of gestures that he had originally perfected while reading the balcony scene from *Cyrano de Bergerac.* "You know that—"

"I'm not having any kid, Pedersen," she repeated vehemently, the level of annoyance rising in her voice. "It's men who want kids. All men want kids. And do you want to know why all men want kids?"

Pedersen and I looked at one another bewilderedly. "Who are you asking?" I asked.

"Either of you," she snapped. "Do you know why men—"

"I give up," I said. "Why?"

"Because men don't have to go through the goddam pain, that's why," and with that she gave the contents of the mixing bowl one more emphatic stir and stormed back into the kitchen.

"She'll come around, Sy," whispered Pedersen with a broad smile. "Women love kids. They can't live without them. Come to think of it, Sy, it's about time you started to give some thought to having a kid yourself."

"I don't like kids," I replied.

Pedersen laughed and slapped me on the back. "Don't be ridiculous, Sy. Everybody loves kids. Kids are wonderful. Where would the world be without any kids? The woman does all the work, Sy. Remember that. You just come home at night and pet the little fucker on the head. It's wonderful, Sy. A wonderful feeling. You come home at night and you pet the little bastard on the head and you say to yourself, 'That is my kid. The blood of my blood. The flesh—' "

"Let's sit down in the living room," I suggested, "and talk about the book."

"What book?" asked Pedersen.

"The book I'm going to write about you," I replied. "The book I flew all the way from—"

"I know, I know what book you mean," he proclaimed, waving me silent. "I know exactly. And I've been getting together all these papers, all these documents for you to look at. Come on, they're all in the file cabinet in the living room."

"It's all here, man," he continued a moment later, as he pulled a fat manila file folder out of an old-fashioned wooden two-drawer file cabinet. "Everything is here. Programs from the community-theater stuff I did in New Mexico. My *Hamlet* paper. All the—"

"Where's all the prison stuff, Ken?" I asked. "All the documents and notes you said you took while you were—"

"Oh, I-I had a hard time pulling all that stuff together, man," stammered Pedersen. "And the moving. A lot of that stuff I think was lost, or maybe just misplaced, when we did the—"

"Lost?" I exclaimed. "Misplaced? How could you—"

"Calm down, man," said Pedersen soothingly, trying to placate me. "Calm down. It's all probably around here somewhere, in a box or something. It's just that I'm not so sure we should accent the prison experience in the book, if you know what I mean. I'm just not so sure we should accent it."

"Ken," I began impatiently, "what you call the prison experience is an important—"

"I know, I know," he whined pathetically. "And in many ways I think it was important to me, important to me as a person and to the development of my philosophy. But there's the real world to consider, too, man, the materialistic aspect of things, like jobs and automobiles and refrigerators. You're not too big on the materialistic side of things, I know, but still you've—"

"Is the journal around here someplace?" I asked, sifting through the papers, trying to hide my annoyance. "Do you have the journal around here someplace?"

"Journal?" asked Pedersen.

"Yes," I said tartly, "the journal. The journal you kept that spring when—"

"Ah, yes!" he exclaimed, raising a forefinger in recognition, wagging it slowly back and forth, and then abruptly closing his fist again and dropping it to his side. "It's gone, man. The journal is gone."

"It's gone?"

"I destroyed it, Sy," stammered Pedersen nervously, as he stuck out his forefinger once again and made repeated jabs with it in the direction of the kitchen. "I found it while we were packing our stuff to move out here, and . . . and I threw it away."

"Ken," I demanded in utter disbelief, "why did you do that?"

"Because I came to realize," he began haltingly, now taking out a handkerchief and wiping his brow with it, "I came to realize that the journal represented a part of my life that was, well, that was sick, man, a part of my life that was sick. And in the interests of my own mental health, I decided that the best thing to do was surmount that aspect of my past, to surmount it and free myself from my dependence on its artifacts and symbols, so that—"

"You destroyed it."

"Yes," he answered quietly, "I did."

"It was your idea to destroy it," I persisted, knowing full well that it hadn't been.

"Well, Marjory and I discussed it," admitted Pedersen, now jabbing his forefinger frenziedly in the direction of the kitchen, "we had one of our heart-to-hearts about it, as we have always had, as has always been our custom, and we agreed that destroying the journal would be a sort of rite of passage, a moving away from a past that was full of let's call them errors and onward and upward into a bright new future."

I glowered at him angrily, unwilling to say anything that might let him off the hook. Ken Pedersen was one of those people who are deathly afraid of dead air, who will talk themselves into oblivion unless someone comes to their rescue by interrupting or asking questions.

"And then of course there was Tracy, Sy. Tracy and I were endeavoring to establish a committed relationship, one based on shared vulnerability and mutual trust, and holding onto that journal was like clinging to an old, bygone relationship, one that had—"

"Ken," I interrupted angrily, "I flew all the way out here to do this book about your life. It is a book that we have discussed doing for years. It—"

"I know that," he said softly. "You're right. We've been talking about it for years."

"And now," I continued, "I come out here and I find that we can't deal with two of the most important periods of your life, the fifteen months you spent in prison, plus the spring in your senior year of high school when you had your nervous breakdown. Now—"

"You're wrong, man," exclaimed Pedersen suddenly. "No, let me stop you here because you're really getting into this thing that is one hundred percent wrong. You can deal with those things. You can deal with prison and the spring I had my breakdown. Hell, no one knows better than I do that the book would be nothing without them, that without those things you might as well forget the project entirely, might as well get on the next plane and go home."

"My sentiments exactly," I mumbled dryly.

"Well I'm not suggesting that," insisted Pedersen. "I'm not suggesting that at all."

"What are you suggesting, Ken?" I asked.

"Well, let me finish and I'll tell you, man. Just let me finish and I'll try to explain it. I'm just suggesting that we change the emphasis a little, that we make the book less of a documentary, less of a total nonfiction thing and more like something a little different."

"More like what, Ken?"

"Well," he stammered, clasping his fingers behind his back and shifting uneasily from one foot to the other, "well, more like a, sort of more like a novel."

"More like a what?"

"More like a novel." He seized the manila file folder and thrust it toward me. "There's tons of stuff in here you can use, tons of it. We'll just change all the names and everything, kind of change the—"

"Ken," I said, as casually as I could manage, "Ken, that is just a terrible idea. It—"

And that is when Tracy stepped cheerfully into the living room, bearing a serving tray piled high with our dinner. "Save the rest of it for later, fellas," she burbled triumphantly. "Dinner is served."

■ ■ ■

The next morning Ken got up early and drove Tracy to work, and then he and I ate breakfast and went out for a walk. The book idea seemed dead to me, at least for the time being, unless I could come up with some ingenious way to salvage it, so I decided to just let it go for awhile, kind of take a vacation from it for a day or two, and then either work up a new angle on it or forget it altogether.

We walked along a sidewalk down a steep hill, past lavish ranch-style houses guarded from the outside world by massive stone walls adorned with vines of ivy and brightly colored flowers.

"You ought to get up to San Francisco," remarked Pedersen.

"You ought to get up to San Francisco while you're here and get a look at one of those topless shows. I think you might really like them."

"Good, eh?"

"Well," mused Pedersen thoughtfully, "I didn't really like them. But you might like them. I think it's possible you might like them. And in any case they're—"

"Why didn't you like them?" I asked.

"Oh, I liked them," he replied, struggling to come to grips with his ambivalent point of view, "I just didn't really like them. They lack an essential—"

He broke off in mid-sentence and began again. "You remember the strip shows we used to go to together in Chicago, right?"

"Sure I remember."

"Well," he began again haltingly, his own viewpoint on the issue still not fully formulated, "those shows were somehow your quintessential—well, look, let me tell you about the San Francisco things."

"Okay," I replied. "Go ahead."

"Well first," he explained, now beginning to gesture tentatively with his hands, "you go into this fabulous nightclub type place. Luxurious. Businessmen on expense accounts. Couples. Everybody elegantly dressed. Smoking Tiparillos. Everybody is—"

"I get the picture," I interjected. "Go on."

"Okay, good," he laughed self-consciously. "Good. You've got the picture. Now overhead, there's this incredible chandelier, there's this chandelier that looks like it came out of Versailles or someplace. The sonovabitch probably weighs three tons." He put his hand to his forehead and paused thoughtfully.

"It's okay, man," I said reassuringly. "I understand. Go—"

"I'm just trying to latch onto exactly what it is, Sy, that's all," explained Pedersen. "I'm just trying to really be clear on this before I launch into my thing about it. There's this elegant decor, this ambience of elegance, elegant men, elegant women, this kind of superior, sophisticated, upper-middle-class type of elegant ambience. And then there is this chandelier, this god damned motherfucking Versailles chandelier."

"Come on, man," I urged impatiently, "try to get to the point."

"Okay," he replied. "The lights dim. There's no jerking of

the lights or anything. There's just this slow dim, this perfect slow dim, and the chandelier starts to come down, they start to lower this goddam eight-ton chandelier toward the ground."

"I like it already," I laughed. "Where did you say this place was?"

"San Francisco, man. They have dozens of these places in San Francisco. But don't stop me now. Because now I'm really starting to home in on the—"

"I'm sorry," I apologized. "Go—"

"So the chandelier is lowering, lowering, and the music is playing. The ceilings must be goddam fifty feet high, it's like they went and had their ceilings made by the same guy that did the Chartres Cathedral, so it takes a really long time for the chandelier to lower. Meanwhile the music is playing, really loud, really raucous music, but the kind of melodic raunchy music that is not really raunchy, if you know what I mean. It is the kind of music that middle-class white people think spades probably fuck to."

He was in such obvious earnest about his explanation that I couldn't help laughing.

"Now look, Sy," he remarked, mildly offended, "if you're going—"

"No," I replied. "I'm sorry. Really. Please go on. I won't—"

"All right," he relented. "So the music is playing and the chandelier is lowering, it keeps on lowering until it is, say, ten feet or so off the floor, and as it comes down, you can see that there is this chick standing on the chandelier, this glossy, sexy blond chick with long blond hair halfway down to her ass and this swimsuit type costume that completely covers up her pussy but totally reveals these outrageous fifty-inch tits. Then—"

"Fifty inches?" I exclaimed incredulously.

Ken waved his right hand limply from the wrist, pooh-poohing the fifty inches. "It's silicone, man," he spat disdainfully, "they all use silicone. But it still looks good. Don't get me wrong. It still really looks good."

"I'll take your word for it," I replied skeptically. "I—"

Pedersen cupped his hands out in front of his chest to show me exactly how fifty-inch tits would look. "They stand right out there, man. They stand right out there like those bullets on a Cadillac car. And they are fucking rigid, man. Fixed. Like—"

"I don't like tits like that," I remarked.

"You like hangers," observed Pedersen.

"That's right," I nodded. "When you take off their bra, there should be this avalanche of—"

"That's because you're still looking for the mother, Sy," noted Pedersen thoughtfully. "Unconsciously, you are still—"

"Oh, please, Ken," I cut in irritably, "go on with—"

"Well, that's it," shrugged Pedersen. "That's really all there is to it. She does this go-go type dance on the chandelier—man, the tits are so close, it's like a 3-D movie, man, you think you can take the aureoles in your mouth—and then the chandelier goes back up to the ceiling and the girl disappears. For two hours. Then they do the whole fucking thing all over again."

"And you didn't like it," I remarked.

"No," he affirmed. "I didn't."

"Why not?"

"I'm not sure why not. Except it has something to do with the ambience and the kind of philosophical attitude, the kind of existential quintessentials that are at work in the situation."

"I don't think I understand any of that," I admitted.

"Well," he continued, "do you remember Lada Bazooms?"

"No," I replied, "I don't."

"Come on," prodded Pedersen, "you remember. In Chicago. The day you came to the hospital to see the kid, we went—"

"I didn't go with you that day," I remarked. "I had to go back to sleep. You went by—"

"That's right," he nodded. "You're right. I went alone that day. But it doesn't matter. The strippers we saw in Chicago were sleazy, right?"

I laughed. "They certainly—"

"Succulent, right?" he went on. "But sleazy. They shook their pussy, they shook their tits, they turned around and gave you a whiff of their asshole, right?"

"Right."

"There was none of this what the spades call 'seditty' shit, that is, an attempt to insert class into something that basically is not supposed to have any class. I mean," he continued, his tone becoming urgent now, more intense, "I mean that when you go to a strip show, you go there for sex and meat, right? You go there to jerk off, right? You go there to flong your dong and yell obscenities at the hairies, right? I mean, that's what it's all about, right? Right?"

"Well," I mused aloud, "I suppose—"

"Suppose, shit, Sy," exclaimed Pedersen impatiently. "Stop spending so much time supposing. You go there because it is what it is, don't you? You go to a strip show because it is what it's supposed to be. It's vulgar, it's obscene, it's—they're waving the shit in your face and you have your meat in your hand and you are screaming for more. Right?"

"Right."

He took a deep breath, exhaled, and went on. "Who do you see when you go to a strip show? You see sailors, right? Guys in the service, right? They're on leave. Horny as hell. They are going blind from lack of pussy. And then there are these raincoat characters, you see one fuck of a lot of raincoats, because you have these older guys—guys from skid row, guys from the suburbs whose wives won't give them a blowjob or won't dress up in sexy costumes for them or wear chicken feathers in their hair, or sequins, man, or whatever it is these guys really need—and these guys come there in their raincoats and lots of them are jerking off into their raincoats."

He paused a moment to catch his breath and gauge my reaction to what he had said.

"I understand you, man," I remarked, slowly nodding my head, "but I'm not sure I—"

"The people who go to the sleazy strip-show parlor in Chicago," continued Pedersen, now looking me intently in the eye, "the people who go to this place, who sit down in these come-stained seats, who do all these lurid, existential types of things, they are all frankly expressing a need. It is a real need, a gnawing need that they have, that probably deep down we all have. The people are what they are. The chicks are what *they* are. It's all on the up-and-up and up front where you can smell it and taste it."

"But—" I interjected.

"But," Pedersen went on, "the elegant topless show in San Francisco is not on the up-and-up, it is not up front where you can smell it and taste it. The people who go to it have this same need the other people have, but they're afraid to express it, they're afraid to express it even to themselves, man, much less to their friends and neighbors. Because society, man, society is scared shitless of this need. So they dress it up in this elegant ambience. They wear three-piece suits, man. They drink martinis. They have this phony shit-ass music that gives it all this kind of raunchy respectability. They bring their wives or their chicks along. The bitch on the chandelier is kind of a little worn around the edges, man, so she has a taste of your whorish ambience, you imagine that probably if you were alone and you met her at a bar she'd be an easy fuck, but she doesn't actually wave it in your face, meaning she doesn't actually do anything that's sexy in a vulgar or threatening kind of way, she doesn't assault you with her sexuality, there's no meat to it, there's no real meatiness, so she takes on the aspect of some sort of *performer*—you'll notice they call them topless *dancers*—so it takes it out of the realm of sex and meat and puts it in the realm of show biz, and when you and your wife leave the goddam place, and you hand the parking attendant your parking receipt and you drive home in your Lincoln Continental, with the goddam sun roof, you don't have to confront that sexual *need,* because you and your wife can joke with one another about the *dancer* that you saw and whether she was *talented* or not and you're safely buffered by this whole concept of show biz."

He was excited now, and angry, angry and self-righteous, and he was waving his arms around like a giant octopus on the brink of ejaculation.

"Let me tell you something, Sy," he exclaimed shrilly, nearly yelling, "let me tell you something that will sum it all up for you. When you go to see the topless show in San Francisco, all over the place there are all these Tiparillos. When you go to see Lada Bazooms at the Majestic, you don't see any goddam Tiparillos."

We were in an open, grassy park now, not far from some museum, and we sat down to rest on one of the wooden benches lining the asphalt pathway that wound through the grass. In a makeshift chicken-wire structure about thirty yards away, bare-chested archaeology students on loan to the museum were using large metal strainers to sift through tiny fragments of fossilized dinosaur bone like forty-niners panning for gold.

"I saw my father," said Pedersen finally, breaking a long silence. "I went down to Malibu and I had this long heart-to-heart talk with my father."

"Your real father?" I asked. "The—"

"Right," replied Pedersen, nodding his head. "I went down to his place in Malibu and I had this long heart-to-heart talk with him."

"How did you find him?" I asked. "What did—"

"Marjory told me," replied Pedersen matter-of-factly. "I told Marjory I was moving to California and I wanted to find my dad, and so she looked in her address book and came up with his address and phone number."

"But—you didn't actually know she had that, did you?" I asked. "You didn't know—"

"No," he acknowledged, "I didn't. But actually, she never said she didn't have it. She never said she did have it. She just never mentioned it. So by not ever mentioning it, she made me think she didn't have it. But I guess she did have it. I guess she had it all along. So when I told her Tracy and I were moving to California, and that I really wanted to find Walt and—"

"Walt's your father."

"Right. So when I told her we were moving to California, and that I was serious about finding him, she just said okay and opened up her address book and gave me the information."

"I thought he moved around a lot, your father. I thought he lived with—"

"Not in the last six or seven years," explained Pedersen. "I mean, he's always lived off women, he's always lived off one woman after another, first one woman, then another. But for the past six or seven or maybe it's even eight years now he's been living with this one woman, Erica, he's been living just with—"

"And nobody else."

"That's right. Nobody else. She has this beach house over in Malibu and they're living down there."

"Did you meet her too?"

"Yeah, I met her. She's—"

"Is she good-looking?"

"I don't know about that. Not especially. I'd have to say not especially. She's in her fifties, Sy. I mean, for a woman in her fifties—no, I'd have to say she's not especially attractive. She has charm, though. She radiates a certain special sort of charm."

"I thought your father was addicted to beautiful women," I remarked.

"No," replied Pedersen thoughtfully, "no, I never said that. That's not what he's into, my father. First of all, he's into women who have money. I mean, it doesn't have to be lots of money, it's not like he's on a money trip, it's not like he's especially into money, they just have to have enough money so that they can support him without his having to work.

"But," he continued, "given that they have enough money to support him so that he doesn't have to work, so he can live in a modest, comfortable, relaxed sort of way without having to work, he's not into physical beauty or big tits or—"

"He's searching for inner spiritual qualities," I said sarcastically.

"Yes, that's right," nodded Pedersen, either missing my meaning or choosing to ignore it, "that's exactly it. He's after these inner qualities, these essences, these kinds of existential—"

"Do you think he's found them in Erica?" I asked.

Pedersen paused a moment. "Yes," he answered, "I would say he has. I would say he's found them in Erica at least for the time being."

"And he's been with her for a long time," I added. "Six or seven years is a long time. Has he usually been with one woman for such an extended period of time?"

"He was with Marjory for that long," replied Pedersen.

"What about after Marjory? What about the others?"

"No, I would say after Marjory he was with them maybe two years, maybe three, but never as long as six or seven. I would say six or seven has been about the longest since Marjory."

"Is he happy?"

"Yes."

'You're sure."

"Absolutely. If he's unhappy at all, if he harbors any unhappiness at all, it's the unhappiness of someone who, in the back of their mind, is always searching. He's happy with Erica, he's content with his life, but in the back of his mind he's always searching for the perfect woman, for those existential essences. It's like a wanderlust of the soul. His body is fixed in Malibu, but his soul—"

"His soul wanders freely among the stars."

"That's right. That's it exactly. That was quite poetic, Sy, quite eloquently—"

"Thank you."

For a moment, we were silent.

"What does he do?" I asked.

"What does who do?"

"Your father. He lives with Erica at her beach house in

Malibu. He has no job. What does he do? To pass the time? Does he have hobbies? Does—"

"No," replied Pedersen with a thoughtful shake of his head, "no hobbies."

"Does he have . . . interests?"

"You mean like hobbies?" asked Pedersen.

"Well, maybe not hobbies," I replied, "but like interests. Does he read, or—"

"Sometimes he reads. But he doesn't usually read. I don't think he likes to read. My father's a very direct man, Sy, he's very direct. He reaches for the essences of things, he reaches for the very molecular fabric of things that gives things their essence. Reading is much too indirect for him, too remote, too—"

"Too sterile," I suggested.

"Yes, that's it. Too sterile. Too removed from the life of the senses."

"Then what does he do all day?"

"I don't understand."

"When he gets up in the morning, what does he do?"

"He gets dressed. He eats breakfast."

"And then what?"

"He goes to the beach."

"Does he bring a radio?"

"No. No radio."

"Does he bring a deck of cards?"

"No. No cards. That would be too much like reading."

"I guess I can see that. Does he spend the whole day at the beach?"

"Yes, the whole day."

"Does Erica come with him? Does she go to the beach with him?"

"Sometimes. But not usually. I think he said she doesn't really like the beach."

"Does he swim? Does your father swim?"

"Yes. He swims. He's a good swimmer."

"Is that about it then? He lies on the beach? Every now and then he goes in the water?"

"He talks to women, Sy. My father is a man who loves women. He loves everything about them. He's not hung up about women the way you and I are, the way everyone we know is hung up about them. He revels in women. He revels in their essences. He explores—"

"Is he ever unfaithful to Erica?"

"Never. My father is never unfaithful to a woman, Sy. He doesn't need to be. That's a whole ego thing. It's a whole sick need. My father is beyond that. He has never been unfaithful to a woman. Ever. I'm sure he was never unfaithful to Marjory. I'd bet my life on it. They support him. He is faithful to them. Eventually, he moves on, but even then he never hurts them. He moves on, yet they still adore him."

"Does Marjory still adore him?"

"Yes, Sy, I think she does. But—"

"But what?"

"But Marjory is a very mature, demanding woman, Sy. She's very rooted in a certain way of perceiving life and perceiving reality. My father is boyish, in a way he's still a boy. In a way he's never grown up. He's immature in a way. But he's not rooted, the way Marjory is. He's not—"

"He's not limited."

"That's right. Thank you. He's not limited. Marjory is mature. Grown up. Realistic. She stays rooted. But my father, my father soars."

"He wanders freely among the stars."

"That's right." For a moment, Pedersen paused. "You're not making fun of that, are you, Sy?" he asked.

"No, I'm not."

"Good."

"So what happened?"

"What happened when?"

"When you saw him? What happened when you saw him?"

"I don't know what you mean. Ask me questions and I'll—"

"Did you call him on the phone, or did you just go there and—"

"The phone. Marjory gave me his phone number and I just called him on the phone."

"Who answered?"

"Erica answered. She said he was at the beach, and he would call me back. And he did."

"What did you say to him when he called you back?"

"I said I was living in Los Angeles and I wanted to see him. And he said okay, I could come anytime I wanted, and did I want to come over that evening, or did I want to meet him at the beach tomorrow?"

"What did you say?"

"The beach."

"You thought that would be more private, that you would be able to speak to him alone there, away from Erica."

"I guess so. I don't think I really thought about it. He just presented me with these two alternatives and I picked one. I picked the beach. I never really gave any thought to why I picked the beach. It just—"

"Okay. So you said you'd meet him at the beach the following day. What happened then?"

"Well, the next day I got up early and I drove Tracy to her job, and then I went over to Malibu and I met him on the beach. He—"

"Did you recognize him? Did you know right away who he was?"

"He's my own goddam father, Sy."

"Well, Jesus Christ, Pedersen," I exclaimed, "I know that. But you haven't laid eyes on the man in over twenty years. It's been over twenty goddam years since—"

"He has sent me some letters, Sy. Postcards, really. When I was a boy, he used to—"

"Letters do not tell you what the man looks like, Ken. They do not help you locate a lone man on a beach full of—"

"The beach was pretty empty, actually," corrected Pedersen. "It was still morning, and the beach—"

"You went to the beach, and you knew right away which man was—"

"Yes, right away. You don't forget what your father looks like, Sy. It's like imprinting—with ducks. You see him once, you remember. So I didn't have any trouble. He was lying on the beach on this orange-and-black Mexican blanket, on a blanket that looked like it came from Mexico, and I walked right over to him and that was that. I knew the minute I saw him that he was my father."

"What did you do then?"

"I sat down on the blanket, I sat down across from him on the blanket. He was very cordial, very friendly. He's a very cordial, charming man, my father. Very open. Very—"

"Did you talk?"

"Yes."

"For Christ's sake, Pedersen. What did you talk about?"

"Everything. We talked about everything. We talked for about two hours. I would say I did most of the talking. I asked a lot of questions. We talked for about two hours."

"What were some of the things you talked about? What kinds of questions—"

"I asked him why he left Marjory."

"What did he say?"

"He said that Marjory was, is, a very fine woman. Very strong. A very powerful woman. A very—"

"Your father doesn't like powerful women."

"No, Sy, you're wrong. He likes powerful women. But only if they're powerful in a certain kind of way."

"What didn't he like about Marjory?"

"He said she's a very fine woman. A very strong woman. But also that she's very controlling, much too controlling, and also she was always after him to get a job, get ahead, make something of himself, which, of course, he never wanted to do. My father never felt the need to make something of himself, Sy. He always was something. He didn't need—"

"What else didn't he like about Marjory?"

"He said she wasn't very good in bed, not very good in the rack department."

"Was that the way he put it, not very good in the—"

"No. Rack is my expression. Not very good in the rack is my way of putting it. He said he wasn't very happy with the way she did the trick, not very enamored of—"

I couldn't help laughing. "I'm sorry," I apologized. "I didn't mean to—"

"That's okay, Sy. Really, that's okay. I laughed, too. At the time he said it, I have to admit it sounded awfully funny. He—"

"Did he tell you why he felt Marjory was—"

"He said she was too self-controlled, too much into exercising self-control. She couldn't let go, she wouldn't allow herself to let go. She was always into controlling herself. He said it got to the point where the only way he could get her to let go, the only way he could get her to express any emotion, would be to get her really pissed off. If he got her angry enough, he said it only happened maybe two or three times in the whole time he knew her, he said if he could get her really angry enough, she would just get hysterical, she would start crying and screaming and tearing at her hair and—"

"Marjory?"

"Yes, Sy. Marjory. She would start screaming and yelling. She would tear at his face with her fingernails and try to scratch out his eyes with her fingers."

"This is what used to turn your father on?"

"Not turn on exactly, Sy. Not exactly turn on. But I guess it was his only means, the only way he knew of breaking down that emotional barrier, of trying to establish some sort of, let's call it an emotional rapport between them. He said it got to the point where their whole marriage consisted of his doing everything he could to get her to get hysterical, and her doing everything she could to keep her cool and keep herself from getting hysterical. And it went on like that for a long time, for a pretty long time, and after a while—"

"After a while he just gave up and left."

"Right."

"Good for him. It all sounds like a losing proposition to me."

"Me too."

"What else did you talk about?"

Pedersen ran his hand through his hair and thought for a moment. "Oh, I told him about Elaine, and Mrs. Willoughby, and the prison experience. I told him about my *Hamlet* thesis."

"Was he interested in that?"

"The *Hamlet* thesis?"

"Right. Was he—"

"Oh, yes he was. Very interested. And I told him about Tracy and about how we've come out to Los Angeles to make names for ourselves in acting. But mostly I didn't talk to him about those things. Mostly I talked to him about that spring with Sandy and all the—you remember the time I told you all about that spring?"

"The spring with Sandy. The spring you wrote about in your journal."

"Yes, that's right. That spring. Mostly I told him all about that spring and about being beaten up and about being institutionalized. He already knew about my breakdown. I guess every now and then he's been in contact with Marjory, and I guess she told him about the breakdown. So I told him all about my breakdown, about the spring with Sandy and all those things I wrote about in my journal, and I asked him if he could help me. I told him it was really important for me to validate my past, to explore the reasons for my breakdown so that I could validate my past and escape the grip of the past so as to be able to live life fully in the present. I told him I needed to know the specific causes for my breakdown, the specific reasons why I had that breakdown at that particular time, what it was that—"

"And what did he say? Was he able to help you? Did he have any answer to—"

"No. No specific answer, no."

"Well, what did he do? Did he say anything when you—"

"First he just paused a minute. He was lying face down on the blanket, he had his right elbow on the blanket, and he kind of made a fist with his right hand and rested his chin against his fist, with his thumb extending underneath his chin. He didn't say anything. All he did was pause for a minute. Then he sat up. He sat up and he rubbed some suntan lotion on his arms and brushed some sand off his legs. He was sitting up, you know, with his knees pulled up under his chin and his hands clasped together around his legs, holding his knees, and for a moment he was very serious and very pensive. And then he smiled at me, this really broad, open, wonderful smile, his whole face opened up into this wonderful smile, and while he was smiling at me his eyes twinkled, his blue eyes twinkled like a little boy's who's just found a pirate treasure buried in the sand, and then he shrugged, and he started to laugh."

"What did you do?"

"At first I was bewildered. I thought maybe his mind had snapped and he was out of his mind. But then it became, it became infectious. All of a sudden I started laughing, too. Now we were both laughing. We were both laughing like crazy. And every time the laughter would peak, every time it would seem like the laughter had peaked and was about to die down, he would smile at me again, that same twinkly smile, and he would shrug at me again, that same little boy's shrug, and then we would start laughing again, laughing and laughing, until finally we were both so exhausted from laughing we couldn't laugh any more."

"Did he say anything else?"

"Anything else about what?"

"Did he have anything to say about your breakdown except to look at you and shrug?"

"Have you ever heard of Zen koan, Sy?"

"Yes, I have. I've always thought they were pure bullshit."

"Well, after we'd both stopped laughing and recovered from the laughing, he looked at me and he said, 'We know the sound of two hands clapping. What is the sound of one hand clapping?' "

"You mean he's read Salinger's *Nine Stories,* too," I remarked.

"No," continued Pedersen, dead serious, "I think he was trying to tell me that I would never know why I had the breakdown, that the breakdown was just one of life's mysteries, and I think the koan was his way of saying that I can't just rely on reason, on pure rational thinking, to get me through life, that life has its irrational, mysterious aspect that has to be accepted, and appreciated, and that my struggle to unravel the reasons for my breakdown now, so many years later, is really just a way of being mired in the past, of being mired in the past and unable to live life fully in the present. So—"

"So you've decided to forget about the breakdown."

"Yes," replied Pedersen thoughtfully, rising slowly from the bench. "Yes, I have. I just don't think it matters anymore."

■ ■ ■

It wasn't quite yet noon when we wandered into a luncheonette wall-paneled in make-believe wood and seated ourselves in a corner booth beneath a painting on black velvet of a spear-wielding black huntress, her supple thighs gleaming and her swollen nipples straining to burst the fragile bonds of a leopard-skin bikini, sprawled sensually across the carcass of a leopard in a sumptuous midnight jungle.

Our waitress had long straight blond hair down to her shoulders, and blue eyes flecked with sunlight like an undersea grotto on a warm day in summer, and on her left wrist she wore a Mickey Mouse wristwatch with a bright, shiny red patent-leather band. Holding her order pad in her Mickey Mouse hand, she felt behind her ear with her right hand for a pencil that wasn't there, then searched futilely for it in the pouch of her apron and then finally in the pocket of her tight blue jeans.

"My goodness," she laughed melodiously, "it looks like I've lost another one. Would you believe that's the third one I've lost this morning?"

"You know what Freud would say about that, don't you?" I asked. "He'd say—"

"I'm hip," she laughed again with a carefree toss of her head. "I know what he'd say. He'd say I can't wait to get the hell out of here and go swimming, which is true. I just can't wait to get the hell out of here and go for a swim."

"Where do you go?" I asked.

"Swimming?" she asked incredulously. "Where do I go swimming?" She extended her left arm sideways from her body and pointed a gleaming crimson fingernail toward the open front door. "We got a whole ocean out there, man," she replied liltingly. "Where on earth you from that—"

"New York," I answered hastily, gesturing toward Pedersen. "I'm out here from New York visiting my friend Ken. I'm—"

She appraised me with a sideward glance, her hands on her hips, a tone of playful suspiciousness resonating softly in her voice, but her blue eyes danced, like opals dancing, and her pupils had opened as wide as they could open, like the mouths of black velvet caverns at the bottom of a deep blue sea.

"You're not from L.A., are you?" she asked. "I didn't think you were from L.A. But you're not from New York. You don't have an accent. You don't say Noo Yawk, like—"

"I lived for a long time in the Midwest," I explained. "It—"

"Like Wisconsin?" she asked. "Did you live in Wisconsin? I have an aunt in—"

"Chicago," I said. "I went to school in Chicago. Then I—"

"And now you're visiting out here," she noted. "How long are you out here for?"

"Maybe forever," I replied, smiling broadly up at her.

"Seriously," she laughed, blushing ever so slightly, her blue eyes dancing, "how long?"

"I'm not exactly sure," I answered. "Probably at least a few—"

Elsewhere in the restaurant a dish clattered loudly to the floor. The waitress glanced around uneasily. "Listen," she said quietly, lowering her voice, "I-I don't mind talking, the place is pretty near empty so I don't mind. But I ought to find myself a pencil. I ought to at least look like I'm—"

"Hey, Ken," I interjected. "Do you have a pencil? Come on, man, give her a pencil."

Pedersen unclipped a felt-tip pen from his shirt pocket and handed it to the waitress, who removed the cap and placed the pen in her right hand, stiffly poised above her order pad. "Go on," she remarked, glancing perfunctorily to her right and left. "You were going to tell me how long—"

"At least a few months probably," I replied. "I'm out here to write a book. But my friend here, he works nights. And I don't know this city at all. I would really love it if you'd have dinner with me and maybe show—"

"Tonight?" she asked.

"Sure," I nodded. "Any night. If tonight's—"

"I don't think tonight's good," she mused quietly, tapping the end of Ken's pen against her lower row of perfect teeth, "but tomorrow's probably—"

"You don't have to have any qualms about going out with my friend Sy," chimed in Pedersen out of nowhere. "He's an amazing guy. He's really fantastic with women."

My jaw went slack. The waitress stiffened slightly and her eyes widened. "He is?" she asked, her eyes darting uneasily from Pedersen to me and then back to Pedersen.

"Better keep an eye out, though," warned Pedersen with a sly wink. "These New York writers can be devastating, especially—"

"I-I guess it must be nice to be so devastating," stammered the waitress, now visibly nervous, "but—"

"Look," I interrupted irritably, my mind racing to find some way to retrieve what was now obviously irretrievably lost, "my friend didn't . . . there's no point in—"

"Don't worry," smiled the waitress wanly, ill at ease but trying to hide it, "it doesn't matter. But I really should take your order now, or—"

"How about the dinner we were going to have together?" I asked hopelessly.

"Oh, I don't think I can do that," she replied hastily, practically jumbling her words together. "Tonight I can't, and anyway I've got this boy friend. He's real jealous. If he—oh Jesus," she exclaimed in mid-sentence, interrupting herself, slapping her forehead with the heel of her palm as though chastising herself for some act of idiotic forgetfulness, "I didn't even get you guys any water. Jesus, I'm sorry. Just a minute. Let me go get you some water." And she fled.

"Pedersen," I fumed angrily, "why the fuck did you do that?"

"Do what, Sy?"

"Damn you, Pedersen. You know what you did. Why the fuck did—"

"Honestly, Sy," he stammered, smiling a shit-eater's smile accompanied by a short nervous laugh, "I don't know what you mean. You mean with the chick? You mean—"

"I had it made with that chick," I barked accusingly, glaring at Pedersen across the table. "Why did you fuck it up?"

"I didn't fuck it up, man," he whined. "I was trying to help you out. I was trying to help you get it. It needed that extra boost, didn't you see that, man? She was on the edge. She needed that extra boost to tip her over the edge. I was trying—"

"Ken," I interrupted irritably, "she was about to make a date with me for tomorrow night, and you screwed it up. You gave her this lascivious wink, and you—"

"Me, lascivious, Sy?" exclaimed Pedersen shrilly, starting to fidget. "I wasn't being lascivious. Listen, Sy, she was a skag, man. This is California, man. The whole state is hairyville, man. All they have out here is fucking wall-to-wall hairies. She was a skag, man. I just wanted to save you from wasting—"

"She is not a skag, Ken," I snapped. "She is an extremely beautiful woman. And for some reason completely unbeknownst to me, you—"

"Look," replied Pedersen confidently, "she was a skag, that's all there is to it. I don't want to see my best pal wasting his time on a skag. Besides, Tracy knows all kinds of incredible pussy, man. She's a young woman, right? So she just has to be in contact with scads of succulent pussies. I'll talk to her about it tonight, after she gets off from work. I'll talk to her first thing about setting you up with some pussy."

"God damn it, Ken," insisted the voice coming from the kitchen in an angry, urgent whisper, "I just don't *know* any—"

"God damn it, Tracy," snapped Pedersen, his voice becoming shrill, "you're a girl, aren't you? How can you possibly not—"

Tracy was in the kitchen, fixing dinner. Pedersen was in there with her, cajoling, insisting, getting pissed off. Even though I couldn't see either of them from where I was sitting, I could tell by the sound of Pedersen's voice that he was waving his arms about.

I was in the living room reading a newspaper, reading some dumb, boring article about how the local state mental hospital was dumping mental patients into the community, people were getting all hot and bothered about having all these loonies loose in their community, unzipping their flies in public, flapping their arms like seagulls, stuff like that, mostly harmless stuff, but disturbing to your average citizen nevertheless. I didn't really care much about the loonies being set loose in the neighborhood, mostly I was trying to get over how pissed off I was at the way Pedersen had fucked up my chance to score with the waitress, in fact I was trying as best I could to ignore Ken and Tracy, but since the kitchen had no door on it, that was impossible.

Every now and then their voices would be drowned out by the sound of the blender. There are people, Tracy was one of them, who cannot eat anything without first whipping it to liquid shit in a blender, so that by the time they serve it to you it looks as though somebody already ate it and then threw it up. I think there is something about making food in blenders that is inherently crazy and anti-life.

"I just don't *know* anybody, Ken," cried Tracy angrily, no

longer even making any attempt to maintain a whisper, "and that's final."

"What about Gloria?" demanded Pedersen. "Gloria what's-her-name."

"Gloria Konstant."

"Right. Gloria Konstant. What about her?"

"She's married."

"That's all right. I don't think Sy'll give a shit about that. I'll go ask him."

"She's married, Ken," insisted Tracy, clearly exasperated. "She's married and she won't do it."

"Then how about Barbara, the one with the big tits?"

"You mean Pat."

"Barbara, Pat, what the fuck's the difference? She has big tits, doesn't she? I mean the one with the big—"

"I don't think that would work out."

"Why the fuck not?"

"I don't think she's Sy's type. I don't think—"

"Oh fuck! What the fuck is this shit?" yelled Pedersen angrily. "What kind of fucking asshole shit is this? Let's let Sy decide whether—"

"And probably more important," interrupted Tracy, "I don't think Sy is—"

"Now god damn," shrieked Pedersen. "God damn. She's got two tits, doesn't she? She's got a pussy, doesn't she? Well then why don't we just let Barbara and—"

"Pat," hissed Tracy icily. "Her name is Pat. She—"

"I don't give a good god damned fuck *what* her name is," yelled Pedersen. "I don't give a god damned fuck. My best friend is—"

"Then get him some pussy yourself," retorted Tracy coolly. "If it's that important to you, go out and do it yourself. Don't bother me with it. Just—"

Pedersen's voice was calm now, eerily calm. "Okay, Tracy," he shrugged, "you're right. This time I think you're one hundred percent right."

Pedersen emerged from the kitchen into the living room, his left hand stuffed in his trousers pocket, his right hand trembling, his face fixed in a frown designed to conceal his rage beneath a mask of thoughtfulness.

"Come on, man," he announced quietly. "We're going out."

"Now?" I asked, putting down the newspaper. "Right now? Before—"

"Right now," he repeated calmly, scooping up the car keys off a wrought-iron white end table. "Come on. We'll go for a drive. Maybe we'll stop and have a quick bite to eat while we're out."

I rose from my chair and followed Ken to the door. I glanced into the kitchen, hoping to be able to catch Tracy's eye and maybe give her a sympathetic shrug, but her back was toward me, she was whistling some loud tune, way off key, and she was washing something in the kitchen sink with both faucets turned on full blast. Above it all was the whirr of the blender.

"God damn it, Ken," I demanded, as we exited from the apartment building and strode toward the curb, "where the fuck—"

"We're going out to chase some pussy, Sy," he replied calmly. "We're going out for a drive and find you a big, fat, succulent hairy."

He opened the car door on the driver's side and slid inside, then leaned over and unlocked the front door on the passenger side. "Come on, man," he urged cordially, "come on inside."

The car lurched away from the curb in patented Pedersen fashion and hurtled insanely down the quiet residential street. It was already dusk, the sun setting bloody in the distance like a colossal ball of clotted blood.

"Now look, Ken," I chided. "You know as well as I do that this is not a good time to be chasing hairy. It's not even six-thirty. All the little hairies are still—"

"No," replied Pedersen, cutting me off, "you're wrong. This is California. Here in California this is the ideal time of day to pursue the hairy. Out on the interstate, there are all these hitchhikers. Every one more succulent than the next one. They wear tight blue jeans and micro-miniskirts and sometimes those California hippie leather hats. You know those leather hats I mean?"

"Yes," I acknowledged, "I do. I've seen—"

"And right around now," continued Pedersen, hunched over the steering wheel, embracing the steering wheel, and peering intently through the windshield as if trying, with his gaze, to penetrate a dense fog, "right around this time of day, around dusk, they are thinking that it will be dark soon and that it is high time they found someplace to spend the night and maybe pick up on some steaming cock. So don't tell me my business, Sy. Don't start trying to give me lessons in how to chase the hairy, because when it comes to chasing hairy, I'm the one who wrote the goddam book."

Out on the coast highway connecting Los Angeles with San Francisco, the cars whizzed past like an armada of robot bumblebees, whizzing, buzzing, making a beeline for the hive. And then suddenly we saw her, trudging along the shoulder, straining to bear the weight of a bright red fiber glass gasoline can, carrying it a few feet, setting it down, switching it to the other hand, staggering forward a few more feet, setting it down again.

As long as I live, I will never forget her, the way she looked is fixed indelibly, forever, in my mind, the tight white shorts she wore, rolled up at the cuffs, the fabric strained to the dissolving point by the luscious cheeks of her firm, round ass; the flimsy, nearly sheer, scarf-style blouse, leaving her entire back naked except for a single thin ribbon of silk tied in a bow, and exposing, in front, hanging there like ripe mangoes behind the gossamer curtain of nearly transparent silk, her firm, pendulous breasts with their distended purple nipples and gigantic aureoles; and lastly, her soft, light-brown hair, which was all but invisible beneath the long white scarf which she had wrapped round and round her head like a turban.

Pedersen lurched off the highway onto the shoulder, like a Ferrari making a pit stop in the Indy 500. He leaned across my lap and yelled out the window: "Hey there. Where you headed?"

The girl had already set down the gasoline can, she was bending over, in the process of picking it up again, when she heard Pedersen's voice just behind her, calling out to her through the open car window.

She straightened, leaving the gasoline can lying on the ground, while placing her right hand against the small of her back in the manner of someone who is fearful of straining their back. As she rose to her full height, she looked to be about five-foot-ten, maybe even six feet, her breasts came alive like a pair of woodchucks trapped in a gunnysack.

"Oh, I'm trying to find my car," she replied with a sigh, pointing down the highway with her left hand while keeping her right hand pressed firmly against the small of her back. "My poor car ran out of gas about a mile or two over yonder, but I think this highway must be some kind of magic highway, you know what I mean? Some kind of fantasy highway that just keeps growing longer and longer with every step you take."

"We'd be happy to—" began Pedersen.

"Oh, would you?" exclaimed the hairy. "Would you really? Oh if you would give me a lift I'd be so grateful, I'd really be so awfully grateful. I'd owe my life to you. I'd actually owe you my life. You have no idea what kind of wear and tear carrying this gasoline can exerts on your body."

"You get in the back with her, Sy," instructed Pedersen, leaping out of the car and seizing the gasoline can. "I'll put this on the floor in the front."

"I really owe you two my life," she exclaimed, as Pedersen gunned his automobile back onto the highway, his rear wheels scooping up gravel from the shoulder and then spitting it out again. "I really owe you both my life. I walked so many miles with that thing. First it was empty, then it was full. It seems like I just walked miles and miles with it."

"What kind of a car do you have?" I asked.

"Oh, just a battered old Karman Ghia," she replied. "Just one of those Karman Ghias with, you know, a bashed-in front end. They're all like that. They've all got front ends that've gotten themselves bashed in. I don't think there's a one of them over two weeks old that—but I don't really care about that anyway. I hate to drive anyway. It's just that out here, it doesn't—"

"Why do you hate to drive?" inquired Pedersen from the front seat.

"Oh I've hated to drive ever since the accident," she replied. "I've absolutely hated even being in a car since I had my accident. I mean, I wasn't actually driving then, I mean someone else was doing the actual driving, but it's all the same to me, it's just been a downer to be in a car ever since that time I had my accident."

"What happened?" I asked.

"Oh, it was such a long time ago," she sighed. "I was so young then. It was such a long time ago. I was eighteen. I was much prettier then. I mean, probably I was never really beautiful, or anything like that, but I was really young then, I was like really at my peak. I—"

"I think you're at your peak now," I said casually.

"Oh no," she disagreed, wide-eyed, shaking her head, "not now. That's nice of you to say, I think you two are both really nice, but that's not true now. I have all these wrinkles now, and if you look real close you can see these gray hairs I have now. I wouldn't even tell you my age now, I just would never reveal it, I just think every girl should just commit suicide as soon as she reaches thirty, it just seems nobody wants you once you reach thirty anyway. So you might—"

"You were going to tell us about the accident," I remarked.

"Oh, it was just so scary, it was such a downer, I don't really like to talk about it, you know. Because it's such a downer to talk about it. It's so depressing, you know what I mean?"

"Yes," laughed Pedersen. "We—"

"I was just eighteen," she continued, "I was just eighteen. And would you believe it, it was our first date. Our very first date. I had never been out with the guy, or dated him, or anything. It was just our first date. And he had been drinking. And he had borrowed this car from this friend of his. Actually, he hadn't really borrowed the car at all. It was more like he had stole it. I mean, not really stole it, I mean it was a friend of his and all, but borrowed it without asking, I mean his friend just wasn't home so he figured his friend wouldn't mind if he borrowed it so he hot-wired it in his friend's driveway and that's how he picked me up in it.

"And he'd been drinking, you know. Maybe not a lot. He had this job, he had this job of some kind where the guys would sneak out back and drink, you know what I mean, there are guys who have jobs like that, where they can drink, so when he picked me up in the car he had already been drinking, and then while we were driving along we were both taking sips out of this bottle he'd brought. I can't remember if—"

"How did the accident happen?" I asked.

"Oh, it was a horrible accident," she replied. "It was a really horrible, death-defying, horrendous accident. But nobody really knows how it happened, I mean nobody really knows exactly how it really happened. I mean there were no eyewitnesses, and I don't remember anything that happened, I mean my whole mind just went completely blank the moment it happened, to this day I cannot really remember exactly what happened, I cannot remember the actual impact. But I've seen pictures. You know, the police took pictures. And for years everyone hid them from me, I mean the police never even showed me the pictures, and for years my father had copies of them, he had copies of these pictures, but they looked so awful, they looked so horrendous, that he hid them from me so I wouldn't see them and get upset about them, so I wouldn't just freak out at seeing how close to death I really came in that accident.

"See, there was this intersection, it was an unmarked intersection, it was an unmarked intersection somewhere out in the country somewhere, it was in Delaware, that's where I used to live, and this huge tractor-trailer arrived at this intersection at the exact same moment as our car, and the tractor-trailer smashed into the passenger side of the car, where I was sitting, it just smashed into the passenger side and spun off the road and carried the car careening into this grocery store, which was just demolished. The car looked like a ravioli can that had had a cherry bomb exploded in it, that's how it—"

"Was anybody killed?" I asked.

The girl laughed wistfully. "No, nobody. The guy I was with, his name was Tom, all he needed was this band-aid to cover up this tiny cut over his left eye. And the driver of the semi, he just walked away from it, too. But I—I was really smashed up. I mean, I was really incredibly racked up. I was unconscious. Tom got out of the car and walked around to my side and he looked in the window and he saw me just lying there, you know, I was just lying there inside the car and I was covered with blood, I was completely covered in my own blood from head to foot."

"Did Tom get you out of the car?" asked Pedersen.

"Ha!" laughed the girl sarcastically. "Ha! It took the fire department three hours to pry me out of that car, it took them three hours to get me out of there. The car was just a pile of twisted scrap. It was like a cheap ravioli can that—Tom and the truck driver were both certain I was dead. Everyone on the scene just took their time getting me out of there because they all just assumed I was dead."

"But you weren't dead," I remarked.

"No," she replied, "but everybody thought I was. I was such a mess. I was a complete bloody mess. And I was unconscious. Everybody just assumed I was dead."

"Then what happened?" asked Pedersen.

"They took me to the hospital and they rushed me into emergency surgery. I was still unconscious. They had to cut all my clothes off of me because my clothes were completely caked in my own blood. And then they wheeled me into surgery. They never thought I'd get out of surgery alive. And that's when I regained consciousness for the first time. That's—"

"When?" asked Pedersen.

"In the operating room," replied the girl. "That's when I regained consciousness. I will never, ever forget that moment. I was lying on the operating table, but of course I didn't know that, I didn't know that because I'd been unconscious for more than three hours, ever since the accident, and there were these lights, these bright lights, the lights of the operating room were shining down on me."

"And?" prodded Pedersen.

"And I regained consciousness. I regained consciousness, but my eyes were caked with blood. I couldn't open my eyes, because my eyes and my eyelids were just caked in gobs and gobs of blood. You can't imagine it, nobody could imagine it. Nobody could imagine how many gobs and gobs there were. And so I regained consciousness, but I couldn't see, I was conscious, but I still couldn't see. And so I was sort of peering through my eyelids, I couldn't open my eyes at all, but the bright lights from the operating room were so bright that they were shining through my eyelids, you know what I mean, the bright lights from the operating lights were shining through my sealed eyelids. And I remember what I thought. I'll never forget what I thought. I thought to myself, 'This is heaven, and I'm dead!' "

"Jesus Christ," I exclaimed. "What happened then?"

"I moved or something, I guess I must've moved, and I guess the doctor must have seen me move. He kind of touched my arm. My eyes were all caked with blood and my mouth was all caked with blood, all I could see were those heavenly bright lights, and I said to the doctor, it was the first thing I said, the first thing I said after the accident, I said, 'Am I dead?' And the doctor said, 'No, my dear. You're not dead. But you have been very badly injured, and you must try to lie very, very still.' "

"What turned out to be wrong with you?" asked Pedersen.

"Ha!" laughed the girl again. "What didn't turn out to be wrong with me? Everything was wrong with me. Every bone in my body was broken. My legs were broken, my arms were broken, my wrists and ankles were all broken. My nose and jaw were broken. A whole bunch of my fingers were broken. Almost every single one of my ribs was broken. For months, I just lay there in the hospital, all wired together. I lay in this bed, wired together,

I was like lying there held together with wire, and twice a day they would turn me, they have to turn you so you don't get bedsores and infections, so two orderlies would take my arms, and two more would take my legs, and twice a day they would turn me over. I'm not a person who can endure pain, I have never been good at enduring pain, and you can't imagine how much pain there was, twice a day they would turn me, two orderlies were on my arms, two more orderlies were on my legs, and I would scream, god they could hear me down the hall and down the stairs and everyone in the dining room would hear me twice a day when they turned me, I would scream because never in my whole life have I felt pain like the pain I would feel twice a day when—"

"But you survived it," I commented. "You got better and you survived it."

"What happened to the guy?" inquired Pedersen.

"What do you mean?" asked the girl.

"Well, you know," replied Pedersen, repeating his question, "what ever happened to the guy? Did you ever—"

"He came to see me in the hospital once or twice," answered the girl. "He came to see me once or twice while I was in the hospital. But that was all. I never saw him again after I got out. He never came to see me after that initial once or twice. He didn't like the way I screamed when they turned me, it gave him the creeps to be around there when they were turning me, and also I think he was embarrassed about the accident."

"I should hope so," I exclaimed. "Was there ever any sort of insurance settlement? I mean, I'm not suggesting that insurance would've—"

"There was some little settlement," she replied, "but not much of one. There was never too big of a settlement. First of all, they never could really establish who was at fault. I mean, Tom said the truck driver was at fault and he said we were at fault, but no one ever really found out for certain. And then it was really against us that Tom had been drinking, and then it was even more muddled up by the fact that the car itself had kind of been stolen, so it was questionable whether we actually had any coverage and, well, I have to admit I don't really understand it. Anyway, I came out pretty well from it all. Sometimes my fingers still hurt, sometimes I have these pains in my fingers, but my main problem now is I'm getting pretty old, I don't like to get into how old I am, I mean it's depressing, it's not so bad for a guy but for a girl it's depressing, it seems like thirty is coming up on me pretty fast and that's got me really depressed."

Up ahead on the highway, parked on the shoulder just a short ways up the road, stood a battered purple Karman Ghia, forlorn and battered. "Hey, Ken," I cried, tapping him on the shoulder, pointing out the window toward the Karman Ghia, "that's—"

Pedersen floored the accelerator and rocketed past it. "Hey, where you going, man?" I exclaimed. "That's her—"

"I just thought we'd drive for awhile," replied Pedersen casually, squinting into his rearview mirror as the crumpled Ghia shrank into a purple polka-dot in his rearview mirror. "I just thought we'd drive for awhile, have some fun, enjoy the sunset, have some fun, maybe stop for a bite to eat or something."

The girl folded her arms in front of her on the back of the front seat and stared placidly out the windshield. "Oh, sure," she nodded, "that'd be cool. I'd rather be here with you two than alone in that old car anyway. I don't really like driving that much, especially alone, I mean I hate being alone anyway, and like I've never been able to really enjoy driving a car since my accident, even though I wasn't actually driving the car when the accident happened. I mean, I was just a passenger. But anyway, I've just never been able to really get into it since then, like there's always this little voice in my mind that's jangling me, you know, this voice that jangles me whenever I drive. So I'm in no hurry. I'd rather be with you two. You two really saved my life, I mean it. I mean I really like where your heads are at, to pick me up like that. I mean carrying that heavy gasoline thing was really doing these terrible ravaging things to my body, so I—"

"I thought maybe we could drive somewhere and have some fun," remarked Pedersen, glancing furtively into the rearview mirror to observe her reaction. "I thought it might be fun to—"

"Oh, sure," replied the girl agreeably, now resting her chin on her folded arms on the back of the front seat, "that would be nice, I mean it would be really nice to go somewhere with you guys and make it, I mean you guys really saved my life today, I mean it, so it would be really nice to make it, but I don't think I can."

"Why not?" inquired Pedersen.

"It's this ovary, man. I've got this really wasted ovary in my body and it's ruptured, or inflamed, or whatever it is, I mean this ovary has like a mind of its own, and it's inflamed, and the doctor said, at least for awhile, I shouldn't—"

"You could give us both some head, though, right?" asked Pedersen.

"Oh, sure," replied the girl amiably. "Head? Sure, anytime. I mean I'd really like to go down on you guys, you just have no idea how you saved my life back there, I just wanted you to know that I'd really like to ball you, you know, it would really be a gas to ball you, but I can't because I have this flaky ovary rolling around in my body."

It was almost completely dark now. Only a single band of sunlight still shimmered on the far horizon. Outside on the highway, most of the passing cars had turned on their lights.

She was sprawled across the back seat now, her legs stretched out on the floor behind the driver's seat, her head resting a foot or two from my lap. I pulled out my throbbing cock and extended it toward her smiling face. She cupped the head in one hand and ran her tongue flirtatiously across the tip.

"Oh, wow," she murmured softly, "you are really gigantic, did you know that? I mean it's so thick. The veins are so—"

"Take it in your mouth," I whispered.

She grasped my cock firmly in her fist and then ran her fist up and down the shank. She took the head in her mouth and caressed it with her lips. "Oh, I really want to," she said softly, "I really want to, but not here. I mean, look at all those cars out there. Somebody will—"

"Nobody will see us," I cajoled impatiently. "Go on. I want you to eat it."

"Do you really think so?" she insisted. "Do you really think no one can see us?"

"Not if we're scrunched down like this," I said. "Not if—"

"Oh, I don't think so," she replied nervously. "I think if they look they can still see us. I mean, I really want to go down on it. You're so gigantic. It's so," she giggled, "it's so big and juicy. And your friend, he's so nice, too. I really want to go down on him too. But maybe it's old-fashioned, I mean maybe you think it's really silly, I mean maybe you think I'm really being silly, but I just feel shy about—"

"We'll take the next turnoff," called out Pedersen from the driver's seat. "There's some woods there, you know. I mean, like there's some woods and some sort of picnic area. No one'll be there at night. We'll go there."

"Will that be all right?" I asked.

"Oh, sure," nodded the girl. "As long as there aren't all these cars, you know, as long as there aren't all these people looking at us in all these cars. Because I really want to go down on you, you know. I mean both you guys are so nice, you really saved my life when that huge gasoline can was just completely enervating my body."

Pedersen swerved off the highway onto the exit ramp, then turned into an area of picnic tables and overflowing refuse cans nestled in a wooded area not far from the highway. He braked to an abrupt halt in front of a refuse can piled high with garbage, then cut off the ignition and turned out the headlights. It was dark. Nearby you could hear crickets chirping, and in the distance you could hear the whizz of automobiles whizzing down the highway toward San Francisco and beyond.

The girl reached behind her and untied her blouse. Her huge breasts jiggled free, revealing the purple nipples all plump and distended. Kneading her nipples slowly between her fingertips, she licked her lips with the tip of her tongue, then hungrily took her left breast in her mouth and began to suck on it. Finally letting it drop from her mouth, she leaned over and, taking my bulging cock in her hand, plunged it far back into her mouth, taking every last inch of it into her mouth, caressing my balls gently with her fingers while she rammed my cock softly against the back of her throat.

Then, withdrawing my cock halfway and cupping it gently in both hands, she stroked the head lovingly with her tongue, licked a glistening drop of come off the tip, and then, with a low, sensual murmur of pleasure, drew my cock far back into her mouth again and began swallowing the mammoth spasms of come I was shooting between her soft, red lips. As she pulled gently away from me, her eyelids fluttered, and semen spilled down her lower lip.

Pedersen couldn't wait to have some, too. Leaping out of the car on the driver's side, he wrenched open the back door and climbed in the back, unzipping his fly as he knelt down on the back seat. Turning away from me, and now facing Pedersen, the girl grabbed Pedersen's cock and sucked it deep in her mouth.

She had drawn it back out again and had started to exclaim how big it was, when all at once Pedersen cut her sentence short by ramming it hard into her mouth. Lying back against the seat, catching my breath, I could see her throat muscles twitching spasmodically as she struggled to swallow Pedersen's tremendous load of come without gagging. By the time Pedersen had finished unloading his wad, her eyes were tearing and she was gasping for air.

"It's always better to stick it in their mouth, Sy," warned Pedersen sternly as he zipped up his fly. "Their pussy is filled with corrosive juices that have the power to rot your dick off."

I don't think five minutes passed before I was ready for seconds. While I held my cock in my right fist, she leaned down and took my balls in her mouth, licking my balls and then my asshole while I gently kneaded my cock with my own right hand. And then, just as I was about to come again, I put my left hand on the nape of her neck and pulled her head up toward my cock and pumped a fresh wad of semen into her mouth. Of all the chicks I've ever had, I don't think I've ever known one who swallowed come as good as she did.

Pedersen clambered back into the front seat and turned on the headlights, then reached over to his right and opened the glove compartment. Inside the glove compartment was a Polaroid camera.

"Hey," exclaimed Pedersen, his eyes sparkling. "Listen to this really great idea!"

Withdrawing the camera from the glove compartment and springing open the lens, Pedersen lifted the camera to his eye and peered through the viewfinder, as though he were about to take a picture of the girl in the back seat. It was much too dark in the car to take anybody's picture, but the girl, sprawled in the back seat with her blouse on the floor somewhere and her turban askew, hastily jerked up a forearm to cover her face.

"Listen to this really fabulous idea," repeated Pedersen brightly. "We'll all go outside and stand in front of the car, and I'll take some snapshots of the hairy sucking us off in the light of the headlights. There's even a self-timer on this thing, so I can like mount it on the hood and we can all—"

"I-I don't really want to do that," stammered the girl. "That's just really not what I'm into. It's—"

Pedersen was kneeling on the front seat. He set the camera

down on the seat beside him and squinted intently down at her. "Why not?" he asked.

"It's just not my thing, you know?" pleaded the girl, anxious to please, apologetic. "I mean, you guys, both you guys, are really great guys, you know? You really saved my life back there, and you really rescued me from having all this wear and tear on my body. And I really liked going down on you. I really loved going down on both of you. You both have really incredible cocks and it really gave me a rush when you let me go down on you. And I'd really like to even do it again if you want to, as soon as you're ready. It's just—"

"It's just what?" asked Pedersen, his eyes narrowing.

"It's just the pictures, man," continued the girl, her hands now twitching in her lap as though they were mice with epilepsy, "it's just the idea of pictures, man, it's just the whole—"

Slowly Pedersen removed his wristwatch. He held it in his left hand and began to wind it. "Now look," he said calmly, peering down at the girl as he wound his wristwatch, "you are a whore, right?"

"Huh?" said the girl.

"I mean," continued Pedersen, carefully placing his watch back on his wrist and refastening the tiny buckle on the watch-band, "I mean," he repeated, "you are a complete and total slut, right?"

The girl glanced nervously at me, then back at Pedersen. Her upper lip quivered, but she did not speak.

"I mean, we picked you up on the highway, you and your gigantic tits, you drove out into the woods with us, you sucked us off like there was no tomorrow. What do you think that is, normal?"

"I never said I was normal," whispered the girl hoarsely, some of the words catching in her throat. "Exhibitionism isn't normal either, you know. It's—"

"You know," began Pedersen thoughtfully, cutting her off, "you know, you get to a point in your life, you get to a point in your life where you get sick and tired of taking shit from one hairy after another. You just get sick of it. And you decide, you decide that some sort of gesture is needed, some sort of grand gesture that will put you on record, once and for all, as being opposed to it, as being in opposition to this constant, never-ending hairy horseshit. Because Sy knows what I mean, and Walt knows what I mean, and I think everyone, even the newspapers and magazines, even the people on television, are beginning to realize that expression is being snuffed out, that the rising tide of suffocating hairy horseshit is suffocating everyone's expressions out."

He reached out his hands imploringly to the girl sprawled wide-eyed and uncomprehending in the back seat. "You know what I mean, don't you?" he implored her. "You understand the implications and you accept them, isn't that so?"

"I-I think so," stammered the girl.

Pedersen nodded gravely. "Good," he said simply. "That's very good."

He reached down to retrieve something, the camera I thought, but when his hands came up again he was grasping the gasoline can, its cap was off, and he was sloshing gasoline all over the girl in the back seat. The girl emitted a faint gasp of stunned disbelief.

I lunged violently forward and grabbed Pedersen's forearm. "GOOD GOD!" I yelled at the top of my lungs. "PEDERSEN! NO!!"

Wrenching his forearm free of my grasp and gripping the gasoline container in his opposite hand, Pedersen drew back his fist and sent it smashing like a jackhammer into my left ear. I hurtled backward against the door handle and tumbled out the car door onto the ground, and when I touched my hand to my aching ear I felt warm wet blood trickling down my fingers from inside my ear.

Through the car window I could see Pedersen still crouched in the front seat, he was striking a match on a paper matchbook, and then he grasped the lighted match between his thumb and forefinger and flipped it ever so gently into the back seat, time seemed to stand still as it fell, it was like a firefly glowing, or like a tiny falling star, falling, falling, into the back seat, and then whoosh, how can you describe what happened then except to say whoosh, and then—WHOOSH—the whole back seat was aflame, and the girl in the back seat, she was on fire, too.

Pedersen flung himself out the car door and rolled like a tumbleweed along the ground. The automobile's headlights played on the picnic tables and on the garbage piled high in the refuse cans, and in the back seat the girl was waving her arms about, frantically waving them, like a drowning diver in a flaming sea, the whole back seat of the car was in flames around her and she was sobbing and waving her arms about, and then the front seat of the car was on fire, too, the inside of the car was a wall of fire, the girl had stopped sobbing, you could hardly see her now through the raging fire, and now the outside of the car was on fire, too, tongues of flame swarmed over the roof, consuming the windshield wipers and crackling along the hood.

And that was when the gas tank exploded, I was in the clear, so was Pedersen, we were both in the clear when the gas tank exploded, fragments of the flaming automobile hurtled into the air, they formed a flaming, spinning jigsaw puzzle high in the air, ragged chunks of human flesh rose skyward with them, arms and thighs and entrails tumbled wildly through the air. And then the gruesome stuff descended, clattering on the tops of the picnic tables, drenching the ground around them in a rainfall of gore.